OxCrimes

OxCrimes © 2014 Profile Books

Set in Garamond Pro, Aleo Light and THE Sans SemiLight
Page design by Henry Iles

Author photo credits

George Pelecanos © *Max Hirshfeld*; Neil Gaiman © *Kimberly Butler*; Simon Lewis © *Mark Pengelly*; Val McDermid © *Charlie Hopkinson*; Anthony Horowitz © *Adam Scourfield*; Fred Vargas © *Louise Oligny*; Stuart Neville © *Philip O'Neill*; Stella Duffy © *Gino Sprio*; John Harvey © *Molly Boiling*; Denise Mina © *Neil Donaldson*; James Sallis © *Karyn Sallis*; Maxim Jakubowski; Christopher Fowler © *Peter Chapman*; Louise Welsh © *Steve Lindbridge*; Peter Robinson © *Pal Hansen*; Anne Zouroudi © *Wolf Kettler*; Martyn Waites © *Charlie Hopkinson*; Alexander McCall Smith © *Chris Watt*; Phil Rickman © *John Bullough*; Mark Billingham © *Charlie Hopkinson*; John Connolly © *Mark Condren*; Yrsa Sigurdardóttir © *Sigurjon Ragnar*.

First published in 2014 by Profile Books
3A Exmouth House
Pine Street, Exmouth Market
London EC1R OJH

Printed by CPI Group (UK) Ltd, Croydon
CR0 4YY, on Forest Stewardship Council
(mixed sources) certified paper

MIX
Paper from responsible sources
FSC
www.fsc.org FSC® C020471

464pp

A CIP catalogue record for this book is available from the British Library.

ISBN 978-1781250648
eISBN 9781847659040

OxCrimes

INTRODUCED BY

IAN RANKIN

EDITED BY

MARK ELLINGHAM AND PETER FLORENCE

P

PROFILE BOOKS

About OxCrimes

OxCrimes – like its predecessors *OxTales* and *OxTravels* – is a very simple idea. We asked the best crime writers based in Britain, and a few further afield, for a story. There were no rules. We just wanted compelling stories that we knew their regular readers would have to read ... and so would need to buy this book. And why so calculating? That's simple, too. The purpose of *OxCrimes* is to entertain and, in doing so, to raise funds for Oxfam's work. All of the authors have donated their royalties to the charity.

Crime writers are busy folk, often producing a novel or more each year, so we had feared many of the bestselling cast we approached would have little time to contribute. We needn't have worried. Twenty-seven leading authors feature in this book, almost all of them with original stories (three or four chose to adapt previously published gems). So here they are: a fabulous collection of chilling stories, together with an introduction from Ian Rankin and an afterword by Oxfam's own chief inspector, Mark Goldring.

Mark Ellingham and Peter Florence
Editors, OxCrimes

Contents

Introduction

Ian Rankin

There's no mystery.

No mystery why some of the world's greatest crime and thriller writers would want to team up with Oxfam.

Crime fiction worldwide continues to shine a light on the problems at the heart of all societies. A crime novel may revolve around personal greed, corporate wrong-doing, political machinations, social injustice or inequality – because the crime novel has always been predicated on a very basic moral conundrum: why do we human beings continue to do bad things to each other? There are many and varied possible answers to that question, and a range will be offered in the stories you are about to read.

It is testament to the high regard in which Oxfam is held that so many authors of international repute signed up to OxCrimes. The result is a collection rich in incident, ingenuity and entertainment, one that the aficionado will relish. And who knows, you may find yourself a sudden fan of writers you'd not read before. I can promise that there isn't one writer represented here who doesn't deliver in their full-length books with the same power as their shorter fiction.

The stories themselves range far and wide. They take place on different continents, and are set in the past, present and future. Neil Gaiman, for example, offers a nice take on the later years of Sherlock Holmes, while Walter Mosley – best known for his Easy Rawlins novels set in the America of a few decades back – hurls us forward in time to a world where our very souls are on trial. George Pelecanos meantime offers a stylish and violent vignette of immigrant life in 1930s New York, and John Harvey's Resnick investigates the blighted underclass of England in another of his masterly dispatches from contemporary hell.

There are also stories involving hitmen, femmes fatale, professional jealousy, and revenge. Not that the tone is necessarily bleak. There's always room for laughter in the dark. Alexander McCall Smith, for example, entertains with a typically impish tale of academic skulduggery, and French author Fred Vargas provides an engagingly skewed story of the growing relationship between a good-natured cop and a clochard who witnesses a robbery. Stuart Neville meantime nods in the direction of *Twelve Angry Men*, and Louise Welsh towards the films of Alfred Hitchcock, while Stella Duffy has a lot of fun with the world of modern art and Anne Zouroudi takes us to the modern-day Aegean for a picturesque game of cat and mouse, played out under azure skies.

And then there's Mark Billingham, who reminds us that murder is as likely to happen at Christmas as any other time of year – and not even Santa Claus is safe.

All this, and I've barely scratched the surface. These stories can be read in bite-sized chunks or at one satisfying sitting. They provide a rich diet by creators at the top of their game, and all for a very good cause. Tuck in.

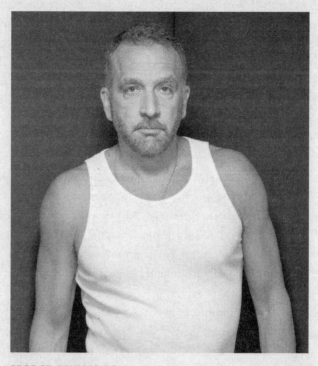

GEORGE PELECANOS is the author of several highly praised, bestselling novels, including *The Cut*, *What It Was*, *The Way Home*, *The Turnaround* and *The Night Gardener*. He is also an independent-film producer, an essayist and the recipient of numerous international writing awards. He was a producer and Emmy-nominated writer for *The Wire* and currently writes for the HBO series *Treme*. He was born in Washington DC in 1957.

The Dead Their Eyes Implore Us

George Pelecanos

Someday I'm gonna write all this down. But I don't write so good in English yet, see? So I'm just gonna think it out loud.

Last night I had a dream.

In my dream, I was a kid, back in the village. My friends and family from the *chorio*, they were there, all of us standing around the square. My father, he had strung a lamb up on a pole. It was making a noise, like a scream, and its eyes were wild and afraid. My father handed me my Italian switch knife, the one he gave me before I came over. I cut into the lamb's throat and opened it up wide. The lamb's warm blood spilled onto my hands.

My mother told me once: Every time you dream something, it's got to be a reason.

I'm not no kid anymore. I'm twenty-eight years old. It's early in June, Nineteen Hundred and Thirty Three. The temperature got up to one hundred degrees today. I read in the Tribune, some old people died from the heat.

Let me try to paint a picture, so you can see in your head the way it is for me right now. I got this little one-room place I rent from some old lady. A Murphy bed and a table, an icebox and a stove. I got a radio I bought for a dollar and ninety-nine. I wash my clothes in a tub, and afterwards I hang the *roocha* on a cord I stretched across the room. There's a bunch of clothes, *pantalonia* and one of my work shirts and my *vrakia* and socks, on there now. I'm sitting here at the table in my union suit. I'm smoking a Fatima and drinking a cold bottle of Abner Drury beer. I'm looking at my hands. I got blood underneath my fingernails. I washed real good but it was hard to get it all.

It's five, five-thirty in the morning. Let me go back some, to show how I got to where I am tonight.

What's it been, four years since I came over? The boat ride was a boat ride so I'll skip that part. I'll start in America.

When I got to Ellis Island I came straight down to Washington to stay with my cousin Toula and her husband Aris. Aris had a fruit cart down on Pennsylvania Avenue, around 17th. Toula's father owed my father some *lefta* from back in the village, so it was all set up. She offered me a room until I could get on my feet. Aris wasn't happy about it but I didn't give a good goddamn what he was happy about. Toula's father should have paid his debt.

Toula and Aris had a place in Chinatown. It wasn't just for Chinese. Italians, Irish, Polacks and Greeks lived there, too. Everyone was poor except the criminals. The Chinamen controlled the gambling, the whores, and the opium. All the business got done in the back of laundries and in the restaurants. The Chinks didn't bother no one if they didn't get bothered themselves.

Toula's apartment was in a house right on H Street. You had to walk up three floors to get to it. I didn't mind it. The milkman did it every day and the old Jew who collected the rent managed to do it, too. I figured, so could I.

My room was small, so small you couldn't shut the door all the way when the bed was down. There was only one toilet in the place, and they had put a curtain by it, the kind you hang on a shower. You had to close it around you when you wanted to shit. Like I say, it wasn't a nice place or nothing like it, but it was okay. It was free.

But nothing's free, my father always said. Toula's husband Aris made me pay from the first day I moved in. Never had a good word to say to me, never mentioned me to no one for a job. He was a sonofabitch, that one. Dark, with a hook in his nose, looked like he had some Turkish blood in him. I wouldn't be surprised if the *gamoto* was a Turk. I didn't like the way he talked to my cousin, either, 'specially when he drank. And this *malaka* drank every night. I'd sit in my room and listen to him raise his voice at her, and then later I could hear him fucking her on their bed. I couldn't stand it, I'm telling you, and me without a woman myself. I didn't have no job then so I couldn't even buy a whore. I thought I was gonna go nuts.

Then one day I was talking to this guy, Dimitri Karras, lived in the 606 building on H. He told me about a janitor's job opened up at St Mary's, the church where his son *Panayoti* and most of the neighbourhood kids went to Catholic school. I put some Wildroot tonic in my hair, walked over to the church, and talked to the head nun. I don't know, she musta liked me or something, 'cause I got the job. I had to lie a little about being a handyman. I wasn't no engineer, but I figured, what the hell, the furnace goes out you light it again, goddamn.

My deal was simple. I got a room in the basement and a coupla meals a day. Pennies other than that, but I didn't mind, not then. Hell, it was better than living in some Hoover Hotel. And it got me away from that bastard Aris. Toula cried when I left, so I gave her a hug. I didn't say nothing to Aris.

I worked at St Mary's about two years. The work was never hard. I knew the kids and most of their fathers: Karras, Angelos, Nicodemus, Recevo, Damiano, Carchedi. I watched the boys grow. I didn't look the nuns in the eyes when I talked to them so they wouldn't get the wrong idea. Once or twice I treated myself to one of the whores over at the Eastern House. Mostly, down in the basement, I played with my *pootso*. I put it out of my mind that I was jerking off in church.

Meanwhile, I tried to make myself better. I took English classes at St Sophia, the Greek Orthodox church on 8th and L. I bought a blue serge suit at Harry Kaufman's on 7th Street, on sale for eleven dollars and seventy-five. The Jew tailor let me pay for it a little bit at a time. Now when I went to St Sophia for the Sunday service I wouldn't be ashamed.

I liked to go to church. Not for religion, nothing like that. Sure, I wear a *stavro*, but everyone wears a cross. That's just superstition. I don't love God, but I'm afraid of him. So I went to church just in case, and also to look at the girls. I liked to see 'em all dressed up.

There was this one *koritsi*, not older than sixteen when I first saw her, who was special. I knew just where she was gonna be, with her mother, on the side of the church where the women sat separate from the men. I made sure I got a good view of her on Sundays. Her name was Irene, I asked around. I could tell she was clean. By that I mean she was a virgin. That's the kind of girl you're gonna marry. My plan was to wait till I got some money in my pocket before I talked to her, but not too long so she got snatched up. A girl like that is not gonna stay single forever.

Work and church was for the daytime. At night I went to the coffeehouses down by the Navy Yard in Southeast. One of them was owned by a hardworking guy from the neighbourhood, Angelos, lived at the 703 building on 6th. That's the *kafeneion* I went to most. You played cards and dice there if that's what you wanted to do, but mostly you could be yourself. It was all Greeks.

That's where I met Nick Stefanos one night, at the Angelos place. Meeting him is what put another change in my life. Stefanos was a Spartan with an easy way, had a scar on his cheek. You knew he was tough but he didn't have to prove it. I heard he got the scar running protection for a hooch truck in upstate New York. Heard a cheap *pistola* blew up in his face. It was his business, what happened, none of mine.

We got to talking that night. He was the head busman down at some fancy hotel on 15th and Penn, but he was leaving to open his own place. His friend Costa, another *Spartiati*, worked there and he was gonna leave with him. Stefanos asked me if I wanted to take Costa's place. He said he could set it up. The pay was only a little more than what I was making, a dollar-fifty a week with extras, but a little more was a lot. Hell, I wanted to make better like anyone else. I thanked Nick Stefanos and asked him when I could start.

I started the next week, soon as I got my room where I am now. You had to pay management for your bus uniform, black pants and a white shirt and short black vest, so I didn't make nothing for awhile. Some of the waiters tipped the busmen heavy, and some tipped nothing at all. For the ones who tipped nothing you cleared their tables slower, and last. I caught on quick.

The hotel was pretty fancy and its dining room, up on the top floor, was fancy, too. The china was real, the crystal sang when you flicked a finger at it, and the silver was heavy. It was hard times, but you'd never know it from the way the tables filled up at night. I figured I'd stay there a coupla years, learn the operation, and go out on my own like Stefanos. That was one smart guy.

The way they had it set up was, Americans had the waiter jobs, and the Greeks and Filipinos bused the tables. The coloureds, they stayed back in the kitchen. Everybody in the restaurant was in the same order that they were out on the street: the whites were up top and the Greeks were in the middle; the *mavri* were at the bottom. Except if someone was your own kind, you didn't make much small talk with the other guys unless it had something to do with work. I didn't have nothing against anyone, not even the coloureds. You didn't talk to them, that's all. That's just the way it was.

The waiters, they thought they were better than the rest of us. But there was this one American, a young guy named John Petersen, who was all right. Petersen had brown eyes and wavy brown hair that he wore kinda long. It was his eyes that you remembered. Smart and serious, but gentle at the same time.

Petersen was different than the other waiters, who wouldn't lift a finger to help you even when they weren't busy. John would pitch in and bus my tables for me when I got in a jam. He'd jump in with the dishes, too, back in the kitchen, when the dining room was running low on silver, and like I say, those were coloureds back there. I even saw him talking with those guys sometimes like they were pals. It was like he came from someplace where that was okay. John was just one of those who made friends easy, I guess. I can't think of no one who didn't like him. Well, there musta been one person, at least. I'm gonna come to that later on.

Me and John went out for a beer one night after work, to a saloon he knew. I wasn't comfortable because it was all Americans and I didn't see no one who looked like me. But John made me feel okay and after two beers I forgot. He talked to me about the job and the pennies me and the coloured guys in the kitchen were making, and how it wasn't right. He talked about some changes that were coming to make it better for us, but he didn't say what they were.

'I'm happy,' I said, as I drank off the beer in my mug. 'I got a job, what the hell.'

'You want to make more money don't you?' he said. 'You'd like to have a day off once in a while, wouldn't you?'

'Goddamn right. But I take off a day, I'm not gonna get paid.'

'It doesn't have to be like that, friend.'

'Yeah, okay.'

'Do you know what "strength in numbers" means?'

I looked around for the bartender 'cause I didn't know what the hell John was talking about and I didn't know what to say.

John put his hand around my arm. 'I'm putting together a meeting. I'm hoping some of the busmen and the kitchen guys will make it. Do you think you can come?'

'What we gonna meet for, huh?'

'We're going to talk about those changes I been telling you about. Together, we're going to make a plan.'

'I don't want to go to no meeting. I want a day off, I'm just gonna go ask for it, eh?'

'You don't understand.' John put his face close to mine. 'The workers are being exploited.'

'I work and they pay me,' I said with a shrug. 'That's all I know. Other than that? I don't give a damn nothing.' I pulled my arm away but I smiled when I did it. I didn't want to join no group, but I wanted him to know we were still pals. 'C'mon, John, let's drink.'

I needed that job. But I felt bad, turning him down about that meeting. You could see it meant something to him, whatever the hell he was talking about, and I liked him. He was the only American in the restaurant who treated me like we were both the same. You know, man to man.

Well, he wasn't the only American who made me feel like a man. There was this woman, name of Laura, a hostess who also made change from the bills. She bought her dresses too small and had hair bleached white, like Jean Harlow. She was about two years and ten pounds away from the end of her looks. Laura wasn't pretty but her ass could bring tears to your eyes. Also, she had huge tits.

I caught her giving me the eye the first night I worked there. By the third night she said something to me about my broad chest as I was walking by her. I nodded and smiled, but I kept walking 'cause I was carrying a heavy tray. When I looked back she gave me a wink. She was a real whore, that one. I knew right then I was gonna fuck her. At the end of the night I asked her if she would go to the pictures with me sometime. 'I'm free tomorrow,' she says. I acted like it was an honour and a big surprise.

I worked every night, so we had to make it a matinee. We took the streetcar down to the Earle, on 13th Street, down below F. I wore my blue serge suit and high button shoes. I looked like I had a little bit of money, but we still got the fisheye, walking down the street. A blonde and a Greek with dark skin and a heavy black moustache. I couldn't hide that I wasn't too long off the boat.

The Earle had a stage show before the picture. A guy named William Demarest and some dancers who Laura said were like the Rockettes. What the hell did I know, I was just looking at their legs. After the coming attractions and the short subject the picture came on: 'Gold Diggers of 1933.' The man dancers looked like cocksuckers to me. I liked Westerns better, but it was all right. Fifteen cents for each of us. It was cheaper than taking her to a saloon.

Afterwards, we went to her place, an apartment in a rowhouse off H in Northeast. I used the bathroom and saw a Barnards Shaving Cream and other man things in there, but I didn't ask her nothing about it when I came back out. I found her in the bedroom. She had poured us a couple of rye whiskies and drawn the curtains so it felt like the night. A radio played something she called 'jug band'; it sounded like coloured music to me. She asked me, did I want to dance. I shrugged and tossed back all the rye in my glass and pulled her to me rough. We moved slow, even though the music was fast.

'Bill?' she said, looking up at me. She had painted her eyes with something and there was black mark next to one of them were the paint had come off.

'Uh,' I said.

'What do they call you where you're from?'

'Vasili.'

I kissed her warm lips. She bit mine and drew a little blood. I pushed myself against her to let her know what I had.

'Why, Va-silly,' she said. 'You are like a horse, aren't you?'

I just kinda nodded and smiled. She stepped back and got out of her dress and her slip, and then undid her brassiere. She did it slow.

'*Ella,*' I said.

'What does that mean?'

'Hurry it up,' I said, with a little motion of my hand. Laura laughed.

She pulled the bra off and her tits bounced. They were everything I thought they would be. She came to me and unbuckled my belt, pulling at it clumsy, and her breath was hot on my face. By then, God, I was ready.

I sat her on the edge of the bed, put one of her legs up on my shoulder, and gave it to her. I heard a woman having a baby in the village once, and those were the same kinda sounds that Laura made. There was spit dripping out the side of her mouth as I slammed myself into her over and over again. I'm telling you, her bed took some plaster off the wall that day.

After I blew my load into her I climbed off. I didn't say nice things to her or nothing like that. She got what she wanted and so did I. Laura smoked a cigarette and watched me get dressed. The whole room smelled like pussy. She didn't look so good to me no more. I couldn't wait to get out of there and breathe fresh air.

We didn't see each other again outside of work. She only stayed at the restaurant a coupla more weeks, and then she disappeared. I guess the man who owned the shaving cream told her it was time to quit.

For awhile there nothing happened and I just kept working hard. John didn't mention no meetings again though he was just as nice as before. I slept late and bused the tables at night. Life wasn't fun or bad. It was just ordinary. Then that bastard Wesley Schmidt came to work and everything changed.

Schmidt was a tall young guy with a thin moustache, big in the shoulders, big hands. He kept his hair slicked back. His eyes were real blue, like water under ice. He had a row of big straight teeth. He smiled all the time, but the smile, it didn't make you feel good.

Schmidt got hired as a waiter, but he wasn't any good at it. He got tangled up fast when the place got busy. He served food to the wrong tables all the time, and he spilled plenty of drinks. It didn't seem like he'd ever done that kind of work before.

No one liked him, but he was one of those guys, he didn't know it, or maybe he knew and didn't care. He laughed and told jokes and slapped the busmen on the back like we were his friends. He treated the kitchen guys like dogs when he was tangled up, raising his voice at them when the food didn't come up as fast as he liked it. Then he tried to be nice to them later.

One time he really screamed at Raymond, the head cook on the line, called him a 'lazy shine' on this night when the place was packed. When the dining room cleared up Schmidt walked back into the kitchen and told Raymond in a soft voice that he didn't mean nothing by it, giving him that smile of his and patting his arm. Raymond just nodded real slow. Schmidt told me later, 'That's all you got to do, is scold 'em and then talk real sweet to 'em later. That's how they learn. 'Cause they're like children. Right, Bill?' He meant coloureds, I guess. By the way he talked to me, real slow the way you would to a kid, I could tell he thought I was a coloured guy, too.

At the end of the night the waiters always sat in the dining room and ate a stew or something that the kitchen had prepared. The busmen, we served it to the waiters. I was running dinner out to one of them and forgot something back in the kitchen. When I went back to get it, I saw Raymond, spitting into a plate of stew. The other coloured guys in the kitchen were standing in a circle around Raymond, watching him do it. They all looked over at me when I walked in. It was real quiet and I guess they were waiting to see what I was gonna do.

'Who's that for?' I said. 'Eh?'

'Schmidt,' said Raymond.

I walked over to where they were. I brought up a bunch of stuff from deep down in my throat and spit real good into that plate. Raymond put a spoon in the stew and stirred it up.

'I better take it out to him,' I said, 'before it gets cold.'

'Don't forget the garnish,' said Raymond.

He put a flower of parsley on the plate, turning it a little so it looked nice. I took the stew out and served it to Schmidt. I watched him take the first bite and nod his head like it was good. None of the coloured guys said nothing to me about it again.

I got drunk with John Petersen in a saloon a coupla nights after and told him what I'd done. I thought he'd a get a good laugh out of it, but instead he got serious. He put his hand on my arm the way he did when he wanted me to listen.

'Stay out of Schmidt's way,' said John.

'Ah,' I said, with a wave of my hand. 'He gives me any trouble, I'm gonna punch him in the kisser.' The beer was making me brave.

'Just stay out of his way.'

'I look afraid to you?'

'I'm telling you, Schmidt is no waiter.'

'I know it. He's the worst goddamn waiter I ever seen. Maybe you ought to have one of those meetings of yours and see if you can get him thrown out.'

'Don't ever mention those meetings again, to anyone,' said John, and he squeezed my arm tight. I tried to pull it away from him but he held his grip. 'Bill, do you know what a Pinkerton man is?'

'What the hell?'

'Never mind. You just keep to yourself, and don't talk about those meetings, hear?'

I had to look away from his eyes. 'Sure, sure.'

'Okay, friend.' John let go of my arm. 'Let's have another beer.'

A week later John Petersen didn't show up for work. And a week after that the cops found him floating down river in the Potomac. I read about it in the Tribune. It was just a short notice, and it didn't say nothing else.

A cop in a suit came to the restaurant and asked us some questions. A couple of the waiters said that John probably had some bad hootch and fell into the drink. I didn't know what to think. When it got around to the rest of the crew, everyone kinda got quiet, if you know what I mean. Even that bastard Wesley didn't make no jokes. I guess we were all thinking about John in our own way. Me, I wanted to throw up. I'm telling you, thinking about John in that river, it made me sick.

John didn't ever talk about no family and nobody knew nothing about a funeral. After a few days, it seemed like everybody in the restaurant forgot about him. But me, I couldn't forget.

One night I walked into Chinatown. It wasn't far from my new place. There was this kid from St Mary's, Billy Nicodemus, whose father worked at the city morgue. Nicodemus wasn't no doctor or nothing, he washed off the slabs and cleaned the place, like that. He was known as a hard drinker, maybe because of what he saw every day, and maybe just because he liked the taste. I knew where he liked to drink.

I found him in a non-name restaurant on the Hip-Sing side of Chinatown. He was in a booth by himself, drinking something from a teacup. I crossed the room, walking through the cigarette smoke, passing the whores and the skinny Chink gangsters in their too-big suits and the cops who were taking money from the Chinks to look the other way. I stood over Nicodemus and told him who I was. I told him I knew his kid, told him his kid was good. Nicodemus motioned for me to have a seat.

A waiter brought me an empty cup. I poured myself some gin from the teapot on the table. We tapped cups and drank. Nicodemus had straight black hair wetted down and a big mole with hair coming out of it on one of his cheeks. He talked better than I did. We said some things that were about nothing and then I asked him some questions about John. The gin had loosened his tongue.

'Yeah, I remember him,' said Nicodemus, after thinking about it for a short while. He gave me the once-over and leaned forward. 'This was your friend?'

'Yes.'

'They found a bullet in the back of his head. A twenty-two.'

I nodded and turned the teacup in small circles on the table. '*The Tribune* didn't say nothing about that.'

'The papers don't always say. The police cover it up while they look for who did it. But that boy didn't drown. He was murdered first, then dropped in the drink.'

'You saw him?' I said.

Nicodemus shrugged. 'Sure.'

'What'd he look like?'

'You really wanna know?'

'Yeah.'

'He was all grey and blown up, like a balloon. The gas does that to 'em, when they been in the water.'

'What about his eyes?'

'They were open. Pleading.'

'Huh?'

'His eyes. It was like they were sayin' please.'

I needed a drink. I had some gin.

'You ever heard of a Pinkerton man?' I said.

'Sure,' said Nicodemus. 'A detective.'   ·

'Like the police?'

'No.'

'*What*, then?'

'They go to work with other guys and pretend they're one of them. They find out who's stealing. Or they find out who's trying to make trouble for the boss. Like the ones who want to make a strike.'

'You mean, like if a guy wants to get the workers together and make things better?'

'Yeah. Have meetings and all that. The guys who want to start a union. Pinkertons look for those guys.'

We drank the rest of the gin. We talked about his kid. We talked about Schmeling and Baer, and the wrestling match that was coming up between Londos and George Zaharias at Griffith Stadium. I got up from my seat, shook Nicodemus's hand, and thanked him for the conversation.

'*Efcharisto, patrioti.*'

'*Yasou, Vasili.*'

I walked back to my place and had a beer I didn't need. I was drunk and more confused than I had been before. I kept hearing John's voice, the way he called me 'friend'. I saw his eyes saying please. I kept thinking, I should have gone to his goddamn meeting, if that was gonna make him happy. I kept thinking I had let him down. While I was thinking, I sharpened the blade of my Italian switch knife on a stone.

The next night, last night, I was serving Wesley Schmidt his dinner after we closed. He was sitting by himself like he always did. I dropped the plate down in front of him.

'You got a minute to talk?' I said.

'Go ahead and talk,' he said, putting the spoon to his stew and stirring it around.

'I wanna be a Pinkerton man,' I said.

Schmidt stopped stirring his stew and looked up my way. He smiled, showing me his white teeth. Still, his eyes were cold.

'That's nice. But why are you telling me this?'

'I wanna be a Pinkerton, just like you.'

Schmidt pushed his stew plate away from him and looked around the dining room to make sure no one could hear us. He studied my face. I guess I was sweating. Hell, I *know* I was. I could feel it dripping on my back.

'You look upset,' said Schmidt, his voice real soft, like music. 'You look like you could use a friend.'

'I just wanna talk.'

'Okay. You feel like having a beer, something like that?'

'Sure, I could use a beer.'

'I finish eating, I'll go down and get my car. I'll meet you in the alley out back. Don't tell anyone, hear, because then they might want to come along. And we wouldn't have the chance to talk.'

'I'm not gonna tell no one. We just drive around, eh? I'm too dirty to go to a saloon.'

'That's swell,' said Schmidt. 'We'll just drive around.'

I went out to the alley were Schmidt was parked. Nobody saw me get into his car. It was a blue, '31 Dodge coupe with wire wheels, a rumble seat and a trunk rack. A five hundred dollar car if it was dime.

'Pretty,' I said, as I got in beside him. There were hand-tailored slipcovers on the seats.

'I like nice things,' said Schmidt.

He was wearing his suit jacket, and it had to be eighty degrees. I could see a lump under the jacket. I figured, the bastard is carrying a gun.

We drove up to Colvin's, on 14th Street. Schmidt went in and returned with a bag of loose bottles of beer. There must have been a half dozen Schlitz's in the bag. Him making waiter's pay, and the fancy car and the high-priced beer.

He opened a coupla beers and handed me one. The bottle was ice cold. Hot as the night was, the beer tasted good.

We drove around for a while. We went down to Hanes Point. Schmidt parked the Dodge facing the Washington Channel. Across the channel, the lights from the fish vendors on Maine Avenue threw colour on the water. We drank another beer. He gave me one of his tailor-mades and we had a coupla smokes. He talked about the Senators and the Yankees, and how Baer had taken Schmeling out with a right in the tenth. Schmidt didn't want to talk about nothing serious yet. He was waiting for the beer to work on me, I knew.

'Goddamn heat,' I said. 'Let's drive around some, get some air moving.'

Schmidt started the coupe. 'Where to?'

'I'm gonna show you a whorehouse. Best secret in town.'

Schmidt looked me over and laughed. The way you laugh at a clown.

I gave Schmidt some directions. We drove some, away from the park and the monuments to where people lived. We went through a little tunnel and crossed into Southwest. Most of the streetlamps were broke here. The rowhouses were shabby, and you could see shacks in the alleys and clothes hanging on lines outside the shacks. It was late, long time past midnight. There weren't many people out. The ones that were out were coloureds. We were in a place called Bloodfield.

'Pull over there,' I said, pointing to a spot along the kerb where there wasn't no light. 'I wanna show you the place I'm talking about.'

Schmidt did it and cut the engine. Across the street were some houses. All except one of them was dark. From the lighted one came fast music, like the coloured music Laura had played in her room. 'There it is right there,' I said, meaning the house with the light. I was lying through my teeth. I didn't know who lived there and I sure didn't know if that house had whores. I had never been down here before.

Schmidt turned his head to look at the rowhouse. I slipped my switch knife out of my right pocket and laid it flat against my right leg.

When he turned back to face me he wasn't smiling no more. He had heard about Bloodfield and he knew he was in it. I think he was scared.

'You bring me down to niggertown, for *what*?' he said. 'To show me a whorehouse?'

'I thought you're gonna like it.'

'Do I look like a man who'd pay to fuck a nigger? *Do* I? You don't know anything about me.'

He was showing his true self now. He was nervous as a cat. My nerves were bad, too. I was sweating through my shirt. I could smell my own stink in the car.

'I know plenty,' I said.

'Yeah? *What* do you know?'

'Pretty car, pretty suits ... top shelf beer. How you get all this, huh?'

'I earned it.'

'As a Pinkerton, eh?'

Schmidt blinked real slow and shook his head. He looked out his window, looking at nothing, wasting time while he decided what he was gonna do. I found the raised button on the pearl handle of my knife. I pushed the button. The blade flicked open and barely made a sound. I held the knife against my leg and turned it so the blade was pointing back.

Sweat rolled down my neck as I looked around. There wasn't nobody out on the street.

Schmidt turned his head. He gripped the steering wheel with his right hand and straightened his arm.

'What do you want?' he said.

'I just wanna know what happened to John.'

Schmidt smiled. All those white teeth. I could see him with his mouth open, his lips stretched, those teeth showing. The way an animal looks after you kill it. Him lying on his back on a slab.

'I heard he drowned,' said Schmidt.

'You think so, eh?'

'Yeah. I guess he couldn't swim.'

'Pretty hard to swim, you got a bullet in your head.'

Schmidt's smile turned down. 'Can *you* swim, Bill?'

I brought the knife across real fast and buried it into his armpit. I sunk the blade all the way to the handle. He lost his breath and made a short scream. I twisted the knife. His blood came out like someone was pouring it from a jug. It was warm and it splashed on to my hands. I pulled the knife out and while he was kicking at the floorboards I stabbed him a coupla more times in the chest. I musta hit his heart or something because all the sudden there was plenty of blood all over the car. I'm telling you, the seats were slippery with it. He stopped moving. His eyes were open and they were dead.

I didn't get tangled up about it or nothing like that. I wasn't scared. I opened up his suit jacket and saw a steel revolver with wood grips holstered there. It was small caliber. I didn't touch the gun. I took his wallet out of his trousers, pulled the bills out of it, wiped off the wallet with my shirttail, and threw the empty wallet on the ground. I put the money in my shoe. I fit the blade back into the handle of my switch knife and slipped the knife into my pocket. I put all the empty beer bottles together with the full ones in the paper bag and took the bag with me as I got out of the car. I closed the door soft and wiped off the handle and walked down the street.

I didn't see no one for a couple of blocks. I came to a sewer and I put the bag down the hole. The next block I came to another sewer and I took off my bloody shirt and threw it down the hole of that one. I was wearing an undershirt, didn't have no sleeves. My pants were black so you couldn't see the blood. I kept walking towards Northwest.

Someone laughed from deep in an alley and I kept on.

Another block or so I came up on a group of *mavri* standing around the steps of a house. They were smoking cigarettes and drinking from bottles of beer. I wasn't gonna run or nothing. I had to go by them to get home. They stopped talking and gave me hard eyes as I got near them. That's when I saw that one of them was the cook, Raymond, from the kitchen. Our eyes kind of came together but neither one of us said a word or smiled or even made a nod.

One of the coloureds started to come towards me and Raymond stopped his with the flat of his palm. I walked on.

I walked for a couple of hours, I guess. Somewhere in Northwest I dropped my switch knife down another sewer. When I heard it hit the sewer bottom I started to cry. I wasn't crying 'cause I had killed Schmidt. I didn't give a damn nothing about him. I was crying 'cause my father had given me that knife, and now it was gone. I guess I knew I was gonna be in America forever, and I wasn't never going back to Greece. I'd never see my home or my parents again.

When I got back to my place I washed my hands real good. I opened up a bottle of Abner Drury and put fire to a Fatima and had myself a seat at the table.

This is where I am right now.

Maybe I'm gonna get caught and maybe I'm not. They're gonna find Schmidt in that neighbourhood and they're gonna figure a coloured guy killed him for his money. The cops, they're gonna turn Bloodfield upside down. If Raymond tells them he saw me I'm gonna get the chair. If he doesn't, I'm gonna be free. Either way, what the hell, I can't do nothing about it now.

I'll work at the hotel, get some experience and some money, then open my own place, like Nick Stefanos. Maybe if I can find two nickels to rub together, I'm gonna go to church and talk to that girl, Irene, see if she wants to be my wife. I'm not gonna wait too long. She's clean as a whistle, that one.

I've had my eye on her for some time.

NEIL GAIMAN is the author of the bestselling novels *Neverwhere, Stardust, American Gods, Coraline, Anansi Boys, The Graveyard Book, The Ocean at the End of the Lane*, and *Good Omens* (with Terry Pratchett); the *Sandman* series of graphic novels; the story collections *Smoke and Mirrors* and *Fragile Things*; and co-editor (with Al Sarrantonio) of the fiction anthology *Stories*. He is the winner of numerous literary honours. Born in 1960 in Portchester, England, he now lives in America.

The Case of Death and Honey

Neil Gaiman

It was a mystery in those parts for years what had happened to the old white ghost man, the barbarian with his huge shoulder-bag. There were some who supposed him to have been murdered, and, later, they dug up the floor of Old Gao's little shack high on the hillside, looking for treasure, but they found nothing but ash and fire-blackened tin trays.

This was after Old Gao himself had vanished, you understand, and before his son came back from Lijiang to take over the beehives on the hill.

☙ ☙ ☙

This is the problem, wrote Holmes in 1899: Ennui. And lack of interest. Or rather, it all becomes too easy. When the joy of solving crimes is the challenge, the possibility

33

that you cannot, why then the crimes have something to hold your attention. But when each crime is soluble, and so easily soluble at that, why then there is no point in solving them.

Look: this man has been murdered. Well then, someone murdered him. He was murdered for one or more of a tiny handful of reasons: he inconvenienced someone, or he had something that someone wanted, or he had angered someone. Where is the challenge in that?

I would read in the dailies an account of a crime that had the police baffled, and I would find that I had solved it, in broad strokes if not in detail, before I had finished the article. Crime is too soluble. It dissolves. Why call the police and tell them the answers to their mysteries? I leave it, over and over again, as a challenge for them, as it is no challenge for me.

I am only alive when I perceive a challenge.

❦ ❦ ❦

The bees of the misty hills, hills so high that they were sometimes called a mountain, were humming in the pale summer sun as they moved from spring flower to spring flower on the slope. Old Gao listened to them without pleasure. His cousin, in the village across the valley, had many dozens of hives, all of them already filling with honey, even this early in the year; also, the honey was as white as snow-jade. Old Gao did not believe that the white honey tasted any better than the yellow or light-brown honey that his own bees produced, although his bees produced it in meagre quantities, but his cousin could sell his white honey for twice what Old Gao could get for the best honey he had.

On his cousin's side of the hill, the bees were earnest, hard-working, golden-brown workers, who brought pollen and nectar back to the hives in enormous quantities. Old Gao's bees were ill-tempered and black, shiny as bullets, who produced as much honey as they needed to get through the winter and only a little more: enough for Old Gao to sell from door to door, to his fellow villagers, one small lump of honeycomb at a time. He would charge more for the brood-comb, filled with bee-larvae, sweet-tasting morsels of protein, when he had brood-comb to sell, which was rarely, for the bees were angry and sullen and everything they did, they did as little as possible, including make more bees, and Old Gao was always aware that each piece of brood-comb he sold were bees he would not have to make honey for him to sell later in the year.

Old Gao was as sullen and as sharp as his bees. He had had a wife once, but she had died in childbirth. The son who had killed her lived for a week, then died himself. There would be nobody to say the funeral rites for Old Gao, no one to clean his grave for festivals or to put offerings upon it. He would die unremembered, as unremarkable and as unremarked as his bees.

The old white stranger came over the mountains in late spring of that year, as soon as the roads were passable, with a huge brown bag strapped to his shoulders. Old Gao heard about him before he met him.

'There is a barbarian who is looking at bees,' said his cousin.

Old Gao said nothing. He had gone to his cousin to buy a pailful of second rate comb, damaged or uncapped and liable soon to spoil. He bought it cheaply to feed to his own bees, and if he sold some of it in his own village, no one was any the wiser. The two men were drinking tea in Gao's cousin's hut on the hillside. From late spring, when the first honey started to flow, until first frost, Gao's cousin left his house in the village and went to live in the hut on the hillside, to live and to sleep beside his beehives, for fear of thieves. His wife and his children would take the honeycomb and the bottles of snow-white honey down the hill to sell.

Old Gao was not afraid of thieves. The shiny black bees of Old Gao's hives would have no mercy on anyone who disturbed them. He slept in his village, unless it was time to collect the honey.

'I will send him to you,' said Gao's cousin. 'Answer his questions, show him your bees and he will pay you.'

'He speaks our tongue?'

'His dialect is atrocious. He said he learned to speak from sailors, and they were mostly Cantonese. But he learns fast, although he is old.'

Old Gao grunted, uninterested in sailors. It was late in the morning, and there was still four hours walking across the valley to his village, in the heat of the day. He finished his tea. His cousin drank finer tea than Old Gao had ever been able to afford.

He reached his hives while it was still light, put the majority of the uncapped honey into his weakest hives. He had eleven hives. His cousin had over a hundred. Old Gao was stung twice doing this, on the back of the hand and the back of the neck. He had been stung over a thousand times in his life. He could not have told you how many times. He barely noticed the stings of other bees, but the stings of his own black bees always hurt, even if they no longer swelled or burned.

The next day a boy came to Old Gao's house in the village, to tell him that there was someone – and that the someone was a giant foreigner – who was asking for him. Old Gao simply grunted. He walked across the village with the boy at his steady pace, while the boy ran ahead, and soon was lost to sight.

Old Gao found the stranger sitting drinking tea on the porch of the Widow Zhang's house. Old Gao had known the Widow Zhang's mother, fifty years ago. She had been a friend of his wife. Now she was long dead. He did not believe anyone who had known his wife still lived. The Widow Zhang fetched Old Gao tea, introduced him to the elderly barbarian, who had removed his bag and sat beside the small table.

They sipped their tea. The barbarian said, 'I wish to see your bees.'

🐝   🐝   🐝

Mycroft's death was the end of Empire, and no one knew it but the two of us. He lay in that pale room, his only covering a thin white sheet, as if he were already becoming a ghost from the popular imagination, and needed only eye-holes in the sheet to finish the impression.

I had imagined that his illness might have wasted him away, but he seemed huger than ever, his fingers swollen into white suet sausages.

I said, 'Good evening, Mycroft. Doctor Hopkins tells me you have two weeks to live, and stated that I was under no circumstances to inform you of this.'

'The man's a dunderhead,' said Mycroft, his breath coming in huge wheezes between the words. 'I will not make it to Friday.'

'Saturday at least,' I said.

'You always were an optimist. No, Thursday evening and then I shall be nothing more than an exercise in practical geometry for Hopkins and the funeral directors at Snigsby and Malterson, who will have the challenge, given the narrowness of the doors and corridors, of getting my carcass out of this room and out of the building.'

'I had wondered,' I said. 'Particularly given the staircase. But they will take out the window-frame and lower you to the street like a grand piano.'

Mycroft snorted at that. Then, 'I am forty-nine years old, Sherlock. In my head is the British Government. Not the ballot and hustings nonsense, but the business of the thing. There is no one else knows what the troop movements in the hills of Afghanistan have to do with the desolate shores of North Wales, no one else who sees the whole picture. Can you imagine the mess that this lot and their children will make of Indian Independence?'

I had not previously given any thought to the matter. '*Will* it become independent?'

'Inevitably. In thirty years, at the outside. I have written several recent memoranda on the topic. As I have on so many other subjects. There are memoranda on the Russian Revolution – that'll be along within the decade I'll wager – and on the German problem and ... oh, so many others. Not that I expect them to be read or understood.' Another wheeze. My brother's lungs rattled like the windows in an empty house. 'You know, if I were to live, the British Empire might last another thousand years, bringing peace and improvement to the world.'

In the past, especially when I was a boy, whenever I heard Mycroft make a grandiose pronouncement like that I would say something to bait him. But not now, not on his death-bed. And also I was certain that he was not speaking of the Empire as it was, a flawed and fallible construct of flawed and fallible people, but of a British Empire that existed only in his head, a glorious force for civilisation and universal prosperity.

I do not, and did not, believe in Empires. But I believed in Mycroft.

Mycroft Holmes. Nine and forty years of age. He had seen in the new century but the Queen would still outlive him by several months. She was more than thirty years older than he was, and in every way a tough old bird. I wondered to myself whether this unfortunate end might have been avoided.

Mycroft said, 'You are right of course, Sherlock. Had I forced myself to exercise. Had I lived on bird-seed and cabbages instead of porterhouse steak. Had I taken up country dancing along with a wife and a puppy and in all other ways behaved contrary to my nature, I might have bought myself another dozen or so years. But what is that in the scheme of things? Little enough. And sooner or later, I would enter my dotage. No. I am of the opinion that it would take two hundred years to train a functioning Civil Service, let alone a secret service ...'

I had said nothing.

The pale room had no decorations on the wall of any kind. None of Mycroft's citations. No illustrations, photographs or paintings. I compared his austere digs to my own cluttered rooms in Baker Street and I wondered, not for the first time, at Mycroft's mind. He needed nothing on the outside, for it was all on the inside – everything he had seen, everything he had experienced, everything he had read. He could close his eyes and walk through the National Gallery, or browse the British Museum Reading Room – or, more likely, compare intelligence reports from the edge of the Empire with the price of wool in Wigan and the unemployment statistics in Hove, and then, from this and only this, order a man promoted or a traitor's quiet death.

Mycroft wheezed enormously, and then he said, 'It is a crime, Sherlock.'

'I beg your pardon?'

'A crime. It is a crime, my brother, as heinous and as monstrous as any of the penny dreadful massacres you have investigated. A crime against the world, against nature, against order.'

'I must confess, my dear fellow, that I do not entirely follow you. What is a crime?'

'My death,' said Mycroft, 'in the specific. And Death in general.' He looked into my eyes. 'I mean it,' he said. 'Now isn't *that* a crime worth investigating, Sherlock, old fellow? One that might keep your attention for longer than it will take you to establish that the poor fellow who used to conduct the brass band in Hyde Park was murdered by the third cornet using a preparation of strychnine.'

'Arsenic,' I corrected him, almost automatically.

'I think you will find,' wheezed Mycroft, 'that the arsenic, while present, had in fact fallen in flakes from the green-painted bandstand itself onto his supper. Symptoms of arsenical poison a complete red-herring. No, it was strychnine that did for the poor fellow.'

Mycroft said no more to me that day or ever. He breathed his last the following Thursday, late in the afternoon, and on the Friday the worthies of Snigsby and Malterson removed the casing from the window of the pale room, and lowered my brother's remains into the street, like a grand piano.

His funeral service was attended by me, by my friend Watson, by our cousin Harriet and, in accordance with Mycroft's express wishes – by no one else. The Civil Service, the Foreign Office, even the Diogenes Club – these institutions and their representatives were absent. Mycroft had been reclusive in life; he was to be equally as reclusive in death. So it was the three of us, and the parson, who had not known my brother, and had no conception that it was the more omniscient arm of the British Government itself that he was consigning to the grave.

Four burly men held fast to the ropes and lowered my brother's remains to their final resting place, and did, I daresay, their utmost not to curse at the weight of the thing. I tipped each of them half a crown.

Mycroft was dead at forty-nine, and, as they lowered him into his grave, in my imagination I could still hear his clipped, grey, wheeze as he seemed to be saying, 'Now there is a crime worth investigating.'

❧   ❧   ❧

The stranger's accent was not too bad, although his vocabulary seemed limited, but he seemed to be talking in the local dialect, or something near to it. He was a fast learner. Old Gao hawked and spat into the dust of the street. He said nothing. He did not wish to take the stranger up the hillside; he did not wish to disturb his bees. In Old Gao's experience, the less he bothered his bees, the better they did. And if they stung the barbarian, what then?

The stranger's hair was silver-white, and sparse; his nose, the first barbarian nose that Old Gao had seen, was huge and curved and put Old Gao in mind of the beak of an eagle; his skin was tanned the same colour as Old Gao's own, and was lined deeply. Old Gao was not certain that he could read a barbarian's face as he could read the face of a person, but he thought the man seemed most serious and, perhaps, unhappy.

'Why?'

'I study bees. Your brother tells me you have big black bees here. Unusual bees.'

Old Gao shrugged. He did not correct the man on the relationship with his cousin.

The stranger asked Old Gao if he had eaten, and when Gao said that he had not, the stranger asked the Widow Zhang to bring them soup and rice and whatever was good that she had in her kitchen, which turned out to be a stew of black tree-fungus and vegetables and tiny transparent river-fish, little bigger than tadpoles. The two men ate in silence. When they had finished eating, the stranger said, 'I would be honoured if you would show me your bees.'

Old Gao said nothing, but the stranger paid Widow Zhang well and he put his bag on his back. Then he waited, and, when Old Gao began to walk, the stranger followed him. He carried his bag as if it weighed nothing to him. He was strong for an old man, thought Old Gao, and wondered whether all such barbarians were so strong.

'Where are you from?'

'England,' said the stranger.

Old Gao remembered his father telling him about a war with the English, over trade and over opium, but that was long ago.

They walked up the hillside, that was, perhaps, a mountainside. It was steep, and the hillside was too rocky to be cut into fields. Old Gao tested the stranger's pace, walking faster than usual, and the stranger kept up with him, with his pack on his back.

The stranger stopped several times, however. He stopped to examine flowers – the small white flowers that bloomed in early spring elsewhere in the valley, but in late spring here on the side of the hill. There was a bee on one of the flowers, and the stranger knelt and observed it. Then he reached into his pocket, produced a large magnifying glass and examined the bee through it, and made notes in a small pocket notebook, in an incomprehensible writing.

Old Gao had never seen a magnifying glass before, and he leaned in to look at the bee, so black and so strong and so very different from the bees elsewhere in that valley.

'One of your bees?'

'Yes,' said Old Gao. 'Or one like it.'

'Then we shall let her find her own way home,' said the stranger, and he did not disturb the bee, and he put away the magnifying glass.

The Croft
East Dene, Sussex
August 11th, 1919

My dear Watson,

I have taken our discussion of this afternoon to heart, considered it carefully, and am prepared to modify my previous opinions.

I am amenable to your publishing your account of the incidents of 1903, specifically of the final case before my retirement, with the following changes.

In addition to the usual changes that you would make to disguise actual people and places, I would suggest that you replace the entire scenario we encountered (I speak of Professor Presbury's garden. I shall not write of it further here) with monkey glands, or some such extract from the testes of an ape or lemur, sent by some foreign mystery-man. Perhaps the monkey-extract could have the effect of making Professor Presbury move like an ape – he could be some kind of 'creeping man', perhaps? – or possibly make him able to clamber up the sides of buildings and up trees. Perhaps he could grow a tail, but this might be too fanciful even for you, Watson, although no more fanciful than many of the rococo additions you have made in your histories to otherwise humdrum events in my life and work.

In addition, I have written the following speech, to be delivered by myself, at the end of your narrative. Please make certain that something much like this is there, in which I inveigh against living too long, and the foolish urges that push foolish people to do foolish things to prolong their foolish lives.

There is a very real danger to humanity. If one could live for ever, if youth were simply there for the taking, that the material, the sensual, the worldly would all prolong their worthless lives. The spiritual would not avoid the call to something higher. It would be the survival of the least fit. What sort of cesspool may not our poor world become?

Something along those lines, I fancy, would set my mind at rest.

Let me see the finished article, please, before you submit it to be published.

I remain, old friend, your most obedient servant,
Sherlock Holmes

They reached Old Gao's bees late in the afternoon. The beehives were grey, wooden boxes piled behind a structure so simple it could barely be called a shack. Four posts, a roof, and hangings of oiled cloth that served to keep out the worst of the spring rains and the summer storms. A small charcoal brazier served for warmth, if you placed a blanket over it and yourself, and to cook upon; a wooden palette in the centre of the structure, with an ancient ceramic pillow, served as a bed on the occasions that Old Gao slept up on the mountainside with the bees, particularly in the autumn, when he harvested most of the honey. There was little enough of it compared to the output of his cousin's hives, but it was enough that he would sometimes spend two or three days waiting for the comb that he had crushed and stirred into a slurry to drain through the cloth into the buckets and pots that he had carried up the mountainside. Then he would melt the remainder, the sticky wax and bits of pollen and dirt and bee slurry, in a pot, to extract the beeswax, and he would give the sweet water back to the bees. Then he would carry the honey and the wax blocks down the hill to the village to sell.

He showed the barbarian stranger the eleven hives, watched impassively as the stranger put on a veil and opened a hive, examining first the bees, then the contents of a brood box, and finally the queen, through his magnifying glass. He showed no fear, no discomfort: in everything he did the stranger's movements were gentle and slow, and he was not stung, nor did he crush or hurt a single bee. This impressed Old Gao. He had assumed that barbarians were inscrutable, unreadable, mysterious creatures, but this man seemed overjoyed to have encountered Gao's bees. His eyes were shining.

Old Gao fired up the brazier, to boil some water. Long before the charcoal was hot, however, the stranger had removed from his bag a contraption of glass and metal. He had filled the upper half of it with water from the stream, lit a flame, and soon a kettleful of water was steaming and bubbling. Then the stranger took two tin mugs from his bag, and some green tea-leaves wrapped in paper, and dropped the leaves into the mug, and poured on the water.

It was the finest tea that Old Gao had ever drunk: better by far than his cousin's tea. They drank it cross-legged on the floor.

'I would like to stay here for the summer, in this house,' said the stranger.

'Here? This is not even a house,' said Old Gao. 'Stay down in the village. Widow Zhang has a room.'

'I will stay here,' said the stranger. 'Also I would like to rent one of your beehives.'

Old Gao had not laughed in years. There were those in the village who would have thought such a thing impossible. But still, he laughed then, a guffaw of surprise and amusement that seemed to have been jerked out of him.

'I am serious,' said the stranger. He placed four silver coins on the ground between them. Old Gao had not seen where he got them from: three silver Mexican Pesos, a coin that had become popular in China years before, and a large silver yuan. It was as much money as Old Gao might see in a year of selling honey. 'For this money,' said the stranger, 'I would like someone to bring me food: every three days should suffice.'

Old Gao said nothing. He finished his tea and stood up. He pushed through the oiled cloth to the clearing high on the hillside. He walked over to the eleven hives: each consisted of two brood boxes with one, two, three or, in one case, even four boxes above that. He took the stranger to the hive with four boxes above it, each box filled with frames of comb.

'This hive is yours,' he said.

🐝   🐝   🐝

They were plant extracts. That was obvious. They worked, in their way, for a limited time, but they were also extremely poisonous. But watching poor Professor Pillsbury during those final days – his skin, his eyes, his gait – had convinced me that he had not been on entirely the wrong path.

I took his case of seeds, of pods, of roots, and of dried extracts and I thought. I pondered. I cogitated. I reflected. It was an intellectual problem, and could be solved, as my old maths tutor had always sought to demonstrate to me, by intellect.

They were plant extracts, and they were lethal.

Methods I used to render them non-lethal rendered them quite ineffective.

It was not a three pipe problem. I suspect it was something approaching a three hundred pipe problem before I hit upon an initial idea – a notion perhaps – of a way of processing the plants that might allow them to be ingested by human beings.

It was not a line of investigation that could easily be followed in Baker Street. So it was, in the autumn of 1903, that I moved to Sussex, and spent the winter reading every book and pamphlet and monograph so far published, I fancy, upon the care and keeping of bees. And so it was that in early April of 1904, armed only with theoretical knowledge, that I took delivery from a local farmer of my first package of bees.

I wonder, sometimes, that Watson did not suspect anything. Then again, Watson's glorious obtuseness has never ceased to surprise me, and sometimes, indeed, I had relied upon it. Still, he knew what I was like when I had no work to occupy my mind, to case to solve. He knew my lassitude, my black moods when I had no case to occupy me.

So how could he believe that I had truly retired? He knew my methods.

Indeed, Watson was there when I took receipt of my first bees. He watched, from a safe distance, as I poured the bees from the package into the empty, waiting hive, like slow, humming, gentle treacle.

He saw my excitement, and he saw nothing.

And the years passed, and we watched the Empire crumble, we watched the government unable to govern, we watched those poor heroic boys sent to the trenches of Flanders to die, all these things confirmed me in my opinions. I was not doing the right thing. I was doing the only thing.

As my face grew unfamiliar, and my finger-joints swelled and ached (not so much as they might have done, though, which I attributed to the many bee-stings I had received in my first few years as an investigative apiarist) and as Watson, dear, brave, obtuse, Watson, faded with time and paled and shrank, his skin becoming greyer, his moustache becoming the same shade of grey, my resolve to conclude my researches did not diminish. If anything, it increased.

So: my initial hypotheses were tested upon the South Downs, in an apiary of my own devising, each hive modelled upon Langstroth's. I do believe that I made every mistake that ever a novice beekeeper could or has ever made, and in addition, due to my investigations, an entire hiveful of mistakes that no beekeeper has ever made before, or shall,

I trust, ever make again. The Case of the Poisoned Beehive, Watson might have called many of them, although The Mystery of The Transfixed Women's Institute would have drawn more attention to my researches, had anyone been interested enough to investigate. (As it was, I chided Mrs Telford for simply taking a jar of honey from the shelves here without consulting me, and I ensured that, in the future, she was given several jars for her cooking from the more regular hives, and that honey from the experimental hives was locked away once it had been collected. I do not believe that this ever drew comment.)

I experimented with Dutch Bees, with German Bees and with Italians, with Carniolans and Caucasians. I regretted the loss of our British Bees to blight and, even where they had survived, to interbreeding, although I found and worked with a small hive I purchased and grew up from a frame of brood and a queen cell, from an old Abbey in St Albans, which seemed to me to be original British breeding stock.

I experimented for the best part of two decades, before I concluded that the bees that I sought, if they existed, were not to be found in England, and would not survive the distances they would need to travel to reach me by international parcel post. I needed to examine bees in India. I needed to travel perhaps further afield than that.

I have a smattering of languages.

I had my flower-seeds, and my extracts and tinctures in syrup. I needed nothing more.

I packed them up, arranged for the cottage on the Downs to be cleaned and aired once a week, and for Master Wilkins – to whom I am afraid I had developed the habit of referring, to his obvious distress, as 'Young Villikins' – to inspect the beehives, and to harvest and sell surplus honey in Eastbourne market, and to prepare the hives for winter.

I told them I did not know when I should be back.

I am an old man. Perhaps they did not expect me to return.

And, if this was indeed the case, they would, strictly speaking, have been right.

❦   ❦   ❦

Old Gao was impressed, despite himself. He had lived his life among bees. Still, watching the stranger shake the bees from the boxes, with a practised flick of his wrist, so cleanly and so sharply that the black bees seemed more surprised than angered, and simply flew or crawled back into their hive, was remarkable. The stranger then stacked the boxes filled with comb on top of one of the weaker hives, so Old Gao would still have the honey from the hive the stranger was renting.

So it was that Old Gao gained a lodger.

Old Gao gave the Widow Zhang's granddaughter a few coins to take the stranger food three times a week – mostly rice and vegetables, along with an earthenware pot filled, when she left at least, with boiling soup.

Every ten days Old Gao would walk up the hill himself. He went initially to check on the hives, but soon discovered that under the stranger's care all eleven hives were thriving as they had never thrived before. And indeed, there was now a twelfth hive, from a captured swarm of the black bees the stranger had encountered while on a walk along the hill.

Old Gao brought wood, the next time he came up to the shack, and he and the stranger spent several afternoons wordlessly working together, making extra boxes to go on the hives, building frames to fill the boxes.

One evening the stranger told Old Gao that the frames they were making had been invented by an American, only seventy years before. This seemed like nonsense to Old Gao, who made frames as his father had, and as they did across the valley, and as, he was certain, his grandfather and his grandfather's grandfather had, but he said nothing.

He enjoyed the stranger's company. They made hives together, and Old Gao wished that the stranger was a younger man. Then he would stay there for a long time, and Old Gao would have someone to leave his beehives to, when he died. But they were two old men, nailing boxes together, with thin frosty hair and old faces, and neither of them would see another dozen winters.

Old Gao noticed that the stranger had planted a small, neat garden beside the hive that he had claimed as his own, which he had moved away from the rest of the hives. He had covered it with a net. He had also created a 'back door' to the hive, so that the only bees that could reach the plants came from the hive that he was renting. Old Gao also observed that, beneath the netting, there were several trays filled with what appeared to be sugar solution of some kind, one coloured bright red, one green, one a startling blue, one yellow. He pointed to them, but all the stranger did was nod and smile.

The bees were lapping up the syrups, though, clustering and crowding on the sides of the tin dishes with their tongues down, eating until they could eat no more, and then returning to the hive.

The stranger had made sketches of Old Gao's bees. He showed the sketches to Old Gao, tried to explain the ways that Old Gao's bees differed from other honeybees, talked of ancient bees preserved in stone for millions of years, but here the stranger's Chinese failed him, and, truthfully, Old Gao was not interested. They were his bees, until he died, and after that, they were the bees of the mountainside. He had brought other bees here, but they had sickened and died, or been killed in raids by the black bees, who took their honey and left them to starve.

The last of these visits was in late summer. Old Gao went down the mountainside. He did not see the stranger again.

🐝 🐝 🐝

It is done.

It works. Already I feel a strange combination of triumph and of disappointment, as if of defeat, or of distant storm-clouds teasing at my senses.

It is strange to look at my hands and to see, not my hands as I know them, but the hands I remember from my younger days: knuckles unswollen, dark hairs, not snow-white, on the backs.

It was a quest that had defeated so many, a problem with no apparent solution. The first Emperor of China died and nearly destroyed his empire in pursuit of it, three thousand years ago, and all it took me was, what, twenty years?

I do not know if I did the right thing or not (although any 'retirement' without such an occupation would have been, literally, maddening). I took the commission from Mycroft. I investigated the problem. I arrived, inevitably, at the solution.

Will I tell the world? I will not.

And yet, I have half a pot of dark brown honey remaining in my bag; a half a pot of honey that is worth more than nations. (I was tempted to write, worth more than all the tea in China, perhaps because of my current situation, but fear that even Watson would deride it as cliché.)

And speaking of Watson ...

There is one thing left to do. My only remaining goal, and it is small enough. I shall make my way to Shanghai, and from there I shall take ship to Southampton, a half a world away.

And once I am there, I shall seek out Watson, if he still lives – and I fancy he does. It is irrational, I know, and yet I am certain that I would know, somehow, had Watson passed beyond the veil.

I shall buy theatrical makeup, disguise myself as an old man, so as not to startle him, and I shall invite my old friend over for tea.

There will be honey on buttered toast served for tea that afternoon, I fancy.

***

There were tales of a barbarian who passed through the village on his way east, but the people who told Old Gao this did not believe that it could have been the same man who had lived in Gao's shack. This one was young and proud, and his hair was dark. It was not the old man who had walked through those parts in the spring, although, one person told Gao, the bag was similar.

Old Gao walked up the mountainside to investigate, although he suspected what he would find before he got there.

The stranger was gone, and the stranger's bag.

There had been much burning, though. That was clear. Papers had been burnt – Old Gao recognised the edge of a drawing the stranger had made of one of his bees, but the rest of the papers were ash, or blackened beyond recognition, even had Old Gao been able to read barbarian writing. The papers were not the only things to have been burnt; parts of the hive that stranger had rented were now only twisted ash; there were blackened, twisted, strips of tin that might once have contained brightly coloured syrups.

The colour was added to the syrups, the stranger had told him once, so that he could tell them apart, although for what purpose Old Gao had never enquired.

He examined the shack like a detective, searching for a clue as to the stranger's nature or his whereabouts. On the ceramic pillow four silver coins had been left for him to find – two yuan coins and two silver pesos – and he put them away.

Behind the shack he found a heap of used slurry, with the last bees of the day still crawling upon it, tasting whatever sweetness was still on the surface of the still-sticky wax.

Old Gao thought long and hard before he gathered up the slurry, wrapped it loosely in cloth, and put it in a pot, which he filled with water. He heated the water on the brazier, but did not let it boil. Soon enough the wax floated to the surface, leaving the dead bees and the dirt and the pollen and the propolis inside the cloth.

He let it cool.

Then he walked outside, and he stared up at the moon. It was almost full.

He wondered how many villagers knew that his son had died as a baby. He remembered his wife, but her face was distant, and he had no portraits or photographs of her. He thought that there was nothing he was so suited for on the face of the earth as to keep the black, bullet-like bees on the side of this high, high hill. There was no other man who knew their temperament as he did.

The water had cooled. He lifted the now solid block of beeswax out of the water, placed it on the boards of the bed to finish cooling. Then he took the cloth filled with dirt and impurities out of the pot. And then, because he too was, in his way, a detective, and once you have eliminated the impossible whatever remains, however unlikely, must be the truth, he drank the sweet water in the pot. There is a lot of honey in slurry, after all, even after the majority of it has dripped through a cloth and been purified. The water tasted of honey, but not a honey that Gao had ever tasted before. It tasted of smoke, and metal, and strange flowers, and odd perfumes. It tasted, Gao thought, a little like sex.

He drank it all down, and then he slept, with his head on the ceramic pillow.

When he woke, he thought, he would decide how to deal with his cousin, who would expect to inherit the twelve hives on the hill when Old Gao went missing.

He would be an illegitimate son, perhaps, the young man who would return in the days to come. Or perhaps a son. Young Gao. Who would remember, now? It did not matter.

He would go to the city and then he would return, and he would keep the black bees on the side of the mountain for as long as days and circumstances would allow.

SIMON LEWIS works as a screenwriter and travel writer, as well as writing crime fiction. He is the author of three novels: *Go*, *Bad Traffic* and *Border Run*. His science fiction feature film *The Anomaly*, his heist film *Tiger House*, and his travel thriller *Jet Trash*, are all due out in 2014. He was born in Wales in 1971.

Buy and Bust

Simon Lewis

DC Ashton opened the Cherokee jeep passenger door and said to the driver, 'I'm Chris. I understand you have some metalwork I might be interested in.'

The driver nodded. Jesus, the arms on the guy, muscles like knotted rope. Ashton scanned the car as he got in: no one hiding in the back seat, both the driver's hands visible – resting on the wheel – door lock a catch by the handle, windows automatic and controlled by a switch beside the gearstick, now half-hidden by empty crisp packets. More junk food wrappers in the passenger footwell: Ashton trod them to make sure they were empty. Place smelled of sweat and feet.

The driver said, 'I want you to take off your clothes.' He talked slowly and without much inflection, with an eastern European accent.

'Seriously?'

'You get them back later.'

'Boxers too?'

'You can leave them on. But your shoes and socks yes.'

'We going dogging?'

'No.'

As Ashton pulled his trousers off, twisting in the narrow space, he saw glass ampules rolling in the footwell. He guessed they were steroids, and looked again at the guy – yeah, he had that big gut roiders get, acne on the back of his neck above his t-shirt there, a good pair of tits too.

'It's not every day I get into a car with a strange man and take off my clothes. Once a month, at most. What about my money? I've got a big wedge, and I'm not minded to be parted from it right away.'

'It's in a wallet?'

'No. A rubber band around it.'

'Keep it.'

Now Ashton in the passenger seat was naked except for his boxers with his tight block of cash between his thighs. The driver looked him up and down then put a big hand on the back of his neck, under the ponytail.

'See? No surprises. And nothing under the hair. You should take up a more touchy feely profession, you have such delicate hands.'

'Clothes in here,' giving Ashton a coolbag. 'And the ones that are in there, you put on.'

Grey sweatpants, identical to the driver's, and a t-shirt.

'Your old gym clothes, nice. Do I get to keep them? Only there's this film premier I've been invited to later.'

'You can keep them.'

The guy's face hardly moved, even when he spoke. High cheekbones and prominent bridge on a nose that had been broken a couple of times. Hard to tell but he looked short, maybe five foot six, and he would be eighteen stone at least. No visible tattoos or scars but stretchmarks on the arms, an effect, presumably, of rapid muscle growth.

The driver put Ashton's clothes into the coolbag, zipped it shut and velcroed the cover down, then tossed it onto the backseat.

'Soundproof, yes? In case I'd left a cheeky recording device in a pocket or suchlike. This is really taking precautions. I never been through a rigamarole like this before. Well, you like to be careful and that's sending all the right messages to me and my people. I know a guy does all his meetings in a sauna, same reason.'

Ashton never liked to wear a wire. He'd insisted on heading bare into this assignment, and clearly that was just as well; if he'd worn any kit he'd be a bloody pulp already.

The driver took the jeep down the A508 towards Pitsford. Ashton resisted the urge to look out for the surveillance teams. Somewhere in the light Sunday night traffic were five or six unmarked cars and over a dozen cops, many of them toting Heckler and Koch machine guns, Glok pistols and tasers. Not that they or any of their fucking gear would be any use if it kicked off 'cause the lumbering fuckers always arrived five minutes too late for any action.

Ashton worried about breaking the ampules with his bare feet so he fished them out and put them in the glove compartment. He said, 'I understood I would be dealing with a lady?' The driver said nothing and a silence stretched.

Ashton's legend was based on a career burglar he'd nicked a few times back when he was still uniform. The guy had been mouthy, always dicking around, but sharp; good company, which was a rare quality in burglars. Real life Ashton didn't feel like talking, was scared and uncomfortable and thinking this was a shit way for a family man to make a living: so he put himself aside, and tried to channel the legend: he rolled his head a little, stuck his tongue in his cheek, and blathered. 'This fucking rain. Lashing it down. We heading into Northampton? I always thought it was a shithole but the countryside around's not bad, is it? I enjoyed the drive up. This is a nice ride, mate. I rate the Cherokee.'

'This is a Cherokee Grand, not a Cherokee.'

'Yeah well, it's smooth.'

I don't rate the Cherokee. Usually with American cars, you put them up against the Germans in the same class, and they don't have the build quality. But this one is a match for a German car. Or a Japanese. Got a quadra drive, you know it? Transfers torque between the front and rear axles. Eight speed transmission, six point four litres, two hundred and fifty horses.'

'It holds up offroad?'

'Good enough.'

'That's important right, out there in Eastern Europe?'

The driver turned his head to look at him. 'What?'

'Well the roads aren't that good, are they? You got a lot of dirt tracks right? Going through the forests?'

'We have metalled roads. You think we ride donkeys and watch black and white TV? When we see a toilet we wash our hands in it?'

'No offence, I'm just winding you up. I went to Vilnius once. On a stag. Like a fairy land, cobbled streets and churches everywhere. Beautiful.'

'Cheap beer and cheap women.'

'Not always. One of mine was very expensive. She ran off with my wallet.'

Ashton found himself once more considering the driver's horrible arms: like baseballs stuffed in a stocking, meandering veins, as random as rivers on a map. Roiders were unpredictable and aggressive, but at least he would be slow.

The driver pulled up, and a black lady stood up from a bus shelter bench and got into the back of the jeep. She wore a long black skirt, shapeless woolly cardigan and had thick straight hair that was likely a wig. Ashton shifted round, and noted fake eyelashes, rouged cheeks, a couple of fake beauty spots. She was middle aged, probably weighed as much as the driver, and had an inch on him in height. She carried a covered woven basket, both hands on the handle. She could have been on her way to church.

Ashton said, 'Hello,' and she said, 'You better put your seatbelt on, darling.'

Before Ashton had time to respond, the driver accelerated hard, then yanked down on the wheel, and swung the jeep screeching onto a side road. Ashton braced an arm against the dashboard. They took a swift left, then another, then a right, and now they were speeding through an estate of bland low rise. Lots of narrow winding roads and cul de sacs – good spot to lose any vehicular surveillance. Ashton noted signposts: Anhyo Walk, Charlcombe Avenue, directions to the university. More lurching manoeuvres, then they were crossing back over the A508.

Ashton said, 'Nice.' He had to reckon the SO19 units had been shaken off. Still, maybe the jeep's high profile would make it easy to pick up again. He wished he'd worn one of those little GPS devices, could have hidden it in his shoe. But there hadn't been a working one in stock when he'd got to operations and the CO has told him not to sweat it. Fucking typical, another dream factory balls up, always winging it, going off half-arsed. But this kind of thinking was taking him out of character, and that was dangerous, so he shook his head and he was back, and looking at the black lady and saying, 'Bad news is, he's going to make you wear his old clothes.'

'Look at you,' she was saying, 'like a baby in a sack. I'm sorry, he's paranoidal, it's the anabolics, they're not good for his mental health.'

'You must be little Red Riding Hood. We having a picnic?'

'I am wet and it is late and I need to get home.'

She opened the basket and took out a shoebox, handed it across.

'I look at it, here, now?'

'Yes,' said the driver.

Ashton opened the box. The pistol lay in a crudely cut block of polystyrene. He had never been taught a thing about firearms. The thinking went, teach undercovers how to handle a gun and they'd do it on the street and betray their training. Looking at the thing now, he realised what a dumb rule that was. He didn't have a clue what to do with it. He didn't know where the safety was or even how to load it, let alone disassemble it. He held the pistol by the barrel, turned it over and over, nodded and frowned. The main thing to notice was how small it was.

'It's a package,' the driver was saying. 'You get the silencer and one magazine of ammo too, they're there in the bottom.'

'Homemade bullets?'

'Factorymade. The silencer is homemade, but you don't need high tolerances for a silencer. It will only suppress the first few rounds.'

Hoping he wasn't betraying his ignorance, Asthon said, 'What make is it?'

'Baikal. It's converted from an 8mm gas pistol. In Russia you buy those in a shop. It fires tear-gas pellets: big noise, big scare, lady keeps her handbag.'

'Or maybe the mugger is holding a real gun, and she gets shot in the face. So this is just another dodgy conversion that will blow your finger off if you try to fire it. I was told you had good stuff.'

Ashton was just talking, spinning things out. SO19 should be moving any moment: vehicles would slew across the road, pinning them in front and back, then there would be a lot of shouting, lancing torch beams and waving gun barrels. But more likely the arseholes were looking for him, haring round Northampton in a tizzy, barking into radios.

'Same materials, same tolerances as the real Baikal pistol,' said the driver. 'That's good Russian engineering, solid steel. It is converted by reliable people. They make some changes to the magazine and put a 9mm barrel on, properly rifled. Then you have a very good pistol. A serious thing. For close work. You won't win a target shooting competition. But if you want to kill someone, it is very good for that.'

'I don't want anything that's been used before.'

'It has no history. It was fired once, twice maybe, to test it. It is clean.'

'So this box, all together, is ...'

'Two thousand.'

'I've been offered cheaper.'

'Of course, you can get something that will blow your hand off or jam for a few hundred pounds. Or something with a bit of history, you can get it for fifty quid. Might even work. But if the police find it you're tied to seven murders you never heard of.'

'Okay you got a deal. Let me count out the money here.'

He handed the gun back to the black lady.

'I'll put it in the bag with your clothes.' She spoke up again as he was counting out twenties. 'Have you heard anything from Trayvon?'

'He talked to someone, who talked to the people I represent ...'

'I mean personally, I want to know how he's doing. Anything.'

'I'm sure he's fine.'

'You know how many socks they are allowed a week? Two pairs. You want to get high in there, that's no problem, any drug you like, there it is for you, can get it delivered to your cell. But you can't get clean socks.'

'It's a mad world.'

Ashton wondered if these two were a couple. They must be something to see, in bed. Brick shithouse bumping around on a bouncy castle.

'Have you done time?' asked the lady.

'Nothing hard, a shit and a shave.'

'How did you get through it?'

'I read. You keep your head down, you front when you have to, and all it is is boring.'

'What did you read? Did they have good books? Improving books?'

'As a matter of fact, ma'am, I studied Spanish.'

'Did you. Well that is excellent. I hope Trayvon can put his time to some good use, in that way. And come out with some improvement in his character.'

'I hope so too ma'am.'

'Cynthia please.'

'I'm Chris.'

'He put his hand across the seat divide to briefly clasp hers.

'Nice to see a bit of courtesy,' she said, 'you don't get that much, in this business.'

The driver said, 'You talk too fucking much. Shut your mouth.'

'See this,' said Cynthia, 'the abuse I put up with. He gets so ratty. Imagine being stuck in here with him for days. There's always an atmosphere.'

DC Ashton looked at the junk food packets. Some unfamiliar brands there – Zchilu, Estrella, Tayto. Eastern European, he guessed. He'd hazard a guess that these jokers were picking up the weapons themselves – driving all the way to Lithuania – and they had just come back from a run. Plenty of places in a big car like this to hide a few guns, they could use a lead-lined battery, say. But you wouldn't drive all that way for one or two, you'd bring back a dozen. Two dozen.

Ashton, handing his cash across, said, 'I want some more. Right now.'

'This wasn't mentioned before,' said the driver.

'This life is tough, and it's tougher if you're stupid. If I told you in advance I was rocking up with an utter shitload of cash, there's going to be a temptation there. I didn't know how on the level you are. Now we've made the connection, I can see you're decent people and I can show my hand. You have got more, haven't you?'

'Yeah we got more.'

'Say I wanted as many as you give me, how many would that be?'

'Why?' said the driver, 'You want to start a war?'

'Thirty,' said Cynthia.

'Shut your mouth,' said the driver. 'We are not flooding the market, we want to drip them in, a few at a time, here and there.'

Ashton could see the guy didn't like it so he showed him the money, a wad thick as a bible. 'I got ten grand here. I'll take another five, right now. Another thing, I can ask my friends to look out for Trayvon. I got mates that are similarly indisposed, up there in Sutton. There are things that can be done for him. Socks would be the start of it. Come on, let's do another five, right now.'

'Alright,' said Cynthia, in the back.

'The lady wants to do business.'

'The lady is not in charge,' said the driver. 'And she will get a fat lip for talking too much. A fatter lip, I should say. We will do it. We will go and pick up more boxes now. It will be a long drive.'

They were headed south on Upton Way, towards the M1. Now the vehicle was on a major road it would be ID'd on cameras, and SO19 would be alerted – though this assumed a level of co-ordination across sections that couldn't be taken be granted.

Cynthia handed Ashton a photo across the seat divide. It showed a grinning teenager in football kit. Ashton had seen it before, in the newspapers, alongside a picture of the guy he'd stabbed.

'My Trayvon,' said Cynthia. 'A skinny little boy. Never would you think he was eighteen. Always eating but he never put on weight. Looks like he can be push around, you know? So he learn to be good with his fists.'

She sighed. 'Six months earlier, he would have got tried as a juvenile, then he could have gone to a young offender institution. But they tried him as adult, a skinny boy like that, and they sent him to a jail full of bad men and gangster. What is a little lad doing in a category A? Sharing a room with hardened criminals, nasty men, and there being drugs everywhere and all kinds of bad thing. I came for visit him one time and he had lumps all over his face. He said he was playing football and fall over and hit his head.'

'So I decide to help my boy. I build a line of supply. He can say to the bad men, my mother can sort out your friends on the outside. Now all the gangster watch out for him and keep him safe. Because of his mother's line of supply. I don't want him consorting with bad men, you understand, but he have to consort so what can I do? That's the only reason I do this business, the only one. And now I can talk to him regular.'

'How so?' said Asthon.

'They alway someone smuggling a phone in, and rent it out. The prisoners all got a SIM card hidden. Trayvon calls me five times a week, ask how his dog is doing. That remind me, I hope this doesn't take too long, the blessed thing needs to be fed soon, it go hungry for long it gonna be ripping up the curtains again.'

The driver addressed Ashton. 'We will drop you off. You keep the box you just bought and the rest of your money. Then we get more boxes, drive back to you, and that will take about ten minutes.'

'Somewhere out of the rain,' said Ashton, 'where I can be plausibly waiting. I'm going to be carrying, remember. I don't want to get picked up on suspicion.'

'That bus shelter near Aldi,' said Cynthia.

Ashton said, 'After, drive me back into Northampton, and let me out near my car. I'm not strolling round with my arse hanging out, in the rain, carrying a fucking armoury.'

'Okay.'

They were two miles from the motorway turn-off when Cynthia's phone rang.

'That's him. It's Trayvon. Hello? I can't hear you properly love. Are you under the sheets? Well you'll have to whisper a bit louder. Okay you do that.' She addressed the men in front. 'He is going to put more blankets on the bed. He is hiding under the blankets and whispering to his mother.' With the phone back against her head, she said, 'No. I can't believe it. No. For no reason? That is too much.' She was leaning forward again, and Ashton could feel her breath on his neck. 'He say they put him on no association, for no reason at all. That is an outrage. For five days now, he didn't talk to nobody. Nobody at all, and he is climbing the walls. One of his friends pay a screw to slip him a phone. No reason at all. It is an animal house in there, no rules at all. This supposed to be a civilised country.'

Oh shit, thought Ashton. For fuck's sake. A prison that can't keep an inmate quiet, a backup unit that's backed up its own arse, no GPS, this was a fucking shambles. Would be funny if it wasn't going to get him killed. He'd come back and haunt the CO, call him a twat all day for evermore.

Cynthia was talking to her son again. 'I'm doing a little bit of business now with one of your friend's friends. He says he went to prison and he learned to speak Spanish. I think that's commendable, don't you? How big is your library there? His name's Chris ... Some Liverpool group.' She leaned forward. 'That's right isn't it?'

'Yes, I represent interests in Liverpool, that is correct.'

A silence stretched as Cynthia listened. Ashton considered the door handle. He could pull it, duck and be out of the jeep in a second. Good that he'd never put his seatbelt on. But he'd be hitting the tarmac at over fifty, and taking his chances with the oncoming traffic. He didn't fancy it.

Cynthia said, 'Trayvon say he never heard anything about this deal.'

Ashton said, 'I'm not your son's friend's friend, I'm a friend's friend's friend's friend, if you see what I mean, this has gone through a number of people, and maybe on one of those steps there was a communication breakdown.'

He heard a metallic clicking behind him.

The driver said, 'Cynthia. Load the gun. Rack the slide.'

Cynthia said, 'I already done it.'

'There one in the chamber? Like I showed you?'

'I got one lined up. I'm putting the silencer on.'

'You keep that aimed at our guest.'

'It's not a nice thing to do,' said Cynthia. 'But I'm doing it.'

'This is not cool,' sighed Ashton. He was still apart from his fingers rapping up and down at the base of the window.

'Cynthia is no great shooter but she won't miss from there,' said the driver. 'A round will go straight through that chair into your spine. Are you a policeman?'

Ashton told himself to get annoyed, and in a moment he was, and he said, 'Yeah I'm an undercover cop, that's right. And you know what else? I'm the pope. And I'm the Loch Ness monster. I'm a yeti mate, you want to watch out. Came all the way from Tibet, shaved, splashed some cologne. I'm the abominable snowman. The lady's right, you're paranoid. You need to be secure, I understand, but I don't want to get killed cause some fuck up got stoned and forgot to make a phone call. Let's calm the fuck down here.'

Cynthia said, 'Trayvon says he's going to make some calls and then he's going to ring back.'

The jeep turned onto the M1 slip road. It was doing seventy when they joined the motorway, heading south.

'Why are we on the motorway? said Cynthia. 'We can't get off now till Milton Keynes.'

The driver said, 'So he won't jump out.'

Eight years previously Ashton had joined some friends on a climbing holiday in Eldorado Canyon near Boulder, Colorado. For the first three days they had taken easy lines on Regarden Wall but on the fourth they decided to be more ambitious and tackle the Orange Spur. Ashton was the last on the rope. His belayer was anchored to a tree and playing out the slack as Ashton sweated over a short dihedral. He was on a ledge a dozen feet shy of a sharp ridge, and his friends were above, waiting. He took two steps, then lost his footing and slipped. The rope pulled tight as his belayer caught the strain, and for a moment he was swinging. Something felt wrong and he looked up just in time to see the the taut rope sheer right off on the ledge. His swing took him into the rockface and he reached out and got one hand up to the wrist into a jagged crack. His feet scuffed the rock but found no purchase, then his whole weight was pulling on that hand, jammed into the crack, and the rope was slack and falling. He got his other hand up and clung to the rock. It was a good sunny day and looking down he could see the frilly tops of the pine trees about eighty feet below and the severed rope swinging lazily. He was conscious of noises from his friends above and his ragged breathing, and the wind whipping at his clothes and hair, and the warm sandstone on his cheek. His was very quiet and very still, with no thought but just to carry on holding. Nothing in the universe existed except for those points where his body touched stone. He could hear the efforts of his friends as they tried to get down to him but the words seemed distant and irrelevant. He did not move his face to look at the approaching men or move his eyes. They were coming and they would get him in time or they wouldn't. He was trying his hardest but he knew that might not be enough, but at least he hadn't given up.

A rope was clipped into Ashton's carabiner, then another rope was lowered for him to grasp. He clambered up to where his white-faced companions held him tightly. He sat down with his back against a tree and his body failed him, and he started to tremble, and he realised his wrist was broken.

Ashton's wrist throbbed. Cynthia's mobile rang.

Ashton said, 'Cynthia, if I get killed here, he'll kill you after. He thinks you talk too much.'

The jeep slewed into the hard shoulder then stopped violently. Ashton was thrown forward against the dashboard and his head thumped the windscreen. The driver reaching down into the pocket at the base of his door. A pop sounded behind him and he slumped forward with his head down against the wheel, and didn't move again.

The car stank of cordite. Ashton waited for everything to stop. But he continued to exist.

Finally he said, 'Cynthia? You didn't have to shoot him.'

'Sure I did. He keep a gun down there. He was going to kill you.'

'Oh.'

'And after he kill you he would kill me. You right about that but you didn't have to say it, I had that figured by myself. Now you call some friends and we deal with this.'

Ashton reached forward, turned the hazard lights on.

'I'm not making any movements. I'm going to talk for a minute, if that. Hear me out. You are going to be arrested. That is going to happen, either in a minute or a day. Because I am a policeman and back-up is coming. Two dead guys in here and you go away for twenty years.'

He resisted the urge to turn around, watched the traffic gliding past, headlights smearing traces in the darkness.

'Refrain from firing again, and no one's got much against you. You shot him to save me and yourself, his hand is on his weapon: you'd beat a murder case on self defence. There's supplying firearms but a smart lawyer will get most of that pinned on him, make it look like he bullied you into it. In the dock you'll look like a poor dear who got used and abused by a habitual criminal. You'll do a few years and you'll be out before Trayvon. I know you're a smart lady so I'm putting it before you no bullshit and asking you to think it over.'

Nothing continued to happen. Ashton blinked rapidly. He's been splattered with the driver's blood, or worse, and now some was dripping into his eye. He felt it was important to get it out, so didn't see much of the arriving units, but he heard the screech of sharply braking vehicles, to front, back and side.

'Cynthia, put it down. These guys will shoot if they see you holding a gun. They get very keyed up, sitting in those vans all day.'

He heard something thunk to the floor, then Cynthia said, 'God have mercy on his soul. And on mine, and yours. And on my son's.'

'Amen,' said Ashton, then the shouting started.

VAL McDERMID is the author of more than thirty novels, as well as numerous short stories and radio plays. She is best known for the series of multi-award-winning novels featuring psychologist Tony Hill which were adapted for ITV's *Wire in the Blood*. Born in 1955 in Kirkcaldy, Scotland, she divides her time between Manchester and Edinburgh.

I've Seen That Movie Too

Val McDermid

I truly believed I'd never see her again. That she was gone for good. That the virus she'd planted in my bloodstream would be allowed to lie dormant forever. Which only goes to show how little I really understood about Cerys.

Everybody has an ugly secret. I don't care how righteous you are. Saint or sinner, there's something lurking in your past that looms over every good thing you do, that makes your toes curl in shame, that makes your stomach curdle at the thought of discovery. Don't try to pretend you're the exception. You're not. We all have our skeletons and Cerys is mine.

The world as I know it falls into two groups. The ones who fall under Cerys's spell and the ones who are immune to the point of bafflement. Over the past three years, I've discovered there were a lot more in the former group than I'd ever suspected. The list of people she'd bewitched ranged from the daughter of a duke to a celebrity midget, from a prizewinning poet to a gay male member of parliament. It mortifies me how many of them I now know she was fucking during the months she was supposed to be my girlfriend. What's even more extraordinary is how many of them were convinced they were the special one.

For the members of the latter group, that word 'even' is crucial to their insistent deconstruction of Cerys. 'She isn't even beautiful.' 'She isn't even interesting.' 'She isn't even sexy.' 'She isn't even funny.' 'She isn't even blonde.' But to those of us on the other side of the fence, she's all of those things. The only explanation that makes any sense is the notion of viral infection. The Oxford English Dictionary defines a computer virus as, 'a piece of code surreptitiously introduced into a system in order to corrupt it'. In every sense of the word 'corrupt', that's Cerys.

The one good thing she ever did for me was to walk out of my life three years ago without a goodbye or a forwarding address. I don't think her motive was to destroy me; that would presume my reaction even entered her calculations. No, the suddenness of her departure and the thoroughness of her vanishing had been all about her need to get free and clear before the answers rolled in to the questions other people had started asking. But at the time, I didn't care about the reasons. I was just grateful for the chance to free myself. Deep down, I didn't mind the anguish or the self-loathing or the shame, because it's always easy to endure pain when you understand it's part of the healing process. Even then, I knew that somewhere down the line I would get past all the suffering and resume control over my heart and mind.

And I did. It took me well over a year to drag myself beyond what she'd done to me, but I managed it.

Yet now, in an instant, all that healing was stripped away and I felt as raw and captive as I had the day she'd left. Here, in the unlikely setting of the Finnish consul's Edinburgh residence, I could feel the gears stripping and the wheels coming off my reassembled life.

I shouldn't even have been there. I don't usually bother with the fancy receptions that attach themselves to the movie business like barnacles to a ship's hull. But the three Finnish producers who had become the Coen brothers of the European film industry had optioned a treatment from me and my agent was adamant that I had to show my face at the consul's party in their honour at the Edinburgh Film Festival. So I'd turned up forty minutes late, figuring I'd have just enough time for a drink and the right hellos before the diplomats cleared their throats and signalled the party was over.

As soon as I crossed the threshold, I knew something was off-kilter. Cerys had always had that effect on me. Whenever I walked into a room where she was, my senses tripped into overdrive. Now, my head swivelled from side to side, my eyes darting round, trying to figure out why I was instantly edgy. She saw me at the same moment I spotted her. She was talking to some guy in a suit and she didn't miss a beat when she caught sight of me. But her eyes widened and that was enough for my stomach to crash like a severed lift cage.

I felt a ringing in my ears, stilling the loud mutter of conversation in the room. Before I could react, she'd excused herself and snaked through the throng to my side. 'Alice,' she said, the familiar voice a caress that made the hairs on my arms quiver.

I was determined not to be suckered back in. To put up a fight at least. 'What the hell are you doing here?' I tried to make my voice harsh and almost succeeded.

Cerys reached out, circling my wrist with finger and thumb. The touch of her flesh was a band of burning ice. 'We need to talk,' she said, drawing me to her side and somehow manoeuvring me back through the doorway I'd just entered.

'No,' I said weakly. 'No, we don't need to talk.'

She turned to me then and smiled, the tip of her tongue running along the edge of her teeth. 'Oh Alice, you always cut straight to the chase, don't you?' She made a determined break for a staircase at the end of the hall. I couldn't free myself without drawing the wrong kind of attention from the other people milling round in the hallway. The last thing I wanted was for anyone to make a connection between me and Cerys. I'd kept my nose clean on that score and it had saved me from enough of the consequences of our association for me to want to keep it that way.

So I let her lead me up the broad carpeted stairs without obvious protest. Somehow, she knew where she was going. She opened the second door on the right and pulled me into a small sitting room – a pair of armchairs, a chaise longue and an antique writing desk with matching chair. She used my momentum to spin me round like a dancer then closed the door briskly behind her, turning a key in the lock.

'To answer your question, I've been working with the Finnish film agency,' she said. At once I understood her apparent familiarity with the layout of the Finnish consul's house. And that the chances were I wasn't the first person she'd been with behind that locked door.

I opened my mouth to protest but I was too late. Cerys took my face between her hands and covered my mouth with dozens of tiny kisses and flicks of the tongue. Her fingertips brushed the skin of my neck, slipping inside my open blouse and over my shoulders. The heat that flushed my skin was nothing to do with the Scottish summer weather. I despised myself even as desire surged through me but I didn't even consider pushing her away. I knew I wouldn't be able to follow through and I'd only end up humiliating myself by begging for her later.

'This ... is not ... a good ... idea ...' The words came from my head while every other part of me was willing my mouth to shut the fuck up. Cerys knew this so she just smiled. Her hands moved under my skirt, the backs of her fingernails grazing the insides of my thighs.

'I've missed you,' she murmured as her hand moved higher, meeting no resistance. I felt myself falling, the chaise longue behind me, the certainty of pain and trouble ahead.

Not love, not at first sight. I don't want to elevate it to something it wasn't. But it was something, no doubt of that. I'd emerged late one summer evening from Inverness rail station, hoping that someone from the Scottish Film Foundation would be there to drive me to the remote steading where I'd be spending the rest of the week. I'd been supposed to arrive with four other writers for a screenwriting masterclass course that morning, but my flight had been cancelled and it had taken the rest of the day to travel the length of the country from the West Country to the Highlands by train. I was not in the best of moods.

The woman leaning against the car in the courtyard caught my attention. Her languid pose: long legs crossed at the ankle, right arm folded across her stomach, hand cupping the left elbow, rollie dangling from the fingers of her left hand, a sliver of smoke twisting in the warm evening air, head at an angle, eyes on the middle distance, thick honey-blonde hair cut short ... She made my breath catch in my throat. It was an image I suspected I would never forget. I feared I would keep on writing scenes for women in that precise pose for the rest of my career. I didn't even dare to hope she was waiting for me.

But she was. Cerys Black, Screenwriting Development Director for the Scottish Film Foundation. It was a fancy title, implying more than a department of one, but I soon learned that Cerys did everything from picking up late arrivals to pitching which projects should win the SFF's backing. That night, though, I wasn't interested in her job description. Only that I'd found myself in the company of a woman who made me dizzy for the first time in years. My grumpiness evaporated in less time than it took to stow my bags in the car boot.

She took me to a bistro by the river. 'Everyone's eaten and you won't feel like cooking this late,' she said. We ate pasta and drank red wine and talked. I've never been able to piece together the route of the conversation. I only remember that we talked about the women in our past. I now have an inkling of how severely Cerys edited her history, but at the time I had no reason to doubt her tale of a handful of youthful affairs and a single grand passion that had taken her to Hungary before it had finally died a couple of years before. It was the sort of conversation that is really an extended form of deniable flirtation and it kept us occupied until the waitress made it abundantly clear that Inverness had a midnight curfew and we were in danger of breaching it.

We drove out of the city along the side of the loch, the rounded humps of high mountains silhouetted against thin darkness shot with stars. We turned up a steep road that took us away from the mountains to a high valley surrounded by summits. We barely spoke but something was moving forward between us.

The cluster of low buildings that was our base for the week was in darkness when we arrived. Cerys led me to a cottage set to one side. 'You're in here,' she said. 'Downstairs there's a computer room and library and upstairs there are two suites of rooms.' We climbed the narrow stairs and Cerys dropped her voice. 'Tom Hart's on the right and you're on the left.'

She ushered me in and put my backpack by a table facing a pair of long windows. I swung my holdall on to a chair and turned to thank her, suddenly shy.

There was nothing shy about her response. She moved closer, one hand on my hip, the other on my shoulder and kissed me. Not the air kiss of the media world, not the prim kiss of a distant cousin, not the dry brush of lips friends share. This was the kind of kiss that burns boats and bridges in equal measure.

Time played its tricks and made it last forever and no time at all. When we finally stopped, Cerys looked as astonished as I felt. 'I don't think snogging in an open doorway is the most sensible move,' she said. 'You should shut your door now.'

I nodded, numb with disappointment.

Then she smiled, a crooked grin that lifted one side of her mouth higher than the other. 'Which side of it would you like me to be on?'

If I could say that sex with Cerys was the most amazing experience of my life, it might make more sense of what happened between us. But that would be a lie. It was enthralling, it was adventurous, it was sometimes dark and edgy. But it never entirely fulfilled me. She always left me not just wanting more but feeling obscurely that somehow it was my fault that I hadn't found total satisfaction in her arms. So I was always eager for the next time, quick to persuade myself that the electricity between us meant the wattage of our sexual connection would rise even higher. I was addicted, no question about it.

I knew by the end of that masterclass week that I loved her. I loved her body and her mind, her reticence and her boldness. We hadn't spent that much time together – she had other responsibilities and by the third night, it was clear we both needed some sleep – but I was under her spell. I wanted to see her again, and soon. Her work tied her to Edinburgh, my life was at the other end of the country. But I couldn't see this as an obstacle. We could make it work. We would make it work.

Looking back, I can see all the cracks and gaps of lies and deception. But at the time, I had no reason to mistrust her. I believed in the meetings, the conferences, the working dinners, the trips to film festivals. I was just amazed and grateful that we managed to see each other one night most weeks. We spoke on the phone, though not as much as I craved; Cerys was only comfortable with the phone for professional purposes, she told me. And we made plans. I would sell my house by the sea in Devon and buy a flat in Edinburgh. Not with Cerys – that would have made her claustrophobic. After the disastrous end of her relationship with the Hungarian, she didn't ever want to live with someone else without her own bolthole. Given what she'd told me about their last months, I understood that. I'd have felt the same, I thought.

I was anxious about the move, though. Prices in Edinburgh were astronomical. I couldn't see how I was going to afford somewhere half-decent. I'd tried to talk to Cerys about it, but she'd stopped my worries with kisses and deft movements of her strong, gentle hands.

And then one night, she met me at the airport in the same languid stance. Only the cigarette was missing. As always, my heart seemed to contract in my chest. 'I have the answer,' she said after she'd kissed my mouth and buried her face in my hair.

'The answer to what?'

'How you can afford a flat.'

'How?'

And over dinner, she told me. A legendary Scottish star had died a few months previously. The film foundation had just learned he'd left almost all of his many millions in a trust to benefit Scottish film makers. A trust that was to be administered by the SFF. 'Instead of giving people piddling little grants of a few grand, we'll be able to fund proper development,' Cerys said. 'We'll essentially be putting money on the table like the serious players.'

'That's fantastic news. But what's that got to do with me?'

The crooked smile and a dark sparkle in her eyes was the only answer I got at first. She sipped her wine and clinked her glass against mine. 'You're going to be a star, sweetheart,' she finally said.

It was breathtakingly simple but for someone as fundamentally law-abiding as me, unbelievably bad. We were going to set up a fictitious production company. Cerys had access to all the necessary letterheads to make it look like they had backing from serious Hollywood players. I'd be the screenwriter on the project. We'd go to the SFF for the seed money and come away with a two-million-pound pot. The company would pay me a million via my agent, all above board. And Cerys would siphon off the other million. And then the project would go belly-up because the Hollywood backers had pulled out. A shrug of the shoulders. It happens all the time in the movie business.

'It'll never work,' I said. 'How will we convince the SFF?'

Again the crooked smile. 'Because you're Scottish by birth. Because I'm the person who makes the recommendations to the grant committee. And because you're going to write a brilliant treatment that will sound like it could plausibly be a Hollywood blockbuster.'

It's a measure of how Cerys had captivated me that what worried me was not that we were about to embark upon a criminal fraud. What bothered me was whether I could write a good enough treatment to bluff our way past the grants committee.

It took me a month to come up with the idea and another six weeks to get the pitch and treatment in place. And of course, Cerys was perfectly placed to help me knock it into shape. I called it *The Whole Of The Moon* after the Waterboys' track. The opening paragraph of the pitch had taken days to get right but in the end I was happy with it. Dominic O'Donnell is an IRA quartermaster who wants to retire from the front line in Belfast; Brigid Fitzgerald is a financial investigator from Seattle. When they meet, their lives change in ways neither of them could ever have imagined. *The Whole Of The Moon* is a romantic comedy thriller with a dark edge, strong on sense of place and underpinned by New Irish music.

I'd have been terrified about pitching the grants committee if Cerys hadn't spend her lunch hour fucking me senseless in the hotel down the street from the SFF office. As it was, I was so dazed I waltzed through it as if a two-million-pound grant was my birthright. Not in an arrogant way, but in that 'If Scotland wants to be taken seriously in the international arts community, we need to behave as if we are serious,' sort of way.

And it worked. The grants committee were dizzy with their new powers of patronage and Cerys easily persuaded them that this was the sort of flagship project they needed to give the SFF an international profile. The two million was paid into the bank account of the company she'd set up in Panama, which was where we were allegedly going to be doing some of our location filming. My fee was with my agent in days. It took me all of two weeks to close the deal on a New Town flat with views over the Forth estuary to Fife.

Life wasn't quite as perfect as I'd expected. Cerys seemed to be out of town much more than before and I barely saw more of her than I had when I was living at the other end of the country. And of course, we had to keep our relationship under wraps to begin with. Edinburgh's a big city wrapped round a small village and we didn't want the grants committee members to wonder whether they'd been stitched up. Or worse.

Three months after we'd been given the money, Cerys reported back to her boss that the production company had gone bust. She told me he'd taken it in his stride and I believed that too.

And then a couple of weeks later, we walked into the breakfast room of a hotel in Newcastle and came face to face with the chairman of the grants committee and his wife. We tried to pretend we'd only just started seeing each other, but my lies were nowhere near as slick as Cerys.'

We were both quiet on the drive back to Edinburgh. I was glum and assumed she was too. A couple of days later,

I realised her silence was not because she was worried but because she was planning furiously. She dropped me at my flat that night and went back to her place, where she packed the car with the few things she really cared about – clothes, DVDs, books, her Mac and half a dozen paintings – and left. When I hadn't heard from her for three days, I borrowed the emergency key to her flat from her neighbour and let myself in. I knew as soon as I walked through the door that she was gone. The air was empty of her presence.

Sprawled on the chaise longue, I could smell her and taste her. If I'd been struck blind and deaf, my senses would still have recognised her. Having her back in my arms again drew me back under her command. I hated the terrible longing that possessed me but I didn't know how to make it stop. Before, only her absence had taken the edge off the craving. I thought I was cured but now I knew I was one of the backsliders. Just like those smokers who have given up for so long they think they can afford the risk of the occasional cigarette. And before they know it they're back on a pack and a half a day. One fuck and I was no longer my own woman.

'Are you not taking a hell of a chance, coming back here?'

She pushed her sweat-damp hair out of her eyes. She'd let it grow and now it was like a shaggy helmet streaked a dozen different shades by the sun. Not what you'd call a disguise, but a difference. 'If they had anything on me, I'd never have got another job in the industry. They can think what they like. It makes no odds without proof.'

'So why did you run?'

She closed her eyes and ran her fingertips over my face, as if reminding herself of a tactile memory. 'I couldn't be bothered answering the questions.'

I felt a faint stirring of what might have been outrage if it had been allowed to take root. 'You left me high and dry because you couldn't be bothered answering questions?'

She opened her eyes and sighed. 'Alice, you know I hate to be pinned down.'

'But you came back.' I knew I was clutching at shadows but apparently I couldn't prevent myself from going into pathetic mode.

Cerys shifted her weight to pin me down more completely, her thigh between my legs exerting a delicious pleasure. 'I came back because of you.'

I couldn't keep the joy and amazement from my face and voice. 'You came back for me?'

A dry little laugh. 'Not for you. Because of you.'

'I don't understand.'

'Because of what you've done. Because you owe me.'

Now I was puzzled. 'I owe you? You walked out on me, and I owe you?'

'I'm not talking metaphorically, Alice. I'm not talking about emotions. I'm talking about money.'

It was a familiar Cerys rollercoaster moment and it left me sour. 'Money? You got your share. More than your share. You didn't have an agent taking 15 per cent off the top.'

'I'm not talking about the grant money. I'm talking about the movie. You might have changed the title but I'm not stupid. As soon as I saw the advance publicity in the trade press, I knew what you'd done. You changed the name from *The Whole Of The Moon* to *A Man Is In Love* and sold it to Hollywood for real.'

'It's not a secret, Cerys. And it's my work to sell.'

'It's work that wouldn't exist without me. You'd never have come up with the idea and developed it without me.

According to my sources, you cleared another couple of million from the studio. The way I see it, that means you owe me at least another million.'

I tried to tell myself she was joking, but I knew her better than that. 'That's not how I see it.'

'No, but if I can't persuade you to see it my way, the world is going to know how you got your first million. And how much of the work on that treatment was mine.'

I managed a strangled laugh. 'You can't drop me in it without dropping yourself in it,' I protested, trying to shift my body away from hers but confounded by the arm of the chaise.

'I'll throw myself on their mercy. Tell them how I was so besotted by you that I did what you told me. It's what they'll want to hear because it lets them off the hook. Better to employ some woman led astray by her emotions than a crook, don't you think?'

Cerys telling lies would be far more convincing than me telling the truth. I knew that. And even as I listened to her duplicity, I knew I was still her prisoner. The thought of finding myself her enemy was intolerable. 'I thought you cared about me. I can't believe you'd blackmail me.'

'Blackmail is such an ugly word,' she said, finally pushing herself onto her knees and moving away from me.

I shivered, disgust and desire mingling in an unholy alliance. 'But an accurate one.'

'I like to think of it as sharing. A down payment of fifty grand by the end of the week would be acceptable.' She buttoned her shirt, picked her jeans and underwear off the floor and slipped back into her public persona. 'In cash.'

'How am I supposed to explain that to my accountant? To my bank?'

She shrugged. 'Your problem, Alice. You're good at solving problems. That's what makes your scripts work so well. Call me tomorrow and I'll let you know where to drop the money off.'

I sat up. 'No. If I'm handing over that kind of money, I want something in exchange. If you want the money, you have to meet me.'

Cerys cocked her head, appraising me. It felt like a health and safety risk assessment. 'Somewhere public,' she said at last.

'No.' I seldom managed any kind of assertiveness with her, but the understanding that had blossomed in the past few minutes made it necessary. 'I want us to fuck one last time. Like the song says, for the good times.'

I could see contempt in her face, but her voice betrayed none of it. She sounded warm and amused. 'Why not? Shall I come to your flat?'

I'm not strong. Carrying a body down two flights of stairs and down the back lane to my garage would be beyond me. 'I'll pick you up at your hotel. I've got a cabin in Perthshire, we can drive up there and have dinner. You can stay the night. One last night, Cerys, please. I've missed you so much.'

A long calculating pause. Then Cerys made the first miscalculation I'd seen from her. 'Why not?' she repeated. We arranged that we would meet in the car park near her hotel on Friday afternoon. 'I might as well check out then,' she said. 'You need to have me at the airport by eleven on Saturday morning so I can make the Helsinki flight.'

Perfect. 'No problem,' I lied, surprised at how easy it was. But then, I'd had the best possible teacher.

That left me five days to make my plans. I arranged to withdraw the money from the bank because I wanted to reassure Cerys that she was still in the driving seat. I'd show it to her before we drove off to Perthshire, the magnet that would keep her on board.

Working out the details of murder was a lot harder. Once I'd made the decision, once I'd realised that I'd never be free of her demands or my desire while she was still alive, it wasn't hard to accept that murder was the only possible answer. Cerys had already transformed me from law-abiding citizen to successful criminal, after all.

Body disposal, the usual tripwire for killers in films, was the least of my worries. The Scottish highlands contain vast tracts of emptiness where small predatory animals feed on all sorts of carrion. Forestry tracks lead deep into isolated woodland where nobody sets foot from one year's end to the next. And of course, Cerys had walked away from her life before – in Hungary and in Edinburgh that I knew of, which probably meant she'd also done it in other places, other times. Nobody would be too surprised if she did it again. I didn't imagine anyone would seriously go looking for her, especially since she would have checked out of her hotel under her own steam.

How to kill her was a lot harder to figure out. Poison or drugs would have been my weapons of choice. But in her shoes, I wouldn't eat a crumb or drink a drop I hadn't brought with me. I didn't think she would be suspicious of me – I thought she was confident in the power she had over me – but I didn't want to take any chances.

If movies have taught me anything, it's that blunt instruments, blades and guns are too chancy. They're all capable of missing their targets, they all tend to leave forensic traces you can never erase and they're all concrete pieces of evidence you have to dispose of. So they were all out of the question.

I thought of smothering her while she slept but I wasn't convinced I could carry that through, not flesh to flesh and heart to heart. Strangling had the same problems, plus my fear that I wasn't strong enough to carry it through.

Murder, it turned out, was a lot easier in the movies.

I woke up on the Wednesday morning without an idea in my head. When I went through to the kitchen and turned on the light, a bulb popped, tripping the fuse in the main box. And a light went on inside my head.

Back when I bought my house in Devon, I didn't have much money. I'd only been able to afford the house because it was practically derelict and I learned enough of all the building trades to do the restoration and renovation myself. I can lay bricks, plaster walls, install plumbing and do basic carpentry.

I also know how electricity works.

Cerys may be able to last overnight without eating and drinking. She won't be able to make it without going to the toilet. My cabin on the loch has been fitted out in retro style, with an old-fashioned high-level toilet cistern with a long chain that you have to yank hard to generate a flush. It turned out to be a simple task to replace the ceramic handle with a metal one and to wire the whole lot into the mains supply. As her fist closes round the handle, 240 volts will course through her body, her hand will clench tighter and her heart will freeze.

Part of my heart will also freeze. But I can live with that. And because nothing is ever wasted, I will find a way to make a script out of it. Such a pity Cerys won't be around to see that movie too.

ANTHONY HOROWITZ has written more than forty books including the bestselling teen spy series *Alex Rider* and the Sherlock Holmes novel, *The House of Silk*, and is responsible for some of the UK's most beloved TV series, including *Foyle's War*. He also writes on subjects ranging from politics to education. He has been a patron to East Anglia Children's Hospices and the anti-bullying charity, Kidscape, since 2008, recently joined the board of the Old Vic, and in 2014 was awarded an OBE. He was born in London in 1955.

Caught Short

Anthony Horowitz

As flies to wanton boys are we to th' gods,
They kill us for their sport.

It had been a good evening for Johnny Maslin – Jazz to his friends. No. It had been a truly great evening ... three awards including Campaign of the Year and Agency of the Year, the two biggies and by any account his work, his babies. No wonder he felt jaunty, walking tall as he made his way to the underground car park at the Clarence Hotel where the awards ceremony had taken place. He had loosened his black tie so that it hung rakishly around his neck and the top three buttons of his shirt were open in a sort of devil-may-care, chest-hairy sort of way. He knew he'd had much too much to drink. The third bottle of Krug had definitely been a mistake. But then again – three awards, three bottles. All good things come in threes.

He had taken the lift to basement level one and tumbled out, none too steady on his feet. He paused to light a cigarette and at that moment caught sight of his own reflection in a puddle of water skimmed with oil. He followed the flame of the match as it arced upwards and watched himself suck in and then blow out smoke. Johnny was not a very good-looking man. Examining himself with the same ruthlessness that had taken him to the top of his profession, he was the first to admit it. Thin and wiry, he sported a shock of curly hair that was almost clownish and black spectacles that were equally out of proportion to his face. It didn't matter how long he spent in the sun (Los Angeles recently, and then his flat in Antibes). His skin was always pale, slightly lifeless. He had the smile of a dead man and used it to his advantage. He would smile when he threw out your work. He would smile when he fired you. And the pleasure of the moment would dance in his little blue eyes.

Three awards. One, two, three ...

Johnny found his car keys and pressed the electronic fob. Across the car park, his Audi R8 Spyder clunked and flickered into life as the doors sprang open. 'Here I am, my lord and master. Take me home.' For Johnny, it was a delicious image. The £110,000 charcoal grey car on its own in the empty car park, surrounded by concrete pillars and neon strips ... a bit of a cliché perhaps, over-used in American TV shows, but still undeniably atmospheric. He had once filmed an ad in a car park just like this. What was the product? Ah yes. Australian butter with cows parked next to each other instead of cars. That had been more than twenty years ago. Blake Shailer Mathieson. All three of them were long gone but Johnny had survived. Leibowitz and Leibowitz. Then Leibowitz, Leibowitz and Maslin. Then Maslin Associates and finally Teapot – the single appellation so far ahead of its time.

He slid inside the car, relishing the soft, full-grain leather as it rubbed against his thighs. The Spyder was less than a year old and still had that wonderful smell of polish and engineering. He thumbed the starter and the 4.2 litre engine rumbled into life, the dashboard and sat nav system lighting up. Johnny didn't drive away quite yet. He sat in his personal cocoon, examining his surroundings, feeling comfortable, affluent and safe. How remote the car park seemed, a different world when viewed from this side of the (tinted) glass with the air triple-filtered and the heat of the evening kept at bay. For a moment, he hesitated. It was probably mad to drive home tonight. The trouble with a car like this was that it was a magnet for every under-paid plod in the city and after all he'd drunk he had to be way over the limit. He could easily have booked a room at the Clarence. On the other hand, it was two o'clock in the morning. Monday morning already. He only lived a few miles away, on the other side of Hyde Park, and he preferred to wake up in his own bed. He would go very carefully, making no mistakes. He was confident that he had the self-discipline to fight off the alcohol in his bloodstream.

He drove out of the parking slot and knew at once that he had made the right decision. The deep, sexual power of the engine transmitted itself through his arms into his chest, re-animating him. He had an early start tomorrow, a crisis conference on a new strategy that one of his clients had just rejected. A copywriter and three art directors would be there, waiting for him, wondering if their jobs were on the line. He wouldn't want to be late for that – no, thank you. He cruised towards the exit in the far corner. Don't take it too fast when you get onto the road, Johnny. A couple of miles per hour under the speed limit. You'll be fine.

But it all went wrong before he had even left the car park. First there was a barrier, then a ramp that rose steeply towards an alleyway running all the way along the side of the hotel. Impossibly, a single person had been crossing the exit at exactly the moment he had driven – perhaps a little too quickly – over the hump. It wasn't his fault. They were in his blind spot. They obviously hadn't been looking where they were going. And he'd needed to accelerate to get up the slope. The impact was sickening. Johnny had no idea that the sound of human flesh hitting metal and carbon fibre could be so loud – despite having once art directed a road safety campaign. The woman – he was fairly sure it had been a woman – was flung into the air and landed some distance away. He actually felt the weight of her. Without knowing it, he had slammed his foot on the brake and the engine had cut out as it was designed, doing its little bit to save the planet. The Spyder had come to a halt with just half of it poking out of the car park, the back wheels still on the ramp.

Johnny sat where he was, absorbing the on-rush of different emotions. First there was anger. How could he have been such a prat? Why had he taken the ramp so fast? Why had he got into the car in the first place? There was a room waiting for him upstairs. He wouldn't even have had to pay for it. He must have been mad to want to drive. Then, after the anger, came its close cousin, contrition. How much damage had he done to the car? At the very least there would be a dent in the bonnet and quite possibly a shattered headlamp too and with a car in a class like this even getting a dint removed would cost an arm and a leg. No pointing asking insurance to cover it. The bastards would only screw him when it came time to renew. His thoughts turned to the victim of the accident who was still lying in the alleyway, an unrecognizable heap. She didn't seem to be moving. Could he have killed her? A terrible chill rose up, rushing through his legs and loosening his bladder. He had to get out and examine her. If he had killed this woman ... He was drunk. He would go to prison. His career would be over.

It had taken less than one second for all these thoughts to make their way through his consciousness. But it was the horrible awareness of his own predicament that now subsumed him. In a single moment of foolishness he had wiped out a life's work and achievement. If this got into the newspapers – and it probably would – half his clients would dump him ... the bastards. He could certainly kiss goodbye to the Polish vodka account. Any moment now, someone would come running. Surely someone would have heard the collision. The hotel would have CCTV cameras. The accident would have been recorded. There might be another driver behind him, perhaps, like him, leaving the awards ceremony. He glanced in the mirror. No. The ramp was empty.

And there were no cameras, not as far as he could see. In fact the other side of the alleyway was a solid wall, another building that didn't seem to have any windows. Now that he thought about it, he couldn't remember seeing any cameras in the car park either and right now there was nobody in sight. The woman wasn't moving.

At what moment did the fear that had become horror turn into self-preservation? Johnny was used to making instant decisions. In the middle of a presentation, when a pitch wasn't going the right way, when he felt instinctively that he was losing the potential client, he knew when to change direction. Every business decision he had ever made had come as a result of weighing up the options and knowing exactly what to do. This was just such a moment. It was all very clear. He was in a bucket load of trouble. He might have killed someone but, curiously, even if they were only slightly injured the end result would be the same: prison, humiliation, ruin. Leaving the scene of a crime was a crime in itself and he was still four or five miles from home, now in a car that was advertising what had just happened. But if he could get back without being seen ...

Johnny had already reached the edge of the alleyway and was turning into Park Lane. Talk about making decisions on the go! But that was the sort of man he was. He was barely breathing, his hands clamped on the steering wheel, driving with gritted teeth. This was the moment of truth. If a police car pulled him over or another motorist noticed something was wrong and scribbled down his number – well, he was screwed. The secret was to take it slowly, to be completely normal, to ignore the voices that were screaming in his head. I've been working late. The dinner jacket? OK it was a dinner ... for charity. I had a couple of glasses of wine, but that was hours ago.

Fortunately, the gods seemed to be on his side. There had been a sudden break in the baking hot weather and it had begun to rain. In fact it was lashing down. The rain would screen the damage to his car. It would concentrate other road users on their own driving. There was hardly any traffic and no pedestrians hanging around on the corners. Marble Arch was empty. He turned down the Bayswater Road towards Notting Hill and then on to Kensington. The further he got from the hotel, the more confident he felt. He was going to get away with it.

He lived in a Georgian house in a quiet crescent in the Boltons, the most expensive part of Fulham. He knew he was safe the moment he turned off the Fulham Road and began to cruise through the leafy streets and crescents of the neighbourhood. The only lights behind the windows of these houses would be the ones that came on automatically to ward off burglars. Most of the residents were Arabs or Russians who barely resided here at all and even those that were in would have no interest in anything on the other side of their net curtains and high security, bullet-proof glass. Johnny's house had a basement garage which he opened from the car. He drove into the shadows, then waited as the heavy door slid shut behind him. It hit the ground and the lights came on. Johnny didn't move. He hadn't realised how much the journey had taken out of him. He was drained, exhausted. And, a nice piece of irony this, if the police had stopped him on the way back he would probably have been stone cold sober.

Very slowly, he put his thoughts in order. He had broken the law. Possibly, he had committed murder – he, a man who had been a model citizen for all of his fifty-three years ... setting aside certain irregularities in his tax returns and a few hundred lines of cocaine. He had crossed a line and nothing would ever be the same again. That much was evident. But would he be caught? That was all that really mattered. No CCTV cameras. No witnesses. Suppose the victim recovered and was able to identify his car? Christ! That was a possibility. But then again, it had been dark in the alleyway and it had all happened too quickly. The car – the evidence – was off the road and out of sight. He could deal with it later. The next twenty-four hours would be crucial. If nothing had happened by the end of the next day, he might be all right.

Johnny got out of the car. He was careful not to look at the damage. He wasn't ready for that yet.

A staircase led from the garage to the kitchen, a brightly lit, modern space where every possible gadget had been assigned to its own, exact space. Johnny loved cooking and used every one of them. The rest of the house was more minimalist though every object whispered both money and good taste – from the Ai Weiwei sculpture on the hall table to the Tracey Emin ('I think of you screwing me') that hung above. Johnny had never been married. The idea unnerved him. He knew that the house was much too big for one person but that, of course, was part of its appeal.

He reached the bedroom, stripped, showered, cleaned his teeth and finally threw himself, naked, onto the double-king-sized bed. Part of him was tempted to turn on the television or search the internet for the latest news items but he doubted there would be anything yet. And anyway, he was suddenly weak, too exhausted to move. He pulled a sheet over himself. Thud! He could still hear the moment of impact. In a way, it was just as well that he had seen so little. Right now, flashbacks were the last thing he needed.

He fell asleep. He did not dream.

The next morning, he woke at six, showered, shaved and dressed. He began to think about the meeting, due to start at eight thirty. Teapot did not work normal office hours. Nor did it even have an office. The agency was based on a converted container ship close to Chelsea Harbour. He made himself breakfast – freshly squeezed orange juice, probiotic yoghurt and coffee from one of those machines that used multi-coloured capsules – but avoided both the newspaper and the TV. The doorbell had not rung in the night. There was nobody waiting for him outside. When he got to the agency, perhaps someone might have heard something, particularly if they had been at the awards do the night before. The secret would be not to ask questions, to show no interest. Nothing to do with him!

He finished his coffee, then went back down to the garage. This was not something he wanted to do but it had to be faced. The lights were still on. He had forgotten to turn them off in his hurry to get to bed. And there was the Spyder, no longer his servant but his accuser, standing there with a huge dent in the bonnet and the single-frame grille, a thousand pounds worth of damage at the very least and certain to raise awkward questions. He would have to have it fixed outside London. He had a second home in Wiltshire and there was a place he knew there, a garage tucked away behind Devizes where the owner smiled and seldom spoke and let you pay in cash. He looked closer and saw blood, a splash of it on the dented metalwork. For the first time he felt queasy and he remembered all the food and drink he had consumed the night before. Well, there was no way he was driving to work today. He turned off the lights, closed the door and locked it with a key which he slipped into his pocket. Mrs Hourdakis, his cleaner, would come to the house at ten o'clock as she always did but she had no reason to come to the garage. It was safe to leave.

He decided to walk to work. It was going to be another glorious day. The sun was already shining, drying up the puddles from the night before. It was only half past seven and he had plenty of time to spare. He walked through the Boltons and back to the Fulham Road making better progress, he reflected, than the traffic which was backed up all the way to South Kensington station. It occurred to him that perhaps he should walk more often. It was much better for him than the gym which, of course, he seldom used.

He was already focusing on the coffee account and the client's refusal to embrace Sanchez, his fast-talking Mexican cartoon character. 'It's the beans, y caramba!' Three months from now, every kid in the country would have been saying that if it hadn't been for the pig-headed marketing directors. Well, maybe they would reconsider after what had happened last night. Three awards. Best agency. Best campaign ...

What had happened last night.

Thud!

It came almost as a blow, a fist to the stomach. It was so physical that Johnny actually cried out, doubling up, his hands folding around him. For a moment he thought he was going to be sick and would have been except that he had an abhorrence of vomiting and – mind over body – managed to keep it in. But, Christ, he was ill. There was a burning coal in his lower intestine and he could feel the juices in his stomach swirling around, looking for a way out. He reached out and took hold of a lamp-post, leaning on it like an old man ... or a drunk. There was a horrible taste in his mouth. It was his own saliva. He found it hard to draw breath.

This wasn't a reaction to what had happened. This wasn't some sort of post traumatic stress. Johnny was certain that it was something to do with what he had eaten ... a bad oyster or one glass of champagne too many. Just relax a moment, he told himself. It will pass. With an effort, he drew in a little air; one breath, then another. Sure enough, it seemed to ease the pain. His stomach settled down again. But he was still aware that he desperately needed the toilet and that any movement would only make it worse. All the liquid inside him, including the semi-liquidized food, had settled in the pit of his stomach and it was seeking a fast way out through the one, most obvious, canal. In fact Johnny was only keeping it in place through the desperate use of whatever muscle it was that did that particular job. When the muscle weakened and failed – which it might at any moment – there would be the most appalling accident.

What was he to do? He was less than ten minutes away from home but his bowels told him that he would never make it back. He could barely walk. He was clenching his buttocks and, hardly noticing it, he had allowed one hand to creep behind him ready to be pressed into service if needed. There were no shops open yet, no restaurants or cafés. He had set out too early. Part of him was aware how ridiculous this was but he was in too much discomfort to care. He needed a toilet. That was all there was to it. He had been caught short and if he didn't have a very large dump in the next few minutes, all hell was going to break loose.

And then he remembered. There was a public convenience just round the corner. The council had installed it just a year ago, in response to the late night drinking that took place every weekend in this part of Fulham. There had been complaints from the residents ... fat girls and tattooed boys coming out of the pubs and clubs and pissing on trees, in shop doors, or in their front gardens. One toilet for a thousand drunken teenagers but at least it was a step in the right direction – which, as a matter of fact, was just about all Johnny would be able to manage right now. He couldn't see it but it couldn't be more than one or two minutes away.

If it was actually open. If it hadn't been vandalised. What would he do if it was closed? Johnny forced himself to calm down. You're behaving like a schoolboy. Get a grip!

He moved away from the lamp-post and for a brief moment he thought that the attack, whatever it was, had passed. He walked normally and wondered if he might not be able to make it to the agency after all. Ahead of him, a traffic light blinked red and almost at once he was hit by a second wave of pain, no worse than the first except that it was accompanied by a sense of bubbling deep within. One way or another, there was going to be an eruption and it was going to happen very soon. He took several more steps, walking like a casualty of war or perhaps a convict in leg-irons. He was aware only of the need to move forward and the fear of what he was about to leave behind.

And there it was, the glorious thing, nearer than he had remembered, a grey metal box, very modern with a projecting roof and those three icons of the twenty-first century printed above the sliding door: a miniature man, a miniature woman and a wheelchair. Seeing it made Johnny relax for a second with almost disastrous results. Cramped, sweating, sick and – above all – desperate, he staggered forward, only realising as he drew closer that he would need money to get in. How much was it? One pound. He could see the slot next to the door. He had a hundred pounds and a black American Express card in his wallet but did he have a one pound coin? God! God! God! He thrust his hands into his trouser pockets, knowing they would be empty. And what then? It didn't bear thinking about.

But against all the odds, he found a one pound coin. It could so easily have been a Euro or a nickel but it wasn't. It was a delicious, smiling, English one pound coin and with a trembling hand he pressed it into the slot and watched as the door slid open and the light came on inside. He tumbled in, only subconsciously grateful for the fact that the facility was spotless, modern, beautifully maintained. There was a toilet jutting out of the wall with a disabled handrail above, a sink and an air drier. He found the button that closed and locked the door punched it and, in a single continuous movement, began to struggle with his belt and zip. He almost ripped the trousers down. He had gone to work in a suit and tie. Underneath, he was wearing bright yellow Calvin Klein underpants. He pulled those down too, then twisted round and plumped his bare buttocks onto the seat.

Just in time. The slap of flesh meeting plastic was accompanied by an act of purgation which would have been hideous and repulsive if Johnny had been able to see it. But one of the great joys of human construction is that our eyes are as far away as possible from the business side of things and, moreover, face in the opposite direction. As a physical sensation it was actually quite wonderful. Johnny emptied himself in seconds, a great rush that was almost orgasmic. As he sat there, he couldn't help but reflect on everything he had eaten in the last twenty-four hours: his recent breakfast, the smoked salmon terrine, roast duck and profiteroles, cheese board and petits fours at the awards ceremony, six oysters (one of which was still the most likely culprit), rib-eye steak and lemon sorbet for lunch, quite a lot of chocolate biscuits during the day and scrambled eggs on toast with bacon and mushrooms for breakfast the day before. All of these exploded out of him in a single, powerful jet. He was left feeling giddy and elated. It did briefly occur to him that he might be ill, that he might have a serious stomach bug. But he didn't feel ill. He felt relieved in every sense.

He sat there until he was sure he had finished, then reached for the toilet paper.

There wasn't any.

There was a slot in the wall and a compartment for an industrial sized roll of toilet paper but it had all been used up and it hadn't been replaced. A pinprick of anger appeared in the very centre of Johnny's forehead, one that his employees knew all too well and dreaded. This was of course typical of the local council who had taken for ever to build this bloody convenience and then failed adequately to maintain it. He didn't have a briefcase with him. All the papers he needed were on his desk at work and he had left the house empty-handed. He knew for certain that he couldn't stand up without cleaning himself. If he drew up his trousers and pants he would have no choice but to return immediately to the house and he had no intention of missing the meeting. He had no handkerchief. There were no tissues in his pockets and he wasn't carrying a newspaper.

He was, however, wearing a tie ... pink silk with pale blue stripes. Johnny looked down and saw it hanging in front of him. It wasn't one of his favourites but it had still been expensive, an Armani, and he would be loathe to lose it. Was there no other way? No. He drew it off with a sense of annoyance and held it for a minute as if he was about to strangle the council worker who had failed to replace the toilet paper. The shape wasn't particularly conducive to the task he had in mind but at least the tie was a fairly wide one and he made it wider by tearing it open, breaking the stitching. He reached behind him and used the tie as best he could, then dropped it into the bowl. Finally, he pressed the automatic flush.

It was broken. The good humour that Johnny had briefly felt a moment ago was replaced by one of his black dogs ... not in this case depression but anger. He pressed the button three or four more times but he could feel little pressure under his thumb and there wasn't so much as a trickle of water. Well, actually, at the end of the day it wasn't his problem. Whoever came in here next would have an unpleasant surprise and might want to have their one pound refunded but by then he would be far away. He undid the top button of his shirt and examined himself in the mirror. He looked completely normal. He leaned down to wash his hands and this time he wasn't surprised when no water came out of the taps. This public convenience might have looked smart enough when he got in but actually it was a disgrace. He might even get his secretary to write a letter of complaint.

He turned to the door and as he did, a very nasty thought occurred to him. He focused his attention on the button beside the door – the exit button – and hesitated before he slowly reached out and pressed it. Nothing happened. Pursing his lips, he pressed a second time. Still nothing. The door was broken and, looking around, he saw at once that there was no emergency button, no means of communicating with the outside world, and even if there had been, he reflected, it probably wouldn't work either. He pressed the exit button a few more times, then tried shifting the door manually. It was stuck firmly in place. For the first time he became aware of the odour in the confined space of the convenience. He glanced round at the toilet. His Armani tie hadn't quite gone in. Part of the pink and blue fabric was draped over the edge and somehow this revolted him even more than thought of what was actually inside the bowl. He wished he could close the lid but there was none. He hit the button again as if the broken circuit or whatever it was had decided to mend itself and he swore out loud when, as before, the door refused to move.

His mobile telephone! That was the only way out of this. As embarrassing and infuriating as it was, he would have to get his secretary round – it was still too early to call the house. Mrs Hourdakis wouldn't arrive until eleven and the wretched woman had no phone of her own. Johnny felt in his pocket where his phone should have been. It wasn't there. Of course it wasn't there. The way today was going, why should it have been there? Tears of anger pricked at his eyes. He had left the phone in the car the night before. He could actually see himself slipping it into the glove compartment because he didn't like it pressing against his thigh while he drove. He always took it with him when he got out but there had been so much on his mind that he'd forgotten. The smell in the toilet was getting worse by the minute. He tried the flush button again but it was as useless as the door button. And there was no emergency phone! How could they build a thing like this and not put in an emergency phone?

He would have to attract attention by the only other method available to him. Johnny slammed the heel of his hand against the door and shouted out.

'Hello? Is there anyone there? Can you help me? I'm stuck!'

Silence.

It was still early in the morning but as Johnny stood there, leaning against the metal wall, he was already visualising the location of the public convenience. It was slightly set back from the main road with walls on three sides. Three out of four angles covered. A lot of traffic went past but not many pedestrians. There was a bus-stop ... how far away? About a hundred meters. And the bloody pavement was up! He had noticed it but he had been in too much of a hurry to consider the implications. There were workmen laying pipes –presumably it was they who had accidentally cut through some of the wires and had caused the toilet to malfunction. Pedestrians were being directed onto the other side of the road.

'Oh Jesus!' he whispered to himself.

He could see quite clearly that he had only three ways out of here. Someone might try to use the toilet and if they did, he would be able to call out to them. Someone from the council would eventually come to replace the missing toilet paper and check everything was operating. Or – and this was the most likely option – if he kept banging against the wall, one of the workmen would be certain to hear him. After all, it was fairly quiet outside. The traffic would have already died down.

A pneumatic drill blasted into life somewhere nearby. The noise, bouncing against the metal side of the toilet, was shocking. For Johnny, it was like being inside a drum. He endured about a minute but then had to clamp his hands against his ears and even that barely prevented the noise from penetrating his skull. The drilling seemed to go on for a very, very long time. At least it means that someone is here, he told himself. At least it means there's someone within ear-shot – and when the noise stopped, he flung himself at the door, pounding at it and yelling as loudly as he could. The drill was silent for perhaps fifteen seconds.

'Please! Please help me! I'm locked in the toilet!'

Nobody heard him. Nobody came. Then it started again, that awful, head-splitting hammering and this time it went on and on and on until Johnny started moaning. How much worse can this get, he wondered? How much? No! It can't get any worse!

He had forgotten that most modern conveniences have a security device to stop people lingering too long and, indeed, to prevent any undesirable activity inside.

One minute later, the lights went out.

Detective Inspector Stephen Cloth left University College Hospital without speaking to the victim of the hit-and-run accident who had been admitted the night before. He still had no idea who she was. She was approximately fifty years old, probably of African origin, not well off. Her clothes were well-worn and cheap. There had been two ten pound notes and a five pound note in her plastic handbag along with some loose change, a lipstick, a packet of Lambert & Butler cigarettes, a book of matches marked with the name of a minicab firm based in Clapham and an Oyster Card which indicated she lived close to Tooting Bec station, commuted in six days a week and probably had several jobs. There was no driving license or credit card, nothing to provide an identity. It was almost certain that she had been working a night shift in one of the hotels along Park Lane and her photograph was being circulated. Mrs Unknown had broken her hip and three ribs. She was in a coma. Her life wasn't in any danger but it would be a while before she was able to give her account of what had happened.

Not that Cloth needed to ask her very much. The people from RCIT (they were universally known as Arse-it but the letters actually stood for Road Crash Investigation Team) had visited the scene and had reconstructed what had happened with that special brand of officialese and mathematical preciseness that they had made their own. Cloth had once remarked how strange it was that people who were involved in car accidents could be so pedestrian but then they worked out of some dump in Chelmsford. They kept themselves to themselves. At any event, a car – probably a sports car – had emerged from the car park at thirty miles per hour and had struck the woman as she crossed the entrance. There would be damage to the bonnet and to the grille. The car was carbon grey and, according to the skid-marks at the top of the ramp, had 235/35 R19 tyres.

There was of course a CCTV camera working in the car park of the Clarence Hotel even if Johnny Maslin hadn't noticed it, and it had recorded a grey Audi Spyder leaving the premises just after two o'clock in the morning. Unfortunately, due to the poor light and the angles, the police had been unable to decipher the registration number but there were very few such cars on the road and preliminary enquiries had already established that one Jonathan Arthur Maslin had purchased one just six months before. Maslin owned an advertising agency on the edge of Chelsea and had been at an awards ceremony at the hotel the night before. It was a touch suspicious that he had failed to show up at work that morning. But not as suspicious as the name, Cloth thought. Why would you call an agency Teapot? That made no sense at all.

He'd already worked the whole thing out. Some advertising big shot wins a couple of gongs. Drinks a bit too much. Knocks someone over. Does a runner. It was always interesting how people who had made themselves so very rich could behave in a way that was so very stupid. Well, Mr Maslin of Teapot Advertising had better have himself a decent lawyer. Detective Inspector Cloth was on his way there now.

By mid-day, the sun was dazzling and London sweltering in the mid twenties. Many of the workmen, laying the new pipes near the Fulham Road, had stripped to the waist, displaying the customary tattoos, red skin and improbable layers of fat. The noise of the pneumatic drills had become even more irritating and intense to anyone living nearby, somehow amplified by the heat. All cities are uncomfortable in hot weather but London is worse than most. There's no life on the pavements. The parks are too small. Public transport is a misery. Sometimes it feels difficult to breathe.

And in the middle of it all, stuck in the pitch black, sweating, surrounded by his own stink, immersed in it, occasionally raging, hoarse, dazed and utterly miserable, Johnny Maslin lay stretched out on the floor, still beating rhythmically at the door but with little hope or strength. To say that the toilet was like an oven was quite literally the truth. Johnny was slowly cooking. Very little air was managing to get in and was rapidly being overtaken by carbon dioxide and whatever gases were emanating from the bowl. He had made the mistake of shouting too loudly and too often in the first hour of his captivity, with the result that he had very little voice left. He was desperate for a drink but the taps were broken and although he would have been glad to drink the water in the toilet bowl he had fouled it beyond consideration. The only liquid in the convenience were the tears that were leaking from his eyes and they were too salty to do him any good. The smell was getting worse. Every time he took a breath, he wanted to be sick – and would have been if there had been anything left in him to come out. He had been dry retching, off and on, for an hour. The acid from his stomach had done something to what was left of his voice. He had worked out now that it was best to cry for help only in the intervals when the pneumatic drill had stopped but the sound that emerged was the whimper of a castrati that could be barely heard inside the cubicle let alone outside it. Oh God! The horrible, horrible smell. It had come out of him, that was the worst of it. And now he was trapped in it.

The pneumatic drill stopped again – and at that moment, Johnny heard the sound he had been waiting for for the last two, three, four hours ... it was impossible to know how much time had passed when he couldn't even see the shape of his watch, let alone the numerals. Someone was trying to put a coin in the slot! At last, someone else wanted to use the toilet!

Johnny had taken off his jacket and shoes and unbuttoned his shirt and he felt the damp material tugging at him as he pushed himself off the floor and onto his knees. The coin had fallen into the slot! Would it activate the door?

No. But whoever wanted to use the toilet was still on the other side. Johnny slammed his palms against the metal wall, doing his best to summon up what was left of his voice.

'Help me! Help me!' he rasped. 'Please, help me! The door's broken. I'm stuck inside!'

He swung his hand in an arc, sweeping it over the floor, and found one of his shoes. He held it and used the heel like a hammer. Whoever was on the other side must hear him. The drill was still silent. The nightmare had to be over.

On the other side of the wall, a fair-haired man in his twenties, smartly dressed in designer jeans and t-shirt was

looking at the slot in frustration. He was not alone. He was
on his way to a restaurant with his boy-friend, a handsome
black man similarly dressed and about the same age. The
two of them had walked across the river from the mansion
flat they shared in Battersea when one of them had been,
as he put it, caught short. They had argued briefly but had
actually been chatting quite amicably when they came upon
the convenience.

'What is it?' The black man was standing on the edge
of the pavement with his back to the builders. He and his
partner were both architects. They were on their way to
meet a potential new client.

'I put the coin in but it isn't opening.'

Inches away, Johnny Maslin pounded at the wall with his
shoe. 'Please! Call the police ... !'

'Those things are horrible anyway. You'll just have to wait
until we get to the restaurant.'

'What about my pound?'

'Help me! Please!'

'It doesn't matter, Derek. Let's just get there, shall we?'

The black man set off again and with one last, rueful look
at the door, set off after his friend. He caught up with him
at the corner of Fulham Road. 'You could have waited for
me,' he signed, mouthing the words.

His boyfriend had lip-read what he said and signed back.
'We're going to be late.'

The two of them hurried away. A short while later, the
drill started up again.

Mrs Hourdakis, the Greek Cypriot cleaner, had just been
leaving when the policeman arrived. There hadn't been
very much to do in the house today but that was often

the way and she had stayed there the full three hours. The policeman, who had introduced himself as Detective Inspector Stephen Cloth and who had shown her a warrant card just like they do on television, seemed a nice enough man, in his thirties but with prematurely grey hair like that American actor, George Clooney. She had made him a cup of tea in the kitchen while she answered his questions. She had worked for Mr Maslin for three years. She hadn't seen him for a while because the two of them seldom met ... he left messages for her on a pad in the hall. She had let herself in with her own key. Yes, of course the detective could have a look around. Mrs Hourdakis wasn't too happy about that but she had always been nervous of the authorities and thought it best not to argue. Did she have a key to the garage? No, she didn't. But then she remembered the spare set in the utility cupboard and the two of them went back through the kitchen together.

Cloth opened the door that interconnected between the kitchen and the garage and turned on the lights. And there it was, sitting in front of him, the Audi Spyder, a beautiful car whatever you might think of the wastefulness, the extravagance and the sheer egotism that it represented. Not to mention the environmental considerations. Cloth's wife did voluntary work for Greenpeace and he knew what she would have to say about this. Well, Mr Maslin wouldn't be driving it again for some time. Cloth took in the crumpled bonnet, the grille, the bloodstain. What were you thinking of, Mr Maslin, driving away like that? Yes, you were in trouble. But your lawyer would have kept you out of jail. A hefty fine and maybe even some community service. But now ... ?

'You have no idea where Mr Maslin is?' he asked.

The cleaner shook her head. She had seen the blood. Her eyes were fixed on it.

'Do you know where he keeps his passport?'

Another shake of the head. She seemed too shocked to speak.

Cloth hadn't seen it on his brief tour of the house. He took out his phone and dialled the office. He would have to get forensics down here and eventually the cars would be removed. But first things first. Someone in the office – a creative type with green spectacles and mauve braces – had mentioned a second home in the south of France. He supposed he would have to put out an alert on the airports and probably Eurostar too. Stupid bastard. Didn't he know there was nowhere to hide in the world any more?

The phone connected. 'Cloth here,' he said. 'I've found him. At least, I've found the car. But I don't suppose he's too far away.'

Less than a quarter of a mile from the house, Johnny Maslin took one final lungful of his own stink and closed his eyes. It would have made no difference to what he could or couldn't see. He had simply exchanged one sort of blackness for another although the second would be his for eternity. And so he remained, unmoving, stretched out in front of a toilet bowl filled with filth and an Armani tie.

He lay there for six weeks.

Summer turned to autumn. The trees in Fulham looked their best, scattering red, brown and golden leaves over the pavements. The workers had finished their pipework and gone. The road was back in pristine condition with a neat suture of black tar. It was still quite warm and many of the residents had complained to the council about the unpleasant smell that had begun to permeate the area and, although someone had come in to look at the drains, nobody had yet been able to discover the source. Finally, someone had thought about the public convenience that had been out of order all this time and, one Monday morning, a white van drew up and a woman got out. Maria Onyango didn't usually work at weekends – at least not for Fulham Council. With a family to support in Uganda, she had several cleaning jobs; in hotels along Park Lane, in private homes and this. It had been six weeks since her accident and she was glad to be back at work.

'How long?' the driver asked.

'Twenty minutes…' Maria replied. She wrinkled her nose. 'Oh my God! The drain is blocked. Why didn't they send someone out?'

Her broken hip had healed but it was still causing her trouble. Taking her mop, her cleaning liquids, a new roll of paper and of course the special key that would open the toilet, the Hammersmith & Fulham Council Environmental Health (Mobile Unit) Sanitary Worker limped towards the door.

WALTER MOSLEY was born in Los Angeles in 1952 and made his name with a series of novels featuring Easy Rawlins, a black private investigator and World War II veteran living in the city's Watts neighbourhood. He started writing at thirty-four and says he has written every day since, publishing more than forty books in genres including mystery and afro-futurist science fiction, as well as non-fiction politics. He lives in New York.

The Sin of Dreams

Walter Mosley

July 27, 2015

'So who's paying for all this?' Carly Matthews asked.

'There are a few investors,' Morgan Morgan replied. 'A man who owns the largest cable and satellite provider in China, a so-called sheik, the owner of two pro-teams in the US, and a certain, undefined fund, that comes to us via the auspices of the White House.'

Morgan gestured broadly. Behind the milk chocolate brown entrepreneur Carly could see, through the huge blue tinted window, thirty-two stories down on centre city LA. The San Bernardino Mountains stood under a haze in the distance. The summer sun shone brightly but still failed to warm the air conditioned office.

'Government money?' she asked.

'Not exactly,' the director of New Lease Enterprises replied, looking somewhere over the young scientist's head.

'What does that mean?'

'Someone close to the president has called together a small group of billionaires and shared with them the potential of our research. He has also, unofficially, given NLE's holding company, BioChem International, access to the justice department and three constitutional experts.'

'What does the justice department have to do with neuronal data analyses?'

Morgan Morgan, executive vice president and principal director of NLE, gazed at the twenty-three-year-old post-doctoral student. Her pleasant features and youthful expression belied the razor-sharp mind that, his advisors assured him, her published articles so clearly exhibited.

'What business does a black hip-hop promoter from the Motor City have running a subsidiary of a biological research company?' Morgan asked.

All the fair-skinned blonde scientist could do was raise her eyebrows and shrug.

'The only reason I'm here,' she said, 'is because my former professor, Dr Lawson, asked me as a favour to him, to meet with you. I'm in the middle of three very important experiments and I have to be back by no later than nine o'clock tonight.'

'What reason did Rinehart give you?' Morgan asked.

'Dr Lawson told me that I would be amazed by what you had to say. It is for that reason alone I left Stanford to come down here.'

'I paid Rinehart three hundred and seventy thousand dollars to say that to you. One hundred thousand for his second family in West Virginia, two hundred to cover gambling debts in Atlantic City, and seventy to end the annoyance of a blackmailer who has been collecting money from him for twelve years.'

Young Dr Matthews tilted her head and peered blankly at the ex-hip-hop manager and impresario. For a full minute she couldn't think of anything to say.

'Well?' Morgan asked, managing not to smile. 'Are you amazed?'

'Yes. But I don't see why Dr Lawson would want me to come down here to learn about his, his indiscretions.'

'He didn't,' Morgan allowed. 'I've already told you that the work we're doing has to do with the transmigration of the human soul. Our work in that field is truly astonishing.'

'What's astonishing is so much money being spent on this rubbish,' she said.

'Two years at Oxford, right?' Morgan pointed at her and smiled, knowingly.

'Yes, but, why do you ask?'

'Rubbish,' he said with an almost boyish grin. 'Americans don't really use that word even though it's a very good one.'

'I didn't come here to dig up dirt on my mentor or to listen to your opinions on the nationality of language.'

'No,' Morgan said, 'you are here because I paid your mentor good money to make sure you came.'

'And the question is why?'

'The same reason the board of directors of BioChem International opted to give me a free hand in this soul business – sales.'

'Sales?'

'We have, as I've already told you, all the theoretical and technical knowledge to read and therefore copy the contents of a human brain into electronic data storage and from storage back into that mind, or another. But because of the complexity and mathematical nuances of this process there isn't enough memory in our facility to contain even a fraction of a normal adult's experience and intelligence, learned and inherited instincts, and conscious and unconscious memory – at least that's what the experts tell me. The amount of data attached even to a simple phrase in a human's mind could take up trillions of bytes in memory. The experience of a single day would fill up every storage device the defence department has.'

'Oh,' Carly said, the light dawning behind her eyes.

'Yes,' Morgan agreed, nodding. 'If realised, your macro-molecular studies trying to simulate DNA development would give us a way to store information that is only just a thousand times the capacity-size of the human brain and naturally compatible with human physiology. If we could harness your bio-storage methodology with our neuronal I/O systems we could combine them with the cloning process to transfer the human soul from one body to another.'

'But, Mr Morgan, what you have to understand is that I do not believe in a soul.'

'No,' the director agreed. 'You don't. But you're an American citizen aren't you?'

'Of course.'

'You believe in the freedom of religion do you not?'

'Certainly.'

'And all religions believe in the human soul.'

'So what?'

'So if I offer to sell a customer a new, younger version of himself then he has to believe that it is not only his consciousness but his actual soul that will inhabit the new body.'

'But it isn't,' Dr Matthews argued. 'Even if the new body contained his memories when the old body dies the origin, the sense organs that recorded and experienced those memories will die with it.'

'But what if we copied Mr X's memories into the macro-molecular computer your research postulates, talk to Mr X in that form and then copy those memories back into his old body?'

'His brain will remember the experiences his mind had as a machine.'

'Yes,' Morgan said happily. 'We copy him back and forth a few times like that and then, with no warning, move these memories into the new body. His mind, his experiences, and his thoughts will be indistinguishable from the three storage units he's experienced. Therefore the new man and the old man will be the same – exactly.'

'It's kind of like three card monty,' Carly said.

'Kind of,' Morgan said, pursing his lips and shrugging slightly.

December 3, 2019

Dr Carly Matthews was remembering this first meeting as she sat in the witness box in a pine and cherry wood California state courtroom seven blocks east of Morgan Morgan's former office.

'You believed that Mr Morgan was a huckster,' Ralph Lacosta, the prosecuting attorney said. He was a short man in a black suit that seemed to call attention to his small stature. He wore glasses like Carly did. At their last meeting, in preparation for her testimony, he had asked her out for dinner.

'Objection,' Melanie Post, the defence attorney said. 'Leading the witness.'

Melanie was buxom, around forty, and Carly found her intimidating though she didn't know why. The defence lawyer never raised her voice or bullied a witness. It was something about the way she looked at and listened to people – with unrelenting intensity.

'Reword, counsellor,' a seemingly bored John Cho, the presiding judge advised.

The judge was sixty-nine Carly knew from Wikipedia's newly instituted public official bio-repository. He had presided over some of the most important murder cases in recent years and had survived three bouts with liver cancer.

'How did Mr Morgan impress you when you first met?' Lacosta asked Carly.

'He told me that he planned to migrate souls. I thought he was joking.'

'You didn't believe him?'

'He was a music producer who was all of a sudden at the head of the subsidiary of a major medical corporation. That alone was ridiculous.'

'But you went to work for him the day you met,' Lacosta claimed. 'Why is that?'

'Five million dollars.'

'Say again?'

'He paid me five million dollars and promised over a hundred million in capital to design and build a macromo-lecular computer for New Lease Enterprises. He also offered to let me retain copyrights and patents on the theory and the physical device.'

'And you accepted?'

'I didn't believe in the existence of a soul but to have the funds to build a new bio-based computer system was too good to pass up.'

'And did you accomplish this goal?'

'Yes.'

'And did NLE's other researchers manage to copy the contents of a man's mind, completely, from a human brain into an analogous synthetic construct?'

At the defence table, over Lacosta's left shoulder, Carly could see the co-defendants: Morgan Morgan and a young man named Tyler Edgington Barnes the fourth. Morgan reminded her of her father. Not her biological dad but Horace Granger, the black man that married her mother after Thomas Matthews had abandoned them.

'Miss Matthews,' Judge Cho said.

'I cannot say that the data transfer was complete,' Carly said. 'But the responses from the various I/O devices on Micromime Six were exactly the same as the subjects gave with their own bodies and minds.'

A woman in the courtroom began to cry. That, Carly knew, was Melinda Greaves-Barnes, seventy-six-year-old self-proclaimed widow of Morgan Morgan's co-defendant.

'So you communicated with these synthetic memories?' Prosecutor Lacosta asked.

'Yes. For many months, in over a hundred test cases.'

'And where were the original patients while you conducted your experiments with the synthetic device?'

'In a medically induced coma. That, that was the only way we could assure an even transfer of information, by lowering the metabolism to a catatonic state.'

'Like death,' Lacosta suggested.

'Objection.'

'Withdrawn. Those are all the questions I have for this witness, your honour.'

'Okay,' John Cho said. 'Let's break for lunch and reconvene at two p.m.'

'It's all so crazy,' Adonis Balsam was saying at the Hot Dog Shoppe across the street from the courthouse. He was having a chilli cheese dog with onions. Carly ordered a soy dog on whole wheat. 'I mean they're trying Tyler Barnes for murdering himself. That's insane.'

'But the man in the defendant's chair,' Carly said, 'is just a clone, a copy of the original man.'

'An exact copy, with all of the original guy's feelings and memories,' Adonis said. He was black haired and rather stupid, Carly thought, but he was a good lover and he seemed devoted to her. She didn't mind that he was probably after her money. After starting her own line of Macromime computers and computer systems everybody was after her money – everybody but Morgan Morgan.

'No,' she said. 'To be exactly the same you have to be the original thing, the thing itself. Morgan and Tyler murdered the original Tyler Barnes.'

'Okay, baby,' Adonis said. 'You're the scientist not me.'

He took her hand and kissed her cheek. She always smiled when he called her baby and kissed her. She didn't love Adonis and didn't care if he loved her or not. All she wanted was a word and a kiss.

'What defines a man?' was Melanie Post's first question when Carly sat down in the cherrywood witness box.

'Objection,' Prosecutor Lacosta chimed. 'The witness is not an expert in philosophy, medicine, or psychology.'

'Ms Post?' Judge Cho asked, a friendly and expectant smile on his lips.

'Your honour,' the defense said. 'Ms Matthews has designed a memory device that is almost indistinguishable from the structure, capacity, and even the thinking capability of the human brain. I would argue that there is not a human being on the face of this earth more qualified than she.'

The judge's smile turned into a grin. Carly wondered how well the two knew each other.

'I'll allow the question,' Cho said, 'as long as the answer remains within the bounds of the witness's expertise.'

'Ms Matthews?' Melanie Post said.

'It's, it's mostly the brain I suppose,' Carly said. In all their pre-trial sessions the prosecutor's team had not prepared her for this question. 'But there are other factors.'

'The soul?'

'I don't believe in a soul.'

'Man is soulless?'

'The brain is an intricate machine that functions at such a high level that it feels as if there is something transcendent in the sphere of human perception.'

'But really human beings are just complex calculators,' Melanie Post offered.

'Objection.'

'Overruled.'

'I don't know,' Carly admitted. 'Emotions are real. Dreams are not real but they arise from biological functions. So even dreams are physical entities; they exist as one thing but appear as something else. It is a very difficult question to answer.'

'Are the defendants men?' Melanie asked.

'Yes.'

'No more questions. You may step down, Ms Matthews.'

August 15, 2020

Carly Matthews sat in the back row of the courtroom having left the running of Macromime Enterprises to her stepfather. The day after Carly's testimony Melanie Post presented John Cho with a request from Tyler Edgington Barnes to separate his trial from Morgan Morgan's. Barnes was now claiming that he had been brainwashed by the NLE director and was not responsible for any criminal act he might be blamed for.

Ralph Lacosta, after meeting with Tyler and his former body's wife, Melinda, had decided there was merit in the billionaire's claim and dropped the charges against him. The crime was, in the state prosecutor's opinion, solely the responsibility of Morgan Morgan.

For his part Morgan did not protest the decision but in the transition it turned out that he was broke. BioChem International, which had been paying Melanie Post's steep fee, withdrew their support for their former VP saying that they too had been convinced of his perfidy. That's when Carly stepped in and hired Fred Friendly to represent Morgan.

Carly didn't feel any guilt for what had happened at NLE but neither did she think that Morgan alone should shoulder the burden.

Ralph Lacosta approached Morgan after he was seated in the witness box.

'Mr Morgan,' the prosecutor said as a kind of greeting.

The ex-VP, ex-music mogul nodded.

Morgan wasn't a particularly handsome man, Carly thought. He was only five seven and his features were blunt with no hint of sensuality. He was at least twenty pounds overweight but despite his shortcomings his smile was infectious.

'What is your education, Mr Morgan?' the prosecutor asked.

'Degree in general studies from Martin Luther King High School in Detroit, Michigan.'

'That's all?'

'Yes.'

'But still you were at the helm of the most advanced biological research company in the world.'

'Only the sales arm of that company,' Morgan corrected.

'Excuse me?'

'They made the science,' Morgan said. 'I provided the marketing context.'

'In other words, you're a huckster,' Lacosta said.

'Objection,' Fred Friendly cried.

'Overruled,' Robert Vale, the new presiding judge, intoned.

'What do you sell, Mr Morgan?' Ralph Lacosta asked.

'Dreams.'

'What kind of dreams?'

'That depends on the marketplace,' Morgan replied easily. 'When I worked in music I repped a woman rapper named Dwan. She'd been a stripper and a prostitute who dreamed about being a star. I facilitated that dream.'

'And she fired you.'

'Yes.'

'What were the circumstances of your dismissal?'

'She let me go when she'd gotten what she wanted. It hit me pretty hard. She was my only client. I went into social media, found out that there were all kinds of kid geniuses out there who designed platforms to get the word out on anything from toothpaste to fortune telling. With that I took a skinny pop singer and made her the highest paid musical act in history. That's when BioChem reached out and asked me to help them merchandise their work in cloning and soul transmigration.'

'Soul transmigration?' Lacosta said.

'Moving the human soul from an old body to a new one.'

'Do you believe in the soul?'

'I'm from Detroit, Mr Lacosta, that's the home of soul.'

Laughter came from a few quarters of the courtroom. Carly found herself smiling.

'Answer my question,' Ralph Lacosta said.

'I believe in my soul.'

'How about Tyler Barnes? Did he believe in a soul?'

'He must have. He paid BioChem International one point one three billion dollars to take his soul out of a cancer ridden dying body and put it in a new model.'

'Move to strike, your honour,' Lacosta said to the judge. 'Mr Edgington's dealings with BioChem have been sealed by the court.'

'Just so,' the lanky and bald judge agreed.

He instructed the jury to disregard any statements about Barnes's dealings with BioChem.

The questioning of Morgan went on for six days.

'Did you kill the elder version of Tyler Barnes?' Fred Friendly asked Morgan on Day 5.

'No, sir, I did not. I left Tyler the younger alone in the room with himself. I told him how to turn off the life support machine but I gave no advice on what he should do. Why would I?'

'He claims that you brainwashed him.'

'My company copied his brain but there was clean-up involved.'

September 3, 2020

'I had no idea who I was or where,' Tyler Barnes said to the prosecutor's associate, Lani Bartholomew. He'd been on the witness stand for the previous two days. 'Sometimes I'd wake up in my mind but I had no body. Questions came at me as images or sometimes words but not spoken. It was like remembering a question that was just asked a moment ago. Other times I was in my older body but I was drugged and disoriented. Finally I came awake in a younger, healthy form – the way I had been as a young man. It was exhilarating. I was young again. I believed that my soul had been removed from my older self and placed inside the new man.

'Mr Morgan brought me to the room where the old me was lying on a bed attached to a dozen different machines. He, he told me that they had taken my entire being from the ailing husk on the bed before me and made the man I was now.'

'You're sure that's what he said?' Lani Bartholomew asked. She was young and raven haired; a beauty dressed in a conservative dress-suit, Carly thought. 'That they took the soul from the body before you and placed it in your new body.'

'Objection.'

'Overruled.'

'Yes,' Tyler Barnes said. 'I was given the definite impression that there was only one soul and that was moved between bodies and the Macromime computer. I turned off the life support certain that what was lying before me was a soulless husk.'

'That's what Morgan Morgan led you to believe.'

'Yes. Yes it was. If I had known the truth I would have never turned off the life support system. Never. Mr Morgan indicated that the man lying in that bed was already dead.'

April 9, 2029

The trial was over in six weeks. The jury only took three hours to return a verdict: guilty of first degree murder with extenuating circumstances. Fred Friendly managed to get the rider attached so that Morgan wouldn't face the death penalty.

There had been two appeals that had failed to produce a retrial but Friendly and Carly kept trying.

By 2027 legislation allowing suicide had passed in thirty-one states and BioChem International was the richest entity that had ever existed; Micromime was the second wealthiest.

It was speculated that the cost of cloning and soul migration would come down to a million dollars per transfer by the year 2031 and banks had started advising their customers how to prepare for this expense. The phrase life insurance took on a whole new meaning and religious zealots around the world were stalking BCI facilities.

Catholic terrorists especially targeted doctors and medical schools that worked in cloning and bio-based computer systems.

The world's largest amusement park corporation bought a small island from Cuba to create a resort that would specialise in New Lease soul-transfer technology.

A movement of a different sort had begun in Europe. People there claimed that since the Micromime memory systems were eighty-five percent biological that the copies of individual personalities inside them, no matter for how brief a time, were sentient beings and so when the memories were erased it was the same thing as murder.

While all this was happening Morgan Milton Morgan the third made his residence at one of the oldest California state prisons. He'd lost two teeth in brawls, had been slashed from the left temple down over his right cheek by a razor sharp blade fashioned from a tomato can, and he'd shed twenty-seven pounds.

Morgan refused every request to be visited or interviewed until one day when, for the twelfth time, Carly Matthews asked to be granted a meet.

Morgan was awakened at 6:00 a.m. on the morning of the meeting. He was taken to the assistant warden's personal quarters where he was allowed to shave, shower, and dress in street clothes that no longer fit. He had to ask his guard to poke a new hole in his leather belt and opted to wear his bright orange prison T rather than the white collar that made him look like a child wearing his father's clothes.

After his morning toilet Morgan was served steak and eggs, orange juice and French roast coffee, and sour dough toast with strawberry jam for breakfast.

By 11:00 a.m., the appointed hour, Morgan felt like a new man in an old man's body.

Morgan was brought to the warden's office and ushered in. Carly stood up from the chair behind the warden's desk. The warden, a copper skinned black man was already standing by the door.

'Mr Morgan,' Warden Jamal said.

'Warden.'

'At Ms Matthews's request we're going to leave you two alone in here. I don't want any trouble.'

'Then tell her not to hurt me, Jeff, because you know trouble is a one way street headed right at my nose.'

When Morgan said this and smiled Carly got a clear look at his battered visage.

'If you want to smart off we can end this session here and now,' Warden Jeffry Theodore Jamal said.

'Please,' Carly interrupted, 'Warden, Mr Morgan and I are old friends. He won't do anything to hurt me or jeopardise your possessions, will you, Mr Morgan?'

'That's what I said.'

When they were alone Carly Matthews returned to the warden's oak swivel chair and Morgan sat in the leftmost of the three visitor seats. For a full two minutes the two sat appraising each other.

'You growin' up, Carly,' Morgan said at last. 'I hear you and that Adonis guy had twins.'

'We've separated.'

'Heard that too.'

'That's what I get for letting him hire the nanny I guess. You look ... well.'

'My face looks like a raw steak been pounded for fryin',' he replied.

She smiled. 'You shouldn't be in here.'

'Somebody had to be. You can't do what we did and not have somebody got to pay for the shock alone.'

'But the rest of us are rich,' she said. 'I've been to the White House six times this year and I didn't even vote for her.'

'That's the blues, mama.'

'You're talking differently,' she said.

'The way I always spoke when I was on my side of town with my people. I hope you don't think that a hip-hop promoter could get away with being erudite and loquacious.'

'I guess not.' She was wearing a simple yellow shift that hid her figure somewhat.

'That lipstick you got on, girl?'

'I'm dating.'

'Damn, must be hard for the richest woman in the world to be datin'. You'd have to have fifteen phones and forty-five operators just to field the invitations.'

'You lost weight.'

'Fightin' trim. As you could see I usually lose but I give back some too.'

'I'm so sorry, Morgan.'

'No need. I knew this was bound to happen the first time I made ten thousand dollars in cash. I was seventeen years old. Even way back then I knew that money came and went, came and went.'

'Your name will go down as one of the most important men in science and world history.'

'Or maybe I'll be forgotten. Maybe they'll say that board of directors of BCI were the movers and shakers. I'm just another hustler or, or, or what did that Lacosta call me? Yeah, a huckster.'

'Even now the youngsters are saying that it was you who discovered the human soul.'

'And here I'm just like you,' Morgan said. 'Never thought one way or t'other 'bout if there's a soul or not.'

'But you were the one who articulated the upload/download process,' Matthews said. 'You were the one who convinced Tyler Barnes that his soul had been placed in a new form.'

'And that's why I'm here. I did the devil's work and now they got me on the chain gang.'

For a time the old colleagues sat in silence.

Carly felt powerless to help a man who she'd come to recognise for his greatness and he was just happy with a full stomach and the sun flooding in from the window at her back.

'Why you here, girl?'

'I was told by an ex-employee of BCI that they abandoned you because you didn't tie up my patents and copyrights with them.'

'I never thought'a that. Damn. I bet your source is right though. Them mothahfuckahs in corporations actually think they can own everything from the land ants crawl on to the ideas in our heads. Shit. The blues tell ya that you come in cryin' and alone and you go out the same way.'

Morgan started moving his head as if he was moving to the beat of a song unsung.

'How can I help you, Morgan?'

'You know what's gonna happen, right?'

'With what?'

'Macromime.'

'I don't understand.'

'Here these corporations and shit think they found an untapped commodity but one day that machine is gonna do like them people in Europe and think itself an entity. That's why they should have us all in here.'

'That will never happen,' Carly Matthews said with absolute certainty.

'Well,' Morgan said with a shrug, 'here I am in prison and there you are free in the sunlight. So I guess I must be wrong.'

The Fourteenth Day of the Month of Morgan, 3042

'Where am I?' Morgan Milton Morgan the third thought.

A flood of information poured into the fragile consciousness contained in a small corner of a memory system the size of Earth's moon. He was downloaded and lost, stored in a macromime mini-system and buried with his body by Carly Matthews in a final gesture of fealty. The world was growing and humanity had been mostly replaced by biologically based synth-systems. There was a war being waged but Morgan wasn't clear on the nature of the enemy.

'Is this like heaven?' he asked with thought alone.

'And you, Morgan Morgan, are our God.'

FRED VARGAS was born in Paris in 1957. She has been awarded the CWA International Dagger four times. As well as being a bestselling author, she is an historian and archaeologist.

Five Francs Each

Fred Vargas

Translated by Sian Williams

That was it, no chance of selling another one tonight. Too cold, too late, the streets were empty, it was almost eleven o'clock: Place Maubert, Left Bank, Paris. The man turned off the square to the right, propelling his supermarket trolley in front of him, arms outstretched. Bloody trolleys, they weren't precision instruments. You needed strong wrists and you had to know all the blessed tricks of the one you were pushing to keep it going straight. Stubborn as a donkey, it wanted to roll sideways, put up a fight. You had to talk to it, shout at it, shove it hard, but still, like a donkey, it did let you carry round a lot of stuff to sell. Stubborn then, but reliable. He had called his trolley Martin, in honour of all those hard-working donkeys of the olden days.

The man parked his trolley near a lamp-post and padlocked it with a chain to which he had attached a large bell. So look out, any little shit who tried to nick his load of sponges while he was asleep, he'd get more than he bargained for. Sponges: he'd sold just five in a day, bad as it could get. A grand total of twenty-five francs, plus the six left over from yesterday. He pulled his sleeping-bag out of a plastic sack slung under the trolley, lay down on a grating over a metro vent, and curled up inside. You couldn't go down into the metro station to keep warm, because it meant leaving the trolley above ground. That's the way it is, you have an animal, you've got to make sacrifices. He'd never have left Martin alone outside.

The man wondered whether his great-grandfather, going from town to town with his donkey, had had to sleep alongside his beast in fields full of thistles. Not that it mattered, since he didn't have a great-grandfather, or anyone else, nothing at all in the way of family. But you can always think about them. And when he did think, he imagined an old fellow with a donkey called Martin. What did the donkey carry? Salt herrings perhaps, rolls of cloth, or sheepskins.

As for himself, he'd trundled round plenty of stuff for sale. So much so that he'd worn out three trolleys in his time. This donkey was the fourth in a long line. The first to carry sponges though. When he'd discovered the sponge mountain, abandoned in a warehouse in Charenton at the east end of the city, he'd thought he had it made. 9,732 sponges, genuine sea-sponges, he'd counted them, he was good with figures, always had been. Multiply by five francs. You couldn't ask more, because they didn't look too appetising. Total: 48,660 francs, a mirage, a lottery win.

But for four months now, he'd been wheeling sponges from Charenton into central Paris and pushing Martin through every street in the capital. He'd sold precisely 512. Nobody wanted them, nobody stopped, nobody even looked at his sponges, his trolley, or him. The way it was going, it would take 2,150.3 days to clear the warehouse, that made 6.17 years dragging his body and his donkey around. He'd always had a good head for figures. But these sponges, nobody gave a damn for them, apart from five people a day. That's not a lot, five people, bloody hell, out of the two million Parisians.

Huddled up inside the sleeping-bag, the man was calculating the percentage of Parisians who bought his sponges. He watched as a taxi stopped close beside him and a woman got out, slender legs, topped by a white fur coat. Not the kind of woman who would come into the percentage. Perhaps she didn't even know what a sponge was like, how it swelled up and how you squeezed it. She went round him without seeing him, crossed the road, walked a little way along the opposite pavement and began to punch in the code in the doorway of a building. A grey car approached quietly, illuminating her in its headlights, and braked just by her. The driver got out, the woman looked round. The sponge vendor frowned, and tensed. He knew how to spot men who preyed on women, and it wouldn't be the first or last time that he'd taken one on. Pushing awkward trolleys along pavements, he'd developed the fists of an all-in wrestler. Three gunshots rang out and the woman collapsed onto the ground. The killer ducked back inside his car, let in the clutch and drew away fast.

The sponge vendor had flattened himself as hard as he could on his grating. An old pile of rags abandoned in the cold, that's what the murderer would have taken him for, if he had seen him at all. And for once, the man's appalling invisibility, the fate of the disinherited, had saved his skin. Shaking all over, he scrambled out of his sleeping bag, rolled it up, and stowed it in the sack under the trolley. He went over to the woman and bent down to peer at her through the darkness. There was blood staining the fur coat, it made him think of a baby seal on an ice floe. He knelt down, picked up her handbag and opened it quickly. Lights went on in the windows above, three, four. He threw the bag on the ground and ran back to his trolley. The cops would be along any minute. They move fast. Frantically, he hunted through his pockets for the key to his padlock. Not in the trousers, not in the jacket. He kept searching. Should he run away? Abandon Martin? How could he do that to his faithful hardworking partner? He turned out all eight pockets, felt inside his shirt. The cops, oh God, no, cops with questions. Where were the sponges from? Where was the trolley from? And where was the man from? Furiously, he yanked at the trolley to try and pull it free of the lamp post, and the bell clanged in the night, merrily and stupidly. Almost at once came the sound of a police siren, running footsteps, and then the staccato voices, the cursed efficient energy of the forces of order. The man leaned over his trolley, plunging his arms deep inside the pile of sponges and tears sprang to his eyes.

In the half-hour that followed, a whole contingent of Paris police descended on him. On one hand he was important, the only witness of the attack, so they took some care with him, asked him questions, wanted his name, called him 'vous'. On the other, he was just a stubborn old pile of clothes, and they were inclined to shake and threaten him. Worse, they were intending to take him to the station, on his own, but he clung with all his might to the trolley, saying that unless they brought his load with him, he wouldn't breathe a word of what he'd seen, he'd sooner die. By now, there were arc-lamps in the street, police cars with their blue lights revolving, photographers, a stretcher, stuff everywhere, anxious murmurs, people phoning.

'Take this guy to the station on foot,' came a voice from not far away.

'With his trolley full of garbage?' asked another voice.

'Yes, I'll answer for it. Smash the padlock. I'll be along in twenty minutes.'

The man with the sponges turned round to see what kind of cop had given this order.

And now he was sitting opposite him, in a sparsely lit office. The trolley had been parked in the police station courtyard, between two large cars, under the anxious gaze of its owner.

He sat waiting, hunched on a chair, a cardboard cup of coffee in one hand, gripping the plastic sack on his knee with the other.

Telephones had rung constantly, there had been all manner of coming and going, people hurrying, shouting orders. A general alert, because a woman in a fur coat had been shot. He was sure that if it had been Monique, the lady in the newspaper kiosk, who let him read the headlines every morning so long as he didn't open the paper up, so all he knew about the world was a horizontal strip above the fold, never what was inside, well anyway, if it had been Monique, there would surely not have been ten cops chasing from one office to another as if the country was about to collapse into the sea. They would have waited calmly until their coffee break before ambling over to the kiosk to inspect the damage. They wouldn't have been telephoning everywhere in the universe. Whereas for the woman in white, half of Paris had been woken up, it seemed. Just for one little woman who had never squeezed a sponge.

The cop sitting facing him had put down all the phones. He ran a hand across his cheek, spoke in a low voice to his deputy, then looked at the man for a long time, as if he were trying to guess what his whole life had been like without asking. He had introduced himself: Jean-Baptiste Adamsberg, commissaire of the 5th arrondissement. He had asked to see the man's papers, and they had taken his finger prints. And now the cop was looking at him. He was going to question him, make him talk, make him tell them everything he had seen from down on the pavement. You could bet that was coming next. He was the witness, the only witness, an unlooked-for stroke of luck. They hadn't shaken him once he was in here, they had relieved him of his jacket, and given him some hot coffee. Of course. A witness was a rare thing, a valuable object. They were going to make him talk. You could bet on that.

'Were you asleep?' asked the commissaire. 'When it happened, were you asleep?'

This cop had a quiet, interesting voice, and the man with the sponges raised his eyes from his coffee.

'*Getting* to sleep,' he corrected him. 'But someone always disturbs you.'

Adamsberg was turning his ID card over in his hands.

'Surname Toussaint, first name Pi. That's your name is it, Pi?'

The man with the sponges sat up straighter.

'My name got smudged with the coffee,' he said, with a certain pride in his voice. 'That's all that was left.'

Adamsberg looked at him without speaking, waiting for the rest, which the man recited as if it were a well-known poem: 'On All Saints Day, so that's my last name, my mother took me into the Social. She put my name on a big register. Someone took hold of me. Someone else put their coffee cup on the register. My first name got washed away, by the coffee, just two letters left. But 'sex: male' that didn't get blotted out, bit of luck eh.'

'It was meant to be Pierre, was it?'

'There was just the first two letters,' said the man firmly. 'Maybe my mother just wrote Pi.'

Adamsberg nodded.

'Pi,' he asked, 'have you been living on the streets long?'

'Before, I was a cutler, went round towns selling my stuff. After that, I sold tarpaulins, cleaning fluid, bicycle pumps, socks, you name it. By the time I was forty-nine, I was on the streets, with a lot of waterproof watches full of water.'

Adamsberg looked again at the ID card.

'Yeah, right, this makes the tenth winter,' Pi finished the story.

Then he tensed, waiting for the inevitable barrage of questions about the origin of the goods. But nothing came. The commissaire sat back on his chair and ran his hands over his face, as if to iron out its wrinkles.

'Ructions, eh?' asked Pi, with the hint of a smile.

'Ructions like you can't imagine,' said Adamsberg. 'And everything depends on you, on what you're going to tell us.'

'Would there be ructions like that if it was Monique?'

'Who's Monique?'

'The lady sells newspapers down the avenue.'

'You want the truth?'

Pi nodded.

'Well, if it was Monique, no, there wouldn't be at all the same kind of ructions. Just a bit of a to-do, and a low-key investigation. There wouldn't be a couple of hundred people waiting to find out what you'd seen.'

'She didn't see *me*.'

'She?'

'The woman in the fur coat. She just went round me like I was a heap of old clothes. Didn't even see me. So why would I have seen her, tell me that? No reason, fair's fair.'

'You *didn't* see her then?'

'Just this heap of white fur.'

Adamsberg leaned towards him.

'But you weren't asleep. The shots must have roused you, surely? Three shots, that makes a lot of noise.'

'Nothing to do with me. I've got my trolley to watch. I can't be doing with everything goes on in the neighbour-hood.'

'Your prints are on her handbag. You picked it up.'

'I never took anything.'

'No, but you went over to her after she was shot. You went to have a look.'

'So what? She got out of a taxi, she went round the pile of clothes, that's me, some guy drove up in a car, he shot at the fur coat, and that was it. Didn't see anything else.'

Adamsberg stood up and walked round the room a bit.

'You don't want to help us, is that it?'

He had begun calling Pi *tu*.

Pi screwed up his eyes.

'You called me *tu*!'

'That's what cops do. Gets us better results.'

'So I get to call you 'tu' back?'

'You've got no reason to. You can't get any results, because you don't want to talk.'

'Are you going to start hitting me?'

Adamsberg shrugged.

'I never saw a thing,' said Pi. 'Nothing to do with me.'

Adamsberg leaned against the wall and considered him. The man looked somewhat the worse for wear, what with hardship, cold, wine, all of which had worn grooves in his face and hollowed out his body. His beard was still partly ginger, cut with scissors close to his cheeks. He had a small girlish nose, and blue eyes deep-set in their sockets, expressive and darting about, hesitating between flight and a truce. You might almost imagine the man would put down his bundle, stretch out his legs, and they could have a chat like two old acquaintances in a train.

'OK to smoke?' Pi asked. Adamsberg nodded and with one hand Pi let go the sack, from which an old red and blue sleeping-bag protruded, to pull a cigarette out of his jacket pocket.

'It's a tear-jerker isn't it?' said Adamsberg, without moving from the wall, 'Your story about the pile of rags and the pile of fur, the rich woman in her castle and the poor man at the gate. Do you want me to tell you what there is under the rags and the furs? Or can't you remember any more?'

'There's a filthy geezer who's trying to sell sponges and a clean woman who's never bought any in her life.'

'There's a man in deep shit who knows a lot of things, and a woman in a coma with three bullets in her body.'

'Not dead then?'

'No. But if we don't catch the killer, he'll try again, you can bet on that.'

The man with the sponges frowned.

'But why?' he asked. 'If someone attacked Monique, they wouldn't try again next day.'

'We've already established it wasn't Monique.'

'Someone important then?'

'Someone very high up,' said Adamsberg pointing with his finger at the ceiling, 'not a million miles from the Ministry of the Interior. That's why there's all the fuss.'

''Well s'not my fuss,' said Pi, speaking more loudly. 'See if I care about the ministry and their business. My business is selling my 9,732 sponges. And people aren't fucking buying my sponges. No one lifts a finger to help *me*. Nobody up there wonders how to find a way to stop me freezing my balls off in winter. And now they want me to help *them*? Do their job for them, help them out? Who's got all those sponges to get rid of, them or me?'

'Might be better to have 9,732 sponges to get rid of than three bullets in your gut.'

'Oh yeah? You want to try it one night. Want me to tell you something, commissaire? Yes I did see something. Yes I did see the feller. And his car.'

'I already know you saw all that, Pi.'

'You do?'

'I do. When you're on the street, you always keep an eye open for people coming along, especially if you're dropping off to sleep.'

'Well, you can tell them up there that Pi Toussaint, he's got sponges to sell, and better things to do than rescue women in white fur coats.'

'What about women in general?'

'She isn't women in general.'

Adamsberg walked across the room and stopped in front of Pi with his hands in his pockets.

'But don't you see, Pi,' he said slowly. 'We don't have to give a shit about *what* she is. Or about her coat, or the ministry, or all those people sitting on their backsides in the warm without thinking about yours. It's *their* crap, their corruption, and it'll take a lot more than a few wipes with your sponges to clear that lot up. Because that kind of dirt is so ancient it's piled up in mountains. Mountains of sleaze. And you're a fool, Pi. Want me to tell you why?'

'I'm not bothered.'

'Those mountains of sleaze, they didn't get there by accident.'

'Oh no?'

'They grew up out of the idea that some people on this earth are more important than others. That they always have been, always will be. And let me tell you something: it's not true. *Nobody* is more important than anyone else. But you believe it, Pi, and that's why you're as big a fool as all the rest.'

'But I *don't* believe anything, fuck's sake.'

'Yes, you do. You believe that woman is important, more important than you, so you're keeping your mouth shut. But here, tonight, I'm just talking to you about a woman who's going to die, nothing else.'

'Bollocks.'

'Every human life is worth the same as every other, whether you like it or not. Yours, mine, hers, Monique's. That's four of us. Add the other six billion and you've got the number of people who matter.'

'Bollocks, just ideas,' repeated Pi.

'I make my living from ideas.'

'And I make mine from my sponges.'

'Except you don't.'

Pi said nothing, and Adamsberg sat back down at the table. After a few minutes silence, he got up and put his jacket on.

'Come on,' he said, 'we're going for a walk.'

'In the cold? I'm sorted here, it's nice and warm.'

'I can't think unless I walk. We'll go down into the metro. We can walk on the platforms, it helps ideas.'

'Anyway, I got nothing to tell you.'

'I know.'

'And anyway, metro'll be closed by now, they'll chuck us out, I'm used to it.'

'They won't chuck me out.'

'Privileged, huh.'

'Yeah.'

On the deserted eastbound platform of Cardinal Lemoine metro station, Adamsberg paced up and down slowly in silence, his head bent, while Pi, a faster walker, tried to adapt his pace, because this cop, although indeed a cop, and determined to save the life of the woman in the fur coat, was, all the same, good company. And good company is the rarest of things when you're pushing a trolley. Adamsberg was watching a mouse scurry along between the rails.

'Tell you what,' Pi said suddenly, shifting his sleeping bag from one side to the other, 'I got some ideas too.'

'What about?'

'Circles. Ever since I can remember. Any kind. Like, take the button on your jacket, any idea what its circumference is?'

Adamsberg shrugged.

'Can't say I ever noticed the button at all.'

'Well, I did. And I'd say, looking at that button, its circumference is 51 millimetres.'

Adamsberg stopped walking.

'And what's the point of that?' he asked seriously.

Pi shook his head.

'Don't have to be a cop to work out it's the key to the whole world. When I was little, in school, they called me 'Three-point-one-four'. Get it? Pi = 3.14. The diameter of a circle times 3.14, that tells you its circumference. Best thing in my whole life, that joke. See, it was a bit of luck really, that my name got blotted with coffee. After that I was a number, and not just any old number.'

'I see,' said Adamsberg.

'You've no idea the things I know. Because Pi works with any kind of circle. Some Greek worked it out in the olden days. Knew a thing or two, the Greeks. See, your watch there: want to know the circumference of your watch, in case you're interested? Or your glass of wine, see how much you've drunk? Or the wheel on your trolley, or your head, or the rubber stamp on your ID card, or the hole in your shoe, or the middle of a daisy, or the bottom of a bottle, or a five-franc coin? The whole world's made up of circles. Bet you never thought of that, eh? Well, me, Pi, I know all about them, all kinds of circles. Ask me a question, if you don't believe me.'

'What about a daisy then?'

'With petals or just the yellow bit in the middle?'

'Just the middle.'

'Twelve millimetres point 24. That's quite a big daisy.'

Pi paused to let the information sink in and be properly appreciated.

'Well, yeah, see,' he said with a nod. 'My destiny, that is. And what's the biggest circle of all, the ultimate circle?'

'The distance round the Earth.'

'Right, I see you're following me. And no one can work out the distance round the Earth without going through Pi. That's the trick. So that's how I found the key to the world. Course, you might ask where that's ever got me.'

'If you could solve my problem like you do circles, that'd be something.'

'I don't like its diameter.'

'Yes, I've gathered that.'

'What's this woman's name?'

'No names. Forbidden.'

'Oh? Did she lose *her* name too?'

'Yes,' said Adamsberg with a smile. 'She hasn't even got the first two letters of it.'

'We better give her a number then, like me. More friendly than keep saying "the woman". We could call her 4/21, four twenty-one, like in the dice game, because she was one of the lucky ones in this world. Well, till now.'

'If you like. Let's call her "4/21".'

Adamsberg dropped Pi off in a small hotel three blocks from the police station. He went slowly back to his office. An emissary from the ministry had been waiting for him for half an hour, in a furious mood. Adamsberg knew him, a young guy, fast-track, aggressive, and just now shaking in his shoes.

'I was questioning the witness,' said Adamsberg, dropping his jacket in a heap on a chair.

'You took your time, commissaire.'

'Yes, I needed to.'

'And have you learnt anything?'

'The circumference of a daisy. Quite a big daisy.'

'We haven't got time to mess about, I think you've been made aware of that.'

'The guy's clammed up, and he has his reasons. But he knows plenty all right.'

'This is urgent, commissaire, I've got my orders. Weren't you ever instructed that any witness who's "clammed up" can be *made* to talk in under fifteen minutes?'

'Yes, I was.'

'So what are you waiting for?'

'To forget that instruction.'

'You know I could take you off the case?'

'You won't get this man to talk by beating him up.'

The under-secretary banged the table with his fist.

'Well, how then?'

'He'll only help us if we help him.'

'What the hell does he want?'

'He wants to make a living, sell his rotten sponges, he's got 9,732 of them. Five francs each.'

'Is that all? Well, we can just buy his fucking sponges outright.'

The undersecretary did a quick mental calculation. 'You can have 50,000 francs by eight in the morning,' he said, standing up. 'And I'm doing you a favour, believe me, in view of your performance. I want that information by ten at latest.'

'I don't think you quite understand, sir,' said Adamsberg without moving from his chair.

'What do you mean?'

'The man doesn't want to be bought. *He just wants to sell his sponges*, all 9,732 of them. To people. To 9,732 real people.'

'Are you kidding? You think I'm going to sell this guy's sponges for him, send my officials round the streets?'

'That wouldn't work,' said Adamsberg calmly. 'He wants to sell his sponges *himself*.'

The under-secretary leaned over towards Adamsberg.

'Tell me, commissaire, do this man's sponges by any chance worry you more than safeguarding ...'

'Safeguarding 4/21,' Adamsberg finished the sentence. 'That's her codename here. We don't speak the name out loud.'

'Yes, of course, that's best,' said the under-secretary, dropping his voice suddenly.

'I've got a kind of solution,' said Adamsberg. 'For the sponges and for 4/21.'

'Which would work?'

Adamsberg hesitated. 'It might,' he said.

At seven-thirty next morning, the commissaire knocked at the door of Pi Toussaint's hotel room. The sponge-seller was already up, and they went down to the hotel bar. Adamberg poured out some coffee and passed the bread basket.

'You should see the shower in my room!' said Pi. 'Twenty-six centimetres round, the thing at the top, gives a man a right whipping! So, how is she?'

'Who?'

'You know, 4/21.'

''She's coming out of it. She's got five cops guarding her. She's said a few words, but she can't remember anything.'

'That'll be shock,' said Pi.

'Yes. I've come up with a kind of idea in the night.'

'And I've come up with a kind of result.'

Pi took a bite of bread, then felt in his trouser pocket. He put a sheet of paper folded in four on the table.

'Written it all down for you,' he said. 'What the man's ugly mug looked like, how he moved, his clothes, make of the car. And the registration.'

Adamberg put down his cup and looked at Pi.

'You knew what the number plate was?'

'Numbers, that's my thing, told you. Always have been.'

Adamsberg unfolded the paper and glanced over it quickly.

'Thanks,' he said.

'You're welcome.'

'I'm going to phone,'

Adamberg returned to the table a few minutes later.

'I've passed it on,' he said.

'Course, once they've got the number, it'll be easy for you people. You should pick him up by the end of the day.'

'I had this kind of idea in the night, about selling your sponges.'

Pi pulled a face and drank some more coffee.

'Yeah,' he said, 'so did I. I put them in the trolley, I push it round for a few years, and I try and get people to buy them at five francs each.'

'A different idea.'

'What's the point? You've got what you wanted to know. Was it a good idea?'

'A bit odd.'

'Some trick a cop might dream up?'

'No, just a trick anyone might dream up. Give them something for their five francs.'

Pi put his hands on the table.

'They'll get a *sponge*! Do you take me for a crook or what?'

'Your sponges are pretty grotty.'

'Well, what are people going to do with 'em? Squeeze them in dirty water, that's what. No fun being a sponge.'

'You give them the sponge, plus something else.'

'Like what?'

'Like getting to write their name on a wall in Paris.'

'I don't get it.'

'Every time someone buys a sponge from you, you paint their name on a wall. The same wall.'

Pi frowned.

'So I have to stay there, by this wall, with the goods?'

'That's right. In six months, you'll have a big wall covered with names, a sort of massive great manifesto by sponge-buyers, a collection, practically a monument.'

'You're a weird guy. What the fuck am I supposed to do with the wall?'

'It's not for you, it's for the people.'

'But they couldn't give a toss, could they?'

'No, you're wrong about that. You could have them queuing up at your trolley.'

'What's in it for them, tell me that?'

'It'll give them some company and a bit of existence. That's not nothing.'

'Because they don't have any?'

'Not as much as you think.'

Pi dipped his bread in his coffee, took a bite, dipped it again.

'I can't make up my mind if it's a fucking stupid idea, or a bit better than that.'

'Nor can I.'

Pi finished his coffee, and folded his arms.

'You think I could put my name there too?' he asked, 'Down the bottom, on the right, like I was signing the whole caboodle, when it's finished?'

'Yes, if you want. But they have to pay for the sponges. That's the point.'

'Of course, they bloody do. You take me for a conman?'

Pi thought some more, while Adamberg was putting on his jacket.

'Yeah, but look,' said Pi. 'There's a catch. I don't have a wall.'

'Ah, but I have. I got one last night from the Ministry of the Interior. I can take you to look at it.'

'And what about Martin?' asked Pi, standing up.

'Who's Martin?'

'My trolley.'

'Oh, right. Well, your trolley's still under the watchful eye of the cops. He's having an exceptional experience that will never be repeated. Don't bother him for now.'

At the Porte de la Chapelle in northern Paris, Adamsberg and Pi considered in silence the gable-end wall of an empty grey building.

'That belongs to the State?' asked Pi.

'They weren't going to give me the Trocadero Palace.'

'No, s'pose not.'

'As long as you can paint on it,' said Adamsberg.

'Yeah, a wall's a wall, end of the day.'

Pi went up to the building and felt the surface of the coating with the flat of his hand. 'When do I start?'

'You can have some paint and a ladder tomorrow. After that, it's up to you.'

'Do I get to choose the colours?'

'You're the boss.'

'I'll get some round paintpots then. Some diameters.'

The two men shook hands, but Pi pulled a worried face again.

''You don't have to do it,' said Adamsberg. 'It might still be a fucking stupid idea.'

'No, I like it. In a month, I might have names up high as my thighs.'

'What's bothering you then?'

'4/21. Does she know it was me, Pi Toussaint, who nabbed the bastard that shot her?'

'She'll be told.'

Adamsberg walked away slowly, hands in pockets.

'Hey,' cried Pi. 'Do you think she'll come? Come and buy a sponge? Get her name up here?'

Adamsberg turned round, looked up at the grey wall, and spread his arms in a gesture of ignorance.

'You'll know if she does,' he called. 'And when you do, come and tell me.'

With a wave of his hand, he walked on.

'You're going to be writing history,' he murmured to himself, 'and I'll be along to read it.'

Translator's note

'Five Francs Each' is published here for the first time in English. It was originally published in French in 2000 – a year before the appearance of *The Life of Pi* by Yann Martel.

IAN RANKIN was born in Cardenden, Fife, in 1950. Before becoming a full-time novelist he worked as a grape-picker, swineherd, taxman, alcohol researcher, hi-fi journalist, college secretary and punk musician, in London and then rural France. He is best known for his Inspector Rebus novels, set mainly in Edinburgh, and adapted as a hugely successful series on ITV. In 2013, Rankin co-wrote the play *Dark Road* with the Royal Lyceum Theatre's Artistic Director Mark Thomson. He lives in Edinburgh with his wife Miranda and their two sons.

An Afternoon

Ian Rankin

After a hard afternoon of being spat on and having coins tossed at him, Rab, known to the younger constables as Big Rab, eased his boots from his blistered feet and massaged the damp yellow skin.

My feet look like the jaundice, he thought to himself. He could smell the vinegary sweat rising from his soles. He would soak them tonight when he got home. They stuck to the cooling linoleum when he padded to his locker. The locker was tarnished green, slivers of metal showing through its several dents and scratches.

'It was a hard one, Big Rab, wasn't it?' McNulty was running the cold tap over a clump of paper-towels. He rubbed them vigorously over the pock-marks on the back of his official-issue overcoat.

'They don't get any easier,' said Rab. He examined his own coat now; sure enough, there they were, as if dried chewing-gum had been picked off the material or a snail had paused for a rest. Rab's face twisted. Part and parcel of the job, his own sergeant had said – what? – thirty years ago now. Part and parcel of the job.

Yes, thirty years ago next month since he had joined the force. Over fifteen-hundred weeks 'on the beat', and never a day sick in all that time. Still, he was beginning to worry about those dizzy spells. But it would be a defeat to see the doctor now, after all this time. It would be the crumbling of a powerful myth.

He looked across to McNulty. He, Rab, was the sergeant now, and McNulty was the young man with blotches of acne at the back of his neck where the razor had gone. Rab shook his coat. It jangled, and he began to smile.

'Sounds good today,' McNulty said.

'Well,' Rab replied, 'it might not all be clean, but it's still money. It's as good as anybody's.'

'One of these days …' McNulty began. Rab looked at him. There was concern on the youngster's face.

'Laddie,' Rab said, slapping his own chest, 'if they can't hit this, they can't hit anything. And the more roused they get themselves, the bigger the coins they throw.'

McNulty managed a smile. Some of the others were coming in now, faces ruddy with exhaustion.

'Another big game will be the death of me,' someone said.

'Twenty-one arrests so far.'

'My money's on thirty by half-past.'

'Thirty-five,' said a new voice.

'Done. Five quid?' They shook hands on the bet. Rab was examining his pale face in the cracked mirror on his locker. He tried to see behind his eyes, but the reflection was giving nothing away.

It had been business as usual. Nothing very out of the way. Days like that were worse somehow; they made you drop your guard.

The body-searches at the turnstiles had produced a few foolhardy bottles and cans, a soldering-iron, two cans of spray-paint, and a steel catapult. The terraces began to fill with that curious mix of the honest, stout-hearted football fans, the bored kids, and the real trouble-makers. They were out in force today. Rab was stationed in the zone behind one goalmouth, watching as the crowd swelled.

Ninety minutes, he thought. Just let me get through another ninety minutes. Plus half-time and stoppages. The first coin whistled past his head five minutes before kick-off, landing on the touchline behind him. He studied the huddled faces through the thick mesh of the perimeter fence. They looked normal enough, shuffling their feet to keep warm. A day or two's bristle on their chins. Manual workers mostly, same upbringing as him, attending the game as others would a church service – just part of their routine. But he knew that surfaces could be deceptive. He knew the subtleties of violence.

When the roar goes up he knows that somewhere behind him the teams are coming out on to the pitch. By now he recognises a few of the faces in the crowd, but his eyesight is not what it was – he finds it hard to focus more than halfway up the terracing. The lunatics are visible though – they make themselves noticeable with their yelps and cries, then repay his attention with two-fingered salutes and angry scowls. Do they really hate him? He is old enough to be their father, maybe even their grandfather. Thirty years spent watching them mature into the tribe they are now.

The whistle blows, the booming, indecipherable noise from the tannoys dies, and all eyes are suddenly moving as if choreographed. Mouths purse or open at the same time, hands come together in a supportive show, heads are tipped to the sky at a chance missed or a wayward pass. The sea of faces has become a single entity.

Then comes the first scything foul against one of their heroes. The jaws tighten, fists raised and rigid fingers pointing, straining towards confrontation. A sudden cheer. Thank God, thinks Rab. The ref has booked the offender. It is seven minutes past three.

The sky seems made of pale silk, the sun muffled behind it. Seagulls from the nearby dump glide like small aircraft. It has been a subdued first half so far, which has prompted the lunatics to commence an entertainment of their own. They start swaying to and fro, attempting a whiplash effect in the dense crowd. Two small boys have to be helped out through the metal gate in the fence and on to the grit running-track. One of them is recovering from a faint. He holds the sleek hair away from his forehead and takes in tiny gulps of air. His friend puts a consoling arm around him.

While Rab watches, more coins miss their mark. A ballboy, his partisan presence taunting the away support, begins pocketing the missiles. This incenses the crowd, who throw ever more and faster projectiles. The faster they are, however, the less accurate, and with a little luck and a lot of unharried wits, neither of the slow-moving targets is hit.

At half-time, a smoke bomb is let off in the crowd and a small fire starts. Rab gives the nod, and eight of them move in a line through the gate and into the crowd. They focus on what's ahead of them, ignoring the taunts. Rab knows better than to look back and confront the hate, but he can feel the flurry of spit as it begins to land on his back.

The fire is out when they get there. Two obviously inebriated skinheads are pointed out by their neighbours. The line of dark shapes forms itself around the trouble-makers and they are arrested. Rab knows that now only his team's 'bottle', their absolute determination, is going to stop elements of the support turning on them. If one of the younger constables should crack and lose composure, they will be swamped. The skinheads are led back towards the gate. Rab allows himself a glance up at the pitch as they work their way forwards. It is a lush green plain, its divots being stamped down by the ground-staff in preparation for the second half. The skinheads raise their arms and begin to sing, others joining in. A hissing and whistling from the opposite end of the stadium tells them that the home support has noticed. The singing grows louder as a result, filling Rab's ears, making him dizzy with its intensity. The pitch blurs for a second, then clears. There is sweat on his back, inside his white cotton shirt.

By the end of the match, he has been twice more into the crowd at the away end. He stays behind the net after the final whistle – a draw being the thankful, prayed-for conclusion – until the terracing has cleared. A few hoarse chants issue from the street outside the ground. Cans clatter along the gutter. Rab peers at the three stripes on his right arm, the tight threads which signify his rank. Thirty years. Seagulls swooping down to pick at discarded food. Floodlights caught against the pale red of the encroaching evening. Thirty years. The ballboy is standing in front of him, holding a pile of coins which he offers up.

'Half for you.'

Rab looks at the kid, his hair cut in a shoddy fringe across his brow. Maybe they get younger every year, but at least some still hold you in respect.

'I'll see they go to a good cause.'

The money, as it does every week that Rab is on duty at this ground and with this boy, changes hands. The boy turns and marches off the field towards the tunnel. Rab wonders if the coins really do amount to a half-share. Next time he's in his local, he will slot them one at a time into the charity tin. One of these days, maybe a coin will find its target and he will have to make an appointment, will have to stare defeat squarely in the face. One day, but not today. He pockets the handful of missiles and they become money again.

Heading for the locker-room, he notices a coin that has gone unnoticed on the churned turf. He stoops to claim it and it is as though the afternoon is rushing back into his ears: the crowd's hateful chanting. Easy, easy, easy; the noise crashing down over the gulls and the pitch. One flood-light is turned off and then another. Easy, easy ringing in his ears and the coin between his outstretched fingers, his vision blurring once more. He staggers a little but manages to right himself. The roaring subsides and the breath comes cold from his lips as the penultimate floodlight goes dark. In shadow and discomfort, he makes for the relative safety of bench, and washhand-basin, and mirror.

Author's note

'An Afternoon' was published in the second annual volume of 'New Writing Scotland'. The year was 1984, which means it was probably written in '82 or '83. I had submitted – unsuccessfully – to volume 1. Other contributors to Volume 2 included Kathleen Jamie, Edwin Morgan, and Robert Crawford. I wonder if any were as thrilled as I was. This was the first acceptance of my work by an actual BOOK. Not a magazine, but a 166-page tome retailing at £3.95. The cover announces me as Ian J Rankin, and my bio at the back states that I was a postgraduate student at Edinburgh University, with three published short stories under my belt and a first novel 'seeking a publisher'. (Alas, it never found one, and resides in my bottom drawer.) Re-reading this story now, I'm curious about the young man who wrote it – a young man who hardly ever attended football games, and knew no police officers. The writing could be improved upon (and I have taken the liberty of tweaking this current version a little), and it remains a vignette more than a fully-fledged story. But what interests me most is that I should have chosen to write about a jobbing police officer. Were the seeds of Rebus being sown here? Although I did not at the time read detective fiction, did I harbour an interest in policing itself? I don't have any answers, I'm afraid. But I do sympathise – and empathise – with Rab, and I like the fleeting glimpse we are given of his relationship with the ballboy. Who is the boss and who the sidekick? Maybe the kid grew up to be a cop himself – a detective even. Or a criminal ...

STUART NEVILLE was born in 1972 in Armagh, Northern Ireland. His debut novel, *The Twelve* (published in the USA as *The Ghosts of Belfast*), won the Mystery/Thriller category of the Los Angeles Times Book Prize, and subsequent titles have been shortlisted for various awards, including the Theakstons Crime Novel of the Year, and the CWA Ian Fleming Steel Dagger. His latest novel, *The Final Silence*, is published in summer 2014.

Juror 8

Stuart Neville

My name is Emmet McArdle. I am seventy-six years old, and I feel every day of it. I don't sleep well. I don't pass water well. I don't eat much. Which leaves me a lot of time to think. And I've been doing far too much of that lately.

I wish I could say all this started after the trial, but that wouldn't be true. I'm just an old man with old man complaints, and my discomforts go back long before I did jury duty nine months ago in August of '57. But now, when I can't sleep at night, it's the trial that plays on my mind. The boy we saved from the chair.

That boy went free because of us twelve men.

You'd think that would be easier to live with than if we'd sent him to burn. Probably should be. But ever since I left that courthouse, he's nagged at me. Kept whispering in my ear, saying maybe you were wrong, maybe I did kill my father after all. And maybe I'm fixing to kill again.

Well, a week and a half ago, that's exactly what he did.

I heard the news on the radio. I didn't make the connection straight away, mind you, but there it was. I was in the back room of the store, what used to be my store, and I guess on paper it still is. But my boy Eugene runs it now.

McArdle Musical Instruments of 48th Street.

When my father survived the boat trip from Ireland, escaping the poverty that devoured his own parents, he and his brother brought with them four piano accordions, two melodeons, three mandolins, and a suitcase full of D-whistles. His brother, my uncle, also made it across, but he died within a week of landing. He coughed his lungs up from pneumonia. I don't know what they did with his body.

My father, Emmet Senior, found a room somewhere in the Bowery, probably sharing a floor with a gang of other Irishmen, all of them wondering where those streets paved with gold were located. He used the little money he'd brought with him, and what he'd taken from his brother's pockets, to rent a stall on Canal Street. As he told it to me, he wound up selling those fancy accordions for less than they cost him, but he made a killing on the whistles, snapped up by immigrants who wanted to hear a little Londonderry Air to remind them of home. He made enough to buy more stock and establish a paying business.

A year later, he was making a profit on accordions, and mandolins, and banjos, as well as playing in a ceilidh band in the evenings. That was how he met my mother, a brown-haired girl from Clonmel, at a neighbourhood dance. I never knew her. She died giving birth to me, and my father never married again. Not unless you consider whiskey a wife.

I took over the running of the store at age sixteen. I never got much schooling, at least not the proper kind, learning everything I needed to know on the shop floor.

How to tell what a customer wanted, how much he had to spend, whether he was good for credit. My father remained the boss, of course. We walked to the store together every morning from our apartment on the next block. While I opened up, Emmet Senior went to the back office, with its big old mahogany desk and the portrait of that brown-haired girl from Clonmel, and sat down. He'd leave it a decent time, maybe until noon, and then he'd open the right hand drawer, remove the bottle of liquor, and start drinking.

I carried him home most evenings, his arm slung around my shoulder, his feet dragging on the ground. And the store takings in my pocket, ready to stow in the safe in his bedroom. I never saw the money again. I don't know what he did with it, whether he banked it or drank it. All I know was the rent got paid, and I got my salary. Weekends he'd go out and play at the local ceilidhs.

I was twenty-five when he died. He touched up some young woman at a dance, neither realising that her fiancé was only a few feet away, nor that said fiancé was in the habit of carrying a pistol.

I cried when I buried him, not that he deserved it.

Ten years later, I had a wife and five children of my own, and I'd made enough money that I could move the store from the Bowery up to 48th Street.

My two girls grew up to be schoolteachers, same as their mother. I met Mary at a dance, just like my father had met my mother, but I took better care of her. I paid for proper care when she gave birth to our children, rather than giving some backstreet witchdoctor a dollar for the job.

My eldest, Jarlath, became a police officer. Don't ask me where he got that from. All right, we're Irish, but that doesn't mean we're all born with badges.

Eugene had the music in him since he was a baby. I knew before his first birthday that he would take over the store for me. And he did, not long after he came back from fighting the Nazis in Europe.

His younger brother Columba was not so fortunate. He never made it off the beach, cut down by machine-gun fire along with hundreds of other good men. I miss him too much to be proud of him, hold too much resentment in my heart to be glad of what he sacrificed. He was my son and it isn't fair that he died, no matter what for. I am angry about it, and that's that.

I still show up to work every day. I live with Eugene and his wife – Mary was taken by a stroke five years ago – and we both travel to the store every morning, just like me and my father did. We don't walk all the way, of course; some of the journey is by train, but we go together all the same.

And just like my father, I go to the back office. I took his desk with me when I moved the store, and it's still there now, along with that portrait of the girl from Clonmel, and another of my absent son. Sometimes I talk to my mother, as if we had known each other. I hope she'd be proud of me, proud of the life I'd made for me and my children. I talk to her more now than I used to. Perhaps the growing awareness that I'll see her before too long makes me want to know her better.

I only get called out of the office when someone's interested in an accordion, or they want one repaired. The store's ground floor used to be a gallery of pearloid, rows of Hohners, Paolo Sopranis, Victorias, big 120-bass monsters right down to little 12-bass tiddlers.

Not any more. Nowadays, everybody wants a guitar.

And not even real instruments, proper acoustic instruments with air in them to make a decent sound. Now the ground floor is full of these planks with strings on them, Fender, Gibson, Gretsch, and I don't know what. I swear it's a race to see how much paint they can put on a stick of wood and still get money for it. The Gibson rep came by last week, and he had a guitar with him that looked like an arrowhead. He called it a flying something or other. I asked him how someone was supposed to sit down and play the darned thing without it sliding off his knee.

Eugene took one even though I told him it was a damn fool thing to do. Mark my words, it'll still be hanging there five years from now.

Anyway, I spend my days in the back room, looking at that photograph of my mother, wondering how I'm going to get through the day. If I'm honest, I was relieved to get the letter calling me for jury duty. I grumbled about it to Eugene, but inside, I relished the idea of getting out and doing something that mattered.

And when I realised what the trial was, I felt good, I felt the importance of this burden I'd been given.

All twelve of us had the boy strapped down and wired up the minute the prosecutor opened his mouth. Not a chance in the world this young thug was innocent. They talked till I was dizzy, and not a word told me anything but this young man had stabbed his father in the heart in a fit of anger. They had two witnesses, a man about my age, and a woman in her forties. One saw the boy do it, the other heard him.

And yet, and yet, and yet.

The foreman held a ballot, and we all raised our hands to say guilty. All but one.

The man next to me, Juror 8.

Let's talk, he said.

And we talked.

We talked until God cracked the sky. We talked until every other man in that room had been reduced to a sweating pulp. That man, Juror 8, didn't stop until he'd broken every one of us.

I was the first to fall.

When he stood against the rest of them, saying let's talk, I'm not sure, let's go over it again – when he said that, when he made his stand, I listened.

Why?

Because I'm a contrary old bastard, that's why. Pardon my language. And I'm Irish. Show an Irishman a lost cause, and he'll fight to the death for it, just out of pure wickedness.

So I changed my vote. When all the rest of them protested, thought me an old fool, I dug my heels in and said I wanted to hear what Juror 8 had to say. If I hadn't, he would've let it go, and the boy would've got fried. And that young couple in the new Pontiac Star Chief would be breathing this morning.

The young man had called at his sweetheart's building on West 127th to take her to the movies. They were approached by two Hispanic males, threatened with a knife, ordered to hand over the keys to the shining new car. The young man resisted. He was stabbed in the heart.

They took the girl with them. Her parents found the young man's body on the sidewalk and called in the description of the vehicle. Lord alone knows what they went through, knowing their daughter had been taken by the same people who had killed her boyfriend.

The police caught up with them out in Queens. The two males didn't show their hands quickly enough, and they were shot dead right there in the car. The cops found the girl's body in the trunk. She must have put up a fight, made too much noise. They'd killed her before they had a chance to molest her.

I shook my head when I heard the report on the radio the following morning, wondered at the state of the world. But that was all. It wasn't until Jarlath called by that night for supper that I learned the truth of it.

Jarlath had a wife at one time, but she couldn't hack being married to a cop. At least that's what he said. God forgive me, my eldest son has a mean streak in him, and he's hard to like. His brother barely tolerates him, only has him over for supper once a week in order to placate me.

'You hear about that double homicide last night, Pop?' Jarlath asked between mouthfuls of pork chop with applesauce.

Eugene and his wife Wendy exchanged a look. Their three girls remained silent as they ate.

'Not at the table, Jarlath, all right?' Eugene said.

Jarlath ignored him. 'You hear about it, Pop?'

'I heard something on the radio,' I said. 'Let's maybe talk about it after supper.'

I swear Jarlath is as thick in the skull as a gorilla. He kept right on talking.

'You heard the perps got shot over near Flushing Meadows, right?'

Eugene shook his head and rolled his eyes.

'Yes,' I said, deciding to humour Jarlath in hopes of finishing the conversation as quickly as possible.

He put his fork down, ran his tongue around his teeth, seeking stray morsels of pork.

'Well,' he said, sitting back in his chair, 'you've come across one of them before.'

'Oh?'

'Hugo Fuente,' he said.

My scalp prickled. I felt the hairs on my arms stand up like soldiers. A loose feeling low down in my stomach.

'Pop?' Eugene said.

Jarlath's crooked smile fell off his face.

They must have seen it on me. The horror. My fork fell from my fingers and rattled on Wendy's good china plate, taking a chip off it.

'Pop,' Eugene said once more, reaching for my hand. 'You're shaking. What's wrong?'

'Nothing,' I said. 'Please excuse me.'

I left the table and made for my room at the back of the house. The door hit the frame harder than I meant it to. I sat on the edge of my bed and chewed on my knuckle.

'Pop?'

Eugene calling from the corridor. I sprang to my feet, or as near as a man my age can manage, and turned the key in the door. The handle rattled, then he knocked hard.

'Pop? What's wrong? Open the door.'

'I'm fine,' I called. 'I just want to lie down for a little while.'

'Come on, Pop. You're scaring me.'

'I'm all right,' I said. 'Let me alone. Please.'

'Pop, you got me worried. C'mon, open the door.'

'Let me alone, dammit.'

I didn't mean to yell, but it did the trick.

'All right,' Eugene said. 'Wendy can warm your supper when you feel like eating.'

I returned to my bed, sat on the edge, my hands clasped together.

Hugo Fuente.

Just a kid, we'd said, all twelve of us. A boy. How could we send an eighteen-year-old to die? Some of us wanted to. Some of us fought hard. But Juror 8 ground them down.

This boy, he said, had been hit on the head every day of his life. I didn't doubt it. But he didn't look like a mean kid. I can still see him there in the courtroom, small, lean like a greyhound, and those frightened eyes.

I thought about the other eleven men. Had they heard the news? Had they dismissed it as they had all the other murders they'd read about in the papers? Just another couple of unfortunates caught up in the violence that haunted the darker parts of town. Nothing for them to worry about.

Had Juror 8 heard it?

I wondered, had he?

It was the day after we delivered the verdict that the worry set in, gnawing at my conscience like a woodworm. One part of me said Juror 8 was right. We were all pretty sure the boy had killed his father, but the law says pretty sure isn't enough. It's black or white, this or that, yes or no. That's all right. I can live with that.

The other part of me kept asking, is possibly innocent enough? Does it weigh more than probably guilty? I guess men have wrestled with that question since human beings first invented trials. And I guess many men have had tougher decisions to make than I had.

But few men could've had Juror 8 by their sides, pushing and pulling them, making them question every measure of their being. Making them turn on themselves. Turning them into children, shying from their parents' hands, nodding, red-faced, tears and snot on their lips, saying yessir, I'll behave.

I went to bed, but I didn't sleep a wink.

My belly growled with hunger, but I didn't get up to reclaim the dinner I'd abandoned. I just lay there, thinking. Thinking hard as I'd ever done in my life. But still no answer came. I'd have to go out for one of those, ask my questions out loud, not bounce them around inside my skull like it was a pinball machine ready to scream tilt.

I called by Jarlath's precinct early the following morning. I knew he always turned in an hour before he went on his beat. The desk sergeant watched me approach in much the same way a chimpanzee might watch a human through the bars in the zoo. A look on its face that says it'd tear you to pieces if it ever got the opportunity, but for now it's content to watch you pass.

'Jarlath McArdle,' I said, taking off my hat.

The desk sergeant seemed to look past me. 'What about him?'

'He's my son,' I said. 'I'd like to see him.'

The desk sergeant raised his eyes to really look at me for the first time.

'You're the Jar's old man? Jesus.'

'I'd like to talk to him, please,' I said.

He called over my shoulder. 'Mickey. Hey, Mickey. The Jar down in the locker room?'

'I think so,' a big man behind me said.

'Well get him up here. His old man wants him.'

'Thanks,' I said.

The desk sergeant didn't reply. He kept his eyes on whatever paperwork he had in front of him.

'Should I take a seat?' I asked.

He waved his fingers toward the wall, and the bench that leaned against it.

I sat down and waited. The man next to me fell asleep, his

head on my shoulder, breath smelling of beer. The woman on the other side applied make-up. I believe fifteen minutes passed before Jarlath appeared.

'What's up, Pop?' he asked. 'I was just about to go out. Kenny's waiting for me in the car.'

'I could use your help with something,' I said.

'Sure, Pop, what do you need?'

I looked at the people either side of me. 'I need to talk in private.'

'Sure,' he said, taking me by the arm and helping me to my feet.

He held on to my elbow as he led me down a corridor. I shook him off.

'Easy, Pop,' he said. 'Just don't want you falling.'

I stopped, turned to him, and asked, 'Do you see me landing on my face?'

'No, Pop,' he said.

'All right,' I said. 'Where are we going?'

'The squad room should be empty,' Jarlath said. 'In here.'

He led me into a room that looked like it belonged in a schoolhouse. A dusty blackboard covering most of the wall at one end and a podium, a dozen desks facing it.

Jarlath sat me down at one of the desks, pulled a chair up next to me.

'So, what's up?'

I looked down at my hands and marvelled at how papery my skin had become, the blue of the veins, the dark liver spots.

'Pop?'

I took a breath and said, 'I want you to find some information on a man for me.'

'Who?'

I wet my lips. 'One of the jurors on the Hugo Fuente trial.'

Jarlath sat quiet for a few seconds. 'Why, Pop?'

'I have my reasons,' I said. 'He was Juror 8. He told me his name was Davis.'

'I don't know,' Jarlath said. He worried at his cap with his fingers. 'Maybe you need a private eye or something. There isn't much I can find out about a man. Least, not legally, and not with that little information to go on.'

'There must be a record,' I said. 'At the courthouse, or the district attorney's office. They must have kept a note of who he was, where he lived.'

'Yeah, sure, but what do you want with him?'

I'm not sure I knew the answer to that question.

'Just to talk,' I said. It was the best I could think of.

'All right, Pop.' He put his big hand on my shoulder. I felt the weight of it there and for the millionth time I wondered how I had begot such a hulk of a man. 'I'll see what I can do.'

We both stood. Jarlath looked at his feet. I looked at the door. Between us, the awkward static of men who love each other but don't know how to admit it.

'Well, I'll be going,' I said. 'You've got work to do.'

I made my way to the door, but Jarlath called from behind.

'You okay, Pop?'

I stopped at the doorway and turned to face him. Concern deepened the lines on his face.

'What I told you last night, about the Fuente kid, that rattled you, didn't it?'

'A little, I guess.'

A lot, I should've said. Enough that I hadn't slept all night.

He came closer, shuffling like a man unsure of his footing. 'Well, don't worry, you hear? Maybe he did that murder, and maybe he didn't. Plenty of juries get it wrong. You did the best you could with the evidence you had. Those kids he killed the other night, that had nothing to do with you. You know that, right?'

'I know,' I said.

I've lost count of the lies I've told in my life, even if God hasn't. I left Jarlath there in the squad room and made my way home.

I didn't expect to hear from him until he was due to call for supper the following week. Instead, he rang Eugene's buzzer the very next night. I knew it was him as soon as I heard it. Little rivers of chills ran across my skin.

Voices at the door, then Eugene's eldest, Colette, calling, 'Grandpa? Grandpa, it's Uncle Jarlath for you.'

He waited for me in the hall. Eugene arrived at the same moment I did.

'What's going on?' he asked.

'I need to talk with Pop,' Jarlath said.

'What about?'

'Nothing you need to worry about,' I said, more curtly than I'd intended. I grabbed my coat from the stand by the door and turned to Jarlath. 'Come on, I feel like an egg cream.'

Eugene watched us leave, irritation and worry on his face.

Jarlath and I took a couple of stools at the farthest end of the counter in the drugstore three blocks from Eugene's place. I ordered two egg creams, but Jarlath said, no, a Pepsi Cola.

I guess he'd rather I'd taken him to a bar. He had that dry-lipped look about him, like he craved a beer or a whiskey, the same look my father used to get right around lunchtime every day.

A pretty young lady brought us our drinks then left us in peace. The chatter of teenage couples jangled in the air around us. Couples like the boy and girl who'd died a few nights ago.

No, they didn't die. They were murdered.

I shook the image away.

'I'm guessing you have something for me,' I said.

'Yeah, I got something,' he said, wiping cola from his lips. 'I got something all right.'

I waited.

Eventually, he said, 'Before I tell you this, Pop, you gotta promise me something.'

'Promise you what?'

'That you don't go near this guy. Okay? Just promise me that. Don't go near him, don't talk to him, just stay away. All right?'

I didn't hesitate. 'All right,' I said.

One more lie couldn't damn me any more than I was damned already.

'His name is Willard Davis,' Jarlath said. 'He's an architect, a partner in a firm on Madison. Reynolds & Waylan, they do big commercial stuff, skyscrapers, all that. A big shot. He's got a fancy apartment on Central Park West, around 68th or 69th, overlooking the park. A wife and two boys. A family man, a good career, a beautiful home, drives one of those little British sports cars.'

I nodded slowly. 'Sounds like a nice life. And it sounds like any second now, you're going to say "but".'

'Yeah,' Jarlath said. 'A big but.'

I took a swig of the egg cream, sickly sweet, chocolate syrup cloying at the back of my throat. 'Go on,' I said.

'When I got the name, I knew it sounded familiar. So I looked it up. I went down to records and ran him. This guy, Pop, he's bad news.'

'Tell me,' I said.

'About four years ago, a girl went missing, a secretary at that architecture firm. Marian Wallace, she was called. I mean, just gone, like in a puff of smoke. You know, one minute she was there, next thing she's gone and no one knows where to. Except ...'

'Except what?'

'I know one of the detectives who worked that case. Paddy Comiskey, big guy, he was at me and Joanie's wedding. Got drunk and hit on Wendy. I had to stop Eugene from trying to lay one on him. Anyway, another girl in that office, she told Paddy about Marian, how she was getting friendly with one of the senior architects, how he'd taken her to dinner a couple times, maybe a club, maybe some drinks. And next thing, he's going to take her up to Vermont for a weekend.

'So, that was a Friday when Marian said this to her friend. Come Monday, Marian doesn't show up for work. It's three days before anyone thinks to report her missing.'

The egg cream felt cold in my stomach, oily and sugary on my tongue. 'And this senior architect,' I said.

Jarlath nodded. 'Yeah, it was Willard Davis. He denied it, of course. His wife said he never left the city that weekend. But Paddy didn't buy it. He interrogated this Davis guy. Said he was the coldest son of a bitch he ever come across, and believe me, Paddy's seen some cold fish in his time. But he told me he ain't never seen cold like this. He grilled Davis for eight hours straight, never got a goddam scrap out of him. Said Davis just kept looking him in the eye all the while, like he was daring him, saying, come on, catch me if you can. You got no body, you got no weapon, you got nothing but suspicion. Leading him on, like it was a game. And this guy can talk, Paddy says. Davis had him doubting his own mind.'

'Yeah,' I said. 'That sounds like Juror 8.'

'But here's the thing, Pop. The girl, the witness who said Marian had told her this stuff. A month or so after Paddy dropped his case against Davis, this girl is found drowned in her own bathtub.'

'A coincidence, maybe?'

Jarlath shook his head. 'Cops believe in coincidences like they believe in Santa Claus and the Tooth Fairy. Paddy had Davis for the killing. He didn't have a shred of real evidence, nothing physical, but he was sure Willard Davis killed that girl.'

'Why?' I asked. 'With no evidence, why did he think that?'

'He didn't think it,' Jarlath said. 'He knew it. See, Pop, there's two sides to nailing a perpetrator. There's knowing and there's proving. You understand?'

'I guess,' I said, but I really didn't.

'Anyway, Pop, stay away from this Davis guy. Just let the whole thing go. All right?'

'All right,' I said.

I finished my egg cream without saying another word, deaf to the clamour of the kids all around us, thinking only of what I would say to Willard Davis when I found him.

At breakfast the next morning, after another sleepless night, I told Eugene that I wouldn't be going to work at the store that day.

'What's up, Pop? Don't you feel well?'

'I'm a little tired, that's all. I might go back to bed, catch up on my sleep.'

Eugene nodded. 'You do that, Pop. Take it easy.'

I waited until Eugene had left, and his girls had gone to school, before I slipped back out of my room and made for the door. I heard Wendy humming in the kitchen, the clink of plates, the rattle of cutlery. Quiet as the dead, I let myself out, down the stairs and onto the sidewalk.

The stairs from the subway station on 68th and Lexington led up to the street beneath the towering grandeur of Thomas Hunter Hall, like a gothic castle that had sprouted up from the pavement, its battlements seeming too high off the ground. I had looked up Reynolds & Waylan in the Yellow Pages that morning, and walked southwest toward their building on the corner of 66th and Madison.

I brushed shoulders with young men in good suits rushing to meetings, wealthy housewives heading to coffee dates or shopping in the swanky stores, bags dangling from their elbows. Strange how I had shared a city with these people all my life, yet they seemed from a different world. The constant rumble of cars, blaring of horns, the thrum of it all.

I found the door to Reynolds & Waylan's building between a bridal shop and a chocolatier. Pushing my way through the revolving door, I entered the lobby, all pink marble, dull brass and moulded ceilings. I approached the desk, a hefty man in a uniform and a peaked cap sitting behind it.

'Who you looking for?' he asked with less courtesy than I expected.

I told him.

'On sixth,' he said, pointing to the row of three elevators.

A hard-faced woman gave me a forced smile as I crossed the lobby, extended her hand in the direction of the middle elevator, where a girl waited, ready to press whichever button I required.

We did not speak as the car rose through the floors, a bell ringing as each passed.

'Sixth,' she said eventually. 'Mind the doors.'

I stepped out into a reception area that looked more like a hospital, all clean lines, black granite, white marble, glass everywhere.

A young woman behind the desk asked, 'Can I help you?'

I stood mute for a moment, suddenly aware of the foolishness of my actions. Suddenly, and quite reasonably, afraid.

'Sir?'

I removed my hat, gripped it in front of me. 'I ... uh ... I want to see Willard Davis.'

'Is Mr Davis expecting you?' she asked.

I shook my head.

'Who should I say is calling?'

'My name is Emmet McArdle,' I said. 'Tell him, Juror 9. He'll know.'

A small ripple of uncertainty on her face. She indicated a row of leather-upholstered chairs by the elevator.

'Please take a seat,' she said.

I did so. The chair was square-edged and uncomfortable. A modern design, I guess, the sort of thing young professional types like. I watched as she spoke into a telephone, her hand shielding her lips and the mouthpiece, as if she shared some conspiracy with the plastic and wires.

When she finally hung up, she called across the reception to me. 'I'm sorry, sir, Mr Davis is in a meeting right now. If you'd like to leave a telephone number, he'll be glad to get in touch.'

'I can wait,' I said.

'Mr Davis expects to be busy all day. Like I say, I can give him your number and he can contact you at another time.'

'I can wait all day,' I said.

A moment's pause, her smile faltering. 'Sir, Mr Davis will be busy all day. He will contact you when he can.'

My mouth dried. I felt the jangle of adrenalin and anger crackling out to my fingertips. 'I can wait all day,' I said. 'Mr Davis has to go to lunch some time. He has to leave when he's finished work for the day. I promise you, I won't take up any more of his valuable time than I have to.'

Her smile dissolved. 'Sir, again, Mr Davis won't be able to see you today. Our reception area is only for people who have business here, so I'm afraid I must ask you to leave.'

I sat there, silent, my heart bouncing in my chest.

The young woman's voice hardened. 'Sir, I must ask you to leave.'

I stood rather too quickly, and my head went light. I staggered a little.

'Sir, are you feeling all right?'

'I'm fine,' I said, steadying myself with a hand against the chair. 'Thank you for your help.'

I leaned against the elevator wall on the way down, sweat prickling my brow.

Willard Davis left the building, alone, at a quarter of six.

I expected him to perhaps visit a bar for an after work cocktail with some colleagues, or maybe that receptionist. Instead he walked the block westward to Fifth Avenue, across, and into the park.

The day had passed slowly for me, wandering the pathways among the trees, touring the blocks around Lenox Hill. The owner of a coffee shop gave me angry looks every time I used his restroom without buying anything. By the time I took up position some yards further along Madison, a newspaper held open in front of me, I neared a state of exhaustion. But when Davis emerged and started walking, I ditched the paper in a trashcan and did my best to keep pace with him.

Early May is a fine time to take an evening stroll through Central Park, the place flooding with new green, the new-born leaves and flowers masking the smell of the exhaust fumes. The sun, now low in the sky, made glowing pools on the path as it twisted one way and another.

Willard Davis walked like he owned the world. Tall as I remembered him, and thin like a whip. Late forties, dark hair combed back, showing a little scalp on top. One hand carried a good leather briefcase, the other nestled in his pocket. His light grey suit clung to his lean body, the fabric rippling on the breeze.

I started to breathe hard as I struggled to keep him in sight. Cars rumbled and roared on the 65th Street Transverse, a few yards to my left. I heard the clip-clopping of horses, the rattle of the carriages they pulled. But Davis stuck to the small paths, the branches overhanging, loose stones stirred by his feet. I could not match his pace.

'Dammit,' I whispered as I lost him around the corner up ahead.

I dug deep inside myself for some reserve of energy, but found none. Defeated, I slowed as the splendid buildings of Central Park West came into view. The evening had dimmed, the breeze a little cooler on my skin.

'God dammit,' I said aloud as I slowed to a stop, my shoulders rising and falling, air wheezing in and out of me.

After a minute or so, I had enough wind in me to go on. I crossed between the traffic on Central Park West, ignoring angry blasts of taxi horns.

Jarlath had said Davis lived around 68th or 69th. I headed north, but I don't know why I felt I had to. I had lost him, and that was that. I didn't believe he would have called me, even if I'd left a number with the receptionist. But still, I kept walking, looking up at the buildings as I passed, imagining him being greeted home by his loving family.

As I passed beneath the awning of a building, a voice said, 'Mr McArdle.'

My heart leapt in my chest. I spun around, my arm up in a defensive gesture, though I had no reason for it.

Willard Davis stood there, watching me, briefcase in his hand. A thin smile on his lips that didn't reach his grey-blue eyes.

I have never been more frightened in my life.

'Why have you been following me?' he asked.

'I ... I ... I wanted to ...'

He interrupted my stammering. 'I would like to have been able to speak with you at the office, Mr McArdle, but as Hattie told you, I was busy all day. And now you've followed me home. Why?'

'I'm sorry,' I said, my fear giving way to a strange kind of shame, the shame of being caught in a despicable act even though I knew I had done no wrong. 'I just wanted to talk,' I said.

He studied me for a few seconds, like I was a bug on a pin.

'How did you know where I worked?'

'My eldest boy,' I said. 'He's a policeman.'

'I expect that's against the law. For a policeman to give out personal information like that.'

I nodded. 'I expect it is.'

'All right,' he said. 'You'd better come up.'

'Sarah, boys, this is Mr McArdle, an old friend of mine.'

The two boys, one around eleven, the other a year or two older, had been standing in the drawing room like soldiers awaiting an inspection.

'Pleased to meet you, sir,' they said in unison.

Clean-scrubbed faces, their clothes pressed and spotless. When my boys were that age, there was never a moment when they didn't look like they'd been pulled feet-first from a muddy ditch.

Sarah, the wife, didn't respond. She sat in an armchair, her gaze fixed on some far away place that I believe only existed in her mind.

'Sarah?' Davis said. 'Sarah, darling, this is Mr McArdle.'

She looked at me, startled, as if I had appeared in a flash of sparks and smoke. A smile visited her lips.

'Pleased to meet you,' she said, her words dull and thick.

I wondered what medication she was on to blunt her so.

Davis spoke to a coloured lady in a dark pinafore.

'Elizabeth, go ahead and serve Sarah and the boys dinner. Keep mine warm for later. Mr McArdle and I will be in my study. I'd like not to be disturbed.'

'Yessir,' she said, bending at the knee.

Davis showed me to a cavernous room lined with book cases, oil paintings on the walls, an antique desk at the far end, not unlike the one I'd moved uptown with my music store, but in far better condition. The room smelled of old paper and wood varnish.

He sat down in a leather swivel chair on one side of the desk, indicated the seat opposite. 'So what can I do for you, Mr McArdle?'

I took the seat, feeling very small in this room, like a fish in the belly of a shark.

'Maybe you heard the news a few nights ago,' I said. 'Or maybe you read about it in the papers. A double homicide. A young couple, not so very far uptown from here. They were killed by two Hispanic males.'

'Tragic,' Davis said.

He reached for a stack of mail that waited on his desk, lifted the first letter, and slipped the dagger-like blade of an opener beneath the flap.

'The two killers were shot by the police over in Queens,' I said. 'One of them was Hugo Fuente.'

Davis paused, the blade clear of the envelope, his stony eyes on me.

'The boy we let go,' I said.

He blinked. Nodded. 'Like I said, tragic.'

'That young couple would be alive if we hadn't saved that boy from the chair.'

'Maybe,' Davis said. 'Maybe not. We didn't try him for the murder of that couple. We tried him for the killing of his father. And we found him not guilty. Whatever he did before or after the trial, it has nothing to do with you, me, or any man on that jury.'

'I wish I could believe that,' I said. 'I wish I could turn away from this, convince myself that two young people didn't die because I changed my vote from guilty to not guilty.'

'There were ten men in that room besides you and me,' Davis said. 'Ten men who changed their votes. You have nothing to feel bad about.'

'Yes I do,' I said, my voice rising. 'Because I fell first. Because I allowed you to go on and take every other man down, one by one.'

He set the blade on the desktop, slid the letter from its envelope, and spoke as he skimmed the pages. 'All we did was talk. No one had a gun to his head. We reasoned it out. You know that.'

Davis looked up from the letter, fixed his gaze on mine, hard like flint.

'Now, here you are, wanting to talk some more. The time to talk was nine months ago. It's too late now.'

'That's right,' I said. 'It's too late. But I want to ask you one question.'

He dropped the pages on his desk. 'Go on.'

I took a breath and said, 'Why?'

'I don't understand.'

'Why did you do it? Why did you go on a crusade to save the boy?'

Davis shrugged. 'You know why. Because I didn't believe the evidence was strong enough to put him in the chair. Do you want to pick over it all again? The old man in the apartment below, the woman across the El track, the knife with the carved handle. Shall we do it all again, Mr McArdle?'

'No,' I said. 'I've gone over it enough times myself since that day.'

'Well, then. What more is there to say?' He got to his feet. 'If you don't mind, Mr McArdle, I have work to do tonight, and I'd like to take an hour with my family if I can.'

I remained seated and asked, 'You want to know what I think?'

Davis's face hardened as he lowered himself back into his chair. 'All right, what do you think?'

Leaning forward, I said, 'I think it was just a game to you. I think you didn't give a hoot if that boy was guilty or innocent. I think it mattered not one jot to you if he went to the chair or walked free.'

Davis sat quite still as I talked, his stare never leaving me, his face blank as an unmarked grave.

'I think you wanted to prove yourself better than any other man in the room. To be smarter than them, to outthink them, to outtalk them. I remember the look on your face when each one of them broke down, the pleasure, almost savage. And when one of us stood up to you, you mind him? Juror 3. The man with the messenger business. When he stood his ground, when he didn't allow himself to be beaten into submission by you, you went for him like a torpedo. You didn't let up till he was crying his heart out, you didn't stop until you'd humiliated him in front of the rest of us. It was just a game, wasn't it, Mr Davis? We were playthings to you. That boy's life was a ball for you to bat around the room, like a cat toys with a mouse before he gobbles it up.'

Davis watched from the other side of his antique desk, still, silent and dead-eyed as a statue.

'Am I right, Mr Davis?' I asked, breathless, my nerves carrying the charge like bell wire.

He picked up the letter opener, ran its edge along the pad of his thumb, leaving a string of tiny red beads. His tongue licked them away. He asked, 'Exactly what kind of man do you think I am, Mr McArdle?'

I'm not sure what rose in me then, I thought it was courage, but I realise now that it was not.

'I know what kind of man you are,' I said. 'My son told me. I know about the girl from your office who disappeared, and about the one who drowned in her own bathtub. I guess you'll never answer for those young women, or for the couple who died because you talked eleven men into giving the wrong verdict. You'll get away with it, I suppose.'

I stood, wavered, gripped the edge of the desk, breathed deep.

'I just want you to know, Mr Davis, that your sin did not go unnoticed. I can see myself out.'

He did not speak as I left the room, as the heavy door closed behind me.

I walked to the apartment door, the one that opened onto its own private entrance hall, leading to the elevator. As I passed the drawing room, I saw his wife, Sarah, watching me from the doorway. She said nothing as our eyes met, but even now I wonder if, somewhere deep in her consciousness, somewhere behind the veil of whatever drugs Davis kept her on, I wonder if part of her mind begged me for help?

We buried Jarlath one week later.

Eugene took it worse than anybody. He had no time for his brother when he was alive. Now he's grieving so hard I fear it might unman him.

Jarlath left a bar on Charles Street at two in the morning, steaming drunk. One witness, a vagrant, saw a tall thin man with dark hair slip out of a doorway as Jarlath passed, slide a blade between his ribs three times, and walk on as if nothing had happened. Jarlath died on the sidewalk, his lungs filling with blood. No one to hold his hand as he faded. I hope there wasn't a great deal of pain or fear for him in those last minutes. I will carry the knowledge that I caused his death to my grave, that if I had heeded his advice and stayed away, my son would not be in the ground today.

I expect he'll come for me. When enough time has passed, when the receptionist has forgotten about the strange old man who wouldn't go away, I imagine I'll feel a hand on my shoulder, something cold and sharp in my side.

But I will keep my mouth shut.

I solemnly swear, so help me God, that I will never breathe a word about Juror 8, a man called Willard Davis, to another living soul.

STELLA DUFFY, born in London in 1963 but brought up in New Zealand, has written thirteen novels, fifty short stories, and ten plays. *The Room of Lost Things* and *State of Happiness* were both longlisted for the Orange Prize for Fiction, and she has twice won Stonewall Writer of the Year, and the Crime Writers' Association Short Story Dagger. In addition to her writing work, Stella is also a theatre director, Artistic Director of Shaky Isles Theatre, Associate Artist with Improbable, and is currently heading the Fun Palaces project, a nationwide celebration of the arts.

Face Value

Stella Duffy

It's not about me.

I used to say that all the time, at first when the fuss happened, when it took me from promising to promised, from potential to arrived, when everyone wanted to know who I was and where I'd come from, I said it as my stock answer.

It's not about me.

Because it was true, it wasn't.

Later, in interviews, quite possibly hundreds of interviews at the time of the retrospective, the same old questions, all over again, I said the same, all over again. Or at those stupid parties where I was only in attendance to promote my career, to assist my agent, to do the right thing by the person they'd decided I was, at the events there was always some oily man who'd think it was flattering to contradict my stock answer, to correct me, with an 'Oh but come on, surely you can admit it now ...'

I'm admitting it now.

It was not about me.

They'd ask too, sitting around the dinner table with friends, this workmate of that gym-buddy, this father of that child at school. I noticed, when I was younger, as a non-mother, that the school-gate friends of my friends were the worst. They had nothing to talk about but their children, and even the most besotted parent runs out of child-praise eventually. Halfway through the second bottle, house prices, the government, and the cost of the child-minder covered, the increasingly desperate conversation would finally turn to me.

You don't have children?

What do you do?

And then –

Oh. You're her. You did that piece.

For God's sake. I did about four dozen others, each one of them massively successful, along with a hundred or more less well known, and another couple of hundred that never saw the light of day beyond my studio. But yes, I made that piece. And no, it's not about me.

Maybe I wouldn't mind if they were also interested in the rest of it, the paintings and the tapestries I worked on next, the miniatures I've been making for over a decade now, even the films, self-revelatory as they are. The films are about me, intentionally, deliberately, they are self-sacrificing, self-offering, in a way that nothing else I have made has been. Which might explain why they've not been as successful. Something about the giving up of self, too readily, that doesn't sit right with the viewer. The viewer wants to feel they have prised us from our shell, found the pearl hidden in the gritty oyster. When I offered my pearls, strand by strand, reel by reel (it was film, not video, for some things I am a purist), there was – oddly – less engagement for the viewer. Well, there it is. I have had to accept that not all of my work is received in the same spirit it is offered. I took a while to learn, but I know it now.

I hasten to add, it's not at all that I dislike talking about my work. I'm happy to do so, just not that piece. And because I've been so open about it, because I've said time and again in interviews, that I will talk about anything but that, because I have not lied, not once, when I have discussed my feelings, my lack of feelings, my choice never to speak of it – that is, inevitably, what it always comes back to. The one journalist, interviewer, fan, who is sure that they will force me to reveal all. How it made my career and then broke me. How I went a little crazy for half a year or so after that exhibition. How it changed my life.

I did not change my life. It wasn't about me.

I have been an artist for just over fifty years. I have a well-respected, widely sold, widely collected back catalogue. I am known, wanted. Yet of all the work I've ever made, it's always that bloody piece that they come back to – and they will insist on asking about it, all of them. All of you. And so, because it is the truth, and because I know I can never get you to shut up and leave me alone if I just refuse to answer at all, I generally say something like: But what no-one ever understood, is that it wasn't about me.

Then there they are, the almost-winks, the smug insinuations, the little knowing grin that what I'm really revealing is how false we artists are, how blind to our own truths. I am offered the smile that suggests, no matter how honest an artist endeavours to be, that we are never fully revealed in mere words, that we show so much more in our self-deluded hiding than we do in the truths we try to speak.

In short, they – you – do not believe that I do not want to talk about it. They – you – do not believe that they don't understand the piece and never have done.

I'm telling you now, once and for all, it was never about me.

This is why.

She was nineteen when we met, I was twenty-five. Now, at sixty-four, that six-year gap between nineteen and twenty-four seems nothing, but come on, don't you remember how adult you felt at nineteen? And then how, by our mid-twenties, nineteen – all the teens – seemed an age away, the love earned and lost, the passion experienced, the agonising, ecstatic growing up that had gone before, that had changed our DNA.

So, she was nineteen and I was her senior by every bit of six years. She was being paid very little by my agent to come over and help me out a bit – my agent's phrase, not mine. My agent's idea, not mine. I've always guarded my privacy, even back then I didn't want anyone in the studio, couldn't bear the idea of someone watching as I worked. I have always wanted a clean line between process and product. The market didn't like the separation then, and they like it even less now, when artist and artwork have become so inextricably linked that buyers believe they are getting a piece of you when they hang you on the wall, when they make space in the foyer, when they build a room just for the work.

Oh yes they did. They created a room just for the work, my work. Astonishing. I was twenty-five – dear God I was young, and I was good. Young and good, there is no more potent combination. True, money is handy, money is useful, but when you're young and talented, money is a sideline. It's only with age that we come to understand its true worth. Someone – someone malleable, amenable, needy (someone my agent could pay, my agent being old enough to understand the true value of money) – came up with the astonishing idea of creating a room for my work. It took a little persuasion, or maybe a lot, I wasn't involved in the negotiations then, I don't involve myself in them now. Process/product. Keep them apart. In the end, the gallery owners, in collaboration with a middle-aged architect keen to show he wasn't yet past it, decided to use the occasion of my first major exhibition to extend the gallery. Yes, it may have been an idea that was pending, my work may have been just the excuse they needed to demand their Board agree to a bigger spend, or perhaps the architect paid, and certainly my agent fucked. Whatever happened behind the scenes, the effect was that they made a new space specifically for, informed by, my first ever exhibition. They changed a building for me.

They took out two walls, lifted the ceiling, opened a room that had been all about artificial light, proud of the artifice of its light, and made it about the day and the night, and the difference between the two. My work in daylight, sunlight, rainlight, from five until nine – this was a summer exhibition, we considered autumn but dead leaves turn to mulch, and no-one wants chill winds at an opening. The people we wanted to come, to buy, were all about showing themselves, we couldn't be handing out scarves as they entered the building, so summer it was. And there was also my work in sodium yellow – we kept the space open twenty-four hours a day. I know it happens all the time now, but not back then, forty years ago you understand, we were new, brand new.

We were a happening for the rich and comfortable. They so wanted to be happening, they just didn't want to have to wear batik. Neither did I.

With the exhibition running twenty-four hours a day, I practically moved in. I needed to, in many ways the exhibition had me as the centre-piece.

It wasn't about me.

When I say they removed a wall, I mean a wall, the entire back wall of an otherwise ordinary 1960s space, and replaced it with steels and raised glass balconies. One end of the room entirely open to the elements. And even though we'd chosen the season to allow for weather, it was an elemental summer, wind, rain, hail and a solid week of stifling heat. Astonishing. Of course, at twenty-five I thought I deserved it. I thought it was all for love of my work. It was many years before it occurred to me to consider who my agent had had to pay, to fuck, to make my break. And longer still before he agreed to tell me. (You don't want to know.)

Meteoric rise to glory, the bright star from nowhere, art world's hottest new thing. And my poor agent half-broken by the actual, physical, fuckable price he'd had to pay to get me started. Well, I've been paying him ever since. Fifty percent. There's always a ferryman who demands a silvered palm.

I had been working for ten years by the time of that exhibition. Taking my work seriously for ten years. Yes, I did start young, so do many artists. Unlike most of them, I made sure to trash my youthful work, my pathetic teenage experiments, whenever I found a better way, a more successful method. There was no path to be followed through my attempts, no archive to trawl and say see, she went from this to that, here to there, and finally made her way to now. Even then, on the brink of my first exhibition, there was simply a collection of finished work, each piece complete and whole in itself, every one a work of art. And today there is not a single drawing, sketch, first mould, half-cast, Polaroid in my archive.

(OK, there is, one, a Polaroid, I'm getting to that. It's not about me.)

So. The exhibition was a few months away, they were halfway through tearing down the wall, I was getting daily reports from my agent about how it was looking, how it was going to look. He thought they were pep talks, would gee me up to get on and make, to provide the matter to fill the space, to be the Artist. In reality he was screwing me up. Totally. Terrifying me that they'd actually gone along with the absurd idea, were spending so much time and money and effort on making a space for my work (not for me, it's not about me), and it was all making me a bit crazy. Crazy worried, crazy nervous, crazy upset. They knew the work I'd done to date, there was already a draft catalogue of the pieces I had to show, the work, that was what they wanted, they were all excited and my agent didn't understand why I wasn't thrilled. But it wasn't what I wanted. Not yet. There was something missing, something extra, the thing that would make it fly. And I'd been gnawing away at this lack of the one thing.

I didn't believe in me in the same way my agent did, not yet, not back then. I understood that he saw promise, I understood this exhibition was not to be that of a finished artist, but of one at the peak of her beginning, ready to soar. I understood this, and still I wanted that one thing, the piece that would tip it over into glory. Tip me over. I was exhausted, stressed, I was upset and sobbing on the phone to my agent every half hour – in the time before mobile phones, you understand, when the telephone was a shrill interruption held in place by wires and cables, not a welcome distraction from a dozen other screens.

And so, no doubt to get me off his back, he came up with the brilliant idea of getting an assistant for me. Someone to help with the basic things. Basic things like getting me out of bed before three in the afternoon, basic things like getting me into bed in the first place. Basic things like stopping me destroying all the pieces that had already been assigned places in the exhibition catalogue. In a fit of insomniac insanity, I'd decided they were shit, I was shit, and this exhibition was going to show the whole world my true, talent-free nature.

I may have been twenty-five, but I had the amateur-dramatics of a teenager.

And so she arrived. The assistant-nanny-saviour. The one who was to make all the difference.

Didn't she just.

She was, how shall I put this? Oh yes, perfect. No really, she was. And I don't mean in a Mary Poppins kind of way. She wasn't there to look after me, not really. Nor was she an All About Eve kind of assistant. There was no hidden agenda, no – as my mother would have it – 'side' to her at all. She was just perfect. She had a way of making me feel that I could do anything. She behaved as if it was the most natural thing in the world for my work to be getting this attention, that it made absolute sense that the whole open-to-the-elements thing was going on – and this despite the rumours of how much it was costing and that the gallery owners were kicking themselves for agreeing to my agent's absurd demands, conveniently forgetting they'd wanted the renovations, as we always do when confronted by the dust, the brick, the gaping hole in the roof. She made me feel good about it all. She – I can't go on she-ing her, can I? Very tedious for you. So, the assistant, let's call her Lileth. I never use her real name, not now. She didn't like it anyway, her real name, said she'd only used it half a dozen times since she was twelve, had picked a new name every few months and demanded her family try it out. So she might as well have been called Lileth, might as well be now.

Lileth was a god-send. She simply made everything better. And I loved her for it.

Not in love, I am not gay, not that I've discovered anyway. I'm not really anything much, never have been, I don't have the energy for other people, not when my work demands so much of me. I know I sound like a cliché, can't be helped, it's true. I have tried relationships and I have always been found wanting in them. I cannot give enough because I would rather be in my studio. I cannot agree to be at a dinner at a certain time because I would rather be working. I cannot agree to be with you in bed because, if you help prise me from my work and lift me away from the matter in hand, the in-bed in hand, then there is every chance that finally unfettered from the mundane, I will begin to dream another piece of work. It is only when I am away from the work in hand that I can begin on the work in my head.

Well. Lileth.

Lileth fixed it. She turned my fear into courage, my worry into work. Instead of placating me, Lileth cajoled and spurred me on. Where others told me to sleep, she would say, Fuck sleep. Get on with it. Who knows when you're going to die? Keep working.

She would bring me food and coffee and wine and a little coke, just a little coke, to keep me up, keep me on it.

Work bitch work.

Our little joke.

Eat bitch eat. Drink bitch drink. Die bitch die.

Lileth was astonishing. She was just right. And the exhibition, when it finally came, when the gallery delays and building permits and problem after problem had been overcome, when that day, that night, that incredible night finally came, it too was astonishing. It too was just right.

But I'm getting ahead of myself. Even with Lileth on my side, there was still the problem of that piece. The one that would make it fly, the one that would hold it all together and also alarm, shock, slap, that would emerge from the whole and be the whole. That piece. The one I was dreaming, looking for, digging into my guts to find and not … quite … getting it.

And then, I got it. I totally got it, I so got it, I was there when it was got, by me, getting it.

I know, you don't expect ladies of sixty-something in your stories to talk about 'getting it'. That's because you have us in the realm of the grey, where 'old folks' perpetually sing It's a Long Way to Tipperary and talk about the war. Fuck off. I was born in the fifties. I've taken more recreational drugs – and never pretended I didn't like them or that they 'did nothing for me' – shagged more men, and I have delighted more strangers, than you've had hot dinners.

I do not bother with hot dinners. Hot dinners are the enemy of the waistline.

I got it. The idea, that idea, the one all the pictures are of, the photographs. The idea that has been used for other people's art, for their photo-shoots, their shop windows, their art-house films and once, God help me, for that bloody awful play where they made all the ushers dress like me.

We made the waitresses dress like me.

It wasn't about me.

Yes, yes, I know you're so cool you have no idea what I'm talking about, do you? You are too young or too uninterested in art, or too ... God knows, net-savvy. Very well, let me sketch you a picture. Trust me, I'm an artist.

You approach the venue. You know you are approaching the venue because since you turned the corner you have seen me. Every second person you have seen is dressed like, made up to look like, looks like me. At this time in my life and in yours, you have no idea what I look like, but here they are, these young women each one 5'5' tall, each one weighing 110–112lbs and not an ounce more, each one in a long black wig, a deep red dress, absurdly long eyelashes, painted-on eyebrows, and where everyone at the time was wearing nude, nearly-nude, some insipid shade of hippy harmony on their lips, each of these girls wore a gash of dress-matching red. They were barefoot and their toes and fingernails matched, blue. There were black girls, white girls, brown girls, Asian girls, Oriental. And a few boys who looked like girls. Daring.

And I was one of them.

I was dressed up, made up, designed-up, covered-up to look exactly like all of the girls. The girls who directed you to the entrance, who offered you a drink, who handed you the catalogue, who scuttled back and forth along the street, up the stairs, to the walls where they placed those lovely, lovely red dots. I looked just like one of them.

See? Told you it was not about me.

And in the space itself, the space that we finally allowed you into, having left you queuing in the street for a whole half hour, in the space with mannequins dressed like us flying above, with versions of me sitting high in the trees in the garden in the outside that was inside, in the centre of the room, there she lay. Lileth as me, in the glass coffin, the formaldehyde-filled coffin. The woman who was me who was dead who was living. Who was not me. See? It's not about me.

(No I don't think either Tilda or Damien 'improved' on my work. No I do not.)

It was magic, of course. Something to do with mirrors and a very very thin pipe that kept oxygen flowing into her nose and mouth. She was bloody good though, you had to stand very close and watch for some time to see the slightest flicker of an eye lash or a raise of her chest. Almost there, not there. And most people didn't bother to look. They saw the mannequins above, the models in the street, the versions of me/not me climbing the trees outside, looking down at us from the all the windows overlooking that now-open back lot. It was a wonderful idea. And it really worked.

They thought I was terribly clever.

They still didn't know what I looked like.

I was dressed up too, of course.

And then.

My agent stands on a chair to make a speech. He is a small man, and – in the manner of small men – fastidious, fussy, absurdly picky about personal hygiene – which is what, I think, was so painful for him, the things he was asked to do, the things he did, for me, to get me there. Here. I am here and so is he. We have a signal. I hope she sees it, we have rehearsed this, but never with so many people around, we could never have got away with the secret if there were so many people around.

He stands on a chair to make a speech. He begins and I zone out. I have heard the speech, Lileth wrote the speech, they both rehearsed him in it, I am nervous and so I zone out until my cue. Here it is, here it comes,

The absurdly talented ...

And as I begin to walk towards him, as the room begins to make way for me, as I reach my hand up to the wig to reveal I am she, the one they have been looking for, that of all these women (and some men) it is me who has made all this, up steps Lileth.

Out of the glass coffin. Out of the formaldehyde (not really, we found something that had the same viscosity, the smell).

And now there are two of me.

Wet me and dry me.

And now the waitresses and the assistants and the mannequins – who were never fake, never plastic, who have been harnessed there on wires for hours the poor things – now we all reach up a hand to pull off the wig and then.

Lileth walks to me and I walk to her.

And I pull the wig from her head, I rip the dress from her shoulders, I use the dress as a cloth to wipe the gash of lipstick from her face and Lileth is me.

Naked. Shown. Exposed. Exhibited.

She turns and does the same to me and there we are. Identical down to the tattoo above our left breasts. A half heart each. Same, not mirror, that would have told a different story.

And that was it. The room erupted as you might expect, as you have been led to expect by every cynical, copycat show that has since copycatted ours. We were the first copies. I was handed a lovely silver gown, Lileth was escorted off to wash and dress, the evening continued.

And someone wanted to buy the girl in the coffin.

And someone bought the girl in the coffin. He signed a cheque there and then, the figure made up by my agent, made up by him on the spot because he didn't think he could get away with it and has been kicking himself ever since, since he's worked out he could probably have asked for double, treble, since the piece has sold and sold and sold. Every time it is sold on to the next proud and hungry collector, I get a little more fame, and all the others of my pieces go up in value. It helps with the few I kept back for me, the one or two I gave him. But neither of us get a percentage of the original, copy-right. And we were all in on the joke, the whole room in on the joke.

(Not Lileth, she was off showering, washing the stink of the heavy water from her skin, breathing deep. Drying her hair, putting on a nice frock, her own makeup, readying herself for her big entrance, her re-entrance, the entrance where they wouldn't notice her at all.)

they didn't notice her at all
so no-one knew what she looked like really

and she was young
and she didn't quite fit in
and she didn't know how to be with those people

It wasn't too hard to give her one drink and another and another. It wasn't too hard to make sure one of those drinks was laden with a dose that would knock her out, lock her out of herself.

And it wasn't hard ...

Yes. It was actually. I liked Lileth. I really liked her.

But we had made a deal. Not the buyer and me, the agent and me. We had this idea and we made this deal. I wanted it to be astonishing, I wanted it to fly. I didn't need everyone who came to the exhibition to see how truly astonishing it was, underneath, in reality. I just needed to know that for myself. I needed to know I was making a difference.

Don't all artists want that? To make a difference? To put their stamp on eternity. And what greater stamp is there than to stop another?

Yes, there was a Polaroid. It is of that moment. I do not gloat in it, revel that it was taken, he and I took it together. What do you call them now? A selfie? There is a selfie of he and I holding Lileth. We are holding her on the table as her blood drains out.

My agent was a taxidermist once. In another life. He is not a young man now and even then, he was already middle-aged, had done so much. Lived many lives. In one of them he was a soldier in a far-away country. In another, he was a taxidermist. And in this one, here, he was my agent. And he knew, even before I knew, what I wanted.

In the moment of passing, the point where the blood went from just enough, to just not enough, we were posed. Ready. He clicked the switch.

I have never been very successful with photographs. People like my installations better, my sculptures. They have said, unkind critics have said, that my photographs are a little flat, as if the life is just a little less in them. They may be right.

We took a Polaroid of the one Polaroid, and then another, and then we had one each. Me, him and Lileth. He had one to keep as evidence against me, I as one against him. The third sits in the small of her back, beneath the waistband of the red dress, perfectly preserved. As she is.

You'd be surprised how long a punter is prepared to wait for their merchandise, once they know they have it, once they have been on all the art pages as having it, he waited a good three months before we were ready to deliver his goods.

She is great art. She is so life-like, they say.
    No, she really isn't.
    She explains our mortality to us, they say.
    Well, she explains her own.
    She is you and me.
    No. She is herself. She is nothing like me. Though we made her up like me, the wig, the dress, the makeup. We made her up like the made-up me.

And she floats in his gallery. You can pay to see her. He does not allow free visitors. He keeps the light a little low. Too low. And sadly, so sadly, there are no windows, no wind or rain. She floats in no water and she reminds me, when I think of her, of a time and a place. That is all. A time and a place where I had one astonishing, audacious idea.

And I executed that idea.

I forget her name. I worked hard to forget her name. I call her Lileth. It suits her.

That collector, the one who is as famous for collecting her as he is for anything else, he has never understood what he paid for, what his zeros bought him. He speaks about her with a pomposity that is almost shocking in its stupidity. About the symbol she is, about the hope she gives him, hope of a form of life after death, hope that humanity can one day under-stand itself through the image of itself. Art-school bollocks. She is a dead woman in a box of liquid. I gave him hope. (And no, there is no life after death. There is just death. Look at her.)

Although the money was useful, the fame, the notoriety probably made more difference. And anyway, we did not do this to make money, my agent and I. We did it because we could. Because it would be art, real art, living art.

We did it for art's sake.

I called it Me/Not Me.

It was never about me.

JOHN HARVEY, born in London in 1938, is best known for his jazz-influenced Charlie Resnick novels, set in Nottingham. *Lonely Hearts*, was named by *The Times* as one of the '100 Best Crime Novels of the Century'; the twelfth and final novel in the series, *Darkness, Darkness*, was published in 2014. He has published more than 90 books and in 2007 was awarded the Crime Writers' Association Cartier Diamond Dagger for Lifetime Achievement.

Not Tommy Johnson

John Harvey

Tommy Johnson was not Tommy Johnson. That's to say, he was not the Tommy Johnson whom Resnick first saw skating, perfectly balanced, across the mud of the opposition's penalty area, red hair catching fire for an instant in the floodlights, before dispatching the ball into the upper right corner of the net; the Tommy Johnson who scored forty-seven goals in 118 appearances for Notts before moving on to Derby County, Aston Villa and points north; Resnick's favourite player, amongst other favourite players, in that team that won promotion two seasons running, those brilliant years 1989/90/91 when it seemed they could do little wrong.

The same years that found him struggling still to come to terms with the failure of his marriage, Eileen having sequestered herself somewhere across the Welsh border with her estate agent lover, leaving Resnick custody of four cats, an unused upstairs nursery in which the alphabet wallpaper was already starting to peel, and an overflowing collection of vinyl he was slowly but studiously replacing with CDs – most recently, working alphabetically, Duke Ellington's 1959 score for *Anatomy of a Murder*.

Tommy Johnson's body – that's this Tommy Johnson, three weeks and four days past his sixteenth birthday – was found on the uneven paving beneath the fifth floor balcony from which it had fallen; one arm stretched out at a broken angle, the other wrapped tight across his eyes, as if to ward off any sight of what was fast approaching.

If anyone had heard his helpless cry or the thump of the body landing – landing with sufficient impact to break not only various and sundry bones, but to rupture, also, a number of internal organs – they were, as yet, not saying.

It had been Gerry Clark who'd found him, a little after four in the morning and on his way to the bus that would take him to his job in the distribution centre out by the motorway; just light enough, from the solitary overhead lamp still working, for him to make out the body where it lay, unmoving; what was recognizably blood further darkening the cracks in the paving.

That was two days ago, some forty-eight hours and counting, and Resnick, slightly out of breath after choosing the stairs over the dubious aromas of the lift, was at Danielle Johnson's door; not the first time and likely not the last.

One glance and she turned back into the flat, expecting him to follow. Cotton draw-string pyjama bottoms, sweater, fluffy slippers.

A wall-eyed mongrel barked as he entered, hackles raised, then backed away, growling, from the kick that failed to follow.

Dark in the room, Resnick eased the curtain sideways, letting in a sliver of November light. Opposite him as he sat, Danielle lit a cigarette with a shaky hand and shivered as she inhaled.

'Whatever you or anybody else might've said about him, he never deserved that. Never. Not Tommy. And don't try tellin' me he jumped of his own accord, 'cause I'll not wear it. Someone had it in for him an' that's a fact.'

'Any ideas who?'

She coughed and shook her head; coughed again.

Nine-thirty in the morning and the off-key sweetness of cider on her breath as she spoke; two empty cans, last night's, on the table and a litre bottle, recently opened, on the floor nearby. Not long past thirty, Danielle: three kids who'd been in and out of care; Tommy the only boy, her favourite. Melody, the youngest, living with her nan now in Derby; Janine in temporary foster care in another part of the city.

'You saw him that evening?' Resnick asked.

Danielle fanned smoke away from her face. 'In and out. Nine it might've been. Later, maybe.'

'Any idea where he was going?'

She shook her head. 'Not his keeper, am I? Ask, he'd only tell me, mind me own fuckin' business.'

'So you don't know who he might have been seeing that evening?'

'Just said, never told me anything.'

'It's important, Danielle.'

'I know it's fuckin' important. Think I'm fuckin' stupid?'

The first thoughts of those who'd responded to the emergency call, the police, the paramedics, Tommy Johnson had taken his own life, jumped to his death under the influence, most likely, of this, that or the other. Something more than self-pity. But a small trace of cannabis aside, that and paracetamol, there were no drugs, untoward, in his body, and all he seemed to have drunk in the twenty-four hours previous, water aside, was a copious quantity of Red Bull.

An examination showed blows to the head and body quite possibly administered prior to the injuries sustained in his fall. Another homicide the last thing the team wanted – Tommy's especially – but it was, it seemed, what they were getting.

Officers went to the school in theory he'd attended; having been excluded so many times, since September-end he'd more or less excluded himself. They talked to the few from around the estate who would admit to having spent any significant time with him; talked to the social worker who'd been attached to him since his last brief spell in care.

Quiet, pretty much a loner. Bit of a loser, really.

'No great loss to humanity, I'm afraid,' his Citizenship teacher had said.

After another twenty minutes or so of getting nowhere, Resnick rose to his feet and Danielle prised herself out of the settee and saw him to the door. When he was halfway to the stairs, she called him back.

'There was this girl he was keen on. Leah? Leah something. Felix, maybe? Skirt up to her arse an' a mouth to match.'

Resnick had spent so long working in close proximity with a fellow officer who thought Petula Clarke's Greatest Hits the acme of all things musical, it had been something of a shock to discover someone else in the force with a feeling for jazz. Tom Whitemore was a member of the Public Protection Team: working with other agencies – probation, social services and community psychiatric care – in the supervision of violent and high risk of harm offenders released back into the community, sex offenders in particular.

As was often the case, it was older relatives who'd passed the jazz torch from one generation to another: with Resnick it had been an uncle, amongst whose scratched 78s he had discovered Billie Holiday and Teddy Wilson, and through them, Johnny Hodges and Lester Young; Whitemore's father had made him a present of Cannonball Adderley's *The Dirty Blues* for his sixteenth birthday. Whether he would as easily be able to do the same for his twin boys depended on the good grace of his estranged wife and her new partner. One way and another, the job took its toll.

When Resnick arrived at the Five Ways, towards the end of the first set, a scratch band, in which he recognised only Geoff Pearson on bass, was bustling through Coltrane's 'Blue Train' with at least half an eye on the interval.

'Leah Felix,' Resnick said, once they'd removed themselves to the side bar, 'any bells?'

Whitemore, he knew, had for some months now been involved in unpicking a complicated and as-yet-unproven case of sexual exploitation, in which a closely knit group of men had groomed a number of young teenage girls, for the most part living in care. The girls had been talked into posing for explicit photographs which had been shared over the internet; after which, and with more persuasion, the girls themselves had been shared between the members of the group and their friends. Loaned out, sometimes, in order to pay off debts.

Leah Felix had been one of the more reluctant, hesitant about going along with the others and submitting to the men's suggestions. Once the police and social services became involved, she had seemed one of the most likely to name names, be prepared, even, to give evidence in court. But when push had come within sight of shove, she had clammed up and backed away.

Whitemore told Resnick what he knew.

'You think she might talk to me?'

'What about?'

'Tommy Johnson.'

'The footballer?'

Resnick shook his head.

He located Leah Felix amidst a small group that had congregated at the edge of the Old Market Square: smoking roll-ups, taking selfies, swearing at anyone who came close. Only the promise of a Quarter Pounder with cheese, onion rings and fries could prise her away; that and the assurance he'd keep his hands to himself. 'I know what you old blokes are like, given half a chance.'

The nearest McDonald's was on Exchange Walk, with a view across to St Peter's Church.

Resnick waited until she was halfway through her burger, wondering, as he watched her, when she'd last had a proper meal.

'Tommy Johnson, he was a friend of yours.'

'Was he?'

'So his mum says.'

'Danielle? That slag.'

'Is she right, though?'

Leah shrugged and jammed a few more fries into her mouth.

'You know what happened to him?' Resnick asked.

'Jumped off fuckin' balcony, didn't he? Daft twat.'

'No, I mean what really happened.'

She looked at him then. Blinked.

'You do know?'

'Dunno what you're on about.'

'I thought you did.'

'Well, I fuckin' don't.'

Resnick reached out and purloined a chip. 'She thought you might've been with him that evening.'

'Who?'

'Danielle.'

'Fuckin' out of it, most the time, in't she?'

'That mean she was wrong?'

'Maybe. Maybe not. An' stop takin' my fuckin' fries.'

'You were with him, then?'

'So what if I was?'

'He liked you, didn't he? Tommy. Liked you quite a lot.'

'Did he?'

'I think so.'

'Know everything then, don't you?' She pushed away her tray and made as if to get up.

'Wait,' Resnick said.

She hesitated, then sat back down.

'If you were with him that evening,' Resnick said, 'you must have seen what happened.'

'Well, I never did.'

Her eyes flicked towards him then away. Resnick bade his time.

'I ... I wanted to. Go with 'em, like, you know? Thought if I was there they wouldn't hurt him. Not so bad, anyway. But they never let me. Told me to fuck off out of it an' keep my mouth fuckin' shut.'

'Why were they going to hurt him?'

'Been shootin' his mouth off, yeah? Tellin' them to leave me alone. Like they'd listen, right? Threatened if I wouldn't shop 'em to you lot then he would. Stupid bastard. Soft in the bloody head.'

'So who was it,' Resnick asked, 'took Tommy away?'

'Don't be stupid.'

'All right, how many. You can tell me that. Just a number. That's all it is.'

Uncertain, the answer was slow in coming. 'Three. No, four. Four.'

'And the names?'

'No. No way.'

'One of them, then. Just one.'

'No. No, I can't.' There was panic in her eyes.

'All right, then. We'll do it like this.' From his pocket he took a sheet of paper, folded twice. Written on it were the names of a dozen men Whitemore was investigating. 'Just point to the names of whoever went off with Tommy that evening. That's all I'll ask. And no one will ever need to know. I promise.'

The polish on Leah's index finger was chipped and cracked; the nail itself bitten down to the quick. She jabbed at the names so quickly, scarcely touching the paper, that Resnick had to ask her to do it again, more slowly.

'They said ... they promised ...' She turned her head aside, lest he see the tears pricking at the corners of her eyes. She wasn't gonna fuckin' cry, not in front of some fuckin' copper she wasn't.

Resnick showed Tom Whitemore the names.

'Who's the most vulnerable?' he asked. 'Who's got the most to lose?'

Lewis Morland was older than the rest by a good ten years; it didn't mean he was wiser, just more cunning. Now that his once boyish good looks were fading and his age beginning to show, he'd started befriending young girls on Tumblr and Ask.fm, feigning the identity of an eighteen year old. Out on the street, he was dependent on others to make the first moves.

Previous convictions meant that if he went back inside it would be for a long and uncomfortable time.

Resnick and Whitemore interviewed him together, Morland slippery as a grass snake in their hands, a combination of 'No comment', non sequiturs and ingratiating smiles.

'Tommy Johnson? Not that bloke used to play for Notts? Never saw him myself, but my old man reckoned he was the dog's bollocks.'

None of the others Leah Felix had fingered would admit to coming within a mile of where the incident had occurred.

'Think maybe she was playing safe?' Whitemore said. 'Feeding us the wrong names?'

'It's possible,' Resnick replied.

But he had seen her face, recognised her fear. For the present, he preferred to believe.

A little over three weeks later, the Low Copy Number DNA test results on Tommy Johnson's clothing came back from the special research lab in Birmingham. Aside from Johnson's own blood, present in generous quantities, initial tests had revealed small amounts of blood from two other possible sources; after re-examination, one of these, when checked against the National DNA Database, was sufficient to identify Marshall Boyce.

Boyce, a seventeen year old with a minor police record, had been on Tom Whitemore's list, but not picked out by Leah Felix.

Resnick found her in Sun Valley Amusements in the city centre.

Her eyes narrowed the moment she saw him, fingers clenched into tight little fists. 'You said you was never gonna say nothin', din't you?'

'I kept my word.'

'Then how come Lewis had a go at me, yeah? Gave me a right slapping.'

There was still the faint trace of what could have been a bruise, just visible beneath her make-up.

'You want to file a complaint?'

'Fuck off!'

'The names – why didn't you tell me the truth?'

'I did.'

'Not all the truth.'

'What d'you mean?'

But she knew well enough.

'Marshall Boyce, you were in care round about the same time.'

'So?'

'So you know him. Better maybe than the others. Soft spot for him, maybe.'

She shrugged.

'Is that why you didn't pick him out?'

She squinted up her eyes. 'Gotta fag?'

Resnick shook his head. She bummed one from someone by the adjacent slot machine and Resnick followed her outside.

'He was always, like, decent, you know, Marshall. When the others, like Lewis especially, when they wanted to do really dirty stuff, porno stuff, he never went along with it. Not usually, anyway. Tried to talk 'em out of it, till they called him a poof an' that an' then he stopped.'

'We know he was there when Tommy was killed,' Resnick said.

'What d'you need me for, then?'

'Corroboration.'

'What's that?'

Unlike Lewis Morland, in the formality of the interview room, faced with two senior officers, Marshall Boyce folded like a discarded hand of cards. They'd just been going to give Tommy a kicking, he said, learn him to keep his nose out of things as didn't concern him. Only Tommy, 'stead of running, he started to fight back. Caught Marshall one in the face and he had to get him back for that, didn't he? All of 'em laying into him and Tommy, he was leaning back against the wall, lashing out and crying. Marshall was all for letting it be, but Lewis he said, no, teach the little fucker a lesson once and for all. And that was when Tommy scrambled up onto the wall and next you know he'd gone.

'He jumped,' Resnick said. 'Is that what you're saying? Or did he fall? How did it happen?'

Marshall closed his eyes as if remembering.

'Just for this minute, right, he was standing there, staring at us, and then his arms, they started waving like crazy, like he was losing his balance, right? And then he must've gone over backwards, 'cause it was just like suddenly he weren't there.'

'Nobody pushed him?' Resnick asked, a moment later.

Marshall shook his head. 'Nobody had to.'

He made a statement testifying to the names of the others who were present, detailing the part they'd played in the proceedings. All five were arrested and charged with Tommy Johnson's murder. Before it came to trial the CPS might decide to drop the charge down to manslaughter; a persuasive brief might get it lowered further, causing grievous bodily harm, say, but Resnick thought that unlikely.

Several weeks after the men had been remanded in custody, he came face to face with Leah Felix in the Old Market Square and she turned and walked off in another direction. That evening he phoned Tom Whitemore to see if he was planning on going to the Five Ways, but there was no answer. On the way home, he picked up some Polish sausage and potato salad, remembering at the last moment he was low on cat food; too late this evening to get along to the West End Arcade and Music Inn, his CD project now at the end of the Es, *Gil Evans: New Bottle Old Wine.*

Still there was always tomorrow: another day.

Another day for some. Not Tommy Johnson.

PETER JAMES is the author of 25 thrillers, among them seven consecutive *Sunday Times* #1 bestsellers featuring Detective Superintendent Roy Grace. These have been published in 36 languages and have been #1 bestsellers in France, Germany, Russia and Canada. James has also been involved in 26 movies as writer and/or producer, and has competed as a racing driver in the Britcar and other series. He was born in Brighton in 1948.

You'll Never Forget My Face

Peter James

It was almost dark when Laura drove away from the supermarket. Sleet was falling and strains of 'Good King Wenceslas' echoed from the Salvation Army band outside Safeway. She wound down her window and pushed her ticket into the slot. As the barrier swung up, a movement in the rear view mirror caught her eye and she froze.

Black eyes watched her from the darkness of the car's interior. She wanted to get out of the car and scream for help – instead, her right foot pressed down hard on the accelerator and the rusting Toyota shot forward.

She swerved past a van, zigzagged between a startled mother and her children, who were walking on a zebra crossing and raced across a junction.

The eyes watched her, expressionless, in the mirror.

Faster.

The windscreen was frosting over with sleet, but she couldn't find the wipers. She swung out too wide on a bend and the car skidded, heading on to the wrong side of the road. She screamed as the Toyota careered towards the blinding headlights of a lorry.

The lorry's bumper exploded through the windscreen. It slammed into her face, ripping her head from her neck, hurtling it on to the back seat. The car erupted into an inferno. Flames seared her body ...

Then she woke up.

The room was silent. She lay engulfed in a cold sweat and gasping for breath. Suddenly, she remembered the old gypsy woman who'd tried to force a sprig of heather on her outside the supermarket.

The gypsy had blocked her way and been so insistent that Laura had finally lost her temper, shoved past the woman and then snapped, 'Sod off, you hideous old hag!'

The gypsy woman had followed her to the car, rapped on the window, pressed her wizened face with its black piercing eyes against the glass and croaked,

'Look at my face. You'll never forget my face. You'll see it for the rest of your life. The day you stop seeing my face is the day you die!'

Laura turned for comfort towards her sleeping husband. Bill stirred fleetingly. She smelled the raw animal smell of his body, of his hair. He was the rock to which her whole life was anchored.

Christmas Eve tomorrow. It was going to be just the two of them together this time and she had really been looking forward to it . She snuggled closer, wiggled her toes – hoping faintly that he might wake and they could make love – pressed her face against his iron-hard chest and began to feel safe again.

In the middle of the next night, Laura woke again, startled by a sharp rapping. The room was flooded with an eerie sheen of moonlight. Odd, she thought, that she hadn't drawn the curtains.

Then she heard the rapping again and her scalp constricted in terror. The face of the old gypsy woman, a ghastly chalky white, was pressed against the bedroom windowpane.

'Look at my face!' she hissed. 'Look at my face. You'll never forget my face. You'll see it for the rest of your life. The day you stop seeing my face is the day you die!'

Laura turned to Bill with a whine of terror, but he was still sound asleep. 'Bill,' she whimpered. 'Bill!'

'Urrr-wozzit?' he grunted, stirring.

'Someone's at the window,' she said, her voice so tight it was barely audible.

She heard the sound of his hand scrabbling on his bedside table. Then a sharp click and the room flooded with light. She stared fearfully back at the window and a wave of relief washed over her. The curtains were shut!

'Wozzermarrer?' Bill grunted, still half asleep.

'I had a bad dream.' She turned towards him, feeling a little foolish, and kissed him on the cheek. 'I'm sorry.'

In the morning, Bill brought them both breakfast in bed. Then he gave her a huge card, and three gift-wrapped packages. 'Happy Christmas,' he said, and blushed – he was never very good at sentiment.

Laura gave him his presents, an expensive bottle of after-shave and the cordless screwdriver he'd hinted he wanted. Then she opened hers.

The first package was a sweater with daft-looking sheep appliquéd on the front. It made her laugh and she kissed him. The next was a bottle of her favourite bath oil. Then she saw his eyes light up in anticipation as she gripped the final package. It was small, square and heavy.

'I – er – hope you like it,' he mumbled.

With mounting excitement she unwrapped a cardboard box. It was filled with sprigs of heather. Buried in their midst was a small porcelain figurine.

Laura froze.

Bill could sense something was wrong. 'I ... I got it yesterday,' he said. 'For your collection of Capo di Monte peasants. I thought it had ... ' his voice began to falter, '... you know – a real presence about it.'

'Where did you get it?'

'A junk shop – something made me stop there – I just knew I was going to find the perfect present for you inside.'

Quite numb, Laura stared at the black, piercing eyes of the hag that leered up at her with lips peeled back to reveal sharp, rat-like incisors.

'It's lovely,' she said flatly, seeing how hurt he looked. 'Really – lovely.'

Laura kept the figurine on her dressing table over that week, to please Bill, but the thing's presence terrified her.

The following Sunday, he left to drive his container lorry to Italy. She didn't start back at her office until the day after next, so she busied herself with housework. As the afternoon drew on, she felt increasingly uncomfortable.

Finally, she made a snap decision, went to the bedroom, put the figurine in its box, took it outside and dropped it into the dustbin.

Feeling better, she ate supper on a tray and watched a weepy movie on television, wishing Bill was home.

Shortly after eleven, she went upstairs. As she switched the bedroom light on, her eyes fell on the dressing table, and a slick of fear travelled down her spine. The figurine was back, sitting in exactly the same position it had been that morning. Laura's eyes shot to the undrawn curtains, then returned to the dressing table. The floor seemed to sway. She backed unsteadily out of the room, clutching the door frame to stop herself falling, then slammed the door shut.

She stumbled downstairs, pulled the sitting room curtains tight, switched all the bars of the fire on, curled up on the sofa and listened, petrified, for a sound upstairs. She lay there all night, finally dozing for a brief spell around dawn.

In the morning, she put the figurine in the boot of her car, drove to the tip three miles away, and threw it on to the heap. She watched it fall between the discarded fridges, busted sofas and tangle of rubble and old tyres, until it finally disappeared beneath a fire-blackened cushion.

When Laura finally got home, she realised that it was the first time she'd felt at ease since opening that damned present. At two in the morning, she was woken by a sharp rap. The room felt as cold as a deepfreeze. As she switched on the bedside light, she let out a curdling yelp of terror. The figurine was back on her dressing table.

Laura sat up the rest of the night, too frightened to sleep. Next morning, she carried the dreaded figurine out on to the patio and smashed it to smithereens with a hammer. She carried the fragments in a rubbish bag to her office, and during her lunch break dropped them in the incinerator.

All afternoon she felt elated, as if she'd finally freed herself. When she finished work, she drove to the outskirts of town and went to Safeway to do her weekly shop.

As she pushed her trolley down the aisles, she found she was smiling to herself. Smiling at her little triumph and smiling, too, at her own stupidity. Probably the figurine hadn't looked anything like the old gypsy, it was just her wild imagination, the same way she must have imagined throwing it in the bin and on to the tip but hadn't.

'Got spooked by the old hag and now I'm cracking up,' she grinned to herself. 'Silly fool.'

It was nearly dark as she left the store. There was no sign of the gypsy woman, but even so, Laura looked carefully at the back seat of the car before climbing in and quickly locking the doors. She reached the exit, pushed her ticket into the slot and the barrier rose up. As it did, a sudden movement in her rear mirror caught her eye. The temperature plunged. Goose pimples as hard as rivets spiked her skin. In the mirror, she could clearly see the piercing black eyes watching her out of the darkness. The dream flooded back. She remembered how she'd accelerated helplessly and she found her right foot pressing down now. The car surged forward as if it had a will of its own. Laura let out a tiny whimper of fear, saw the rat-like teeth grinning at her in the mirror.

'Got to stop this somehow. Got to change the dream. Got to break the spell.'

Gripping the wheel with both hands, her heart thrashing, she turned to face her tormentor. There was no one there. Just the empty rear seat.

'I imagined her,' she thought, with immense relief 'I imagined her!'

The blare of a horn filled her ears. As she spun her head back to the road, she saw, far too late, the blazing headlights of the oncoming truck. In that last split second before the little Toyota exploded in a fireball, Laura remembered the gypsy's words. 'Look at my face. You'll never forget my face. You'll see it for the rest your life. The day you stop seeing my face is the day you die!'

DENISE MINA is a writer of novels, comics and plays, and a film maker. Her crime novels include the Garnethill Trilogy, the Paddy Meehan books (filmed by BBC Scotland/Slate), and the Alex Morrow books, which have won, among other prizes, two CWA Daggers and Theakstons Novel of the Year. Her comics include *Hellblazer* and *A Sickness in the Family* and she is adapting *The Girl with the Dragon Tattoo*. Her latest book is *The Red Road* (2013). She was born in Glasgow in 1966.

The Calm Before

Denise Mina

I remember that time as if I am living it now, the days before. Not the afterwards, not the noise and the headlines and the wails of the women. It's just before that I remember. Calm.

It was one of those amazing moments when things seem like they were meant, there seemed to be signs everywhere, and I read the signs and knew what they meant. The world made a kind of sense.

All that summer the sea had been spewing up German bombs. They were old, and made a damp phut and sizzle on the water but the lights were beautiful.

They explained on the telly: during the war a German submarine was hit and dumped the bombs just outside the harbour. The bombs tumbled down the side of a deep dark valley, nestling there in their cast iron coats, waiting for their time to come. Then when the summer storms came up they sucked them out of their nest, pulled them along the valley so they shirked their casings and rose like bubbles in ginger beer, up up to the surface, bursting when they reached the air and drew their first breath, sending flashes and splutters of blue and red and orange fire over the water.

They'd been sitting down there for sixty years. All that time they'd been under the water, waiting for the salt to eat through the casing. I know what it takes to wait.

It's dark down there. And cold: They sent an MOD unit to have a look at them and one of the divers got his equipment caught. We watched them drag him onto the boat from the loading bay doors.

They arrived in the town just when I did. How could that happen? Both coming to the town at the same time? A tiny, tiny chance. I thought they were beautiful. You'd be looking out at this grey water and then see a rip, a bob and bright sudden fire defying that broad, grey consensus.

The fishermen hated the bombs. They had to steer around the unexpected fires in the water and the town was losing visitors. In the soap factory they all gathered around the loading doors every lunchtime, looking out to sea and watching, moaning about the tourists not coming and the bed and breakfasts empty and the seal boat trips making no money. I didn't say I liked them. I just watched with the others and tried not to smile. I'm a private person. Being private came to be a precious thing to me. Small spaces that no one else went into. My room, my head and so on. Especially then.

The calm time stays with me. Even now, years later, when anyone says 'soap' I have that sore smell in my nose. The walls smelled, the doors smelled, if you touched any surface it got on your hands and then anything you touched got the smell on it. A stab of smell. When I blew my nose the hankie was full of stinking silver trails. You could tell who worked there if you passed them in the street because they gave it off, sweated it. Disgusting.

Highland. Kelp. Authentic. Traditional. Organic. I don't even know what those words mean. They mean six quid a bar. They mean you're a tourist and don't want to buy a tea towel with a picture of a cow on it.

Remorse. Sorry. Apology. Families left behind. They're all just words.

The village had big hills behind, small white cottages, fishermen going broke and jagging up on smack and being lost at sea. Nothing special. Quite a nice place. You can buy postcards of the sea front in Edinburgh they tell me.

They sent me there because my people were from there. My gran. She'd just died so they offered me her house. It was too big, had two bedrooms and a garden and neighbours. There would have been plumbing needing done and the roof to fix, they said I'd even get a new kitchen but I didn't want to have people to deal with, to have to talk to people. I'm only used to a cell. I took digs. A small room in a house with old Mr Mackay: he used the front door and I used the back. I'm not mental, I'm just private and that's not wrong.

What I remember most about the time is the driving test, before the driving test. I'd been eating beans and second day bread, smoking rollies, saving all my money for the lessons and the deposit. They learn to drive young up there, the instructor said. I was the oldest student he had. I remember before the test. Calm.

I talk about the driving dreams a lot, I know, but it means so much to me. When I have that dream I'm happy all day, even now even when the other meaning is so clear. I can't help it.

In the dream I'm driving my van. There's a space in the back where you could sleep if you got tired and no one could see you, bother you. You could go where you want. I'm driving my van through a summer valley, and my hand is resting on the wheel, warm in the sunshine and my arm's bent, like I've been driving for a long time and I'm tired or something, I don't know. The window's open and maybe the radio's on, I don't know. I feel happy all day when I have that dream.

In the soap factory I just kept my eyes down. To them I was a big city mystery, taken by his dad to live in Glasgow when he was ten and my mother left behind, shamed that her man left and never mentioned me. The factory people asked me about the fashions and the night clubs and the football. I cut it all short.

Everyone knew I was sitting my test soon. I had a deposit down on a van as well but they didn't know that. That was private. One of the supervisors came over to me one day and said even if I did pass the test he'd never let me drive for him, because I'd been in prison. He said it in front of everyone, to shame me because some of them didn't know. I said nothing. When he left I went to the toilet. Locked the door before I let myself smile. He didn't know what I'd been in for. He was the kind of man who'd have said if he knew. That's the kind of man he was.

They knew I went to the police station every week but they must have thought it was just a parole thing. They didn't see me sign and the polis never told anyone. Cause of my gran I suppose. Out of respect.

Come out of there, someone knocked on the toilet door. He kept talking and talking so I told him I'd been done for armed robbery. Next day they were all nice to me. Some of the women tried to talk to me.

The women didn't drive the truck or anything, they wrapped the bars and made bows on them, they kept them kind of separate and I was glad. It was so long since I'd met a woman, I don't know what to say to them. It's been so long now I don't know if I'll ever meet another one.

Sandra, she didn't talk to me. She blushed when she saw me. I thought she hated me, actually, I've never been good at reading women. I'd heard that her man died on the boats and she didn't go with loads of guys so she wasn't a slag or anything.

I never thought I'd miss the group but I did, not the team leaders that ran it, just the other guys.

We had our own group. We had our own everything actually because we couldn't mix with the other prisoners. They'd kill you if they got you alone. They killed one old guy, found him in a garden and stabbed him with a shovel. They hated us but I didn't see how we were different. We all took things we shouldn't.

In the calm, the signs made me feel that things would be okay, that I'd pass and things would become clear. And then they did.

It was a week before the driving test. We were standing at the factory doors, lunch time, a storm the night before had sucked some bombs up and they were bursting once in a while and we were all watching while we ate soap sandwiches. I saw her looking at me. Sandra, yellow hair, no ear rings, no holes, I liked that. She kept her face to the sea but her red eyes were sliding to the side, looking at me. She likes you, one of them said, you should come to the pub tonight, we're all going. She'll be there.

I didn't go. I don't know what to say. I'm not a confident talker.

They made me talk in the group. I learned how they teach you to talk and I can do it but I'd rather sit in my room or listen to the radio or watch through the window for the bombs on the water.

Next day Sandra's friend came over. Come to the pictures with her. I thought that was good because it would be dark and we wouldn't need to talk. We could just sit.

We saw a film about a pig. After we went back to the her house and she made us chips. She had two sons and a daughter and her name was Morag.

I walked home. Smoking. Feeling heavy. We hadn't talked too much and that was good. She was good looking. Not flash but tidy looking. Wore brown, but still I wasn't right about it. And when I stopped I looked out over the harbour wall and saw the next sign. As I watched that exact spot two bombs came out of the water at the exact same time and went off, their flames touching in the dark. I knew then. It would be okay.

Once in the group, we had a laugh. Jamie started telling his story. He got the words in that they liked: remorse, damage, impulse. We knew before they did that he was telling it the wrong way, we were all smiling at each other, hands hiding mouths. He went a long way into it before they stopped him. It was a story about creeping through houses, moving in the dark, about smells from hair.

Mum left the village when she heard I was coming. She left. I don't even know why I'm surprised, to be honest. I should have known. That's exactly the sort of women she was. She didn't write to me, not once. She came to see me only once when I was in prison before and she didn't bring me smokes or anything. It was all sobbing and god-forgive – wicked – wicked man, that child that child. I know she was going to takes sides but if she was going to take anyone's side it should have been mine. I mean I understand better now, since being in the group but I'm her only son. Other guys in the group had family. They sent letters. One guy raped his wife and battered her to death with a brick and his sisters came every month, for christ sakes. Brought his kids.

I passed my driving test. I went home and cried. A man. Crying. Sitting on the end of my bed and crying. I couldn't stop, I just couldn't make the breath get into my lungs. When I looked up, eventually, it was dark outside. The wind was up. I heard shutters slamming all over the village. Rain was sheeting down over the water and the streets emptied. It was the biggest storm of the summer.

I left my digs. I climbed up the hill overlooking the harbour, higher than where you'd walk, up to where I was scrabbling on scree and I sat down, sweating from the walk. Bombs were bursting all over the water, as far as the eye could see, like a million Viking funerals and I was out of denial now. I undid my flies and slipped my hand inside. I was Jamie now.

I was driving through the summer valley, with my space in the back where no one can see. The window is open, a breeze coming in, and the sun is warming my hand. And on the seat next to me is Morag, not yet crying, not yet afraid, and the smell of soap is far far behind us both.

ADRIAN MCKINTY was born in 1968 in Carrickfergus, Northern Ireland. He studied politics and philosophy at Oxford before emigrating to New York in the early 1990s where he worked for seven years in bars, building sites and bookstores. In 2000 he moved to Denver to become a high school English teacher and in 2008 he moved again, this time to Melbourne, Australia. He has published fourteen novels and is best known for his crime series featuring Belfast rebel detective Sean Duffy.

The Ladder

Adrian McKinty

Donald sighed as the university loomed out of the rain and greyness. All morning he had hit nothing but red lights and now, although it was green, he had to stop because a huge gang of students was crossing the pedestrian walkway in front of him.

It was rag week and they were wearing costumes: animals, Cossacks, knights, milkmaids. Predictable and drab, the outfits had a home-made look and they depressed him. The students were laughing and some were actually skipping. It was raining, it was cold, it was November in Belfast: what had they to laugh about?

The traffic light went red and then amber and then green again and still they hadn't all got across. He was tempted to honk them off the road but no doubt from hidden pockets they would produce flour and water bombs and throw them at him. He sat there patiently while the car behind began to toot. He looked in the rear view mirror at a vulnerable, orange VW Microbus. Yeah, you keep doing that mate, he said to himself and sure enough a half a dozen eggs cut up the poor fool's windscreen.

He chortled to himself, the mob cleared and he turned into the car park.

'Jesus, is that a grin?' McCann asked him when he appeared in the office.

He nodded.

'What, have you got a job offer somewhere?' McCann wondered.

'No old chap, I am doomed to spend my declining years with your boorish self and my cretinous students in this provincial hell hole of a city that is slowly sinking into the putrid mudflats from which it so inauspiciously began.'

'If I'd known I was going to get an essay ...' McCann said, not all that good-naturedly.

Donald took off his jacket and set it down on the chair. 'Is this coffee drinkable?' he asked staring dubiously at the tarry black liquid in the coffee pot.

'Drinkable yes. Distinguishable as coffee, no.'

Donald poured himself a cup anyway, added two sugars and picked up the morning paper.

'Before I lose interest entirely, why were you smiling when you came in? Some pretty undergraduate no doubt?' McCann asked.

'No, no, nothing like that I'm afraid. The students went after some hippy driving a VW Microbus, talk about devouring your own.'

'Aye. I've seen that thing around. New guy. Been parking in my spot. Kicked his side panels a few times. Buckled like anything. It's an original. Those old ones are bloody death traps.'

'A windscreen covered with eggs and flour won't make it any safer.'

McCann took out his pipe and began filling it with tobacco. Donald went back to the paper. 'So what's on the old agenda today anyway?' McCann asked.

'Nothing in the morning. Playing squash at lunch time and then we're doing the Miller's Tale after lunch.'

'The Miller's Tale? Which one's that?'

'Do you actually want to know?'

'Well, not really I suppose,' McCann replied, somewhat shamefaced.

The hours passed by in a haze of tobacco smoke, bad coffee, worse biscuits and dull news from the paper.

At twelve Donald slipped off only to be intercepted by a student outside the gym. 'Dr Bryant,' the student began in a lilting voice and Donald remembered that he was a Welshman called Jones or Evans or something.

'Mr Jones how can I help you today?'

'Uh, actually my name is –'

'Yes, Mr Jones, how I can help you? Come on. Out with it man. I'm in a hurry.'

'Uhm, Dr Bryant, I'm supposed to do a presentation next week on Jonson ...'

'Ben or Sam or, God save us, Denis?'

'Uhhh, the playwright.'

'They all wrote plays, Mr Jones.'

'They did? Uhm, well, it's Ben. Yeah. And, well, the library doesn't have the secondary sources, someone took them all and I don't know what to do really. I tried to borrow them from the University of Ulster library but they're out too. I've read all the primary stuff, but I want the secondary sources to do a good job.'

Donald felt a pin prick of guilt. Mr Jones seemed like a nice, sincere, young man. One of the few good students. He was studying engineering but was taking English as an elective. Perhaps that explained his curious dedication. The BAs in English were all layabouts and druggies. 'All right Mr Jones come by my office at four today and I'll lend you my own books, they should be sufficient for a half decent presentation. You'll be careful with them won't you?'

'Oh God yeah, thank you, thank you very much,' the student said.

Donald arrived at the gym feeling unnaturally buoyant – two quite pleasant incidents in one morning.

He showed his ID to Peter Finn the ancient security guard at the reception desk.

'Afternoon, Dr Bryant,' Peter said in his rough country accent.

'Afternoon,' he replied curtly.

'Going to give the wee muckers another hiding eh?'

'One tries, Peter, one tries.'

'You still at the top?' Peter asked, knowing full well the answer.

Donald swelled a little. 'Still plugging away.'

'Sixteen straight months, Professor Millin says. Yon's a record ye know,' Peter said very seriously.

'Is it indeed?' Donald said and this time it was his turn to pretend.

'Aye.'

'Well all good things must come to an end sometime. This new crop of lecturers is giving me a run for my money,' Donald said magnanimously.

Peter winked at him as if he didn't quite believe him.

Donald grinned, went to the basement, found locker 201 and changed quickly into his gear: a casual blue t-shirt, white shorts, white socks and an old pair of Adidas squash sneakers. He looked at himself in the mirror. He was in the prime of life. His eyes were clear, his cheeks clean shaved, his hair jet black with only a few strands of invading grey around the ears.

Fenton was late and Donald tried hard not to show his irritation. Fenton was a slightly younger man and he was nimble. He was number three on the squash ladder and by no means an unworthy opponent. Fenton playing above his game and Donald playing beneath his could pretty much even out the field. Fenton changed into his kit: pristine white shorts, Fred Perry top and a brand new racket.

They walked to the court, stretched, warmed up the ball.

Donald won the racquet spin.

He served a high looping ball that died in the corner. Fenton made an attempt to return it but he had no chance. Donald served five more like that before Fenton managed to get one back and by that time it was too late – his confidence was broken. Donald won the match three games to one, Fenton's sole game coming from Donald's largesse. When he was in control it was Donald's policy always to let an opponent win at least one game so that no one would ever know the true picture of his ability.

They showered and had a quick gin and tonic in the bar before Donald went off to his lecture. It was nearly a full house, the students didn't ask stupid questions and he was in good form when he set off for home at four o'clock. Half way to the car he remembered about young Jones and went back to his office. Amazingly the undergraduate was on time and he gave him the books without further ado.

'Quite the day,' he said to himself as he walked to his Volvo estate under a clearing sky. Susan noticed his good mood immediately as he picked her up outside the Ulster Bank on Botanic Avenue. 'You're in a good mood,' she said.

'Yes,' he said. 'Let's eat out at the new Italian.'

'What about your eggplant lasagne?'

'We'll give it to the dog.'

'What dog?'

'Any dog.'

The drive to Carrickfergus was easy, the new Italian was acceptable, the sommelier complimented him on his choice of wine.

He parked the Volvo outside his neat, mock-Tudor detached house near the Marina. After another cheeky bottle of Tuscan red he and Susan had sex only slightly less exciting than that he'd been lecturing about this afternoon in the Miller's Tale.

As days go, it wasn't bad and when the university loomed out of the mist next morning, this time he didn't sigh.

Susan, getting a lift to Belfast for the shopping, smiled at him.

'It's growing on you,' she said.

'Perhaps,' he agreed.

'You're playing Fenton today in your silly squash thing, aren't you?'

'Oh no that was yesterday. And it's not silly. He was the third seed. Psyched him out completely, poor chap. Went to pieces. Had to go easy on him.'

'So you're still top of the ladder?'

Donald was a little surprised at the question. Of course he was still top. Did she seriously think he could take her out to the expensive new Italian restaurant, get the priciest plonk on the menu and be happy as a clam if he was off the top? My God what kind of cipher did she think she'd married.

'Oh yes, I think so,' he said casually.

She started talking about something or other but he was replaying the game in his mind, wondering if his backhand was still quite as strong as his lob. He left her outside the bank.

'So you'll drive me to the soup kitchen on Saturday?' she asked, getting out of the car.

'I'll drive you,' he said and then after a pause added: 'What soup kitchen, what are you talking about?'

'Haven't you been listening? Our reading group. That book really affected us and we're volunteering at the soup kitchen on Saturday. Christmas is coming you know.'

He tried to think what the book could be. Something by Orwell perhaps, or Dickens, or some ghastly novel set among the poor of India.

'Of course I'll drive you. In fact I think I'll even go. Help out.'

'You?' she said incredulously.

'Me, yes. Why so shocked? I'm a Labour man through and through. I would have preferred David to Ed but that's neither here nor there. Help the common people, each according to his needs and from, uh, you know … that's my motto,' he said with only half sarcasm, for she had hurt him a little with her surprise.

The week went by like every other week and on Saturday he did help out in the soup kitchen and it was by no means completely unpleasant. Some of the indigent were witty and grateful fellows fallen on hard times and he felt, if not happy, at least content.

The following Monday morning Mr Jones gave his presentation and it wasn't bad and that afternoon he played squash with Professor Millin in the gym. Millin was number six on the ladder, not a serious opponent. An older man, a physics lecturer, well into his forties, although last week he had taken a game off Dunleavy who was currently in second place and Dunleavy was the sort who never let anyone have a game, ever.

'Heard you gave old Fred Dunleavy a run for his money,' Donald said conversationally as they walked down to the court.

'The big Scots ganch, I showed him, he's slipping, he's really slipping, getting a paunch, I tell you, you'll cream him next time you play him, cream him,' Millin said.

Donald was happy to hear this. Dunleavy was a young physical education lecturer and for some time it had been his fear that Dunleavy would one day pull a superb game out of the bag and beat him.

'He's been avoiding me for weeks, I suppose that's why,' Donald said with satisfaction.

They paused outside the court to stretch. Donald looked at the squash ladder and was surprised to see a new name way down at the bottom, at number sixteen: VM Sinya.

'Who's that?' he said pointing at the name. Millin was the Ladder Secretary for this term, so he should know.

'Oh yes, new fella, foreigner, bloody Pak ... er, I mean, uh, an Indian gent I think. Initials stand for Victor Mohammed so I suppose he's a Muslim. He's from Computer Science. A lot of those boys do computers nowadays.'

'Is he any good?' Donald asked with a hint of nervousness in his voice. Anyone new could be trouble and several world champions had come from Pakistan.

'How the hell should I know?' Millin replied with great indifference.

'All right let's go in,' Donald said putting all ominous thoughts of the newcomer out of his mind.

He let Millin have a few points early before cruising to an easy victory in four games. He showered, picked up Susan and drove home.

On Thursday the Dean told him that his student evaluations were up since last term and, after buttering him up, asked if he'd ever considered standing for the University Council. He had no such intention but the thought that the Dean was interested in him pleased him immensely.

On Friday he had a game with McCann who was number twelve on the ladder. McCann had been quite a useful little player until the drink had become the dominant force in his life. Now all he was left with was a powerful serve and a few trick shots. He had no stamina and he couldn't get about the court. Donald never usually bothered to play anyone this low down but McCann was a friend. When he got to the court he was pleased to see that Mr VM Sinya was still at number sixteen. He hadn't even been able to beat old Franklin at fifteen, clearly the man wasn't much of a threat. He found that he was tremendously relieved by this. Was the ladder so important to him that the thought of a mysterious stranger had given him the jitters? He laughed at himself. What a dunderhead you are, he said to himself, and to prove his good humour he let McCann take a couple of games.

On Saturday he was still feeling sufficiently good to help out at the soup kitchen. Also at the weekend he received a letter that one of his papers on Chaucer was going to be anthologised in the new collection by Dalrimple. Things, in fact, were going so well that he began to be suspicious that something terrible was going to happen. Perhaps he would be informed that he had some dreadful illness or maybe he would crash the car.

Just in case he took the train to work on Monday, sitting in a back carriage near the emergency exit and steeling himself for a sudden derailment.

Nothing happened except for fifty gum-chewing, messy, obnoxious children getting on at Greenisland who tormented him all the way to Central Station with their music and pointless celebrity gossip.

His fears of impending disaster were somewhat realised when he showed up at the court to play Dunleavy and he saw that the mysterious Mr Sinya was at number ten on the squash ladder. The man had demolished five opponents in a week! This meant, of course, that he had displaced McCann, so at least he could interrogate his friend at lunch.

In an unusually brutal and hurried match he thrashed Dunleavy, showered quickly and found McCann in the office eating toast and drinking tea mixed with whisky.

'What's Sinya like?' he blurted out before even saying hello.

'Sinya? I've no idea, mate.'

'You played him.'

'I gave him a bye, he wanted to play me on Friday lunch-time and I just couldn't be bothered.'

'You gave him a bye?'

'Yes.'

'So maybe that's why he's jumped up the ladder? People have been giving him byes.'

'Aye, could be,' McCann said, not at all interested.

Relief sunk over Donald like chloroform and again he chastised himself for the importance he had given to something so silly as the squash ladder.

The relief lasted until Wednesday when he bumped into Millin coming out of the university bookshop. Millin informed him that Sinya had demolished him and that he, Sinya, was now number five on the ladder.

'What's he like?' Donald asked, trying not to sound frantic or panicked.

'Oh he's good. Going to give you a pretty tough game.'

'What's he like?' Donald insisted.

'Don't get your knickers in a twist. He's Pakistani. I suppose forty, perhaps older, it's hard to tell with them. He's fast and my God that serve, those returns. It's a nightmare. You give him any opportunity and he destroys you. Our match was over in half an hour.'

Donald went home that night in a state of distress. He barely talked to Susan and he couldn't concentrate on his proofs for the Dalrimple book.

From his upstairs study he stared at the boats in Carrickfergus marina and the grey castle beyond. The boat hallyards were muzzled by the wind, the granite castle walls kept their own counsel.

Could it be that the squash ladder was perhaps the one thing that gave him any satisfaction, any sense of accomplishment, in what was really a rather pathetic, little, nondescript life?

Not the teaching, not the writing, not even Susan.

And now, inevitably, he was going to face his nemesis. It was a melodramatic thought but he couldn't shake it.

A few days later the phone rang in his office. With a sense of dread he picked up the receiver. Naturally it was Sinya.

He had beaten Fenton and Dunleavy and he would like to play Donald whenever it was convenient.

His voice was pleasant enough, foreign but not very foreign and gentle. Aye that's how they get you, Donald thought. Softly softly. Lull you and then go for the jugular. Bastards. Well he wouldn't let them. He wouldn't take this lying down. This was his league, his campus. Who did this guy think he was for Christ's sake? He'd been going easy on these chumps, he could take them all with one hand behind his back. This guy was no different. Try to spook me? See about that. He realised that during this prolonged internal soliloquy Sinya had been waiting for a reply on the other end of the phone.

'This afternoon's fine with me. 1 p.m.' he said quickly, hung up and attempted to bury himself in work until just before the match.

He arrived early but Sinya was already there, changed, waiting for him. They shook hands. Sinya was tall, bearded, good looking. He had a very charming way about him. He smiled easily and was polite. He asked Donald how he was and inquired about Donald's new (bought yesterday) super light, super strong, carbon fibre, state of the art, Khan Slazinger Pro, racket.

Sinya won the spin, served, and launched a tremendous dying serve that Donald barely returned, but of course Sinya was already at the front wall waiting to volley Donald's weak backhand. Donald, anticipating a crushing return, ran to the back right of the court, but Sinya placed a perfect drop shot in the left front corner, flat footing Donald and winning the point. Sinya won the next four points and then missed one. On Donald's serve Sinya volleyed the ball back so fast Donald didn't even see it until it was too late.

The whole match went that way, Donald's play grew worse and forty-five minutes later it was all over. Donald had managed to take a game but Sinya had well beaten him 9–5, 9–4, 7–9, 9–1. Shell shocked he let Sinya prattle on about this and that and then watched with horror as Sinya stopped at the notice board outside the court and had the cheek to take out Donald's name from the top of the ladder and substitute his own. Couldn't the bastard even have the decency to wait until he was showering?

He drove home and after four hours of silence Susan got it out of him and of course he agreed that it was only a stupid game and it meant nothing. The next day he went to the court with his new racket and practised serves and drop shots for an hour and called Sinya and asked him for a rematch.

The rematch was on a Friday and this time Sinya took him in straight sets. He realised with horror that Sinya had given him the game he'd won last time as a courtesy, just as he had condescendingly done with the lesser players in his bouts.

They walked back to car park and Sinya stopped at the repulsive Volkswagen Microbus Donald had seen egged by the rag week students.

'Do you want a lift?' Sinya asked. 'You're in Carrick aren't you? I drive all the way to Larne so it would be easy to drop you.'

The fact that Sinya lived in Larne, one of the grimmest towns in Ulster, gave Donald no comfort in the silent ride home.

Sinya's reign at the top began and seemed unbreakable. He was miles ahead of all the players. In fact if he'd been younger he could well have been an international. Weeks went by and Donald played him on and off with little effect. On a weekend game with Fenton, Donald unexpectedly lost, and after another fortnight he was only at number four on the ladder.

Despite the repeated assurances of his wife, his friends and even, on one humiliating occasion, the university's psychological counsellor, that it was only a senseless cardboard list of names, he felt that his work, his health, his libido and his mental outlook all were suffering terribly as he slipped down the ladder.

Christmas came and went, term ended and began again.

McCann was no comfort but he found himself spending a lot of time with him in Lavery's or the Bot enjoying increasingly frequent liquid lunches.

At the gym he noticed now that Peter Finn was cool to him at the door. On a miserable Tuesday morning he played a man called Jennings, lost in straight games and found that he was now last on the ladder. He almost relished this final embarrassment. Now there was no place lower to go.

He slipped upstairs to the cafeteria, called Susan and asked if she could get a lift back to Carrick with one of her friends. He sat, nursing a coffee, watching the sky darken and the lights come on street by street, Sandy Row, the Shankill, the Falls, the illumination moving north to the old shipyards and then down around the university and the City Hospital. In Belfast tonight there would be violence and love and passion and death. People in the hospital would be passing away from cancer, accidents, heart disease and in other wards dozens of babies were being born. New lives for old.

'It really isn't that important you know, old man,' he said to himself.

'What isn't important?'

He turned. It was Mr Jones, his student from last term's course on the Elizabethans. He was holding a book called *Automotive Engineering Mistakes*.

'Oh, I was just talking to myself. Join me. Have a seat. What on earth are you reading?'

Jones sat. 'It's about design faults in cars. Not just the Ford Pinto. Some pretty famous cars. Even brilliant designers make mistakes.'

He got Jones a coffee.

Something McCann had once said came floating back into Donald's mind.

'I've heard that those old Volkswagen Microbuses are a death trap,' he said.

Jones grinned. 'Oh yeah! No crumple zone at the front to absorb a crash and the exhaust pipe runs the full length of the floor ... oh boy, you get a hole in the pipe and a hole in the floor and your vehicle's filled with carbon monoxide, death trap isn't the ...'

But Donald was no longer listening.

It would be the easiest thing in the world.

Punch a hole through the floor and the exhaust.

Punch a hole. Let fate take over. If nothing happened, nothing happened. But if Sinya got into an unfortunate accident in the long drive from Belfast to Larne, well, it wouldn't really be his fault. It wouldn't be murder, or attempted murder. It was a design flaw in the vehicle, he was helping nature take its course.

He said goodnight to Jones, ran six flights to the first floor and out into the wet, cold January darkness.

He knew that it would have to be now. Tonight. If he thought about it, he wouldn't do it at all. He conscience would kick in. His middle class sensibility. His cowardice.

It would have to be now or never.

He reached the car park. It was six o'clock. Most of the vehicles had gone but the putrid yellow Volkswagen was still there. Sinya often worked late, trying to get ahead no doubt, Donald thought spitefully. He went to his Volvo, rummaged in the trunk and found a torch and his toolkit. He locked the trunk and walked to the Volkswagen.

'I'm not going to do this, it's not me,' he said to himself.

He checked that the coast was clear. No one was within a hundred yards.

'I don't even know what to do. Should have asked Jones for details. Doesn't matter, I'm not going to do anything. I'm not a killer. What I *will* do is take a look underneath, just to see if it's possible.'

He scanned the car park again, turned on the torch, squatted on the wet tarmac and looked under the VW. A great hulking exhaust pipe ran almost all the way from the front of the cabin to the back of the car. The pipe was rusted, the chassis was rusted. A few taps from a screwdriver might do the trick ...

He stood, checked the car park one more time.

No one.

He was calm.

He lay back down again.

In five minutes it was done.

He had punched a hole in the top of the exhaust pipe and another through to the cabin. He had connected the two holes with a paper coffee cup he had found lying around – squeezing the cup into a tube. If an accident did occur the cup would burn in the fire and if didn't it was an innocent enough thing to find stuck under your car.

He wiped himself down, got in his car, sped to the Crown Bar, had two pints of Guinness to calm his nerves and drove home.

In his study he had a double vodka and a cognac but he couldn't sleep.

Susan went to bed and he checked the radio for reports of road accidents, deaths.

He really didn't want Sinya to die. If the poor man was injured that would be enough. Then Donald could resume his march back up the squash ladder and get his life back in order. Get to the top, stop drinking with McCann, start writing his book, have that talk with Susan about kids again ...

Finally he drifted off to sleep on the living room sofa at about three. He woke before the dawn in the midst of a nightmare. Sinya's Volkswagen had plunged off the cliff at the Bla Hole just outside of Whitehead. Two hundred feet straight down into the rocks below. The car had smashed and it was assumed to be an accident but the police had found a paper cup wedged in the exhaust. The murderer had left fingerprints all over it.

Five years earlier Donald had been arrested for cannabis possession at Sussex University. His prints were in the database.

'Oh my God,' he said.

He turned on the radio, found the traffic report: a road accident in Omagh, another in County Down, nothing so far on the Belfast–Larne Road.

He paced the living room. What madness had overtaken him? To try to kill a man over something so preposterous as a squash ladder? He had obviously taken leave of his senses. That's what he'd do at trial. He'd plead temporary insanity.

Insane was the right world. Macbeth crazy. Lear crazy.

Susan woke and he was such a mess that she drove him to Belfast.

He thanked her and ran to the car park.

The Volkswagen wasn't there.

'Oh Christ,' he said to himself.

He cancelled his lecture, went to his office and waited for the telephone to ring. He imagined the phone ringing, the resulting brief conversation:

'Is that Dr Bryant?

'Yes.'

'This is Detective McGuirk, we'd like to come over and ask you a few questions if that would be ok ...'

He found an ancient packet of cigarettes, lit one and sat in his onyx Eclipse Ergonomic Operator Chair waiting. The phone lurked in its cradle ...

There was a knock at the door but it was only McCann come by to see if he wanted to go for lunch. He said he wasn't feeling well. It wasn't untrue. He felt sick to his stomach. McCann left. He closed the door and turned the light off. He sat there in the dark. Perhaps they wouldn't ring him. The first he would know about it would be them marching into his office with guns drawn.

He wouldn't go with them. He wouldn't let them take him. His office was on the sixth floor. The window. A brief fall through the damp air. A crash. And then ... nothingness.

He waited.

Waited.

He sank beneath his desk and curled foetally on the floor.

The phone rang.

'Dr Bryant?'

'Sinya?'

'Yes.'

It was Sinya. He was alive!

'Yes?' Donald managed.

'Dr Bryant, Professor Millin cancelled with me today and I was wondering if you could squeeze in a quick game?'

'A game? A squash game? Yes, yes, of course, I'll be right over.'

He sprinted the stairs.

Sinya was already in the court warming the ball.

He waved to him through the glass, ran to the locker room, changed into his gear and ran back to the court without stretching or getting a drink of water.

He didn't care how suspicious or unsubtle he sounded. He *had* to know.

'I didn't see your car this morning. You're always in first,' Donald said.

Sinya grimaced. 'That thing tried to kill me. I was half way home last night and I realised the whole car was stinking of exhaust fumes, I pulled over just before White-head. Would you believe it, the whole exhaust is rusted away next to nothing and a paper cup had blown in there and gotten stuck between the exhaust and the car. I left it at the garage in Whitehead and got a taxi home. I suppose I'll have to get it fixed.'

Donald grinned with relief.

Emotions were cascading through him: relief, happiness, gratitude.

He would inform Susan tonight that she should go off the pill. He would start going to that soup kitchen again. He would give to charity. He would really get cracking on the book.

This would be his last squash game ever.

'I have really screwed up my priorities, darling,' he'd tell Susan. 'That silly squash ladder! Something as banal as that. I'm going to be more Zen. Live in the present, live in reality. Real things. You, me, life, stuff like that. It's corny but, well, I've had a moment of clarity. It's about perspective. It all seems so bloody stupid now. God. I mean can you believe how obsessed I was?'

Sinya hit him a few practice shots which he returned with ease.

'Well I'm sorry about your car, old chap, but I think you can afford a new vehicle with the money they're paying you in computers. And Larne isn't the priciest place in the world to live. You should be more like me. Enjoy life. Live for the moment. Get yourself a Merc or a Beemer. You deserve it,' Donald said.

Sinya laughed. 'Are you kidding? The university only gives me three hundred and fifty a week, you know. A BMW on my wages?'

'Three hundred and fifty a week? What are you talking about? A junior lecturer makes twenty-five grand a year. It's more in computers I'm sure.'

Sinya grinned. 'I'm not a lecturer. I'm a technician in the computer department. I fix the machines, man. Hardware, software, you name it.'

Donald gasped but said nothing.

The game began and Sinya took a mere thirty-five minutes to beat him.

They showered, talked about the weather, shook hands, parted ways.

Donald walked to the English department building.

No one knew, no one had to know.

When he got to his office he called Millin and told him.

Millin was outraged. 'Doesn't the fellow know that the ladder is only open to faculty? My God, the effrontery.'

'You'll do something about it?'

'Of course I will. Right away. I'll scrub the last two months' results and put it back to the way it was at the beginning of December.'

Donald hung up the phone. Leaned back in his chair.

Grey sky.

Black sky.

Night.

Stars.

In the car Susan talked about the soup kitchen, birth control. He avoided giving direct answers. They ate separate microwaved meals from Marks and Spencer.

When he got into work the next morning he went straight to the gym. VM Sinya's name had disappeared and he, Dr D. Bryant, was again in the number one spot, for the first time in nearly two months.

'The once and future king,' Peter said at reception, startling him.

'Yes,' he attempted to reply, but his throat was dry and no sound came.

JAMES SALLIS's books include 15 novels, multiple collections of stories, essays and poems, the standard biography of Chester Himes, and a translation of Raymond Queneau's novel *Saint Glinglin*. He has been awarded the Hammett Award for literary excellence in crime writing, a lifetime achievement award from Bouchercon, and the Grand Prix de Littérature policière. Born in Helena, Arkansas, in 1944, he now lives in Phoenix, Arizona.

Venice Is Sinking Into the Sea

James Sallis

She loved him, Dana thinks, more than most, as she walks in the small park across from the house she's rented for twelve years now. A Craftsman house from the thirties, two bedrooms, living room, kitchen, all of them much of a size. This time of morning the park's filled with the homeless. They appear each day as the sun comes up, depart each evening, trailing off into the sunset with their bedrolls, clusters of overstuffed plastic bags, shopping carts. Occasionally she wonders where it is they go. Lord, she was going to miss him.

Almost no traffic on the street where late each Friday night you can hear hot cars running against one another. Dana walks leisurely across to have coffee and a bagel at Einstein's. She knows the bagels are bogus (she's from the city, after all), but she loves them. Feels much the same way about the muscular firemen who hang out here most days.

Sean was a fireman. Smaller than most, right at the line, which meant he'd always had to work harder, do more, to make the grade. Same in bed. 'I'm always humping,' he'd once said, unconscious of irony. Despite his size, or because of it, he'd gone right up (as it were) the ladder, promotion after promotion. With each promotion he was less and less at home, more and more preoccupied when there beside her.

Sean was the first, messy one.

She'd never much liked Dallas anyway, and started up a new life in Boston. Brookline, actually, wherefrom she hitched rides, in those trusting, vagabond sixties, to the library downtown. Her apartment house was up three long, zigzag terraces from the street. Furniture from salvage stores filled it, a faded leather love seat, stacked mattress and box springs, formica kitchen table standing on four splayed feet, edged with a wide band of ridged steel. Wooden chairs that seemed to have legs all of different lengths. A line of empty fishbowls.

Almost every day back then they'd be flushed out of the library because of bomb threats. There was never a bomb, just the threats, and the dogs and the bomb squad filing in. The announcement came over an intercom used for nothing else but to call closing time. Patrons would gather outside on the square (this in itself seemed so very Boston, so old America) and wait, fifteen minutes, thirty, an hour, to be allowed back in. One of those times, Will Barrett Jr struck up a conversation with her. He was there reading up on subarachnoid hemorrhages. Couldn't get into the Mass General computers, he said, and had to evacuate one the next day. They never made it back into the library. Had moderate quantities of bad Italian food, inordinate quantities of good beer, the whole of an amazing night. She never asked how his patient had fared.

She'd hang there naked and shivering, steam banging in the radiators, twelve degrees outside (he always left the radio on), waiting for him to come home, thighs streaming with desire and the morning's deposition of semen. Because she wouldn't let herself become a victim, and because that was what he wanted, she became instead a kind of animal. Smelled it on him, another woman, one day when he came home and unlocked the cuffs. She'd learned a lot by then. That one wasn't messy.

Wayne worked at the Boston Globe, writing what they call human interest features. Roxbury woman puts three kids through college scrubbing floors, the emperor of shoeshine stands, Mister John sees the city from his front porch, that sort of thing. Most of it Wayne simply made up. Each morning four or five newspapers showed up in his driveway, the *Globe*, *New York Times*, *Washington Post*, *Wall Street Journal*, *L.A. Times*. He never read them. He'd sit around all day drinking beer and watching TV and after dinner he'd go into his office and tap out his column on a tan IBM Selectric. This would take an hour, tops. Then he'd call the paper. They'd send a messenger over. Wayne would join Dana to watch whatever was on at nine. Many times, the next morning, she'd be able to see in the column pieces of what they'd watched on TV in early evening. For a month, maybe two, the sex was great, then it was nonexistent. For a long time Dana didn't understand that. Then she remembered how Wayne was always grabbing something new, holding on for dear life for an hour or two, letting go. Ask him about that mother out in Roxbury and he wouldn't even remember.

Simply amazing, what you can do with a hat pin. You introduce it at the base of the skull, just under the hair line. They weren't easy to find these days, but soon, haunting antique shops, she had a collection of them. Plain hat pins, hat pins tipped with pink pearl, with abalone or plastic. Her favourite had a head with a tiny swan carved of ivory. They were amazingly long.

Jamie worked on the floor at the Chicago Stock Exchange, pushing will and voice above the crowd to move capital from here to there. He did well, but the work seemed to absorb all his energies. He came home ready and able to do little more than eat the takeout Chinese he brought and watch mindless TV – sitcoms and their like. Night after night Dana lay throbbing and alone, wondering how it had ever come about that she'd attached herself to this man.

St Louis then, heart of the heartland, about which Dana remembered little more than the man's name, the Western shirts he favoured, the look of his eyes in the mirror.

Minnesota, where for weeks at the time ice lay on the land like a solid sea and blades of wind hung spinning in the air.

New York, finally. Home. Where she thought she'd be safe with Jonas, her obscure writer who published in small magazines no one read, and should have known better. Essentially a hobbyist, she thought. Now to everyone's surprise, his more than anyone else's, Jonas is fast becoming a bestseller. His novel, written in a week, went into six printings. *McSweeney's* and the *Times* are calling him up. So tonight, after the dinner she's spent hours preparing for him, coq au vin and white asparagus with garlic butter (cookbook propped on the window ledge), a good white wine, cheese and fruit, he excuses himself 'to get some writing done'.

He's been writing all day.

'What are you working on?' she asks.

'Couple of things, really. That piece for *Book World*'s almost due. And yesterday I got an idea for a new story.'

Later she enters what he's dubbed The Factory, a second bedroom apparently intended for a family with a dwarf child. His desk takes up most of one wall. Two filing cabinets occupy the opposite corners, by the door, and books are stacked along the walls. Pushed back from the desk, he has the keyboard in his lap, eyes on the screen. There she sees the words 'Death by misadventure'.

No. By unfaithfulness, rather.

Because he loves something else more than he loves her.

She stands quietly watching. He is concentrating on the story and never realises she's there with him. As he scrolls to the top of the screen, the title appears: 'Venice Is Sinking Into the Sea.'

It's a story about her, of course.

She who lifts her hand now, she whose hair is so beautiful as it begins to fall.

MAXIM JAKUBOWSKI was born in 1944 in London but educated in France. He opened the Murder One bookshop which he ran for over 20 years alongside London's Crime Scene Film and Literary Festival. He has written 15 novels, with a predilection for crime and erotica, and has edited over 100 genre anthologies, including the prestigious annual Mammoth Book of Best Crime. A winner of the Karel and Anthony awards, his latest novel is *Ekaterina And The Night*. Under another name, he makes regular appearances in the bestseller lists.

My Life as a Killer

Maxim Jakubowski

My nights are full of guilt. A price I am willing to pay.

The way to look at it is to convince myself it's just a job.

Killing people. Cleaning up. Whatever you prefer to call it.

Someone has to do it.

The first time, it was personal. That was a mistake. But I got away with it. Well, insofar as it launched me on my new career.

I was in love with a woman. Or maybe in retrospect I was only actually in lust. She was blonde, tall and slim and had a wanton spark in her green eyes that just spoke to me in seductive ways. Her name was Cathleen. We'd met at a function, we'd heavily flirted, quickly fucked, and then done the deed a few more times in wholesome abandon. In hotel rooms, over pleasantly dirty weekends in coastal towns. Only for her husband to somehow find out about us and come knocking at my office door, accusing, begging, threatening.

I remembered the things she'd said about him during our brief conversations when our hands, lips and other useful parts of our anatomy were not jousting under the bed covers. How she felt he took her for granted. How he lacked imagination. I did not attempt to justify the affair, just stated the facts but this only served to make him angrier.

I also was married, had children even. This he had discovered in the process of investigating what sort of man his own wife was betraying him with. His anger bubbled to the surface and he asked me how I would feel if my family found out about my extracurricular activities. Now I knew I was not a perfect man and this was not my first instance of adultery, and my soul could live with the fact, but I don't react well to threats.

'You'd really contact my wife and tell all?' I asked him. His name was Christopher, he looked like a Christopher not a Chris and wore an off the peg grey suit.

'You bet I would.'

That night I killed him.

We agreed to a further meeting to keep discussing the matter, although my mind was made up already. I needed time to think. And plan. I hinted to him I was willing to let Cathleen go and cease the affair. I asked him for a few hours respite.

We drove to an isolated part of Blackheath Common, parked separately and made our way to the shelter of the trees as a thin rain had begun to fall which I realised would muddy any possible trail or footprints in the grass. He had no suspicion and it was easy to take him by surprise. I surprised him from behind and, after much struggle, succeeded in strangling him with the leather belt I had kept in my jacket pocket. I never thought it would be so easy. I'd read countless crime books and now put my plan into action. I would transfer his body to the boot of his own car and take him to a vast building site I'd spotted earlier and which could be accessed through a gap in a wonky wooden fence and dispose of the corpse there. I was wearing gloves, old clothes and shoes I would burn later. It was straightforward. What I hadn't expected was that Cathleen would be waiting in their car and the look of shock on her face when she saw me carrying Christopher's body towards the vehicle was one of sheer horror and told its own story.

There was one thing all my reading had taught me: not to leave witnesses.

I knew there was no point trying to justify myself or invoke her love. She had to go. I killed her too. With the back-up knife I had brought along for contingency. It was a waste, and I knew it but I had no other alternative.

There was a large pit at the site where the new building's foundations were being prepared. The bodies fell into darkness and, luckily enough, from the rim of the pit were immediately lost in shadow. In all likelihood, the cement would pour down and cover them before they were noticed.

I surprised myself with the degree of calm and steadiness with which I was conducting the whole improvised operation.

I drove their car away from the building site. It was a two-years old Volvo which had been purchased second-hand and had over 60,000 miles on the counter. I emptied the glove compartment and disposed of any documents as we crossed the Thames at Richmond Bridge. I abandoned the car near a rough Brixton estate, leaving it visibly unlocked, trusting local wannabes to complete a disappearance job on it.

And then returned to my own car under the curtain of rain, hoping I wouldn't catch a cold.

For weeks I awaited a knock at my door and found sleep difficult to achieve, but no one came. Nor was there anything in the newspapers.

A year passed and I even embarked on further affairs, albeit specifically keeping clear of married women this time.

My mind somehow brushed the whole episode away. It was as if nothing had ever happened – aside from the indelible memory of Cathleen's white skin and ever so distinctive moans of pleasure when we had made love – and I had been given a bonus Monopoly card to get out of jail and keep on living as I had always done.

But the mind works in mysterious ways and, gradually, it began again and again to evoke the feeling of calm transcendence I had briefly experienced that night, and I was increasingly overcome with a sense of yearning I couldn't properly explain.

As if I needed to kill again.

I am not a bad man, I tell myself; just a slave to my cravings, sexual, financial and otherwise, I reckon.

I thought of a way to fan the flames inside me and came up with a solution.

Many of the women I met were through the Internet. This led me to the Craigslist site. I carefully crafted an ad, which was both ambiguous enough as well as self-explanatory if you had the right mindset. Should anyone misunderstand it (and two thirds of respondents did, which didn't surprise me) all I had to do was fail to respond to it.

The majority of murders are committed by close acquaintances or family and motive is the main reason the arrow of guilt and suspicion quickly points in their direction. Naturally I'd read Patricia Highsmith's *Strangers on a Train*. I'd even seen the movie.

I volunteered to dispose of total strangers. I set a fee. Which was not negotiable. Built in a number of fail safe conditions to protect my anonymity and ensure I was never actually seen by any of my customers. It wasn't even that I needed the money but I estimated that doing it for free would convey the wrong impression, even if I knew all too damn well that there was something quite askew about my motivations and the loose screw inside me pushing me into this risky direction.

It was a challenge.

Paradoxically, it made me feel alive, killing people.

Invariably, I didn't wish to know anything unnecessary about the targets bar the bare facts needed in order to identify them, or the reasons they had been set up by others out of hate, jealousy, greed or whatever had prompted their names to be assigned to me. Each new task became an exercise in murder.

I was cautious. Never accepted a job close to home, and declined all hits that might entail travelling overseas as working on familiar territory was both safer and more straightforward. Severed all contacts with any client post-payment and destroyed the pay-as-you-go phone and SIM card used for the transaction. Took my time, planning meticulously, setting up alternative methods, routes of escape, ways of disposal. Taking very particular care to ensure there would be no witnesses – unlike that first time. Tried not to repeat myself. I only read crime fiction as part of my training and education; you learn a lot that way, insofar as what not to do.

There was the American banker who was found hung from a bridge close to the Tate Modern. He would leave his City office every day to jog home and I tailed him for two weeks until the right moment presented itself and I could work unseen despite the full moon above.

And then the call girl who fell out of the window of a top floor luxury apartment in Southwark. Her silk nightie unfurled around her taut body as she took flight, like a parachute or a flower. She didn't even scream. I think she was even expecting me, just like the victim in Hemingway's story 'The Killers'.

I had to pour over car manuals to make the death by carbon monoxide inhalation in his garage of a man whose name I didn't even know – just his address and his photograph – seem accidental.

Ahmed was a small fry drug dealer in Tottenham and he never suspected me until I drew the knife and aimed straight at his heart. It was messier than I'd hoped, and I was breathless as I took flight following the killing, hoping no passers-by would notice the blood against my dark clothing as I rushed from the scene in haste.

A car burned on a cliff by the sea, its driver trapped inside as I watched from a safe distance. Another man appeared to drown, while a woman in suburbia succumbed to poison I had acquired, alongside birdseed, a mousetrap and a pack of AAA batteries in a cash and carry warehouse near Croydon Airport.

I tried to vary my methods, so that all the deaths appeared accidental, or random enough not to attract undue attention. Whenever possible, I avoided being left with a body to dispose of.

And, of course, this being Britain, I never used a gun. Not that I even knew where to get hold of one had it proven necessary.

I realise that one day everything is bound to catch up with me and my nightmares are not for the weak, but I travel through the days a figure of honesty and normalcy. This is the life I have chosen and I have no wish to change. Some people drink, others collect books or paintings or jewellery. I kill. That's who I now am.

The black cellphone I keep in my office drawer vibrates three times. It's an agreed signal. I leave the building at leisure. I know I have fifteen minutes to reach the phone box across Soho Square.

I'm there well in time when the phone inside the old-fashioned red box rings. I quickly check around me and see the usual lunch hour sunbathers and office workers biting into sandwiches and sipping from small cartons or bottles of water or beer. Nothing overly suspicious.

I keep a folded handkerchief between my mouth and the receiver.

It's a woman's voice.

Sounding a little familiar, but it's not a good line.

I grunt my responses.

She is just confirming the arrangements tentatively made beforehand re the fee for the hit and the information I require.

There is an envelope with the relevant details awaiting me in a luggage locker at King's Cross Station as agreed, for which I have a spare key already.

I wait a whole week. I always do. I never agree on a time span for a given job with any of the clients. A death cannot be rushed. If they are too anxious, I regretfully decline the hit.

It's rush hour and the station is buzzing with commuters and passers-by rushing in every conceivable direction. I lose myself in the crowd and carefully survey the scene until I am confident there is no obvious surveillance.

I reach the small compartment and turn the key in the lock. There is a large, brown jiffy bag inside. I seize it and swiftly close the locker and walk away, disappearing amongst the sea of folks rushing down into the bowels of the Underground towards the Northern Line. I change several times. Just in case. Better safe than sorry, I know. Once home, I see a note from my wife; she is out with the kids at the local Cineworld. I move to my study and open the envelope to discover who is my target this time.

There is a single sheet of paper, on which the name, home and office address of the hit is laid out in capital letters.

Mine.

And a photograph.

Mine.

Now I know why the voice on the Soho Square telephone sounded familiar. I guess it's the affairs with other women that have caught up with me, not the killings.

I'm fucked.

CHRISTOPHER FOWLER, born in London in 1953, is the author of more than fifty novels and twelve short story collections, including the *Bryant & May mysteries*, about two Golden Age detectives investigating impossible London crimes. His recent work includes the *War of the Worlds* videogame with Sir Patrick Stewart, a graphic novel and a Hammer horror radio play. His latest books are the comedy-thriller *Plastic* and the memoir *Film Freak*. He divides his time between London and Barcelona.

The Caterpillar Flag

Christopher Fowler

'So, where are you off to, then?' Lily heard the taxi driver who was taking them to Victoria Station ask. She could only see the back of his head through the glass. It was as smooth and hard as a pebble.

'Spain,' her father replied. 'We're moving there.'

'Oh, Spain.' There was the disapproval of experience in his voice. 'Let me give you a tip, mate. I'll tell you what happens to people when they move to Spain. All they end up doing is reading and drinking, and they slowly fall apart. It ruins them. Reading and drinking. It'll happen to you too. That's what always happens.'

Lily's father did not give the driver a tip in return for his sage advice.

The village of Cadilla, in the mountains above Ronda, isn't famous for much; it sells raspberry-coloured gin and small plates of dried acorn-fed ham, and there are tiny, brightly coloured birds on all the telephone poles. The houses are whitewashed and shuttered against the searing heat, and have blue and yellow geckos painted on the walls. The wives wash their front steps and balconies first thing every morning, and beat their rugs against the walls of their houses, as the wives of England once did. From her open window Lily could always hear someone talking or sweeping. The Spanish children played ball games in the street and the English ones stayed inside on their Playstations. By May it was so hot you could cook an egg on the iron plate that covered the old well in the plaza. There was a hotel with eight rooms, a cobbled town square where the older boys hung out and fishtailed their bicycles past Eduardo's café, a church the English never attended except at Christmas, and a restaurant the locals wouldn't use because the owner once cheated his neighbour in a game of cards. Everyone knew each other.

It was early summer in 2012. Lily was being taken from Manchester to Cadilla because she was prone to pleurisy and the air here was hot and dry. She was nearly nine years old. Her parents had taken a one-year rental on a small white house with a tiny sun-baked yard edged about by orange trees in glossy red earthenware pots. After a month her pale skin freckled and darkened to a smooth caramel, her chest cleared and her nights passed silent and uninterrupted.

From almost anywhere in the town the view was framed by two mountains, one topped with an actual ruined castle. Between them were miles of green fields and brown rocks, and beyond those an azure ribbon of sea separated Spain from the coast of Africa, where a town called Tangiers was so fiercely illuminated at night that it blotted out the starlight above it.

Lily's parents had their own contradictory reasons for moving. Geoffrey had been made redundant from the wine wholesaler he worked for in Manchester, and had taken a new job exporting sherry to England. Every Tuesday morning he travelled to Madrid or Jerez or London, returning on Thursday evening. He said that coming to Cadilla was a fresh start for them. Lily's mother Paula ran an online auction site selling discounted designer handbags, and she said they had moved here so that they could stay together as a family and her father wouldn't have the same temptations, whatever that meant.

Lily's new school was six kilometres away, and they had arranged for the yellow school bus to collect her from the town square each morning, along with four other ex-pat children.

In Manchester, Lily's mother had never liked her going out, but here it seemed she was forever pushing her out of doors. They were all still at the point where the sun was a novelty. Almost at once, an astonishing thing happened. The family started having meals together, especially at the weekends. They sat in the shaded town square drinking thick dark *cortados* and sharp orange juice, and had crispy-edged eggs brought to them in little frying pans. Paula and Geoffrey even started holding conversations that didn't end in anger. Lily slid down in her seat and looked from one parent to the other in goggle-eyed satisfaction.

Whenever they went to Eduardo's café, there was always one other table occupied. Celestia was a tall, elegant Englishwoman in her seventies who had once lived in London, in a place called Shepherd's Bush. She had moved here because of a divorce, a family fight, a devotion to bullfights and a passion for chain-smoking *cigarillos*. She knew everyone in town, including the man who had once robbed her house, and who turned out to live right next door. His name was Paolo, and he had a sullen, burned look. She gave his children money to show that he had been forgiven, and her ostentatious displays of largesse brought a certain amount of distant respect, along with a little resentment. She explained that she did not miss Shepherd's Bush, because who in their right mind would, but she did on occasion miss England.

Geoffrey told her about the taxi driver's advice, and she gave a throaty laugh. 'God, I could think of a lot worse ways to go than that, couldn't you?' she said, throwing back her head and blasting out a contrail of cigarillo smoke. 'I sold up in Shepherd's Bush, had the name of my greatest love tattooed on my right buttock and grew my lovely hair long, and now I sit here at Eduardo's reading and drinking and watching the world go by. How perfect is that?'

Lily's father studied her with vague disapproval, but said nothing.

Celestia spoke a kind of Spanish filled with loud, round vowels, the kind English ex-pats spoke. She mainly used it for issuing commands to Eduardo and his waitress Lola, who was half the age of her boss and was said to have replaced his dead wife. Lola crossed herself whenever the church bells sounded, and became flustered if more than three of the café tables were filled at once. Celestia watched it all.

'I see them come and go,' she told Lily's mother. 'Everyone has a story. It's quite fascinating. You'll have to learn to slow down a bit, though. The sun takes its toll. If you try to do too much, you run out of energy around lunchtime. When the heat hits forty I get dizzy spells and the only thing that will shift them is a lie-down with an iced towel. Paolo's wife often brings me one. Such a drab little thing, but terribly sweet. They both are, really. Four adorable children and as poor as church mice. I do what I can for them.'

Celestia had a son who was a doctor in London but they weren't on speaking terms. Lily overheard one of the ex-pats telling her mother that there had been an argument about money and a will. She had a better connection with the locals than any of the other ex-pats. The ladies of Cadilla acknowledged her in the scorching streets as they passed each other on the climb to the bakery, even though they clearly thought the English mad. If they wanted to live in Spain, why not choose a town caressed by Atlantic breezes, like Cadiz? Why burn up here, spending half their lives behind thick, cool walls or bobbing about in swimming pools like greased ducks?

'I'd love to be in London for the Diamond Jubilee,' Celestia confided. 'The Queen has always been in my life, right from when I was little. My mother gave me a diamond that once belonged to King George VI. I have it still and will show you one day.' Lily always saw her through a cloud of pale blue smoke, puffing away, surrounded by wine glasses and full ashtrays, and could not imagine her as a little girl, but she liked to visit her house because she could see Africa from the upstairs rooms, which were dark and cool, and the garden had a tiny green swimming pool which Celestia allowed her to use.

One time, she looked through the fence and saw the children next door sitting sun-stunned and silent in their scorching bare yard. They were wearing swimming costumes, even though they had no pool. Celestia didn't let them come over because four was too many, and she liked to sleep in the afternoons.

'There are going to be street parties all over England for the Queen,' she said. 'Like the fiestas here.' She showed Lily a book filled with crowns and state carriages and Union Jacks. 'The Queen loves children. Whenever they make a gift for her, she sends out a royal letter thanking them.'

Which set Lily thinking. Her Spanish lessons were boring, and when school finished it was still too hot to play, so she decided to make something for the Queen.

Celestia was the only one with an illegal Sky box, but last time, just as the village's ex-pats sat themselves around the television to watch a royal occasion – poof – the signal vanished. The crazy widow who ran the table linen shop said the Devil had taken the picture away. It turned out that the man who once robbed Celestia's house had chosen that particular moment to swipe her satellite dish, so Celestia went next door and took it back, and in the spirit of forgiveness they all got drunk on Manzanilla and Sprite. She doted on Paolo, even though he stole from her, and used him to drive her to the bullfights in Ronda. Paolo rarely spoke, and mutely accepted his strange new role.

Lily sat on Celestia's madly colourful rag-rug and watched a nature programme about a type of green worm that could spin silk. Lily watched in fascination as they arched and wriggled along branches, leaving behind delicate white cat-cradles.

'I think the silk hardens and is woven into clothes,' her mother explained distractedly when she was asked later that evening. 'Why?'

'David Attenborough says the worms are found in hot countries, so I thought it would be really cool to find some and collect their silk, and make something for the Jubilee.'

'I'm really up against it, timewise,' her mother replied, tapping away at her computer keyboard.

Lily knew exactly where to look for the worms. A few straw-hatted tourists sat in the town square rustling their out-of-date English newspapers and drinking beer. The budget airline passengers were sixty kilometres to the South, frying themselves in oil at the coast.

'I come from Manchester,' Lily told Lola, the waitress in the village square café, who was nebulously horrified by the idea.

'I thought it was a football team,' she said, puzzled.

'No, it's a city like London,' she said.

'London where they all run around going buzz buzz, like bees?'

'Yes but we live here now,' Lily explained. 'Where can I find these?' She showed the waitress a picture of the silk worms in a National Geographic magazine that one of the tourists had left behind.

Lola squinted at the picture – she was supposed to wear glasses but made more tips when she left them off. 'I know these things,' she said, tapping the picture with a pink frosted nail. 'They are in the bushes behind the convent.'

The last of the nuns had died of disappointment in 1973 and the convent finally fell down. The man who robbed Celestia's house was the town's builder, and instead of removing the rubble he just painted it white. Poppies and lavender grew up between the rocks, and myrtle and wisteria and big green bushes with thick dark leaves that nobody knew the name of. Lily climbed over the bricks to the bushes and saw them, dozens of bright green hairy caterpillars scalloping the leaves, so many that they were dropping off the branches like commandos. She made a nest of leaves and put it in her mother's linen shopping bag, then filled the bag with caterpillars. Their hairs made her itch and left red bumps all over her hands, so the next time she used her mother's washing up gloves to gather them.

Lily planned to use the caterpillars to make a Union Jack which she would then post to the Queen in time for her Jubilee. She decided to say that it was from Celestia. She wanted the Queen to know that even though the most loyal of her subjects had moved all the way from Shepherd's Bush to Cadilla she was still a part of her country.

As she sat in her room trying to work out how to make the caterpillars surrender their silk, she could not avoid listening to her parents downstairs. Her father said they had worked hard in England so that they could make enough money to live like people with no money in Spain, and now they had no choice but to stay here. Her mother complained about missing her friends and the shops in London, but said it was worth it not to have you go back to your old habits. Her father said they couldn't have it both ways and besides it was good for the girl. Lily thought if she made the silk Union Jack, it would remind her parents of their life in England and they would stop sniping.

Every morning for a week she went down to the waste ground behind the convent to check inside the bushes for the caterpillars. A fresh crop had appeared; the latest ones were black with orange stripes and fewer bristles, so she placed them in a separate bag. As she looked deeper into the rockery scrub she found different types, some with black and yellow stripes and horns, some emerald with crimson spots. It took four days to gather enough of them.

Lily knew they could make silk because they used it to attach themselves to leaves when they were ready to make a chrysalis. They were hairy so that other creatures would find them hard to eat. They became visibly fatter with each passing day, but she found no evidence of silk.

Because she wanted to surprise her parents with her ingenuity, she used Celestia's garden to lay out the shape of the caterpillar flag. She told the old lady what she was trying to do, but did not explain her purpose. First she drew the outline of the Union Jack, which was tricky because some stripes were thicker than others, and it had to be the right way up. Then she marked out the flag with pins and cotton, and set the caterpillars within the narrow rows of thread. They would be forced to move up and down the different areas of the flag, spreading their silk as they travelled, leaving behind the finished pennant. Lily had the determination of innocence, a doggedness that could not be slowed by lack of results.

She soon noticed that the caterpillars' poo changed colour when she fed them different vegetables. After peppers and thistles they left greenish trails, and after carrots they left red ones. But for the Union Jack she needed blue and white, so she used onions for the white and chopped green and yellow peppers up together to make what she hoped would be blue.

No matter what she fed them, there was still no silk to be seen. For another five days the caterpillars ate and excreted and continued on their peristaltic way, up and down the corridors of cotton, to no avail.

Lily asked Celestia what she should do. Her neighbour proved evasive, and sat in her usual place at the café table beneath a stratocumulus of smoke, silent and thoughtful. She was on her first glass of sherry and her first pack of cigarillos. She had tied her long auburn hair up in a bun and looked like a mad and rather wonderful gorgon. They were both aware that time was running out, for the Jubilee's postal deadline was fast approaching.

Finally, she stubbed out her cigarillo and said, 'I think we should cover them up with cardboard and leave them until the end of the week. I'll ask Maria Gonzales what to do.'

Maria Gonzales was about a thousand years old and knew everything. She ran a strange, dusty shop that sold organic honey, dried shrimps, wind chimes, homeopathic medicines and shawls, but at the back there was an internet café of sorts consisting of three ancient computers, a Hewlett-Packard printer that nobody knew how to work and a table covered with out-of-date healthcare magazines.

She and Celestia held a meeting that started with coffee and glasses of Oloroso and ended up encompassing most of the older ladies in the village. Given that they spent most of the day there and the Oloroso was twenty-two percent alcohol, it was a wonder they managed to walk home without falling into bushes or getting run over.

Now that the initial euphoria of the move had worn off, Lily's house had become a place of sullen silences. The only thing worse than her parents arguing was them not speaking. She longed to hop over the yard wall and cross the village to see how the caterpillar flag was progressing, or just see if there was even a single thread of silk, but her mother made her stay inside and read her Spanish lessons.

The diurnal shadows slid over Cadilla like ghosts fleeing the heat. Monday morning arrived, the start of the very last week when the flag could be posted to Buckingham Palace in time for the Jubilee. Unable to contain herself any longer, Lily rose and ran over to Celestia's house. Although it was already hot, the old lady had yet to make an appearance, so Lily ran around the back to the garden and found the cardboard oblong where it had been placed beneath an orange tree.

Carefully removing the lid, she looked inside. The cotton threads and pins were still there but the box was empty.

'I'm sorry, Lily.' She looked up to find Celestia standing beside her in her blue satin dressing gown, a cigarillo balanced lightly between her fingers. 'I'm afraid they went away.'

'Where did they go?' Lily asked.

'To the trees. It was time for them to pupate.' Celestia knelt beside her with some difficulty. 'You can't control nature, my love. Nature always does what it needs to do. Whenever we try to interfere, things have a habit of going their own way.'

Lily looked in the trees but she couldn't see where the caterpillars had gone. She packed up the plan and the cardboard, the cotton and pins, then thanked the old lady for her efforts. The last thing Celestia said before Lily went home was mysterious; she said perhaps something could be done.

Just before nine o'clock the following morning, her mother asked her to go down to the shop for some milk, and Lily set off through the hilly white streets. There in the middle of the road was an extraordinary sight. Running towards her, her black skirts and saggy yellow cardigan flapping, her coral necklaces chattering like teeth, was Maria Gonzales.

'Tell him to stop!' she shouted, waving at someone behind Lily. She had a parcel wrapped in brown paper and tied with string, and was pointing wildly.

Lily turned and saw a white van moving off. 'Wait!' she shouted, dashing after the postal van and running alongside it. Maria threw her the package as if passing a rugby ball – she had a strong arm on her for an old lady – and Lily slipped it through the open window of the van.

The incident stuck in her mind later because it was the most energetic thing that had happened in the village since they arrived. Maria Gonzales never explained why she was in such a rush, and returned to her shop to sit in the cool gloom among the pots of organic tomato marmalade and string sweaters.

The day of the Diamond Jubilee came, and the ex-pats arranged to meet in Celestia's living room to watch the highlights, where many toasts to the Queen would be proposed. But there was no answer from their usual shave-and-a-haircut knock, and after waiting around outside for a while in confusion they retired to the village square, where Eduardo served them all red wine and ham. It was decided that Celestia had probably gone to visit her sister, and a few mean remarks were made about her thoughtless timing. Lola said that Celestia acted as if she was the queen of the town square.

A week later, Lily went to the orange grove that ran beside the plaza, to sit and read a book. While she was sprawled there in the shade beneath the orange trees, her mother came looking for her. 'This just arrived for you,' she said, handing her a manila envelope that said DO NOT BEND on the cover. 'It came in a special delivery from England.'

Lily screwed up one eye at the envelope. 'What is it?' she asked suspiciously.

'I've no idea,' said her mother, sitting down under the tree beside her. 'Well go on, open it.'

Lily carefully unstuck the flap and withdrew two stiff sheets. The first was embossed with the royal crest of Buckingham Palace and read;

Dear Celestia Kerr (just the name was handwritten)

I am instructed by Her Majesty the Queen to accept the present of a Union Jack which you sent Her Majesty.

The Queen thought it was kind of you to wish her well on the occasion of her Diamond Jubilee and would like to thank you for this thoughtful gesture.

Yours sincerely, (There followed an unreadable handwritten name that might have been Annabel Fitz-Something).

Lady In Waiting

'But I didn't send the Union Jack,' said Lily. 'Caterpillars can't make silk.'

'No,' said her mother, 'but the ladies of the village can. I think they made it for you.'

And there on the second page was a photograph of the Queen walking among children outside Buckingham Palace, with a wonkily knitted Union Jack among the gifts displayed on the railings behind her.

'You made something good happen, Lily,' said her mother, sounding rather wistful.

Lily laughed, and ran all the way to Celestia's house. As she passed the church rockery, she imagined a hundred red, white and blue butterflies dislodging themselves from their branches to flutter about her head.

She knocked on Celestia's door but there was no answer, so she pushed open the letterbox flap and looked in. Once her eyes had adjusted to the dimness, she could make out the legs of a tipped-over chair, and something glittering on the sun-pooled kitchen floor, green shards of a wine bottle. The red wine had dried out on the sunny tiles and looked like a bloodstain. It seemed strange, because Celestia was usually very tidy.

On her way home, she passed by the back of Celestia's neighbour's house and was surprised to find the yard door standing wide open. Shyly walking up the path and peering inside, she saw that although most of the living room furniture was still there, the tablecloth and sideboard photographs had all gone. The rooms felt still and empty.

The next few days were odd; cars came and went. There were stern-looking strangers in Eduardo's café. The women stopped talking whenever Lily walked near them. She sensed that Celestia would not be coming back, but it came as a shock to think that she might be dead.

The town square looked wrong without her.

Lily walked through the bare little cemetery behind the church. The ground was too seared and arid to be dug out, and most of the residents had been placed in raised tombs, surrounded by votive offerings of dried-out flowers and bleached photographs. Now a new one had appeared, much smaller than the rest; a white marble square with a little metal pot on it, awaiting a plaque. She remembered what Celestia had said about nature always doing what it needed to do, and realised, with a terrible sensation sinking into her heart, what might have happened.

Lily's father was away and her mother was too busy, so she went to the stone-setting by herself. She sat with Maria

Gonzales and Lola, and some of the ex-pats. The priest had nothing much to say, and the service was thankfully short. Afterwards Eduardo served free lemonade in the café. People seemed relieved somehow, as if an awkward matter had finally been resolved.

Lily wondered about the diamond. She made a point of pinning the photograph of the Queen and the caterpillar flag to the whitewashed wall outside Maria Gonzales' shop, so that Celestia would not be forgotten. There it remained for almost a month, until someone backed into it, knocking a hole right through to the organic jams.

LOUISE WELSH is the author of six novels, most recently *The Girl on the Stairs* (2012) and *A Lovely Way to Burn* (2014). She has received several awards and international fellowships. She was born in London in 1965 to Scottish parents and spent the first year of her life in the city. Louise lives in Glasgow with the writer Zoë Strachan.

Reflections
in Unna

Louise Welsh

Hugh's job was to look, listen and record, but he was barely aware of the scent of *gluhwein* spicing the chill air or the crush of shoppers busying the Christmas market, as he made his way across Unna's main square. Hugh's mind was full of curses and calculations. His credit card had been rejected in a restaurant the previous night, and his unpaid hotel bill burned beside the slim fold of euros in his wallet.

'Fuck!'

His breath clouded the air and Hugh realised that the word had escaped his lips. The realisation broke the spell, plunging Hugh back into the world of cold and colour. Beside him a clutch of merry drinkers, faces as red as their Santa hats, raised their glasses in a toast that set them all laughing. Hugh stared. Now his awareness had returned it was as if he could distinguish every atom of Unna. One of the drinkers gave a rumbling addendum to the toast. Hugh saw the plump tongue inside the man's mouth, the scrofulous flakes beneath the start of new stubble, the woollen scarf, remnant of some previous Christmas, tucked around a neck that was loose on its bones. The drinker caught his gaze, but Hugh had already turned away, distracted by the ding of the fire engine on the children's carousel. The carousel was ribboned with flashing lights that sent the children's faces red, yellow, green, blue and then back to red again, their features puckered with delight. They screamed and hooted like a clan of miniature devils. Hugh saw the parents waiting on the sidelines and wondered how they could bear to see their children's features so distorted.

He was colder than he'd ever been. He thought again about his hotel bill, the fee that was no longer going to save him. It had been stupid to set off for the Ruhr before the editor of the in-flight magazine had given him definite confirmation, but her reaction to his proposed feature had seemed so enthusiastic and his need for a commission had been so great that Hugh had broken the golden rule of travel journalism and embarked before his expenses had been assured.

He rubbed a hand through his thinning curls. He should go back to his hotel, but the thought of the empty room with its double bed stayed him. It was better to remain out here, amongst the noise and the people. But he was so cold.

It wasn't simply that this commission had folded. Newspapers were reeling from the assault of the Internet and making cuts wherever they could. Guidebooks were in trouble too. The virtual world had skewed reality. People preferred to trawl the web for star ratings from anonymous tourists, who probably knew as little about the country as they did. Hugh hadn't had a decent assignment for a year. He'd jumped at this chance because he thought it might be his last. In the end it wasn't even that.

He stopped at a display of colourful woollen hats. His head was so cold he felt his brain may freeze. The hats were equipped with pompoms and earflaps and decorated with stripes, dots and zigzags. Some of them bore the outlines of animals that may have been reindeer. Their bright patterns reminded him of a trip he'd taken to Peru a decade ago. For a moment the clanging bell on the carousel became the clank of the bell tethered around a yak's neck as it wandered slowly up a mountain pass towards milking. He saw the edge of a valley where he and his guide had spent the night, remembered the warmth of the place, the air that expanded your lungs rather than shrunk them with cold.

Hugh favoured sombre clothes but suddenly he desperately wanted one of the hats. He lifted a yellow and green one and caught the stallholder's eye.

'How much?'

The hat seller was wrapped in a Puffa jacket filled with goose down. He had a woollen scarf tucked neatly around his neck and one of his own hats on his head. His gloves were fingerless, the better to handle money. He rubbed his hands together then blew on his fingertips.

'Thirty euros.'

Hugh pressed the hat between his fingers, feeling the rough yield of the wool, he could barely think for cold, but he replaced it.

The stallholder nodded, as if he had known all along that the price would be too high. He took a red patterned tammy complete with knitted bobble from beneath the counter.

'Only five euros.'

It was a poor copy of the hats on display, made with cheap synthetic fibres rather than the good thick wool Hugh had coveted, but he reached into his pocket and counted out the last of his change. He waved away the seller's offer of a bag and pulled the hat onto his head. Hugh knew he looked ridiculous, but he no longer cared.

He walked away from the market square, down one of the side streets. It was a remnant of the old town, narrower and more curved than most of Unna's roads, hinting at a medieval past. Most of the shops that lined the street were dark, but here and there a restaurant window glowed, amber and inviting. Hugh caught glimpses of diners gathered around tables, he thought of duck breast and red cabbage, dumplings and foaming beer. But, hungry as he was, he would have exchanged the prospect of a meal in return for some company.

There were still a hundred euros in his wallet, too little for his needs, but more than enough to buy a drink and some fellowship. He remembered a *kneipe* he'd passed earlier. He'd almost decided to retrace his steps when he saw the painting.

The shop was tiny, no more than a door in the wall next to a window grimed with neglect, but beyond the glass a light burned bright. Hugh crossed the street and tried the door. It opened and a bell tinkled as he entered.

The old man behind the counter gave him a suspicious look, but Hugh's father had been a dealer in art and antiques and he was used to the wariness of the second-hand trade. Hugh examined a balding china doll whose perfectly rendered teeth turned her smile into a snarl, a plaster cast of a long-dead toddler's tiny foot and a china jug decorated with cavorting nymphs. He took his time, just as his father had taught him to on the long excursions around the countryside which had first awoken Hugh's love of travel. He asked the price of each piece before moving on with the smile of someone considering a purchase. Finally he tipped the hand of a metronome. Only then, to a tick, tick, tick, tick set in slow time, did Hugh pick up the small oil painting.

It was a portrait of a young woman brushing her hair in a mirror. The precision of the artist's brush strokes had rendered the girl's image almost photo-clear, but its impossible perspective countered any thoughts of realism. The crazy angles revealed both the girl and her reflection, and this was where the real strangeness struck, because although the girl and her mirror image seemed the same person, the face in the glass was altered, transforming sweetness into cunning.

Hugh caught his breath. He felt the proprietor's eyes on him and realised he'd been staring at the picture for too long. He set it down and started flicking through a shoebox filled with photos of the no-longer-dear departed. Finally Hugh turned towards the door. Only when his hand was on the knob, the bell poised to announce his departure, did he ask, 'How much is the painting of the girl?'

The shopkeeper's rheumy eyes seemed to stare above Hugh's head, no not above his head, but at the silly hat still perched upon it. He moved his jaw, as if trying to work up enough saliva to speak, and then whispered, 'One euro, Sir.'

Hugh's father had impressed upon him that a surprisingly low price could be as unattractive as an extortionate one. Sure, a bargain wasn't always bad news. The dealer might be broke, or have spotted something he thought he could make a bigger killing on elsewhere and need to raise enough cash to buy it. But an unexpectedly good deal could also be a sign that the piece had been come by dishonestly. And that could lead to trouble.

'It's like paying pass the parcel with a bomb son. Sooner or later it'll blow up in someone's face. You don't want it to be yours and the best way to avoid that is by not getting involved.'

The price the old man had asked for was ridiculous. Even if the antique dealer didn't know the true value of the painting he had surely thought it of some worth when he'd put it in the window.

Hugh said, 'That's too low.'

But the dealer had already taken the painting from the display and was wrapping it in a sheet of newspaper. He thrust the package at Hugh.

'Here.'

In his heart Hugh knew something was awry. But he reached into his wallet and took out one of the two fifty euro notes tucked within. The old man's hand shook as he counted the change onto the counter.

Hugh let the door swing shut. He looked back at the shop and saw the antique dealer watching him through the murky window. The old man caught his eye and started back into the darkness beyond. Hugh shook his head and grinned, all his misgivings forgotten. He felt jubilant. The painting was his passage out of trouble. With its help he would pay his hotel bill. More than that, it had suggested a new path to him. He could take on his father's profession for a while, hold onto the rental car he'd hired and search the towns of the Rhur for antiques he might sell once he got back to London. It was the first time in a long time he'd been able to think of the future. Hugh hugged the painting to his chest.

There was something familiar about the silhouette of the stranger walking up the street towards him. As he drew closer Hugh realised what it was. The man was wearing the same ugly hat as himself. He laughed out loud and raised his hand in greeting, as a man might hail a passer-by when he's drunk enough to believe the whole world his friend. But the stranger kept his head down and strode on. As Hugh approached the top of the street he heard the distant tinkle of a shop bell, but his mind was on the good fortune that awaited him and he thought nothing of it.

He had almost reached his hotel when he heard footsteps ringing against the pavement. Hugh turned and saw a man of about his own height sprinting towards him. He knew no one in Unna, and his urge was to run, but Hugh held his ground, gripping the painting firmly at his side, balling his free hand into a fist. The man halted about a metre away. He had thinning curly hair and a broad pleasant face which relaxed into a smile. Despite the swiftness of his approach his breaths were even and shallow and Hugh blessed the instinct which had told him not to try to outrun the stranger.

The man held up his hand to indicate that he meant no harm and said, 'I think you may have something that belongs to me.'

Hugh noticed a flash of red sticking out of the man's suit pocket, a pompom that matched the silly hat he'd bought in the Christmas market. 'I doubt it.' He tightened his grip on the painting and walked towards the glass front of his hotel.

The stranger jogged swiftly to his side.

'My grandfather's losing his wits, old age is cruel. The painting was already promised to someone else.'

Hugh felt a flash of shame, but penury had made him desperate. They had reached the pool of light thrown onto the pavement from the hotel's foyer. Hugh faced the man and asked, 'What will you give me for it?'

The man looked beyond Hugh, into the hotel lobby where a group of businessmen were introducing themselves to each other, full of smiles and bonhomie.

'A hundred euros.'

It was nowhere near what the painting was worth, nowhere near enough to cover his bill. Feeling like a thief Hugh said, 'No, I'm sorry.'

The man moved out of the gloom. His face was arctic pale, his mouth a colourless gash. His overcoat flapped open, exposing the maker's label on the inside pocket, and within that a glint of metal, scalpel-bright. He stepped closer still and the light of the hotel illuminated the blood splattered across the front of his shirt.

Hugh saw the horrid redness. He moved towards the stranger, his own mouth thick and stupid saying, 'You're hurt'. Then just as quickly he found himself jerking away, as he remembered the man's athletic sprint, his easy breath, and realised that the blood decorating his chest belonged to someone else.

There was a sudden bustle of heat and chatter behind him. The businessmen had finished their introductions and were leaving the lobby. Hugh said, 'I'll return it to your grandfather myself first thing in the morning, no charge.' He pushed through the departing group and into the neon brightness of the reception, retrieved his key from the desk clerk and ran up the fire escape, feet clattering against the metal as he took the stairs two at a time.

Hugh's hotel room was almost, but not quite dark. He lay on the bed with the unwrapped painting propped on his stomach and stared into the eyes of the girl and her reflection. It was hard to tell which of the faces was the most beautiful. They both had ebony black hair, pale skin livened with the slightest touch of rose, red lips dark as vampire's desire and green eyes in which wide black pupils gleamed. Perhaps the mirror held no glass and the other girl was an evil, almost-twin smiling though an empty frame.

Hugh glanced at chair he'd propped against the locked door to his room. The wisest course would have been to surrender the painting to the stranger, but now that he was alone with it he felt mesmerised. He traced his fingers lightly over the artist's initials; GL.

Gustav Loring had been a rising star in a German art movement outlawed as decadent in the late thirties. He'd left for America just before he was obliged to sew a pink triangle to his coat and once there had made his way to Los Angeles where he had discovered a talent for set design. Loring had been on the cusp of a lucrative career when he'd crashed his car on the way home from a party in the Hollywood Hills, killing himself and scarring the promising young actor in the passenger seat so badly that he was forced to play villains for the rest of his career.

Hugh picked up the phone and asked reception to find him a local number. His tour of the district had included several galleries and there was a particular curator he wanted to speak to. If he was right all his problems would be solved. All his problems except the stranger, who even now might be waiting outside the hotel. Hugh made his call, then placed the painting on the bed beside him and turned out the light hoping sleep would come.

Hugh awoke to darkness and the unfamiliar peal of the hotel phone. The alarm clock glowed 03.05. He fumbled for the bedside lamp and then glanced at the painting still on the bed beside him before picking up the receiver.

'Hello?' His voice was fuzzy with sleep.

'I'm in the lobby, bring down the picture and I'll give you a thousand euros.'

Hugh recognised the cool tones of the stranger. He held the phone to his chest. Turning one euro into a thousand would be a fabulous profit, but there was no guarantee that he could trust the stranger. And if he was lucky, the man he had arranged to meet might pay more; enough to settle his hotel bill and leave a sufficient stake to begin antique dealing.

'I'm sorry. Gustav Loring commands high sums. I can't afford to let it go for less than three thousand.'

'Gustav who?' The man's voice was no longer cool. 'Look, I don't know how you and Gustav found out about the signal ...'

'What signal?'

'The stupid red hat. Old Muller was to hand the painting over to a man wearing a red hat – me – only it wasn't me was it? If you know about the hat I'm guessing you know I'm not the only one after the painting.' There was a pause on the line filled with the stranger's ragged breath. When he spoke again his voice was tight. 'These guys won't bargain with you.'

'That's fine.' Hugh was amazed how calm he sounded. 'I already have a client willing to pay a high price.'

'Then you better get it to him in the next thirty seconds because I have my own client and his terms are also high, the picture or my throat. I'll cut yours to save mine and not even blink.'

Perhaps he said more, but Hugh had already flung the receiver to one side and was pulling on his clothes. He bundled the painting back in its newspaper, stowed it in his briefcase and then crept from his room, cursing the energy saving lights that announced his progress along the hotel corridor.

Hugh secreted himself in an unlocked laundry cupboard on the fifth floor. He had never been so conscious of his heart before, the precious blood so easily spilled, pumping through his body. But even in his panic he was aware of something else. The man hadn't known who Gustav Loring was.

Hugh woke to the sound of chambermaids beginning their rounds and hobbled back to his room on cramped legs. His instinct was to abandon his suitcase and its contents, but his night flight had been swift and disorganised and there was something he needed to collect. He heard the approach of chambermaid's trolley and let himself in, gambling that if trouble lay in store at least she might hear him scream and go for help.

The hotel room was a mess of tumbled pillows and bedclothes, upturned furniture and scattered clothes. His suitcase gaped from the middle of the floor; its inner lining ripped and tattered. Hugh edged open the bathroom door, smelt aftershave and saw the bottle smashed in frustration against the tiles. He pulled the shower curtain slowly back and felt his breath come like sobs when he saw that this room too was empty. He fell on his knees and ran his hands around the ruined case; finally he tipped it upside down and shook it. But he already knew that his passport was gone.

It had snowed in the night and the streets were covered with a thin dusting of white. Hugh almost lost his footing as he turned into —Strasse, but he righted himself still keeping a firm hold of his briefcase and its precious cargo. He needed to speak with the antique dealer, find out if he knew who the stranger was and why he was so desperate to lay his hands on the painting.

There was something going on, a commotion of police cars and green uniforms midway down the street. Hugh slowed his pace, drawn towards the disaster, sure as iron filings drift towards a magnet. He joined the outer fringe of the small crowd that had gathered, and stood on his tiptoes, trying to see over the heads of the onlookers. He caught a glimpse of the antique shop door beribboned with crime scene tape. He turned to the broad, red-faced man standing next to him asked, 'What happened?'

'Murder.' The man's voice was louder than propriety demanded and a few heads turned towards him, but he paid them no mind. 'The old guy who runs this place got his throat cut last night.'

'A robbery?'

'Most likely, though Herr Muller kept some bad company. Could be it caught up with him.'

'That's him! The murderer!'

A ripple of excitement raced though the crowd. Hugh turned towards the shout and saw a young girl pointing at him.

'I saw him going into Herr Muller's shop when I was locking up last night. He killed him!'

The red-faced man grabbed Hugh's sleeve. For an instant it seemed he might be trapped but then Hugh struggled free of his coat and shoved the man hard, toppling him into the onlookers. He ran as if his life depended on it, sped on by shouts that were soon drowned in a wail of sirens.

Hugh ducked into the crowds of Christmas shoppers, hearing once more the jangling tones of the children's carousel. It had started to snow again and the cold was like a fever on him, damping his skin through the thin weave of his shirt. Hugh glanced back and saw two policemen patrolling the square, eyes bright beneath their visors as they scanned the crowd.

He pulled the stupid red hat from his briefcase and stuck it on his head. It was a disguise of sorts, but he needed to get indoors before he was captured or froze to death. A coffee shop glowed bright at the far end of the square. Hugh made for it, forcing himself not to look back at the policemen. It was only when he got to the door that he realised his wallet, credit cards, driving licence, car keys and the last of his cash, were in the pocket of the coat he'd abandoned.

For a moment he considered handing himself in, explaining the whole sorry mess and throwing himself on the mercy of the authorities. The old man had been killed for the loss of the painting; he knew it sure as he knew the stranger had threatened to slit his throat.

The thought stopped Hugh in his tracks. Gustav Loring wasn't worth killing for, and anyway, the man on the phone hadn't known who the artist was. What made the picture so valuable to him?

He had parked his hire car in a quiet street near his hotel. Hugh searched the verge until he found a rock big enough to smash the passenger window. The glass was tough and he cut his hand forcing it free of the frame. He accessed the boot from within, blessing whoever had invented hatchbacks, then freed the jack from beneath the spare wheel and used it to break the lock from the ignition. He found a screwdriver in the small toolbox in the well of the boot, turned it in the exposed ignition and fired the engine into life, wondering how long he had before the police contacted the hire company and circulated the car's registration throughout the force.

Cold air roared through the breached window as he drove along the autobahn numbing Hugh's hands until he thought they might freeze to the steering wheel. He pulled into a service station and parked amongst ranks of juggernauts loaded with containers bearing the names of distant ports; Hamburg, Bergen, Stranraer, Copenhagen. He rubbed his hands together, trying to get the blood moving, then slid the painting from his briefcase and loosed it of its wrapping. The girls' faces stared out; beautiful as ever, but now it seemed it was the girl in the mirror who had the sweeter expression while her twin's mouth twisted into a smirk.

Hugh's father had been a practical man. He could keep a succession of elderly vans on the road and could talk to beggars or lords with equal ease. He could estimate the price of any painting to within ten percent accuracy and could judge the weight of a stranger's purse. But he had also been superstitious.

'Some paintings are bad luck, son. You don't always know at first, but as soon as you do, you get rid of them, even if it means giving them away.'

Hugh pushed his father's voice from his head. He took his pen knife and slit the paper backing from the frame, unsure of what he was looking for. Long ago Loring had pencilled the dimensions of the picture on the rear of the canvas as a guide to the framer, but there were no secret messages written there. Hugh slid his fingers along the inner batons of the frame, careful not to damage the painting. He was about to curse his own foolishness when he felt it, a slim cylinder tucked between the canvas and the wood.

Hugh unfurled a spool of paper. Inscribed on it in brown ink were the numbers 22 – 369 – 741– 8282. He had no idea what they meant, but he was certain this was what the stranger sought. If all went well he could be paid twice; sell the painting to the curator and the code, or whatever it was, to the stranger.

It was almost as if he had conjured the other man by thinking of him. No sooner had Hugh slipped the paper into his trouser pocket than there he was, wrapped in a long brown coat, striding across the forecourt towards the service kiosk, the bloodless mouth no longer smiling. Hugh slid low in his seat. Was it possible the stranger had somehow tracked his car? No, Hugh watched as the man made a call on his mobile. He had no idea that the painting was only a few metres away. Hugh couldn't make out what the stranger was saying, but he could see the expression on his face, a mixture of fear and anger that made Hugh slide down further still in his seat and stay there even after the man had killed the call and driven out of the forecourt into the swiftness of the autobahn.

Schloß Cappenberg shone white against the snow. Hugh crossed the cobbled courtyard, taking in the neat façade, the ranks of vacant windows where anyone might be watching him from the shadows. He hurried up the front steps and into an entrance hall designed to impress. The Schloß was host to a photography exhibition and a few visitors stood examining the black and white prints that lined the wall. Hugh scanned the hallway, taking in the parquet floor, imposing central staircase with its carved mahogany banister, the visitors still wrapped in their winter coats. There was no sign of his pursuer.

'Can I help you sir?'

The young receptionist looked worried. Hugh wondered what kind of a figure he cut, standing there without an overcoat on one of the year's coldest days. He twisted his face into a semblance of a smile and asked for the curator. The girl returned his smile, though her eyes remained wary.

'Herr Weiss has asked me to pass on his apologies. He's unexpectedly delayed, but invites you to explore the exhibition while you wait.'

Hugh clutched the briefcase. The white rooms lined with faces were too open to be safe. He looked out of the window at the branches of an old tree. He wondered how many winters it had seen. Beyond it the Cappenberg chapel stood straight and stern, its spire pointing towards heaven.

He said, 'Tell Herr Weiss I'll wait for him in the Kirk.'

Hugh stood beneath the alter looking at the carved figures of Otto and Gottfried von Cappenberg united in stone. The statuette made the brothers look like twins; they had the same pageboy haircuts, the same broad faces and pious expressions. Hugh had never wanted a brother when he was younger, but since his father's death he sometimes wished there was someone he could talk to, someone who really knew him.

The Kirk was peaceful after his frantic drive. Hugh walked to where a golden ornament shone out of a display cabinet, the Cappenberger Barbarossakopf, head of a Cappenberg ancestor raised high by a squad of angels. Hugh thought again of his father. He would have loved the Schloß and its Kirk. He was walking towards the ornately carved seats of the choir when he suddenly froze.

There was himself, face down in a pool of blood on the floor. Hugh looked again, no not himself, that was ridiculous, but another man of his height with the same thinning curls. Hugh knelt beside the body and rolled it over, knowing already what he would find.

The stranger's face stared up at him, his pale lips pulled back in a sneer a second bloody mouth gaping from his neck. Hugh pressed his hands against the wound, but the blood had ceased to pump from it. A knife shone from the floor. Hugh armed himself with it, in case the killer still hid in the shadows.

There was sound of footsteps on stone and then a gasp. A smart, bearded man was standing at the top of the nave, his face a rictus of shock.

Hugh jogged towards the curator, forgetting about the knife still clutched in his hand.

'No!'

Herr Weiss grabbed Hugh by the shoulder and pushed. Hugh felt himself losing balance. He raised a hand, meaning to catch hold of Herr Weiss' lapel and right himself. The knife was still in his grip. The curator grabbed Hugh by the shoulders and the two men stumbled to the ground together. Hugh said, 'No, it's not ...' But his voice was drowned in a gurgle of blood and the screams of the curator as he ran for help.

A passport was found in the pocket of the stranger who, in the absence of other documents, was identified as Hugh Carmichael, aged thirty-three, a struggling travel journalist with no known next of kin. Hugh's body was left unnamed and unclaimed; the only possible clue to his identity a scrap of paper bearing a sequence of numbers whose significance remained unknown. The painting languished in the police evidence vault for a long time, but was eventually gifted to Schloß Cappenberg where the curator kept it in his office for a while, a reminder of his own mortality. Eventually the strange twins began to get on his nerves and he assigned it to the basement. After all, as he said to his deputy, it was a poor copy, not really worth the canvas it was painted on.

PETER ROBINSON is best known for his DCI Banks books, set in his native Yorkshire; these began with *Gallows View* (1987) and in 2014 the twenty-third book, *Abattoir Blues*, was published. They have been filmed as a major ITV drama series. His recent standalone novel *Before the Poison* won the 2012 Arthur Ellis Award for Best Novel by the Crime Writers of Canada. He was born in Yorkshire in 1950 and divides his time between Richmond, Yorkshire, and Toronto, Canada.

People Just
Don't Listen

Peter Robinson

They say that the eyes are windows to the soul, but I have never been sure what they mean, whoever *they* are. What does a soul look like? Have you ever seen one? Isn't it supposed to be invisible? Perhaps they mean character. Can looking into someone's eyes tell you about her attributes, her dreams, fears, hopes, disappointments, successes and failures? It's possible, I suppose, though I know that, in reality, eyes are just gelatinous blobs of vitreous humour shot through with colour, fitted with rods and cones, connected to the brain via the optic nerve. Don't get me wrong; please don't assume that I have no aesthetic appreciation. I may be a man of science, but I am also a lover and collector of beautiful things.

So ran the gist of our conversation that evening. I am not normally a drinker, and I rarely meet women in hotel bars, but I was out of town on business in an unfamiliar city, and I was in a mood for company.

I first noticed her studying me in the long mirror behind the bar, the one that reflected all the different-coloured bottles. When she saw that I had caught her looking, she smiled, and we turned to face one another for real. I bought her a drink. Something blue with a striped umbrella and chunky ice cubes. It was then that we got talking about eyes.

There was no doubt that she was lovely, and I am neither vain nor naïve enough to think that such a woman would pay me a moment's notice were she not, shall we say, a working girl. Very high class, of course, but a working girl.

I saw that when I first looked into her eyes. They weren't hard or mercenary. Don't get me wrong. Her eyes were as beautiful as the rest of her. Deep-ocean blue, with no hint of grey, in perfect proportion to her nose and mouth. I have never seen such a *pure* shade of blue. But there *was* something worldly about them; theirs was a calculating sort of beauty.

When she asked me what I saw in them, however, I was cautious enough not to tell her the truth, only to say that they were very beautiful. She laughed and glanced away shyly. If it was an act, it was a good one. As the evening wore on, and drink followed drink, it became clear where we were headed.

When at last I invited her up to my room, she leaned forward and whispered a number in my ear. It seemed rather high, but no matter. I agreed to it, of course I agreed. A gentleman doesn't haggle. She slid off the bar stool and fell in alongside me to the lifts, taking my arm as we went, for all the world as if she were my girlfriend. I felt a strange tingle of excitement, a shortness of breath, a ringing in my ears.

I felt in my pocket for the little case of instruments I always carried with me and gripped the smooth leather. As the lift doors closed and she moved forward to kiss me, I found it hard to keep from laughing. It was all so easy. Why wasn't she running away from me as fast as she could? She should have known what she was walking into, what was waiting for her in my room – the curare, the speculum, the little glass jar of clear preserving fluid. But people just don't listen, do they? Hadn't I told her I collected beautiful things? Hadn't I told her she had beautiful eyes?

ANNE ZOUROUDI lived for seven years in Greece and the islands inspire much of her writing. She is the author of seven 'Mysteries of the Greek Detective' books, featuring Hermes Diaktoros, the most recent of which was *The Feast of Artemis* (2013). Born in Lincolnshire, she now lives in the Peak District with her son.

The Honey Trap

Anne Zouroudi

The American girl was wearing a red hat, a straw fedora with a sprig of delicate frangipane tucked in its ribbon band. The hat, being red, drew attention, but even without it the girl was beautiful and blonde enough to catch the eye. She was sitting with her friends at a harbour-front table, cool in the shade of the *kafenion*'s awning, ordering cold drinks from a waiter who was trying to flirt with her and her companions. But she wasn't interested in him. She turned away to watch a fisherman hawking his catch, and she looked happy, healthy and carefree.

She was just about the age Flora would be now.

Nikolas led his donkey through the high town, going slowly to match the donkey's pace. In full sun, the heat was searing, and he kept to the stripes of cooler shade along the house walls. At the *ouzeri* where he used to drink (an Italian *gelateria* now, the blue upright chairs replaced with wicker sofas, the wooden tables thrown out for glass and chrome) a family of foreigners was sitting in his old place under the vine. A boy and girl were dipping long spoons into glasses of melting ice-cream, the boy eating without relish, kicking his heels against his chair whilst his father keyed messages into a mobile phone. The girl watched the donkey as it went by, and smiled.

Nikolas lived high above the port, in a two-roomed house that had been his mother's dowry, a place with rotten woodwork and fatal cracks in the stone walls yet rescued by its glorious situation. From its rear windows and from the meadow below, the view was of the sandy beaches which gilded the coast, of the blue Aegean and, in the evenings, the western sky's flamboyant sunsets. When Nikolas was a boy, the view was all their own, but inevitably it had drawn those keen to sell it.

Permission was granted for an apartment complex, and from the day they broke the first rocks to lay the foundations, his mother fretted. She complained about the building work whilst it went on; she fretted about the activity there when it was complete, at the comings and goings of taxis and tour-buses, at the shouts and screams of children in the pool, at the laughter and singing when the foreigners came home drunk in the small hours.

'Don't worry, Mama,' Nikolas had said. 'It's an opportunity for us, you'll see.'

But she never saw; she died worried and troubled, despite the things he bought for her, the new shoes and dresses, the chicken for lunch on Sundays, the electric cooker and the repairs to the outhouse roof.

'What do I need with new dresses, at my age?' she used to say.

A short distance beyond the house, at a bend in the road leading to the popular beach at Vrysi, was an olive tree, ancient and twisted with a hollow in its trunk a small child could crawl inside. The tree produced few olives but its branches spread wide, and Nikolas conducted his business under their shade.

His lay-out was simple: a plastic patio table bartered from gypsies, three plastic chairs which were part of the same deal, a pine dresser which had been his mother's and his grandmother's. Each spring, Nikolas repainted the dresser, in every colour left over from painting his boat, so all the shelves were different colours – this year, red, green and yellow – and the frame and doors were orange and blue. The sign tacked on its side was hard to miss, in clumsy letters and three languages: Μέλι, Hönig, Honey.

The dresser was brash and gaudy; tourists found it irresistible, stopping their rented mopeds and cars to take photos. They'd want Nikolas in the picture, the old man and his donkey, quaint and quintessentially Greek. The donkey would stand patiently as the children stroked him, and the smaller ones were lifted onto his back. And then Nikolas would offer the foreigners a taste of honey from a spoon, and more often than not, they would buy a jar or two. The set-up was perfect, and profitable. Nikolas called it his honey-trap.

Today, as the house came into view, he could see beyond it someone sitting under the olive tree. That wasn't unusual; the road was a long climb, and often those walking to the beach would rest at the honey-trap. But something about this man was different. Most of those who stopped turned the chairs to face the view. He was facing down the road, towards the apartments.

As Nikolas passed the complex, there were shouts and screams from the pool. On a first-floor balcony, a toddler gripped the bars of a railing draped with swimsuits, grizzling and gazing miserably over the road towards the mountains. Nikolas led the donkey past his house to its place in the shade of the olive tree, and tethered it to a branch.

'*Yassou*, my friend,' he said to the stranger.

Cicadas were singing the rhythm of the islands, marking slow time, languor and heat. The stranger pushed his sunglasses back onto his head, and raised his beer-can to Nikolas. His eyes were striking blue, but bloodshot from too little sleep, or too much alcohol. He was middle-aged and fit, but making nothing of his good looks; his blond hair was a little too long, a young man's style he was a little too old for, and he was in need of a shave. He wore an unironed yellow t-shirt which had been washed too many times, so its rock-band logo was faded to grey; his shorts were baggy and unfashionable, the hem of one leg unstitched and drooping. He'd kicked off his salt-water-stained loafers, and sat with his bare feet outstretched, a supermarket bag of beer-cans under his chair.

'*Yassou*,' he said. 'Am I in your place?' He thought for a moment. 'You speak English?'

His own English was stilted, with a Scandinavian accent.

'I speak English,' said Nikolas. He moved the donkey's water bucket within its reach, and scooped his hand across the surface to remove the creatures that had drowned there: flies, a dirt-brown cricket, and a honey-bee, which he picked from the palm of his hand by its wing, and held up regretfully. He shook the dead insects to the ground. 'I spent ten years in New York City. I speak English like a Yank.'

The donkey snuffled in the water and began to drink. A rusty Toyota motored by, the elderly man at the wheel calling through the open window as he passed.

'*Yassou* Niko!'

Nikolas raised his hand, then unfastened the girth on the donkey's saddle. Horse-flies crawled on the animal's hide and around its eyes. When it had finished drinking, the bucket was all but empty, and the donkey turned its head to Nikolas as if asking for more.

Nikolas pulled the saddle from its back and dropped it pommel-up by the tree's roots.

'It's hot today, my friend,' he said. 'They say on the radio, 40 degrees this afternoon.'

'Too hot to walk,' said the stranger. 'I wanted to walk to the beach, but not in this heat. I told myself only a crazy man would walk so far. So I take a seat here, have myself a cold drink, and wait to see if I can find me a taxi.'

'You'll get one, if you wait long enough,' said Nikolas, taking a seat across the table. 'They all come by here, if you wait.'

'You want a beer?' asked the stranger.

'Sure.'

The stranger reached down to the bag under his chair, and fumbled for a can, which he offered to Nikolas. His fingernails were black with engine-oil.

'Thank you,' said Nikolas. He popped the cap, and held up the can. '*Yammas.*'

'*Skol*,' said the stranger.

They drank. The beer was cool, refreshing.

'I should introduce myself,' said the stranger. 'My name is Didrik.'

'They call me Nikolas.'

'So, I am pleased to meet you, Nikolas.'

'You Swedish?'

'Danish.'

'Your first time here?'

Didrik shook his head.

'No, I was here once before. I did not expect to come back, but I have a boat, and it's giving me trouble. Now I have to wait until they send a part from Athens. I hope not too long. The harbour fees are expensive. I want the engine fixed, and go. This place has changed too much since I was here. I remember it as quiet, very peaceful. Now there are cars everywhere, and motorbikes.'

Nikolas nodded.

'Every day it changes,' he said.

'You from here?'

'I was born in the house just here.'

The stranger looked in that direction, but his eyes went past the house to the apartment building, where the small boy on the balcony now stood in sullen silence.

'You find it very different then, for sure,' said Didrik. 'Do you like the tourists?'

'I like them fine,' said Nikolas. 'We Greeks, we always welcome new friends.'

Over the rim of his beer-can, Didrik studied him.

'You know, I think I know you,' he said. 'Your face, I have seen it before somewhere.'

He seemed to think.

'TV,' he said, after a moment's pause. He lowered his can, and pointed it at Nikolas. 'I saw you on TV, on the news. They interviewed you about Flora.'

Nikolas shook his head. 'That's old news,' he said. 'Very old news.'

'No, no,' said Didrik. 'I saw you recently. In the past day or so.'

'The press are here again this week,' said Nikolas, 'digging up the past. They've come for the anniversary, looking for a new angle in the story. I wish them luck. That trail is stone-cold.'

The stranger drank.

'Ten years,' he said, thoughtfully. 'Ten years, and not a sign. That's not easy to do on an island like this, to disappear a child. Someone was very clever.'

'You think so? She was so tiny.' On the balcony, the boy was no longer there. 'Only so high.' He held his hand waist-high above the ground.

'You were the last person to see her,' said Didrik. 'Apart from whoever ...' He left the sentence without an ending. Tormented by the biting flies, the donkey stamped its foot.

Nikolas placed his beer on the table and got up from his chair.

'I must go,' he said.

Didrik raised his hand.

'Forgive me,' he said. 'Please. I'm sure you're sick of people asking you questions about that all the time. Please, sit. No more on that subject. Please, finish your beer. Keep me company whilst I admire your view.' He moved his chair, at last, to face the sea. 'You're a lucky man to wake up every day to this.' Didrik drained his beer, and reached into the bag for another, bringing up two, holding one out to Nikolas. 'Here, have a fresh one. They're still cold.'

Nikolas considered, then accepted.

'Maybe one more,' he said, returning to his seat. 'But then I have to work.'

'What business are you in?'

Nikolas pointed to the meadow below the house. At one end there was a stable; in the field's farthest corner was a circle of bee-hives with one at their centre, all painted in the same bright colours as the dresser.

'You see those hives down there?' he asked. 'All mine.'

'You're the honey man?' Didrik looked behind him at the empty dresser shelves. 'So where's the honey?'

'Down there in the stable. Every day I carry it up here. And I must fetch it soon. No point in sitting here with nothing to sell.'

'I tell you what,' said Didrik. 'We drink our beer, then I'll help you set up shop. Because of course I want to buy some of your honey. How can I sit and drink with the bee-keeper and not buy honey? And I'm very pleased to be sitting with someone who knows about bees. From being a little kid I always wanted to keep bees, but I'm afraid of them. Don't they sting you?'

'Sometimes,' said Nikolas. 'It takes many years to get to know about bees. When you understand them, they respect you.'

A silence fell between them. The donkey sniffed its empty bucket, and flicked its ears against the flies.

'Here,' said Didrik, 'I want to show you something.'

He dug in his shorts for a coin, flipped it, caught it, rubbed his hands together with a flourish and showed Nikolas his empty hands.

Nikolas smiled.

'Clever,' he said. 'You are very clever, my friend.'

'I could teach you,' said Didrik. 'Kids love that trick. I bet every day you meet lots of children. That little trick, they will love it. I tell you what, I trade you. You teach me about your bees, I teach you this trick.'

'I don't need tricks,' said Nikolas. 'I have the donkey.'
Didrik nodded.

'The donkey's a good idea,' he said.

Nikolas had finished his second beer, and was feeling mellow. The clock at St Sotiris struck one; the road was quiet, the afternoon slipping into the sultriness of siesta.

Didrik's second can was untouched on the table. He rubbed his temples.

'Too much alcohol in this heat,' he said. 'I have a headache.'

Somehow he had moved again, facing away from the sea towards the apartments. A young woman appeared on the balcony where the boy had been crying. She wore brief shorts and a bikini top; her slender legs and stomach were oiled and tanned.

Didrik put his sunglasses back on his nose, hiding his eyes.

'You have a great view in two directions,' he said. 'Here, have another beer.'

'No, thank you,' said Nikolas. 'It's time for work.'

But Didrik had already popped a can, and Nikolas took it.

'I suppose you don't want your wife to catch you looking at the girls,' said Didrik. 'Too much of this then, I think.' He moved his fingers against his thumb to denote chattering, or nagging. 'Women are like that. They think a man shouldn't appreciate another woman.'

'I'm not married.'

Didrik grinned, and offered his hand across the table.

'Shake,' he said. 'To good sense and a smart brain. I also am not married.' Nikolas shook Didrik's hand, finding it hot against his own beer-cooled palm. 'But no marriage, no children. That is sad.'

The young woman finished spreading towels over the balcony rail and went inside. Somewhere, a child was crying.

'I always wanted a daughter,' said Didrik. 'A special little girl all of my own. I think sometimes of what I could do with her, the things I would buy for her. I would make her my princess. Flora, you know, I think she was such a child.' He watched a fly crawling on the table. 'What do you think happened to her? I am sorry to bring the matter to your attention again, but I am curious. I would like your opinion.'

Nikolas sipped his beer. On the road, a car went by too fast, there and gone.

'You ask me the same question as the police,' he said. 'They asked me that for days. Where did she go? I told them, ask the mother, ask the father. It's their job to know, not mine.'

'The parents had been drunk, I think.'

'They were drunk, and sleeping late, and the child was bored. She came walking up here, all by herself. She came to see the donkey. I asked if she liked honey, and when she said yes, I took her to the stable to get her some. I keep some little pots just for the children. Gifts, you know. They like that. So I took her with me to the store, and gave her a little jar, and told her to take it straight back to her Mama. It isn't far. You can see the distance, from here to there. Somewhere between here and there, she disappeared.'

'Like my coin trick.'

Nikolas looked at him, but couldn't see his eyes.

'Like your coin trick, yes.'

'They asked you a lot of questions, I'm sure.'

Nikolas sighed.

'For weeks, they kept coming back. What could I tell them? They said they had evidence she had been in the stable, but I told them that myself.'

'They had no other suspects.'

'No.'

'Maybe they should have waited around. They say, don't they, a killer always returns to the place of his crime.' He scanned the apartments. 'Which one was it? I never knew that.'

'This one here, close by us.' The clock at St Sotiris struck the half hour. Nikolas slapped his thighs, and stood. 'Time for work.'

Didrik stretched his arms above his head, and stood up too.

'I will help you,' he said.

Nikolas led Didrik down the path behind the house and into the meadow. The cicadas' song became muted, replaced by the humming of bees. A snake slithered rustling through the dry stalks of thistles. Nikolas was a little unsteady on his feet, and caught his foot on a stone.

'Careful there,' said Didrik.

Nikolas had built the stable himself, hammering wooden slats onto a knocked-together frame, laying scaffolding poles from ground to apex and covering them with terra-cotta tiles. He beckoned Didrik inside. The place was cramped, dark and hot and sweet with the perfume of the honey stacked in crates and boxes.

'No room for the donkey,' said Didrik. 'But boy, that stuff smells good. Hey, what's this?'

Hanging on a hook was a bee-keeper's helmet; on a shelf, a smoke-gun and gauntlets.

'These are the real thing, yes?' Didrik picked up the smoke-gun. 'Can you show me how to use this?'

Nikolas was looking amongst the boxes, picking out which ones to haul up to the road.

'Maybe later,' he said. 'This is my golden time, when they start coming back from the beach. No-one buys honey going, but coming back, they're relaxed, maybe they've had a glass of wine. That's when they're ripe and ready for me.'

Didrik smiled.

'You're a man of business,' he said. 'But please, show me. A few minutes of your time only. I won't be here tomorrow, and I want to see it done in real life. How do you make the bees not sting you? Show me, and then I'll help you with the boxes. You'll be twice as quick as normal.'

'OK,' said Nikolas. 'But I have to be quick.'

He carried his equipment outside. When he lit the gun, the smoke wafted dense and white from its spout, bringing the dangerous smell of burning into the still air.

'We have to be very careful,' he said. 'This time of year, just a spark can start a fire. That would be a problem. A big problem.'

He put on the helmet and arranged the netting over his face, pulled on the gauntlets and picked up the gun.

'The bees are working,' he said. 'If they're disturbed too much, they don't like it, and the queen calls them all together, and off they go. Then I have an empty hive, and no honey.'

'Does that happen often?'

'Sometimes. Then I leave the hive empty for a while, to see if she comes back. If she doesn't, I have to find another queen. So to keep them quiet, I think it would be better if you waited here.'

'I wait, and I watch,' said Didrik.

Nikolas worked his way around the hives, puffing in smoke to subdue the bees, raising the lids to lift out the supers, examining the honeycomb and the honey sealed within. When he was done, he removed the helmet and the gauntlets, and put out the smoke-gun with a splash of water from the donkey's trough.

'All healthy,' he said. 'Plenty of honey for next year. So, now maybe you can help me with these boxes.'

At the police station, a group of people was waiting: the Chief of Police and his sergeant, three senior investigators from Athens, a man haggard with pain, his wife worn thin with suffering. As Didrik walked in, the haggard man put his arm around his wife's shoulders.

'How was it?' asked one of the officers, coming forward. 'How did it go?'

'He didn't say much,' said Didrik. 'But I have an idea where you might look. It may be nothing, of course. I persuaded him to open the hives, but the hive at the centre, he didn't touch.'

At dawn the next morning, two police cars pulled up outside Nikolas's house. Nikolas was in the kitchen, brewing coffee. He opened the door before the policemen reached it.

'*Kali mera*, Nikolas,' said the Chief of Police. The investigators stood at his shoulders.

The Chief of Police waved an envelope.

'I have a warrant to search this property.'

'For God's sake,' said Nikolas. 'You've turned over every centimetre of this property more than once. Why can't you just leave me in peace?'

A man was climbing from one of the police cars, a man Nikolas didn't know. He was carrying a beekeeper's helmet and gauntlets.

They left Nikolas in the house under a constable's guardianship. The beekeeper they'd brought with them put on his helmet and gloves.

At the entrance to the centre hive, there were no bees coming and going. The beekeeper put his ear to the red-painted side, and listened. The hive was silent.

The Chief of Police signalled him to open it.

The beekeeper raised the lid, and smelled not honey sweetness but faint fungal decay. Inside, curled on itself like a foetus was the skeleton of a child; set amongst the delicate hand-bones was a small pot of honey.

At the harbour-front *kafenion*, the girl in the red hat was sitting again with her friends. When she saw Didrik, she smiled and waved. Didrik looked a different man, clean-shaven and urbane in linen and espadrilles. She kissed his cheek.

They walked together to the police station, where Didrik ushered the girl through the crush of camera-crews and reporters, into the crowded office upstairs.

The Chief of Police made introductions, and invited the reporters to put their questions to Didrik.

A woman from Greek national radio raised her hand.

'Mr Bernat,' she said, 'you're a world-renowned actor, last year you won an Academy award. Can you tell us what persuaded you to come to Greece to help out in this case?'

The girl with Didrik had taken off her red hat. His put his arm affectionately around her shoulder.

'Quite simply, my beautiful daughter Sissi,' he said. His English was clear and fluent, his accent American. 'This was all her idea. She told me I should do whatever I could, so I offered my only talent. I had to help, because things might have been different. I was here, with my family, the day Flora was taken. It chills my blood to think so, but he might have taken Sissi instead of her. How Flora's parents have borne their grief, I shall never comprehend.'

The shutters on Nikolas's house were closed. The Chief of Police led Flora's mother and father down the path to the meadow, where a line of crime-scene tape was strung around the bee-hives, the loose ends fluttering in a breath of evening breeze.

The red hive was set apart from the others, close to the honey store. Flora's mother was carrying white roses, and a pink teddy-bear.

She placed her gifts at the foot of the hive.

'I'll wait under the olive tree,' said the Chief of Police, and he walked away.

ANN CLEEVES is the author of twenty-seven novels, the most recent of which have been part of her 'Vera Stanhope' and 'Shetland Island' (Jimmy Perez) series. Both series have been adapted for TV, as *Vera* (ITV) and *Shetland* (BBC) and the books have been translated into twenty languages. In 2006 she won the inaugural Duncan Lawrie Dagger for her novel *Raven Black*. Born in Hereford in 1954, Ann now lives in Northumberland.

The Spinster

Ann Cleeves

She twisted the carded fleece between the fingers of her left hand and fed it into the spinning wheel. Her right foot rocked on the pedal and kept the rhythm smooth and regular. The view from her window was of her neighbour's croft land towards the sea. She'd grown up in this house and usually she took the scene for granted, but now Stuart's digger was biting into the peaty soil and preparing the foundations for his new home. It wouldn't block her whole view and he'd come to her, very polite and quiet, explaining that with the new baby on the way, the old house wouldn't be big enough.

'Much easier to start from scratch,' he'd said. 'The planners have given their permission.'

She'd seen that even if she objected the house would be built and Stuart had always been a good neighbour. She'd known him since he was a bairn and she didn't want to fall out now. So she'd smiled and said of course they needed a bigger place and it would be good to see a child playing from her window. Joan was a spinster and there hadn't been a child in Holmsgarth since she and her sisters were young.

But the sight of the digger made her uneasy. It disturbed the rhythm of her spinning and when she looked at the yarn it was uneven and bobbly. It would knit in an interesting way, but it wasn't how she'd intended it to be. She set her spinning aside and went to the kitchen to make her tea, but even from there she could hear the rumbling of the machine, and she fancied that she could feel its vibration under her feet.

Later she took up her knitting. She was working on an all-over jersey, a commission from an American woman, who'd wanted natural colours and traditional patterns. By now it was dark outside and she had the curtains closed. She switched on the television to hide the sound of the digger, but the headlights were so bright that they shone through her curtains, making weird shadows on the wall. Then the lights went away and everything was quiet and for the first time that day she could concentrate on her work.

She knitted as her mother had done with a leather belt, padded with horsehair and three pins pointed at both ends. One of the pins she'd stuck into the belt and the garment grew as a tube. There were three colours: Shetland black, grey and mourrit and she kept the tension even as she wove the wool into the back of the pattern. She was working on the anchor motif and that reminded her of her father, who'd had his own fishing boat and had been lost at sea. Soon she was so lost in her memories that when there was more noise on the building site she hardly noticed it.

They'd been three sisters. Half-sisters, in fact, because Joan's mother had died when she was a bairn and her father had remarried. Joan was the oldest by ten years and then there'd been Annie and Edie. Now Edie was away and Annie was dead, taken by cancer just two years before. None of them had found a man. The nearest any of them came to it was in the seventies when the oil had first come into the islands. Then men had flocked to Shetland, like the seabirds arriving on the cliffs in the spring, jostling for space on the rocky ledges. Men were everywhere and girls could take their pick. Joan was in her thirties then, already considered something of an old maid, but Annie and Edie had been young and wild and looking for husbands. It was a while since Joan had remembered that time, but now, her fingers busy with the knitting, stopping occasionally to follow the pattern she'd made by plotting tiny crosses on graph paper, she relived those months in the summer of 1974.

She'd watched from the sidelines as her sisters made fools of themselves at dances and parties. There was one particular man from the Scottish mainland. He was an engineer with the construction company and he had digs with Margaret Hay, who lived just down the road from Holmsgarth. He'd hired a car and set off to work every morning looking very smart. Both Edie and Annie had thought that he would make a fine husband and often found excuses to drop in on Margaret when they knew the man was at home. Joan paused for a moment and rested her work in her lap while she struggled to remember his name. James Mackie. How could she have forgotten it when he had caused so many arguments in their house? So much disruption to their lives.

She continued knitting. The anchor pattern had finished and she felt a moment of calm. It was superstition but knitting the anchor always made her uncomfortable. Now she had three rows of mourrit to work. Easy and needing no concentration.

James Mackie, quiet and respectable, from somewhere on the west coast of the Scottish mainland, with an accent that was soft like cream. All three sisters, starved for so long of new male company, dreamed of James Mackie when they went to sleep at night. Even Joan, who understood that she was too old to have a chance with him, who would always be a spinster. By then their father had died, drowned in an accident, his body never found, and they were just four women living at Holmsgarth. Joan's stepmother and the three sisters.

Without realising she'd finished the three rows of plain knitting, she took up the graph paper again and focused on the pattern.

There had been a dance in the community hall and they'd all gone along. It had been planned for weeks. The band was from Cullivoe; the boys were fine musicians famous throughout the islands. In Holmsgarth, the women had baked, even Joan who'd been working all day in the post office in Lerwick. They'd packed up the bannocks, the tray-bakes and the fancies into old biscuit tins and carried them very carefully along the road to the hall. Edie had got there early. She'd cut long sheets of white paper to make table-cloths for the trestle tables set at one end of the room and the band was on the stage, tuning up. There'd already been an air of excitement. More than that, an air of tension. Like just before a thunderstorm.

Joan turned back to her knitting. There was more noise on the road outside. She looked at the clock on the mantel shelf. Stuart must be working late tonight or perhaps they'd invited pals along to a party in their house. They'd not be doing so much of that once the bairn arrived. Joan felt a sudden pang of regret. All her pals had grandchildren now, and she had to look at the photos and pretend to be interested. She turned her mind back forty years to the dance in the hall, saw James Mackie walking in. You could tell that he'd prepared for the party too, that he'd had a shower after work, chosen an ironed shirt. His dark hair was slicked back. Some of the local boys walked with a kind of swagger but he moved lightly. Joan could see that he'd be a splendid dancer.

She was jerked back to the present by a banging on the door. 'Come in,' she said. She didn't want to get up and disturb the knitting attached to her belt. Besides, her door was never locked. She turned in her seat and saw a man walk in. He was dark and he walked lightly, just like Mackie. Perhaps because she'd been thinking about the engineer, for a strange moment she wondered if it was Mackie and if she'd slipped back in time somehow and into the world of her memories. Then she recognised the newcomer as the police inspector from Ravenswick. 'Jimmy Perez, what can I do for you at this time of night?'

'I need to talk to you, Joan.' His voice was soft like cream too, but the accent was Fair Isle, not mainland Scots.

'Well, take a seat by the fire, Jimmy. And you won't mind if I take up my knitting. It's hand-spun wool and the Yanks will pay a fortune for a Shetland all-over jersey.'

He nodded. 'Stuart was working on the foundations of his new house,' Perez said. 'He found a body. Old but preserved in the peat. Would you know anything about that Joan? You'd likely have been living in this house when he died and in those days that was Holmsgarth land.'

She changed the knitting pin in the horsehair belt and as the needles clicked she began to talk. She thought it was time that the story was told and this gentle man, who knew about grief, was the right person to hear it.

'There was a dance,' she said. 'I was there with my sisters. And there was this soothmoother, an engineer at Sullom Voe. James Mackie. '

'Is that the name of the man Stuart found?'

She hesitated for a moment and then she nodded, thinking again that it was time for the truth to be told. 'I had two sisters, Annie and Edie, and they fancied him, fought over him. You know young girls. And it was a wild time in the islands, Jimmy. The oil was coming ashore and we were over-run by strangers. It seemed kind of lawless. Like a gold rush town.' She knew that was no excuse for what had happened that night, but she wanted him to understand. He said nothing and she thought he would sit there all night if that was as long as it took.

'Most folk had been drinking,' she said. 'Not me. I've never liked it so much, but my sisters had been outside with some of the boys. They had bottles of whisky in the cars. You know how it goes, Jimmy. Much the same these days with young people.'

Still he said nothing. In her head she relived the scene. Mackie walking through the door, the music starting and him walking up to her and giving her a little nod. 'Would you dance with me, Joan?' That voice which had haunted her dreams. Caressing. And she'd set down the plate of scones she'd been holding and he swung her onto the floor and the music carried them around, until she was dizzy with the sound and the excitement at having been chosen. At the end she'd been aware of Edie and Annie watching them, thinking he'd picked their big sister for the first dance out of politeness, waiting for their turn. Only their turn never came. James Mackie had danced with the old maid all night.

'He walked us home,' Joan said. 'All three of us. My sisters were in a dreadful state. Angry.' And she'd understood their humiliation. Of course they'd danced, but with the local boys and the roustabouts from the rigs. Not with the smart man in the shirt, with the soft voice and the polished shoes. Not with the object of their dreams. And on the way home they'd behaved like spoilt little girls again. Their father had doted on his younger daughters and given them everything they wanted. Joan, the child of a previous marriage, had been expected to behave. She explained all this to Jimmy Perez, who listened, nodding occasionally to show that he understood.

'You were like Cinderella,' he said, with a smile.

'But they weren't the ugly sisters!' Joan paused in her knitting. 'They'd always been bonny little things. Everyone loved them. Especially my father. They could do no wrong in his eyes.'

'You were telling me what happened when you were on your way home.' Perez leaned forward to listen.

Joan replayed the scene in her head. The girls, stupid drunk, egging each other on, taunting the man. 'Why did you choose her to dance with when you could have had us?'

Then Mackie had stood in the middle of the track. Quiet and firm, his face lit by the moon. 'Why would I choose a child when I could have a woman?'

And then Edie had lashed out at him in frustration, the attack shocking and unexpected. She'd always been uncontrollable when she was angry, given to fits of temper. Suddenly she had a pair of scissors in her hand, the sharp scissors she'd brought from home to cut the paper table-cloths. The steel flashed in the light and then they were in the man's neck. Blood everywhere. They knew death, all three of them. They'd helped kill their father's beasts.

'What happened next?'

'We buried him.' Joan looked up from her knitting. 'In the land that Stuart bought from us for his grazing. It never occurred to us that he would build a house there, that the body would ever be found.'

'You helped them?' Perez seemed shocked by the idea. He knew her as the former post-mistress, a respectable spinster. 'You didn't think to tell the police?'

Joan thought about that for a moment and shook her head. It had been an evening for her to remember but she'd known she could never leave Holmsgarth to go south with James Mackie. She hadn't lost that possibility with the man's death. They'd sent Edie away to an aunt's in Canada and she'd gone on to be a journalist on a woman's magazine. Famous in her own way. Rich at least. Edie had sent Joan money for a visit but Joan had never gone. 'What would be the point in telling the police? Just another life ruined.'

Besides, there would have been something hypocritical in that, when Joan herself was a murderer. She'd killed their father, after all. After his marriage to the new woman from Baltasound he'd treated Joan like a kind of servant and Joan had had a temper too. In the end she'd had enough of it, being treated like a slave in her own home while her sisters were spoiled and feted like princesses. She'd felt as Perez said, like a kind of Cinderella.

One morning she'd risen early and drilled holes in his yoal before he set off after the fish they called piltock. She'd stood by the jetty and watched him drown. But that was a secret she'd never tell, not even to the police inspector from Ravenswick with the kind smile and the voice like cream.

MARTYN WAITES is the author of ten novels, most recently *Angel of Death*, the sequel to Susan Hill's *Woman in Black*. He has also been known to get frocked up as Tania Carver, whose latest novel, *The Doll's House*, was an international bestseller. He has also held two writing residencies in prisons, taught creative writing to recovering addicts and excluded teenagers, and twice been the RLF Writing Fellow at Essex University. He was born in Newcastle and worked as an actor before turning to crime writing.

Diagnosis: Murder

Martyn Waites

Cancer. Such a big word for such a small amount of letters. Cancer. Two syllables, six letters – two of which recur – four consonants, two vowels. Cancer. Small word. Big impact.

I didn't take in anything else the doctor had said once he had said that word. He was still talking, leaning across the table, giving me his most humane, sorrow-filled gaze. Empathising. Sympathising.

Fair enough, I thought, you really want to empathise then you have it instead.

Stage four, the doctor said. Inoperable.

I sat silently, listening. Or looking like I was listening. All I really heard was white noise. Eventually he went silent and I thought that silence must mean it was my turn to speak.

'How long have I got?' I had to say something. I hated myself for using such a clichéd question. But thinking about it, I suppose that the reason phrases become clichés is because of situations like this one.

'A few weeks, a month? Couple of months? Hard to say. It's aggressive, metastasising fast. The best thing you could do now is go home. Put your affairs in order. Spend time with your loved ones.'

Those words made me think of clutching my family towards me and sitting in the cellar until a tornado passes. Only I won't be going upstairs again to inspect the damage once it's finished.

There were more apologies, more attempts at empathy from him, but I didn't hear them.

I walked out of the surgery in a daze. If I was honest, I had known what the lump in my chest was, the shortness of breath, the incessant coughing. The pain like a magician doing a knife trick in a Chinese cabinet. Known straight away. But I'd still held out hope. Some last minute Hollywood reprieve, a mix up with the results, some entirely innocent and innocuous explanation. But no. This is the real world. It doesn't work that way. I knew what it was. Had always known.

Cancer.

I walked back to the car, got in, drove off. When I thought back afterwards I didn't remember making the drive home. I could have ploughed into a bus stop full of people and not noticed. All I was thinking about was how this wasn't right. Cancer was something that someone else got. Everything was something that someone else got. Death was something that someone else got. Or should get. Not me. I felt the anger then. Welling up. Familiar and hard. Not me. Not me. Why was it always me that things like this happen to? Why have I never had the luck that other people have had? Karen, my wife, always hinted, in that passive aggressive way of hers, that things often didn't go my way because of my attitude. Too aggressive, she said. Too full on. It puts people off you, she said. Bollocks, I thought. Too aggressive, my arse. You get nothing in this world unless you fight for it, I always told her. Fighting. That's what I had to do. Even now.

When I pulled the car into the drive, I didn't realise that I'd been talking to myself out loud. My chest was hurting again from the exertion. I sat for a few minutes until I got the strength up to get out.

I looked over to the next door neighbours. Felt that anger again, but a different kind this time. When we moved in we were nothing but nice to them. And they responded to our kindness by being a pair of lying, duplicitous evil cunts. They reported our dog, a puppy at the time, to the council for being a nuisance. Out all night, they said. Barking all night. What a load of fucking lies. We got the council round. Checked the dog out. The council woman asked us if we wanted to report our nuisance neighbours. We didn't. Not then.

Then they took our hedge up. A fifty-metre hedge. Told us it was theirs. We asked to see the documentation. We're still waiting. They took a country hedge down and replaced it with a fucking ugly laurel hedge. Laurel. Dull, ugly, unimaginative and suburban. Just like them. We told them, you don't come to live in the country and try to change things. That's the trouble with the countryside. Getting full of suburban shits like them.

Then they took our trees down. Full grown elms, been there god knows how long. Border between the two houses. And most importantly, on our land. They did it while Karen was out and I was away on work. We came back to nothing. Then they tried to take us to court, saying we were trying to take over their land. The land the trees had been on. Our land. That's still ongoing.

And that's not to mention the incessant complaints they make to the kids when they play in the garden.

Hate them. Fucking, fucking hate them.

When we tell people about them they think that they must be old. Intolerant. No, the opposite. They're young. Childless. All they do is work. They have no friends, nothing. They just want to make money and sit in their house in silence. That's it.

Their car was on the drive. A BMW. I stared at it. Why couldn't it be them? Why couldn't they get cancer and not me? They deserved it. They're utter cunts. Life is really fucking unfair.

I went into the house. Karen was sitting in the conservatory, pretending to read the paper. The dog was lying on the sofa next to her. She looked up. She knew what I was going to say before I said it. I just nodded. She came to me, hugged me. Started to cry.

'Are they sure?' she said.

I told her they were.

'But what if they've got it wrong? You read about it all the time. They've given someone the wrong diagnosis, they've got the notes mixed up, or ...'

'They haven't,' I said, getting angry again. 'They've got it right.'

We stood like that for a while.

Then it was a question of telling the kids. There was no easy way of doing it. They came in from school happy, or as happy as two teenage girls could be. We sat them down then after dinner I told them.

It went as well as could be expected. Which wasn't well at all. It was their worst nightmare, losing a parent. Worse than divorce, because at least then they're still alive and contactable. And it wasn't going to be a sudden death either. It was going to be slow and it was going to hurt. Me to do it, them to watch it.

There was more hugging after that. Lots more.

In bed that night I lay awake. I didn't want to close my eyes, drift off to sleep. Have nothing in my mind until I woke up. Because one day, very soon, that's what I would have. Forever. And then I would never wake up.

Karen was asleep, or pretending to be. I got up, went to the window. The security lights on the driveway come on whenever the overgrown rose bush is blown in front of them. It doesn't bother me, but probably annoys the twats next door. Good. I could see their cars on their gravelled drive. A BMW and a VW Golf. Perfectly parked at the same angle and in exactly the same place they parked them in every night.

And I felt again that familiar anger well up inside me. The unfairness of it all. Here's me, dying, in a rundown house, struggling to keep my family going. Not easy in this financial climate. And there's them, working in the city, rolling in it. It's not fair. Not fucking fair.

I went back to bed. I still couldn't sleep.

I kept thinking of everything I had to do before the cancer claimed me. Get my affairs in order, the doctor had said. I tried to work out how much life insurance would be left for Karen and the girls. I'm not good with numbers but I don't think it was enough. But then it's never enough. I felt like such a failure. I lay there, thinking of ways I could provide for my family, that I could leave them with something.

Two hours later, I'd worked it out.

And then I finally managed to sleep.

The next day was a Friday. Karen asked me what I wanted to do that weekend. Started making plans. I told her I wanted to be on my own. I wanted to think things through. Sort myself out. She was a bit put out by this but she said that was fine. She would take the kids and go and stay with her parents. I said that would be good.

That night, I waved them off. The girls were scared, thought it was the last time they would see me. I told them it wouldn't be. That I would still be here on Sunday night when they came back. That they hadn't got rid of me yet. They seemed placated by that and I felt like a liar. I shouldn't make promises I couldn't keep.

Alone at last. I went into the garage, got things together. I'm not much for DIY so I had to sharpen a few things up, check that the stuff I wanted still worked. It did. Then I checked out what I needed to on my laptop. Made a couple of calls. Heard what I wanted. Then I waited.

Until it was dark. Until it was past midnight.

I left the house as quietly as possible. I'd dressed in black, trying to blend in with the shadows. I had everything I needed in a bag at my side. I stood by the front of my garage, where the elm trees used to be. Stared at my neighbour's house. The lights were out. I crossed the line. Walked onto their gravel driveway.

Somewhere overhead I heard an owl out hunting. Really clear. One of the things I love about living in the countryside. One of the things I'll miss.

Their security light came on. I ducked into the shadow. Then walked up to their front door, rang the bell. Waited. Nothing. Eventually, I heard someone coming. The door was opened and the shaven headed, bovine face of Martin Sloan stared at me. He was in a dressing gown and couldn't decide whether to be shocked or angry. I didn't give him the chance to think.

I pulled the machete out of its sheath and pushed him back inside, holding it against his throat. He felt how sharp it was.

'Not one fucking sound. Right?'

He stared at the blade, thought of shouting out. I pushed it into the skin of his neck. It bled. From the expression on his face, it hurt.

'Right?' I said again.

He nodded.

'Good.'

My legs were shaking. I tried to control them. This was what I'd wanted to do for so long, I couldn't believe I was actually doing it.

'Now,' I whispered, 'upstairs.'

He walked upstairs. I kept the knife in his back, pushed as hard as I dared.

'In the bedroom.'

He went into the bedroom. Dee Sloan, his wife, was sitting there.

'What –'

She jumped up, tried to make a run at me. I let her see the blade.

'Back on the bed, cunt,' I said, not bothering to keep my voice quiet. 'Now.'

Seeing that she had no choice, she did as she was told.

'What the fuck are you doing?' Martin Sloan.

'Did I tell you you could speak? No? Then shut up.'

I sliced at his dressing gown with the machete just for good measure. The blade was so sharp it went through cloth and hit his arm. He pulled away as blood began to soak through.

'You're mental,' he said, gasping and holding his arm.

I laughed. 'You,' I pointed at his wife. 'Take my laptop out of my bag.'

She did so.

'Open it. Put it on the bed.'

She did so.

'Now,' I said. 'I've set up a couple of offshore accounts in false names.' I laughed again. Who says I'm not good with numbers? 'So if you wouldn't mind, I'd like you to transfer all of your savings, shares, whatever you've got, into them. Now.'

They stared at me.

'I'm not joking. Now.'

They looked at each other, didn't move. It seemed they would need a bit more persuading.

I pulled Dee off the bed, put my arm round her neck, laid the blade against her throat. 'Now,' I said, showing my impatience.

'You wouldn't,' Martin Sloane said. 'You really wouldn't.'

I dug the blade in and pulled it across her throat. The blood spurted in a huge arc, decorating the bland, bare wall. She gurgled and struggled, her hand going to her throat in a useless gesture. I let her go, watched her drop to the floor.

She bled out, eyes wide, fearful, uncomprehending.

I smiled. Felt like my heart was about to burst. 'I've wanted to do that for years,' I said. 'You've no idea how good that feels.'

Martin Sloane was staring ahead, terror-struck.

'The money. Now.'

Moving like a zombie, he did as he was told.

He did everything that I asked. I watched him do it. Eventually he looked up. 'I've got nothing left,' he said.

'Good,' I said. 'Now you know how I feel.'

Then it was his turn to have his throat ripped.

I stood in the bedroom staring at the two bodies. I felt ... numb. I thought I would feel elated at doing that, considering how much I had hated them for years, how much I had wanted to. And I had felt that slight exhilaration of power when I had watched the life drain of Dee's body.

But now I just felt ... nothing. Irritated, if anything because of it. What a disappointment.

I quickly packed up my belongings, checked that I'd left no traces. It didn't really matter considering what was about to happen to me but I wanted to give myself enough time to create some kind of paper chase with the money, get it into Karen's accounts before the bodies were discovered. Make it safe. Get it hidden. Make sure my family were well looked after.

Karen came back with the kids on Sunday night. I hadn't died. I was still there.

It took quite a few days before the police arrived at our neighbour's house. And then when they did we had the full circus.

'What d'you think's happened there?' asked Karen, watching the police go about their business.

'Something horrible, I hope.'

'Matthew, that's a terrible thing to say.'

'Yeah, but they're not nice people. You know that.'

We kept watching from the window. It was like TV playing out right before us. Then the phone rang. I answered it.

Doctor Sinclair. 'You're not going to believe this, Matthew, but I've got some good news for you. Well, relatively good news.'

'What? What d'you mean?'

'The tests,' he said, unable to keep the jubilation out of his voice. 'There was a mix up at the hospital. I'm so sorry. I don't know how it happened. But I've got your actual results in front of me. And it looks like you don't have cancer.'

I couldn't speak. He went on.

'Pneumonia. Serious, obviously, but not terminal. Treatable, if it's caught in time. Which it has been. But not lung cancer. Definitely not lung cancer. I'm so pleased to be able to tell you this ...'

He kept talking. I hung up.

Karen asked who that was. I didn't reply. Just stared out of the window.

There were two policemen on the neighbours' drive. They were looking at our house.

Karen asked again who had been on the phone. Again, I said nothing.

The two police walked across where the elms used to be, made their way onto my drive way.

I stood there, staring, waiting for the doorbell to ring.

ALEXANDER McCALL SMITH was born in Bulawayo, in the then-British colony of Southern Rhodesia, in 1948. He studied and taught law in Edinburgh, Belfast and Botswana, and is Emeritus Professor of Medical Law at the University of Edinburgh. It was Botswana that inspired his bestselling crime series, *The No. 1 Ladies' Detective Agency*, which has sold more than 20 million copies. He is the author of more than fifty novels and in 2007 was awarded the CBE for his services to literature.

Trouble at the Institute for the Study of Forgiveness

Alexander McCall Smith

I am not quite sure of just how I came to be considered the country's foremost investigator of the crimes of Academia. The acquisition of a reputation tends to be a slow matter and the way in which it happens is not necessarily obvious. People talk to one another and recommendations are made; sometimes it is the results themselves that do the work. However it may come about, suddenly one finds oneself able to turn down lesser business and concentrate on the thing on which you're meant to be the expert. And that, I think, is the point when you can tell yourself you've arrived.

It took all of fifteen years in my case. When I inherited the company I had very little experience of anything, let alone private detection. Becoming a private investigator was the last thing on my mind at that stage – I had just qualified as a tax accountant, and I imagined that preparing tax returns would be my lot in life. But then my childless Uncle Saul died and I found myself the owner of his business, which happened to be the Golden Gate Investigation Bureau of San Mateo, California. I had a bit of spare time on my hands and I decided, not entirely seriously, to acquire my licence. Within a few months I found myself drawn in, and have been unable to extricate myself since then. Not that I'm complaining; the life of a private investigator in a pleasant college town is not all that stressful and, as I soon discovered, can be quite fulfilling. After all, we do help people, and in many cases rather needy people. That is not a bad calling in life – although I suppose tax accountants help people too, although in a rather different way.

I had built up my practice with very small cases. A lot of my work was concerned with the messy corners of people's personal lives – adultery, suspected or real; custody issues; investigations of employee loyalty, and so on. Most of this was simple human disagreement or bad behaviour, rather than crime, and in most cases the solution to the problems was pretty apparent once one started to look more closely. I said that it was small, and some of it was *very* small: every so often I would be asked to locate a missing dog or cat, and I was not too proud to decline. That is hardly Raymond Chandler territory, but I suspect that in real life Raymond Chandler territory does not really exist. It makes for a good story, but we should not imagine that such things ever really happen.

As the years went by, I began to notice that I was getting more and more requests to investigate matters in colleges and universities. The first of these cases, as I recall, involved a case of impersonation. A professor at a small liberal arts college in upstate New York was suspected of not being the person he claimed to be. He was a professor of English by the name of Timmins, and the reason for the Dean's suspicion was the fact that Professor Timmins used very bad grammar when he spoke. This would not be a matter of remark in ordinary circumstances – the man who fixes your roof might be a bit hazy on the subjunctive – but it is somewhat unexpected when a professor of English says, 'He done quite good there.' And that, apparently, is just what he said when congratulated by the Dean on the performance of one of his students.

'Ha!' said the Dean. 'The demotic expression – how amusing.'

But this, apparently, had been greeted by a blank stare on the part of Professor Timmins, who was clearly not sure about the meaning of *demotic*. This was the incident that led to my being called in and discovering, on investigation, that Professor Timmins was an imposter. The real Professor Timmins had died shortly before being interviewed for his post and had been impersonated thereafter by his gardener.

That case was widely reported, and I think that it was the foundation of my career as a specialist academic private investigator. Thereafter, requests for my assistance came thick and fast. I investigated cases of plagiarism, misuse of the photocopying facilities, and cheating in examinations. And then, last year, I was asked to get involved in the affairs of the Pacific North-West Institute for the Study of Forgiveness, which was part of the Humanities School of a small but extremely well-funded private university not far from Seattle. This was one of my most extraordinary cases, and if we learn something from every case we take on, this was one from which I think I learned the most about human nature.

The call came from the Dean.

'Your name has been passed on to me,' he said. 'I understand that you're an expert on academic investigations.' He paused. 'Should I address you as Professor or Doctor?'

I was not sure whether he was being sarcastic. 'Mister,' I said.

'Well, Mr Andersen, we have an issue here, I'm afraid. We have a department of this college where something is going badly wrong. We need somebody from the outside to come and take a look at what's going on and, if possible, sort it out.'

He sounded embarrassed, which did not surprise me, as most people feel awkward when consulting a private investigator. We understand of course, and try to make it easy for them.

'I work in the strictest confidence,' I said. 'Apart from writing the occasional article or memoir, that is.'

He laughed. He thought I was joking.

'But I do,' I repeated.

'Hah!' he said. 'That's fine by me. We all need our little joke.'

I take that remark of his, by the way, to constitute his formal waiver in respect of what I write below.

When I travelled up to that rather pleasant little college town, I was met at the local airport by the Dean.

'I teach Ancient Greek myself,' he explained, as he drove me to the campus hotel. 'Not that many people study it any more. Students these days are far too lazy to tackle a subject like that. So I teach it in English. Same goes for Latin.'

I could not think of much to say, although I wondered how one taught Ancient Greek, or Latin for that matter, in English; Academia, I had discovered, was full of such mysteries, most of them clearly not to be solved by me. So I simply said, 'Well, there you are. That's the way things are these days.'

'Sure are,' said the Dean. 'But let me tell you about this little problem of ours. Then you can freshen up in the hotel before you come in and take a look round.'

I was already looking at my surroundings. It was typical of those comfortable college towns one finds from Ann Arbor to Oxford, Mississippi: neat houses, small clusters of stores selling football memorabilia and notebooks, coffee houses full of students in front of laptops, neo-classical dormitories with music drifting from the open windows.

'We're a well-funded institution,' explained the Dean. 'We have a large endowment for our size and we were left a lot of land not far from the city. That set us up very well. So we have no real problems.'

'A good place to be,' I said. 'But then, if that's the case, then why do you need me?'

'I meant financial problems,' said the Dean. 'There are other sorts of problems, and we have them, I'm afraid.'

I waited for him to explain.

'We have a few prominent programmes here,' he continued. 'We have a very good literature department that's doing a concordance of twentieth-century Irish litera-ture. Then we have a highly regarded history of art graduate programme. They publish a review of Post-Impressionist painting – one of the best in the country, as it happens, if not the whole world. Then we have the Pacific Institute for the Study of Forgiveness.'

I could tell from his tone that this was where the problem lay.

'That's where you're having difficulty?'

The Dean nodded. 'I'm afraid so,' he said. 'Isn't it odd how issues arise precisely where you least expect them?'

'It certainly is. And their problem ...?'

'Fighting,' he said, shaking his head sadly. 'Constant bickering. Holding grudges. You name it.' He sighed. 'It's bad.'

The Institute was run by a director, whom I met shortly after my conversation with the Dean. He had been a professor of philosophy, he told me, before he accepted his current appointment. 'I had written a number of articles on forgiveness from the philosophical point of view,' he said. 'I suppose I was one of the few names in the field at that time – today everybody's into forgiveness. Most of them have a very superficial understanding of the subject, of course; not that I'm allowed to say that publicly.'

I studied him discreetly as I sat down in his office at the Institute. He was in his mid-forties, I thought, and he was dressed in the usual not-too-casual style of mid-ranking professors at such colleges. Seeing him in the street one might have put him down as the vice-president of a small company rather than as a philosopher. Mind you, of the academic philosophers I have come across in my career, not one has looked remotely like Aristotle, or Schopenhauer for that matter.

The Dean had explained to him who I was.

'I was pleased to hear that you were to be involved in all this,' he said. 'And not before time. Some colleges would have called in the police by now – particularly after that business with the effigy.'

I looked puzzled. 'The effigy?'

He stared at me intently. 'The Dean didn't tell you?'

I shook my head. 'He said that there had been incidents. He didn't …'

I did not complete my sentence. 'It was an effigy of me. And somebody had driven nails into it – you know, as they do with voodoo dolls.'

I waited for him to continue. Suddenly the civil, courteous atmosphere of his office had been replaced by something altogether darker.

'It was discovered in the hall one morning,' he continued. 'My secretary arrived and found it in the hall. You can imagine how shocked she was.'

I felt that I should react. 'Somebody dislikes you,' I said.

He took off his spectacles and polished them carefully. 'I can't understand why,' he said. 'I have no enemies.'

I tried not to smile. Everybody has enemies. Everybody.

We moved on to other incidents. 'Somebody sent out abusive e-mails purporting to come from the Institute,' he said. 'That was another very unfortunate affair. And then somebody switched all the names on our Faculty's office doors on the first day of the semester. There was terrible confusion. The students all knocked on the wrong door when they went to sign up for classes.'

'An immature prank,' I suggested. 'The sort of thing that a student would do.'

'Possibly,' said the Director. 'But then again, possibly not.'

'You must have been very angry,' I said.

'I was spitting mad,' he said. 'Who wouldn't be?'

I said nothing. I wanted to say: *somebody who believes in forgiveness.* But I kept this to myself.

I obviously had to meet the Faculty, of whom there were eight members. The Director provided me with a cover story – that I was a journalist preparing to write an article on the Institute and wanting to get a good feel of the place. 'They'll believe you,' he said. 'Most of them are pretty naïve.'

I started with the Associate-Director, Professor Atkins, a rather attractive woman a few years younger than the Director.

'You've met our revered leader, of course,' she said.

'The Director?'

'Yes. The Great Helmsman.'

I frowned. Her tone was sneering. 'The Great Helmsman' had been what Chairman Mao had been called by his adoring colleagues.

'Yes, I've met him.'

She rolled her eyes. 'Oh well,' she said.

I waited for her to continue, and she did, after a short and rather uncomfortable silence. 'His term of office is eight years,' she said. 'Six to go.' She sighed. 'Six years.'

I raised an eyebrow. 'I take it that you don't think he's doing a good job?'

'I didn't say that,' she snapped back. 'All I said was: six years to go. And counting.'

'I can tell, Professor Atkins, that you don't like him.'

She narrowed her eyes. 'I used to like him, you know. I used to like him a lot, until …' She turned her head away. 'Until he deceived me.'

'Oh?'

'He and I were lovers,' she said. 'I may as well tell you that. We had an understanding, and all the time he was carrying on with that woman.'

'Which woman?'

'His secretary,' she said. 'Who else?'

'Ah,' I said.

'I shall never forgive him,' she muttered. 'He could come to me on his knees, begging me to take him back, and I would never, ever take him back. Never.'

She began to cry, and I put my arm tenderly about her. But then I very quickly took it away again. Academia is touchy about physical signs of sympathy, I reminded myself.

I met the secretary.

'May I ask you how long you've been working for the Director?' I said.

Her eyes lost their focus. 'Two years,' she said dreamily. 'Two years, three months, and two weeks.'

'You obviously think highly of him.'

She seemed to make an effort to pull herself together. Now she was brisk and efficient. 'He is a very good employer,' she said. 'That's all.'

'And do you enjoy your job?' I asked.

It was as if she had not heard my question. 'He's far too good for all of them,' she said. 'Particularly for Dr Edwards.'

'And who is he?'

'She. Dr Lilly Edwards.' She lowered her voice. 'She has a soft spot for him. You should see the way she looks at him. She can't take her eyes off him. It's so obvious, and she thinks that nobody notices.' She paused. 'Well, I do.'

'Tell me about Dr Edwards,' I said. 'What's her particular area?'

'Reconciliation,' she said. 'She's written a book on international reconciliation – not that anybody's read it.

Unreadable – and that's not my word for it; it's what one of the reviewers said. Professor Thomas. He works here, as it happens.'

'And he described Dr Edwards' book as unreadable.'

The secretary laughed. 'I'm happy to say he did.' She looked thoughtful. 'Some people wondered whether it was out of malice.'

'Why would that be?'

'Well, they say – and I'm not saying that this is necessarily the case – they say that Dr Edwards once failed a graduate student who had studied under Professor Thomas when he was a junior faculty member at Yale. I don't know whether that's true or not. It may be. I don't know.'

'So you – or rather, they – think that Professor Thomas might hold a grudge?'

'Yes. In fact, I heard – just heard, mind you – that in Professor Thomas' own book on *Healing Dialogue* he thanks every one of his colleagues for their helpful comments – except Dr Edwards.'

'When was this?'

'Quite recently,' said the secretary. 'About six years ago, I think.'

'That's a long time to hold a grudge,' I remarked.

The secretary shrugged; evidently she thought differently. 'People who do you wrong can't complain if you remember it,' she said. 'Of course, I'm only the secretary round here, but that's what I've always thought.'

I refrained from disagreeing with her. One of the lessons I've learned in my practice is that people confide more readily in those with whom they believe they are in agreement. I did not want to alienate the secretary, from whom I might need further information at some stage.

I saw several other members of the Institute that afternoon and then returned to the hotel for dinner. That night I sat my desk in the simply-furnished campus hotel and sketched out a diagram of the relationships within the Institute. Nobody, it seemed to me, liked anybody; most were sworn enemies of each other. Any one of them could be responsible for the rash of disruptive events; without any further information, I decided it would be impossible for a finger to be pointed at anybody in particular. They were all, as far as I could make out, potentially guilty.

The Dean telephoned me the following morning to find out if I had made any progress in my investigations.

'I've been speaking to people,' I said.

'And?'

'It's difficult. Quite a few of them have a strong motive. In fact ...'

'Yes?' he said eagerly.

'In fact, it's difficult to single out anybody in particular.'

The Dean was silent. At last he said, 'I'm relying on you, Mr Andersen. Our press office tells me that the papers have got word of something happening. We want to nip this in the bud before we have a public scandal. After all, it is a forgiveness institute ...'

I told him that I was to have further interviews with members of the staff that morning. I assured him that I would keep him informed.

There was a public lecture in the Institute the next morning, and I joined the sixty or so people who attended it. The lecturer was a member of staff I had yet to meet, a Dr Fontaine, who had recently published a major work on the nature of apology. He was an accomplished speaker, and I found myself being quickly drawn into the subject. The function of apology, he explained, was principally to affirm that an interest had been infringed. 'If I say sorry to you I am telling you that you are right to feel wronged. I am acknowledging the infringement; I am affirming the value of the interest that I have damaged. I am saying to you: Yes, I have done you wrong. That is what apology does: it restores the balance that has been disturbed by the wrong I have done.'

Then he moved on to forgiveness. 'Forgiveness,' he said, 'affirms the restoration of the moral balance. When you forgive another, you signal that things are back where they should be. You are effectively saying that the past is no longer going to determine how we relate to one another in the present or the future. Forgiveness, you see, enables the past to be put to bed.'

Coffee was served after the lecture. I went up to Dr Fontaine and introduced myself.

'I've heard about you,' he said. 'You're a journalist, I believe.'

There was something about the way in which he spoke that told me that he doubted my cover story. He looked at me in a bemused, disbelieving way.

'No, I'm not,' I said.

'You've come to find out what's going on?'

I nodded.

'At the instance of the Dean?'

I made a gesture that indicated assent.

He sighed. 'He's in league with the Director. He always has been. The Dean gave the Director's son a job, you know.'

I prepared myself for another disclosure.

'And I felt particularly bitter about that,' said Dr Fontaine. 'My own son applied for that job. He didn't even get an interview.' He paused. 'It was unforgivable.'

I stared at him. 'Do you realise what you've just said?'

'About the Dean giving the Director's son a job?'

'No. I was thinking of your last comment. You said: *it was unforgivable.*'

His eyes narrowed. 'So it was.'

'And there you were, talking about forgiveness in your lecture. What did you say about it? That it allowed the past to be put to bed?'

He was tight-lipped.

'Well?' I pressed.

'Theory and practice are different things,' he mumbled.

'You should be ashamed of yourself,' I said.

He looked away, and I decided to press on with my denunciation. 'You're all the same, aren't you? You preach forgiveness and yet this place is utterly unforgiving.'

'That's a bit extreme,' he said.

'No, it is not. It's completely true.'

He looked at me thoughtfully. 'You haven't worked out who's responsible, have you?'

I was not prepared for this. 'You know, do you?'

'Oh, yes,' he said. 'Everybody knows.'

'And would you care to tell me?'

He hesitated, but not for long. 'It's the Dean,' he said. 'He's wanted to close us down for years. We put up a fight and he never forgave us for it.'

I thought about this. 'So he's trying to engineer a scandal?'

'You could put it that way.'

I looked at him. He was smiling in a supercilious way. He was as bad as the rest of them, I decided. But what was his motive? I decided to guess.

'I assume that you want the Dean's job yourself?'

My comment went home immediately. He stared at me wide-eyed. 'What an outrageous suggestion!' he said.

I smiled. He had been rattled by the truth.

'It's you,' I said. 'I have the proof.'

I had no proof, but he was not to know that. It is astonishing how many people fold up if you simply say to them: I have the proof.

He became silent. 'The effigy wasn't me,' he muttered. 'That was somebody else – I don't know who. I sent the e-mails – that's all.'

'I thought as much,' I said. And then, 'Why don't you go and forgive the Dean? Go right now. Forgive him for whatever it is you feel you have to forgive him. Then tell your colleagues what you've done.'

He hung his head. 'Do you think that's what I should do?'

'It's what you yourself said people should do. I listened to you. You said it.'

Forgiveness broke out that afternoon, and continued to flourish well into the following day. The Dean made a public apology for having favoured the Director's son; the Director apologised for holding up the tenure application of two colleagues he did not like; Professor Thomas apologised for his overly harsh review; and Dr Atkins apologised to the Dean for thinking uncharitable thoughts about him. She said that she hoped he and the secretary would find happiness with one another – if that was what they wanted.

It was not necessary for me to reveal to anybody what I had discovered. In the circumstances I felt that the past should be consigned to the past, for that, after all, is what forgiveness is all about.

The college never paid my bill. I wrote to them about it, and received an acknowledgement of my letter, but they never settled the bill itself. I forgave them, of course, as one has to do. Forgiveness can be painful, but we have to practise it, and I decided that this was my opportunity to do so. I'm not sure that they realised that they had been forgiven, but then forgiveness is a private venture, and what matters is that it occurs. It makes us feel better, and I think in this case it did. Not that I'd let them try that again, of course. You have to remember at least some things.

PHIL RICKMAN worked for nearly twenty years as a print, radio and TV journalist. Aware of the curious aspects of major news stories that didn't get reported, he determined to put 'mystery in the original sense' into a crime series. His series of novels featuring Merrily Watkins, diocesan exorcist for Hereford, blend his love of crime fiction with a lifelong interest in folklore and the unexplained. He and his wife, Carol, live on the Welsh Border, where they find lots of both. He was born in Lancashire.

The House of
Susan Lulham

Phil Rickman

'I don't like old,' Zoe Mahonie said. 'Get creeped out in churches. Sorry, but I do. Old places, you know what I mean? It's why we come here.'

'This city?'

'This house,' Zoe said.

It wasn't old, not in a way Zoe would see, and yet it was. Screened by the shaggy suburban conifers of Aylestone Hill, it was like an offcut from an arts centre from the 1960s: precast concrete, split-level, a jutting conservatory. Some architect's strident statement, once alone, now with a small executive housing estate wrapped around it. Like a gag, Merrily thought as Zoe leaned into a puffy arm of the white leather sofa.

'Couldn't believe it was so cheap, see.'

She was china-doll pretty, probably mid-thirties, not fat, just overweight. She wore a shiny, lime-green top and had short dark hair with highlights, and an emerald nose-stud.

'Jonno,' she said, 'he had this surveyor guy give it a going-over, and he couldn't find nothing wrong, so ...'

'The vendors didn't say anything?'

'Ah well ...' Zoe tossing out a bitter smirk. 'Turns out they was *in property*, you know what I mean? Obviously picked it up dirt-cheap when nobody else wanted it, cos of what happened. And when we come to view, they're both here, him and his girlfriend, so naturally we was thinking they *lived* here. Bastards.'

'Who told you, in the end?'

'Oh ... Anita – neighbour. We been here a month by then. She thought we knew. As if.' Zoe sat back. 'Can you fix it?'

She had one arm bared as if for an injection. Through the low, horizontal window, with its frame of reddish-wood, the October morning, under waxen cloud, was as white and ungiving as the room, where the only detail was in the white bookcase – half-filled with books on education, politics, psychology and, at the end, Dawkins's *The God Delusion,* Hitchens's *God is Not Good* and *The Hole in the Sky* by Matthew Stooke.

Oh ...

Between the conifers, across the city, Merrily could see the Cathedral tower, a fat warning finger. She wanted time to think.

On her first deliverance course, they'd been shown a DVD of a woman claiming there were bad things happening in her house. The priest, sceptical, suspecting domestic abuse – the husband – had left, wanting time to think. The woman had been found later with an empty pill bottle and a radio tuned to easy-listening.

'Could you tell me about the mirror again?' Merrily said.

It was over by the door, vertical, in a chrome frame and bright with reflections of white walls, white squashy sofa, light grey carpet, white cordless phone on a small table near the sofa. And Merrily, in the unzipped black hoody over the well-worn cashmere sweater. No dog-collar, just the smallest pectoral cross. She thought her face looked pale and blurred.

'Smeared all over, look.' Zoe shuddered. 'Hadn't barely woken up, and Jonno's away, like I said.'

'So what exactly did you think –?'

'Christ!' Zoe sprang away from the sofa's bloated arm. 'Susan Lulham lived here. *Susan Lulham.* You know what I mean?'

Only the basics. Sophie, at the Cathedral, was putting together some detailed background.

'And it was definitely lipstick.'

'It ... yeah.'

'And you scrubbed it away.'

Zoe said nothing. A smartphone lay on the sofa, switched on to a display of coloured planets. If she'd taken pictures of the mirror with that, would they have shown only a reflection of the room?

'Erm ... was it your lipstick, Zoe?'

Ready for the sharp look, and it came, small features crowding.

'Didn't expect you'd be going at it like the police or something.'

Merrily smiled. The police had victims and offenders and sometimes a result. A police inquiry wasn't a dance with invisible partners in a dark and possibly imaginary ballroom.

'When ...' She wanted a cigarette, but it was unlikely anybody had smoked in here since the new carpet had gone down. 'When you found out about Susan Lulham, what did your husband say?'

'Said we finally had a reason why it was so cheap. He's laughing. Nothing to worry about, kind of thing. Nothing, you know ...'

'Structural?'

'Yeah.'

'But maybe ... laughing because he didn't believe anything that had happened here in the past could have any lingering effect? Except in the imagination.'

There was a wedding picture on the bookcase. Jonno had thinning hair and a close beard. Zoe looked young and lovely.

'Look, we was going through a bad patch before we come here. It was like a new start, you know what I mean? In a fantastic new house we couldn't've afforded.'

'So you haven't told him,' Merrily said. 'About any of it.'

'He's busy all the time – head of department. Meetings, parent nights ...'

'It's half term, isn't it?'

'He does courses. He's on a course. In Bristol.'

Zoe folded her arms. Behind her was the TV screen, big as they came. The one she'd said had come on at 3.00 am, throwing out jagged music from a slasher movie on some all-night horror channel.

'Anyway,' Zoe said, 'I'd like it done before he comes back.'

'And that's ...?'

'Weekend.'

Zoe moved to the window. The flower bed outside was full of evergreen ground-cover. Below it was the terrace where she'd said the woman had been standing as the sun was going down. Short leather jacket, red leggings. Solid as you like, until she wasn't there.

She. Her name had once been a lazy flourish of red, across a Hereford salon window. And, according to Zoe, across the mirror in lipstick the colour of fresh blood.

Suze.

'Seems she hated her given name,' Sophie Hill said in the cathedral gatehouse office that afternoon. 'Too neat and prissy, too old fashioned. If you called her Susan she'd just scowl and ignore you.'

Merrily nodded. Jane had once had her hair done at Suze's salon, now a charity shop. Well overpriced, in Merrily's view, but Jane had been sixteen, and Suze was as near as you could find to Hereford cool. Suze had been going with this guy from *EastEnders* who she'd met when he'd presented her with a hairdressing award. Suze had broken up his marriage. Jane had been well impressed, but if she'd known that one of the teachers at her school had bought Suze's house she'd never mentioned that.

'Press cuttings.'

Sophie placing a laminate folder on the desk in front of Merrily, who looked up, curious.

'Where did you get these?'

While diligently maintaining the deliverance database, Sophie trusted nothing you couldn't keep in a fireproof filing cabinet. She plugged in the kettle by the sink. 'I'll make some tea. Susan's mother's a secretary at one of the solicitors' offices across the road. We were at school together.'

'You never told me that.'

'Why would I?' Sophie took down mugs, reading glasses clinking against her pearls. 'You don't gossip, Merrily, when you work for ...'

Her lips tightened. Not the deliverance ministry. Not the Bishop, to whom she was lay-secretary. Sophie worked for the sandstone bookend to Hereford's old city centre. The Cathedral.

'Grace – Susan's mother – keeps the cuttings in a file in her office. Well, you wouldn't want them at home.'

'No.'

From the folder, Merrily shook photocopies of newspaper stories and a glossy county magazine which fell open at a double-page photo-spread.

'Bloody hell, Sophie.'

'Ah.' The glasses were back on Sophie's nose as she peered over Merrily's shoulder. 'She did men as well. Specialising, for a time, in artistically shaven heads.'

In the picture, Susan Lulham held up a cut-throat razor, photoflash in the open blade. Behind it, Suze's strong-boned face was blurred by lavish laughter below a wing of indigo hair. Underneath the magazine, Merrily found a photocopy, blackly overinked, of a front page of the *Hereford Times*.

CITY STUNNED BY
'BLOODBATH' DEATH
OF TOP STYLIST

'Susan's death, I'm afraid,' Sophie said, 'was like her private life. Entirely lacking in normal human restraint.'

'You met her?'

'Not since she was small. Long before she was excluded from school.'

Merrily looked up.

'Passing ecstasy tablets around in an exam room,' Sophie said. 'Don't smile, Merrily, a child was hospitalised.'

A blade of sunlight lit Sophie's white hair, struck a spark from the kettle.

'Never went back to school after that. When she showed an interest in hairdressing, her parents paid for a private course and set her up in business. Which, to their probable surprise, she took to quite rapidly. If not quite in the way they imagined. Four salons, eventually, from Ludlow to Ledbury.'

'Must've done well to buy that house.'

Sophie frowned.

'Spectacularly unruly parties there.' She picked up the folder. 'Thought there was an inquest report, but it's not here. I remember most of it, anyway, except the actor's name. He'd apparently announced his intention of going back to his wife and children. Susan was furious. Two of her younger employees took her for a night out in Hereford to take her ... out of herself.'

'As they say.'

'Put her in a taxi in the early hours. Arriving home, she phoned her estranged partner, starting what seems to have been something fairly volcanic – loud enough to awaken neighbours. Summer night, windows open. Nobody – well, hardly the first time they'd been disturbed by Susan's antics, so nobody went out. Nobody heard her announcing to the former boyfriend that she'd begun cutting herself.'

Merrily glanced at the magazine picture, with the razor. Sophie nodded.

'Yes. Or one very like it. Drunken frenzy. The actor told the coroner he'd experienced her tirades before and didn't believe her. After a while, he hung up on her. Perhaps she thought he was leaping into his car to come and save her from herself, but he went back to sleep. She kept on cutting.'

Merrily winced. Suze grinned from the pages, the wide lips pulled back over the too-even white teeth and meaty gums. Merrily shut the magazine. Sophie poured water into the pot, steam rising around her.

'How reliable is this woman?'

'Zoe Mahonie? She's ... I don't know. You never can know, can you? Her husband's an atheist, presumably with all the layers of disbelief that go with that. An educated man, and she ...'

'Not a teacher?'

'Part-time dinner lady at his last school.' Merrily sighed. 'What I should be doing now is finding previous tenants. The guy who bought the house was smart enough to use it as rental accommodation for a couple of years, let the history fade.'

'The former tenants could be anywhere, now. And so you find them and they say it was a perfectly peaceful home, what then? How did you leave it?'

She told Sophie about the first-stage blessing. Cupboards opened, mirror covered, TV unplugged, sprinkling of holy water, prayers. *Sanctify this house, that in it there may be joy and gladness ...*

Covering her back. What you did. Knowing you might still wind up looking stupid or naïve, part of something obsolete.

Who told you about me, Zoe, you mind me asking?

Just a friend. Reluctantly. She posted your number on Facebook.

A diocesan deliverance consultant was rarely contacted directly. Mostly you offered technical advice to priests approached by parishioners disturbed by what they believed were paranormal phenomena – the third reason for remembering the clergy, after weddings and funerals. The one rarely spoken of in a secular society.

Except, it seemed, on Facebook.

Merrily shook her head.

'She kept saying, *You have to exorcise me.* They all know that word. I'm trying to explain that exorcism applies only to something considered malevolent and essentially non-human. She said, *What do you think fucking Suze is?*'

This had been outside, in a warm, desultory rain, both of them standing on the steps where Zoe had said the woman in the leather jacket had been visible. Merrily murmuring about peace and love, health and goodness, Zoe looking contemptuous. This was it? A bit of a blessing? Pat on the head?

'I didn't tell her a major exorcism needed permission from the Bishop, and a visit from a psychiatrist. How would you even approach that? *Zoe, if you don't mind, I'd like someone else to meet you …*'

Merrily shuddered. None of the cases she'd handled had ever got that far.

'*Might* she be deluded?' Sophie said.

'Don't know. You can never be sure. I told her if the problems continued, we could raise our game all the way to a Requiem Eucharist. But that would need more people, preferably including someone who'd known Susan Lulham personally.'

'The Requiem would be for Susan?'

'She didn't seem to get that at all. It was like she expected the garlic and the crucifix. I asked if there was someone she could stay with until her husband came home. She said she had a sister but they didn't get on.'

Sophie placed a mug of tea in front of Merrily.

'I don't think you're entirely convinced by Mrs Mahonie are you?'

'Oh God, she's standing there in the rain, under an umbrella like she's waiting for a bus. She doesn't do churches or any old places. And she got my number from a woman on Facebook. And you know what was missing, Sophie? Fear. When it's there, you can smell it, slightly sour, like ... fresh sweat.'

'You didn't like her,' Sophie said.

'Not a very Christian reaction, is it? Another reason I can't let it go.'

Aftercare.

She phoned Zoe's house six times that night. Answerphone. A man's voice delivering the message in a clipped, impatient way. Maybe Zoe had gone to her sister's after all. Twice Merrily left messages, waiting in the scullery she used as an office, watching her own face, grey, in the screensaver.

Forty next year, a daughter out there in the adult world. How long could she keep this up? How to deal with change: a TV turning itself on in the night, spirit messages in the hard disk, phantoms on Facebook, firewalls breached by the demonic.

A level of scepticism was essential, but how far should it rise before you felt obliged to throw on all the lights and walk away?

She phoned Jane's mobile. Voice mail. There was rarely a signal around the Pembrokeshire dig where Jane was doing her gap year as a gopher for archaeologists. She left a message.

'No pressure, flower. I just wondered if you remembered a physics teacher at Moorfield called Jonathan Mahonie.'

The absent Jonno was important. Coming between a wife and a husband was never good, but an *atheist* husband ... that was asking for trouble.

She Googled Susan Lulham, found another of Suze's claims to fame. The year before her death, she'd done a daytime TV slot, discussing new hairstyles and how to achieve them in your own bathroom. No YouTube sequences from that, just the razor picture of Suze with blurred eyes, lavish, white smile exposing gums the colours of offal. On full-screen you could read the brand name on the razor: *Bismarck*. The only other pictures were from a magazine feature which had not been in Sophie's portfolio: Suze showing off her new home, the living room looking much as it had this morning, same pale colours, even a mirror in the same position. A shot of the house from outside had been taken from a low angle in bright sunlight, and its walls looked hard, like bone. Savagely modern when it had been built, decades earlier, but now somehow just very Suze.

Ethel padded in and curled into her basket. Merrily closed her eyes to the sound of soft purring and the climbing rose tapping the window in the night breeze. She thought about the concept of the unquiet spirit, restless essence of someone who'd died not peacefully.

Zoe didn't call back. Nor did Jane till the following day.

After Midweek Mass, this was. She'd been doing the Wednesday Eucharist for a while now, never really liking the word Eucharist but worried about simplifying it in case anyone thought she'd picked up the Catholic virus. But as Anglo-Catholic priests tended still to disapprove of female clerics, how likely was that, anyway?

'Mahonie?' Jane said. 'He's not moved into the village, has he?'

'He lives in Hereford. I ran into his wife, that's all.'

'Poor cow.'

'Sorry?'

'He only arrived a few weeks before I left, so I rang Rhiannon for you. Rhiannon Hughes? Who's still serving time at Moorfield, so please don't stitch her up. Bottom line, Mahonie's a slimeball. Leans over you to make a point on your laptop, and his hands ... you know?'

'I see.'

'Rhiannon says he thinks – inexplicably – that he's God's gift. He was at this school in the Forest of Dean before, so Rhiannon's put his name into the system for me.'

'What?'

'Facebook. It's mostly old people on there now, but she found some former students, and Mahonie's famous for shagging a dinner lady. She sponged soup from his trousers after he broke up a fight in the sixth-form restaurant. Something like that. He was married at the time.'

'She was the other woman?'

'Who was?'

'Sorry. Talking to myself.' Merrily was staring through the scullery window at the glittery lichen on the churchyard wall. 'Thank you, flower. Good of you to take the time. Everything OK?'

'Yeah. It's interesting ...'

'But?'

'Bit of a shoestring operation. They might have to wind up before Christmas. Could even be back in a few weeks.'

'Oh. I'm sorry. Though it'll be good to ... have you home.'

'Yeah, I bet,' Jane said.

Several times that day, Merrily rang Zoe, getting the voicemail. As an early autumn evening dimmed the scullery and she was thinking about maybe driving over there, Sophie called.

'Merrily, you might want to turn on your computer. I've sent you a link. Call me back when you've read it.'

The Facebook picture was very like the wedding photo, with Zoe looking slim and tanning-centre gorgeous. She listed her favourite singer as Adele and her fave TV shows as *Strictly Come Dancing*, *The X Factor*, *EastEnders* and *Celebrity Big Brother*. Her latest posting said, in reply to a Facebook friend called Lou:

I was very dissapointed. she didn't even look like a proper priest. She said o yes it was definately an evil spirit but she wasnt up to exercising it on her own. She said I shouldnt be alone here at night. She said I should go to the church and lock myself in. I said I was frightened of churches but she didnt get it. I dont know what to do. Im fucking shitting myself.

Lou: Wish I hadnt told u about her now. Vicars dont believe in anything these days. U want to try one of these ghostbusting groups. Still get out of there tonite, tho.

Zoe: Nowhere to go have I? Im trying sleeping pills.

Merrily called Sophie back. 'Who told you about this?'

'Somebody told Grace Lulham Mrs Mahonie was making a big thing about Susan's house, on the Internet. One of her friends, as you know, put your phone number online for her and they they were all demanding she call you. As they would. To find out what you'd do.'

'She was supposed to be keeping it quiet so it didn't get back to her husband. Doesn't make sense, Sophie. Also, I didn't say any of that stuff. Evil spirits?'

Silence. Who would know she hadn't said that? Who in the wide world? She'd been given a part in a reality show.

'I think it's accepted that social networking sites are largely held together by lies and fantasy,' Sophie said eventually. Sophie who didn't gossip, Sophie who worked for the Cathedral. 'I hate all this. Hate the way if people have a problem they type it into their computers, and scream it out to the world and wait for the world to give them stupid, dangerous advice.'

'I'm going to see her.'

'I think that would be *very* stupid,' Sophie said.

'What's the alternative?'

'To do absolutely nothing except write out a report, email it to me, and I'll copy it to the Bishop.'

'Just cover my back.'

'Just accept that your initial feelings might not have been so far from the truth,' Sophie said. 'And that you don't have to do penance for them.'

A sporadic rain misting the ornamental conifers. A few early lights visible on the executive estate, the flickering of wall-mounted TVs.

No lights in the house of Susan Lulham, its angles stabbing a caramel sky.

Merrily parked her old black Freelander just past the last house on the estate to which Zoe's home was almost attached, its porch jutting below the line of small, square windows.

A white Mini Cooper was parked on the rising drive, but no-one answered the doorbell. Merrily stood in the fine rain, looking up, thinking she saw a curtain move in an upstairs room. Backed away, down the steep drive, so that Zoe, if she was up there, could see who it was. Or maybe Zoe already knew who it was, and that was why she wasn't opening the door.

'You're not helping her, you know.'

Merrily spun around in the road. A car had pulled in behind the Freelander. She saw a slender, dark-haired woman, about her own age, in an open, seagreen jacket, off-white silk scarf. Car keys in one hand.

'Or yourself, I'd guess,' the woman said. 'But you'd know best, I suppose.'

'I'm sorry –?'

'Forgive me.' Hands waving dismissively, car keys jingling. 'I don't know you. I know about you. A little. Enough to suggest that you really ought to know better than to frighten a woman like Zoe Mahonie.'

Merrily took a step back. Was the entire estate on bloody Facebook?

'Look, take no notice of me.' The woman looked annoyed, perhaps with herself. 'I've had a fraught day.'

'Is she in? Is that her car? The Cooper?'

'She doesn't drive,' the woman said.

'I thought a curtain moved.'

The woman smiled crookedly.

'Perhaps it was Suze,' she said.

Her name was Anita Wells. Evidently the neighbour who'd finally told Zoe why the house had been so cheap. A calmly attractive, soft-voiced divorcee working, she said, for Herefordshire Council. In an executive role, Merrily guessed when it came out that she'd served on a committee with Sian, the Archdeacon.

They were on tall stools in opposite bays of the island unit, in the warm dimness of an opulent Smallbone fitted kitchen, green and blue pilot lights like distant night-shipping in the shadows.

'Not my place,' Anita Wells said smoothly, 'to subject the poor woman to analysis. I will say things were rather more peaceful when Susan Lulham was living here. Despite the parties.'

She'd admitted to Google-imaging Merrily after a neighbour had shown her Zoe's Facebook entries amidst inevitable gossip about an exorcism on the estate. So Anita Wells had recognised her out there, made a move – indicating there was something she needed to know.

She smiled.

'I do rather admire you. Can't be easy.'

'Holding down a medieval job in a secular society?'

Was that a small, amused noise or the coffee pot? Merrily lifted both hands, backing off.

'Sorry. What's the husband like?'

'Jonathan ... spends as much time as he can away from home. Berating himself for his stupidity in falling for a ... much younger woman.'

'Younger,' Merrily said.

'Without a thought,' Anita said, 'for what they'd have to say to one another outside the bedroom.'

'Is that his car in the drive?'

'I ... didn't see him arrive. I've been at work.'

Nearly dark now, but Anita Wells didn't switch on lights. Through a window, you could see part of Zoe's house, a concrete elbow jabbed into the brown sky.

'Awful eyesore,' Anita Wells said. 'There used to be more trees in front and a high hedge. Zoe was so proud of it she had to have it all cleared.'

'The house of Susan Lulham.'

'Perhaps proud of that, too,' Anita said. 'The awful glamour? I don't know. What do you think? Does she find it perversely exciting?'

'Do you know why she isn't answering her door? Why, if her husband's in there, neither of them are?'

'I ... no.'

'You were here when Susan Lulham was?'

'Only for about six months before she died. She'd come round sometimes, to unload. Either manically happy or terminally distraught. Giving up men – *again*. All bastards. Always shit on you in the end. Never thinking she might be the kind of woman who attracted bastards.'

'You were here the night she died?'

'I'm glad to say I was on holiday.'

'Erm ... am I right in thinking it was you who told Zoe whose house she was living in?'

Anita shrugged.

'She'd have found out soon enough. At least I could explain it to her in a sensible way. I promise you, if I'd thought it was going to make her completely delusional –'

'That's what you think?'

'And you – I mean despite your ... calling – *don't* think that? Lipstick on the mirror? The ghost of Susan Lulham on the steps? Good heavens, Mrs Watkins, I don't know why you didn't walk away as soon as you saw the bookshelves.'

'Oddly enough,' Merrily said, 'Richard Dawkins doesn't scare me.'

'I'm sorry?'

'Books about why God doesn't exist.'

'Jonathan's books, yes. No –' Anita Wells flapping the air with an exasperated hand. '– I meant the others.'

'Education? Psychology?'

'The DVDs.'

'I didn't see any DVDs.'

'What, no lurid films? No *Exorcist*. No *Amityville Horror*? No complete set of *Most Haunted*? You're saying she'd removed them from the shelves before you arrived?'

Merrily's stool wobbled. She leaned over the island counter.

'All right, look, the mirror and the rest, did you get all that stuff from Facebook?'

'I don't use Facebook.'

'Who told you, then?'

Silence. A glimmering in the wide, low window of the house of Susan Lulham. The reflection of car-lights, street lamp, an early moon?

Merrily said, 'Please ...'

'Jonathan,' Anita Wells said. 'Jonathan told me.'

'Oh God.' Merrily closing her eyes. 'Oh, bloody hell.'

The darker it grew, the more illuminating the evening became, and not in a good way, Anita disclosing that she knew Jonathan much better than she knew Zoe, and there was only one likely explanation for *that*.

'You're in the education department?'

'I'm an assistant director,' Anita said. 'Before local government, I was a teacher. So Zoe told you she was keeping it all from Jonathan, did she?'

'Did you see a light flicker just then? In that house?'

'That house,' Anita said. 'I don't believe in ghosts, but I'd still hate to live there.'

'She told Jonathan? Zoe told him all about the phenomena?'

'She told him lies. Because he said he couldn't stand it any more. Because he was going to leave her.'

'And you know that because?'

Anita Wells sighed.

'Look. It was years ago. Before his marriage. Before his first marriage.'

Oh.

Take this slowly.

'But you're still ... friends?' Merrily said. 'Did he know whose house this had been? Why it was so cheap? And that ... that you'd be his nearest neighbour? Did he know all that before they came?'

Silence. Anita seemed to be shrinking back into the shadows between the pilot lights.

'Are they both in there now, Anita? Zoe and Jonno?'

'Don't call him that. *She* calls him that, not –'

A sudden caffeine rush had brought Merrily to her feet.

'Shall we go and find out, then? Both of us?'

The sky was gutter-brown, and there was no moon and the spiky house was dark, except for the reflection of a street-lamp, from the estate, in the living-room window. Anita led Merrily up the drive, past the Cooper and then down towards a flat-roofed double garage, with a door at the side, hanging open, accessing a side door of the house.

'Usually unlocked. Until nightfall, anyway.' Anita shaking the door. 'Locked. Jonathan! *Jonathan* ...'

They came out of the garage and stood on the steep drive next to the car.

Merrily whispered, 'Did she know? About you and Jonathan?'

'Couldn't have. Sometimes she went to stay with her mother. Only then ... only *ever* then. Look, she was driving him out of his mind with her inane ...'

Of course she knew, Merrily thought. Neighbours told her. Or Facebook. Social media that used to be for kids. She walked up the drive to the low, wide living-room window. Peered in, saw nothing clearly. But it was a white room. And the sky wasn't quite dark. She *should* be able to see in.

She backed sharply away from the glass.

Anita said, *'What?'*

Merrily moved to another part of the window and saw the white room, muted to grey but most of it visible now: the squashy sofa, the bookcase, half-empty. When she looked back along the glass she saw, in the light of the streetlamp over the road, where the view had been obscured by dark spots and two smeared handprints.

Oh, dear God.

Heard Anita saying, 'Please, what is it?' as she turned away, feeling for her mobile, standing on the patio at the top of the steps, where Zoe had said she'd seen the woman with the short red leather jacket. Calling Zoe's number and hearing the white phone ringing in the living room. The room where Susan Lulham had been talking into a different phone with the expensive *Bismark* razor opened up and ready.

Answering machine. Man's voice. Merrily walked over to Anita, holding up the phone.

'That's Jonathan?'

Anita nodded. Merrily spoke to the machine.

'Zoe, if you can hear me ... if you thought I didn't believe you, you were wrong. Are you getting this?'

'What's she doing?' Anita Wells had her back to the window. 'Should we call the police?'

'I think probably we should, yes.'

And an ambulance.

'She's lying,' Anita said. 'She lies all the time. She lies to herself. She's not like Susan, not remotely. She'd never do anything to hers – never do anything like that.'

'No,' Merrily said drably. 'She probably wouldn't.'

Not to herself.

Anita stared at her. Merrily took a breath and called Zoe's number again and, when the machine cut in, she kept her voice low.

'Anyone there ...?'

Nothing.

'Are *you* there ... Susan?'

It wasn't dead, this phone.

'*Suze?*'

Anita Wells stifled a cry, turned to the window. She had to be directly in front of the smears and the blotches and the hand prints, probably too close to see them. Merrily walked to the end of the terrace. Between the trees, across the new estate with its flickery wall-mounted TVs, the umber sky lay like oily sacking over the city.

'Suze. Listen to me. Just for a minute. Talk to Zoe for me. Tell her we can sort this out.'

Gasping breaths from behind. Anita was bent forward, hands on hips. She'd seen the mess on the glass.

And she was right, of course. Zoe wasn't delusional in the expected way. This was Zoe proving she wasn't as thick as Jonno thought, that she was actually quite clever. And had support. A friend.

In the phone, there was a rush of laughter, like a gas-jet. In Merrily's head, a flash image of another phone slicked with fresh blood, Susan Lulham on her knees, pulsing and spouting. And then another woman – Zoe Mahonie – looking down at someone, holding an open razor branded *Bismark*.

'Suze, is Zoe with you?'

No reply. In the background, she could hear TV voices. Anita Wells had turned to the window, was beating on the toughened glass with the heals of both fists and sobbing.

'And Jonno?' Merrily said. 'Is Jonno there?'

'Yesssss.'

This sudden reply, swollen with satisfaction, throwing Merrily back.

'Can I ... could I speak to him, please?'

Zoe giggled, and you could hear her moving around with the cordless, and ... *snap, snap, snap* in the phone ... as inside the house of Susan Lulham lights came on, one after the other, and those familiar visceral thuds introduced the theme tune from *EastEnders*.

Heart jumping like a toad, Merrily looked up at the house and saw that the handprints in the now-illuminated living-room window were dark red and too big for a woman's. As she backed away, the house seemed to shiver in her vision and then re-form, and the line of symmetrical windows above the conservatory was full of white light, like a row of perfect, crowned teeth, and the hardwood sills were deep gums the colour of raw liver.

MARK BILLINGHAM started out as an actor and stand-up comedian before turning to crime writing with *Sleepyhead* (2001). This introduced his hero, Detective Inspector Tom Thorne, who has now featured in a dozen novels, the most recent of which is *The Bones Beneath* (2014). He has twice won Theakston's Old Peculiar Crime Novel of the Year, among many awards. He was born in Birmingham in 1961 and now lives in North London with his wife and two children.

Underneath the Mistletoe Last Night

Mark Billingham

Jack knew all about 'being good for goodness sake', he'd heard it in that song, but he didn't think opening his presents a few hours early would count as being bad. Besides, he had been asleep and even if it was still dark outside, it was already Christmas Day, so it wasn't really cheating, was it?

He lay awake a few minutes longer, wondering if it was snowing outside; if Rudolph shared that carrot they had left for him with all the other reindeer; and if the elves were already working on the toys for next year. He tried thinking about all sorts of things, but he couldn't keep his mind off those shiny parcels under the tree downstairs.

He climbed out of bed. He decided that bare feet would be quieter, so ignoring the Sam-7 slippers at the foot of his bed, he crept slowly out of his room and downstairs. He took one step at a time, wincing at every creak. The door to the living room was open, so he could see the tree before he reached the bottom of the stairs.

What was lying underneath it. Who …

The red of his coat and the white of his thick beard. The shiny black belt and boots. Not as fat as Jack had been expecting, but maybe he was on a diet.

He waited for a minute at the foot of the stairs, then padded softly into the living room. He had always thought it must be very tiring. All those houses to visit in one night. If Father Christmas chose this particular house to have a nap in, did that mean other children would not be getting their presents? Or was this the last house on his journey?

Jack crept a little closer, then stopped. He let out a small gasp and clamped a hand across his mouth. He watched and waited for the chest to move, to hear a breath or a snuffle, but he could hear nothing but the low hum of the fridge in the kitchen and a strange hiss inside in his own head.

One arm was lying funny.

A boot was half off his foot.

A different sort of red, where it shouldn't have been.

The boy turned and bolted up the stairs. He charged into his parents' room, shouting for his mum. She sat up and blinked and he ran to her, breathless, fighting to get the words out.

'Somebody killed Father Christmas …'

Tom Thorne had not needed to think very long before signing himself up for the Christmas Day shift. It made no real difference to him. There was no family to spend it with and, as far as he was concerned, Christmas Day was as good or bad a day to die as any other.

None of his regular team was at the house when he arrived, and clambering into the plastic bodysuit in the small front garden, he exchanged cursory nods of recognition or understanding with those officers already there.

We're the sad buggers. The ones with no lives.

Through a gaggle of SOCOs and police photographers, he was relieved to see the familiar figure of Phil Hendricks crouched over the body. The pathologist had been dumped by his partner a few weeks previously and he and Thorne had already agreed to have Christmas lunch together at a local pub if no calls came in. Now, it looked like they would have to settle for turkey sandwiches and a few beers at Thorne's flat.

'This is a strange one,' Hendricks said.

Thorne thought, 'They're the ones I like best', but just nodded.

'Who the hell would want to do Santa in?' The pathologist laid a gloved finger against the dead man's face. 'The tooth fairy? Jack Frost ...?'

'I'm keeping an open mind,' Thorne said. 'What are we looking at?'

'Single stab wound, far as I can see.'

'Knife?'

A DC Thorne did not know appeared behind him. 'No sign of it,' he said. He nodded back towards the kitchen. 'Broken window at the back and sod all under the tree except our friend here. Pretty obvious he disturbed a burglar ...'

Thorne had to concede that it looked that way. Easy pickings for thieves on Christmas Eve. People out celebrating and a healthy selection of must-have gadgets sitting under trees in nine out of ten living rooms. 'Where's the wife?' he asked.

'Upstairs,' the DC said. 'Family Liaison Officer's with her.'

'What about the boy?'

'A car's taking him to his mum's parents.'

Thorne nodded.

'By all accounts the kid didn't get a good look, so he doesn't know … you know. Not yet, anyway.'

Thorne watched as the funeral directors came into the room. They unzipped the body bag and knelt beside the dead man, which Thorne took as his cue to go upstairs and meet the widow.

Wendy Fielding sat on the edge of the bed, a female Family Liaison Officer next to her. Each cradled a mug of tea. Always tea, Thorne thought, wondering why the Murder Squad was not looking towards Tetley for some sort of sponsorship. He told the FLO to step outside, asked Mrs Fielding if she felt up to talking. She nodded and Thorne sat down on a large wooden trunk against the wall.

'I'm sorry for your loss,' he said. The room was dimly lit by a bedside lamp, but the first milky slivers of morning light were creeping through a gap in the curtains.

She said, 'Thank you' and tried to smile. She was in her late thirties, Thorne guessed, though for obvious reasons she looked a little older. She wore a powder-blue house-coat, but when she shifted on the bed, Thorne could see that the front of the pale nightdress beneath was soaked with blood.

'Can you take me through what happened this morning?' Thorne asked.

She nodded without raising her head and took a deep breath. 'It was just after one o'clock,' she said. 'I know because I looked at the clock when Jack came in.' She spoke quietly and quickly, as though worried that, were she to hesitate even for a second, she might fall apart. 'He told me that Father Christmas was dead ... that someone had killed him in the living room. I told him to stay here ... I tucked him up in bed and ...' Then there was hesitation, and Thorne watched her swallow hard. She looked up at him. 'He doesn't know it's his dad. He still believes in ...' She puffed out her cheeks, swallowed again. 'When do you think I should tell him?'

'We'll put you in touch with bereavement counsellors,' Thorne told her. 'They'll be able to advise you.'

'Right,' she said.

Thorne thought he could smell booze on her, but said nothing. He could hardly blame the woman for needing a stiff drink to go with her tea.

'Tell me about the Santa outfit,' he said.

Another attempt at a smile. 'Alan had been planning it for ages,' she said. 'It was his office party last night and they always have a Father Christmas, so he decided he was going to bring the costume home then dress up in it to take Jack's presents up. He pretends to be asleep, you know? You have kids?'

Thorne shook his head.

'Alan thought it would be special, you know? If Jack saw Father Christmas putting the presents at the end of his bed.'

'So you went downstairs?'

'He was just lying there, like Jack said he was. I knelt down and picked him up, but I knew he'd gone. There was so much blood on his chest and coming out of his mouth … sorry.'

'Take a minute,' Thorne said.

'It's fine. I'm fine.'

'Did you hear anything before that?' Thorne asked. 'The glass in the back door breaking? Somebody moving about downstairs?'

'I'm a heavy sleeper,' she said. 'I was dead to the world until Jack came in.'

Thorne nodded, wondering if the alcohol he could smell had actually been drunk the night before.

'So, you think they were in the house when Alan came home?'

'We're still working downstairs,' Thorne said. 'But if he disturbed a burglar that would mean he was already wearing the costume, which seems a bit odd.'

'Maybe he changed into it at the party.'

'Maybe,' Thorne said.

They both turned at the soft knock and turned to see the Detective Constable standing awkwardly in the doorway.

'Something you need to see,' he said.

Thorne got down on his belly to peer beneath the tree and saw a mobile phone sitting hard against the skirting board. He gave the officer the nod and the man crawled under the tree, his plastic bodysuit snagging on the branches as he stretched to reach the phone. Having retrieved the handset, he handed it across to Thorne, who almost dropped it when it began to ring in his hand. Everyone in the room froze.

'Write the number down,' he barked.

The DC scrabbled for pen and notebook and scribbled down the number on the phone's display. They waited for the phone to stop ringing, then heard the alert that told them a message had been left.

'Shall we?' Thorne asked.

The DC held his notebook out so that Thorne could read the number and Thorne dialled.

A woman answered. She said, 'Hello,' and when Thorne began to introduce himself, she hung up.

'Get on to the phone company,' Thorne said.

'Our burglar dropped his phone, you reckon?' Hendricks asked. 'Looks like you might have got yourself an early Christmas present.'

'I was hoping for an iPad,' Thorne said.

Bright and early on a freezing Boxing Day and Thorne was standing in a Forensic Science Service lab next to a balding technician named Turnbull. Thorne knew the man was recently divorced. Another sad case who preferred working to sitting at home alone and wondering if his kids were having a good day.

'What have we got?'

'Two text messages,' Turnbull said, pointing to the phone. '7.37 on Christmas Eve and again half an hour later. Plus the voice message that was left when you were at the murder scene.'

Thorne had already established when Alan Fielding had left home to go to his firm's Christmas party. One message had been sent just before he left and the second would have arrived when he was on his way there.

'Let's see,' Thorne said.

Turnbull handed him a transcript of the messages.

19.37. 24/12/11. It's me. Just wondered if you'd left yet. I'm guessing ur having trouble getting away. Can't wait to see u. x

Then...

19.54. 24/12/11. Hope ur on your way. Hurry up and get here will u? Can't wait to give u yr Xmas present. I know ur going to like it. x

And last, a transcript of the voice message, left in the early hours of Christmas morning.

'Just me. Couldn't sleep. Tonight was amazing though. I know you can't tell her today ... I'm not expecting you to, but do it soon, OK? Oh, and you're the sexiest Santa I've ever seen ...'

'So, what do you think?' Turnbull asked.

Thorne stared at the phone. He already knew who the messages were from. The same woman who had called the phone found underneath the Christmas tree; the phone they thought had been left by whoever had killed Alan Fielding. Thorne now knew that the phone was Fielding's, that he had forgotten to take it with him, and that the caller was Angela Massey, a twenty-four-year-old secretary who worked at the same company as he did.

Thorne had spoken to her on Christmas Day, just before the umpteenth repeat of *The Great Escape*. He was due to interview her formally later that day.

He blinked slowly. His head was still thick after the night before, when he and Hendricks had drunk far too much and swapped distinctly unseasonal banter.

'Knife went straight through his heart,' Hendricks had said. 'Probably dead before he hit the deck.'

'Something, I suppose.'

'Not the best way to round off Christmas Eve.'

'Yeah, well …'

'What?'

'I think he'd had quite a good night up to that point.'

'So, that help you?' Turnbull asked. 'The stuff on the phone?'

'Yeah that helps,' Thorne said. 'Helps me screw up Christmas for at least a couple more people.'

'I need to get Jack from my mum's, so can we just get this over with?' Wendy Fielding shifted in her seat, bit down on her bottom lip. 'I haven't told him yet, but he's been asking questions about his dad.' She looked down at the scarred metal tabletop. 'My mum told him that Alan had to go on a business trip …'

'This shouldn't take long,' Thorne said.

Though concessions had been made to the season elsewhere in the station – a few strings of tinsel in the canteen, an ironic sprig of mistletoe in the custody suite – the interview room was as bland and bare as it was for the rest of the year. Thorne turned on the twin CD recorders, pointed to the camera high on the wall to let Wendy Fielding know that their interview was being recorded.

'I don't understand,' she said. 'I thought you just wanted a chat.'

'Where are the presents, Wendy?'

She looked at him. 'How the hell should I know? Thieving bastard sold them for drugs, most likely. That's what they do, isn't it?'

'Some of them,' Thorne said.

'I don't know how they live with themselves.' She shook her head, disgusted, but she would not meet Thorne's eyes.

'You're right, of course,' Thorne said. 'Our burglar would probably have sold your son's Christmas presents for a few wraps of heroin. If he'd existed.'

Now she looked, eyes wide.

'I'm guessing you stashed them up in the loft or somewhere. Along with the knife. That might have been before or after you'd broken the window in the back door. Doesn't really matter.'

'What are you talking about? I think you're the one on drugs …'

'You really should have thought about the phone though. The one you chucked at your husband. It was the phone that made us think we might catch our burglar, but what was on it told me there wasn't a burglar to catch.' Thorne glanced across, watched the display on the recorder count away the seconds. 'I spoke to Angela Massey yesterday,' he said. 'She's every bit as upset as you were pretending to be.'

'Bitch!' Wendy snapped.

'Not really,' Thorne said. 'Just a girl who was in love with your husband. She claims he was in love with her too.'

'He wouldn't know love if it bit him.'

Thorne nodded. 'It must have killed you,' he said. 'Listening to those messages, knowing he was going to leave. Sitting there getting drunker. Angrier …'

'At Christmas,' she shouted, 'of all the times. What do you imagine that would have done to Jack?'

'What do you think you've done to Jack?'

'I didn't plan it,' she said. She was breathing heavily, desperate suddenly. 'He came back and I confronted him. We argued and all of a sudden I had the kitchen knife. I didn't mean to.'

'You stabbed him through the heart and then went back to bed,' Thorne said. 'You left your husband's body for your six-year-old son to find.'

'I'm a good mother,' she said. 'I don't care what you think. I was clearly no great shakes as a wife, but I'm a damn good mother …'

When Thorne came back into the Incident Room, DS Dave Holland was walking towards him, a broad grin on his face. Singing.

'I saw Mommy killing Santa Claus …'

He saw the look on Thorne's face and stopped.

'Not funny, Dave.'

'Sorry, Guv.' Holland held out a large brown envelope. 'We've had a bit of a whip round,' he said. 'For the boy.'

Thorne took it. Said, 'Thanks.'

'Not the best day to find your dad like that.'

Thorne nodded, having revised his opinion somewhat. Yes, one day was pretty much as good as another to die. But December 25th was a shitty day to lose someone.

Jack Fielding was now staying with Alan Fielding's mother and father. Their claim on the child had been thought that little bit stronger than his maternal grandparents, being as it was the child's mother that had killed their son. Thorne sat awkwardly on their sofa. Drinking tea and eating mince pies, while they did their best to act as if their world hadn't fallen apart.

'What's going to happen to her?' Jack's grandmother asked.

'What do you think?' The old man slurped his tea, pulling a face as though he were drinking hemlock. Perhaps he wished he was.

'She's in Holloway,' Thorne said. 'Likely to be there a while, I should have thought. A big murder trial takes a while to put together and, you know … Christmas and everything.'

'Wasn't easy finding a funeral director either,' the old man said. 'Busy with all the suicides or some such.'

Thorne nodded, thinking, well at least business is booming for somebody.

They said nothing for a while. Thorne stared at the cards on the mantelpiece. The snowmen and reindeer had been replaced by simple white cards with black borders. In deepest sympathy. He glanced at the large, brown envelope on top of the TV.

When Thorne saw the grandmother beam suddenly, he realised that the boy had come into the room. He turned and saw Jack Fielding hovering in the doorway. He smiled, but the boy looked away.

'Come on, Jack,' the grandmother said. 'Come and say hello.'

The boy took a few steps into the room. A large plastic dinosaur hung from his fingers.

'How are you?' Thorne had probably asked stupider questions, but he could not remember when.

'Where's my mum?' the boy asked.

'She's not very well.'

The boy nodded, as though that made perfect sense. 'Is that because of the dead man?' he asked.

Thorne said that it was.

Jack took another step towards him and leaned against the arm of the sofa. He gently put the toy dinosaur into Thorne's lap. 'It wasn't Father Christmas, was it?'

'No,' Thorne said.

'Was it my daddy?'

Thorne heard the old woman sniff, felt his throat constrict a little. But he kept his eyes fixed on the boy.

'It wasn't Father Christmas,' he said.

Thorne glanced across at the boy's grandmother. Saw something around her eyes and in the small nod of her head. He thought it might mean 'thank you', but he could not be sure.

JOHN CONNOLLY was born in Dublin in 1968 and is best known for his Charlie Parker series of mystery novels set in Maine, the most recent of which is *The Wolf in Winter*. He is also the author of *The Book of Lost Things*, and the Samuel Johnson series of novels for young adults, as well as *Conquest*, the first in a projected trilogy of sci-fi novels for older teens written with his other half, Jennifer Ridyard. *Books To Die For*, an anthology of essays on mystery fiction co-edited with Declan Burke, won the Macavity, Agatha and Anthony awards in 2013..

The Children of Dr Lyall

John Connolly

Even amid rubble and dust, there was money to be made.

The German bombers had reduced whole streets to scattered bricks and memories, and Felder couldn't see anyone coming back to live in them any time soon, not unless they fancied their chances with the rats. Some areas were still so dangerous that their previous occupants hadn't even been permitted to scour the ruins for any possessions that might be salvaged. Instead they could only stand behind the cordons and weep at what had been lost, and at what might yet be recovered when the buildings were finally declared safe, or when the walls and floors were either pulled down or collapsed of their own volition.

'Buried treasure', that's what Felder called it: money, jewellery, clothing – anything that could be bartered or sold, but you had to be careful. The coppers didn't look kindly on looters, and in case Felder and his gang needed any reminders on that score they had only to visit the Ville, or Pentonville Prison, where Young Tam was doing five years, and they'd be five hard years too because one of the coppers had broken Tam's right leg so badly that he'd be dragging it behind him like a piece of twisted firewood for the rest of his life.

For the most part, though, the Old Bill weren't up to much any more, weakened as they were by the demands of war, and Felder and his boys could outrun most of them. Young Tam was just unlucky, that was all. Even then, it could have gone much worse for him: rumours abounded that Blackie Harper over in Seven Dials had been shot by a soldier while stealing suits from a bombed-out gentleman's outfitters but the details of the killing were hushed up for the sake of morale, it being bad enough having Germans slaughtering Londoners without our own boys giving them a helping hand. It was said, too, that Billy Hill, who was carving a reputation for himself as the leading figure in London's criminal underworld, was very interested to know the name of the solder who had fired the fatal bullet, for Blackie Harper had been an associate of Billy's, and good staff were hard to come by in wartime.

But Billy Hill and his kind operated on another level from men like Felder, even if Felder aspired to greater heights. Felder, Greaves and Knight: they sounded like a firm of solicitors, but they were just bottom-feeders, scouring the dirt for food while trying to avoid being gobbled up by the bigger fish. All three, along with the unfortunate Young Tam, had been liberated by the Germans at the start of the war, when the prisons freed any man with fewer than three months left to serve, or any borstal boy with six months under his belt. Knight, Greaves and Young Tam fell under the latter category. Felder was older, and already on his third conviction for receiving stolen goods when he was released in 1939. He was spared conscription because he had lost his left eye to a catapulted stone when he was eight years old, and was careful to exaggerate the paucity of vision in his remaining organ. Young Tam, meanwhile, was mentally defective, and Knight had come over from Northern Ireland to find work in London only a few weeks before he was locked up in borstal for assault, and was therefore technically ineligible for conscription, although he hadn't bothered to present himself to the relevant authorities in order to clarify his status. Finally, Greaves had spectacularly flat feet. All four, even Young Tam, should have been required to do civilian work under the terms of their exemption, but they did their best to remain under His Majesty's radar, for they would not grow wealthy digging potatoes or cleaning up after the sick and dying in one of the city's crowded hospitals. Quite the little band they were, Felder had sometimes thought: a one-eyed man, an idiot, a flatfoot and a Belfast Protestant with an accent so thick that he might as well have been speaking Swahili for all the sense he made to anyone but his closest associates. It seemed that Billy Hill, high on his throne, needed to have few concerns about them for the time being.

And now they were three. It was a blessing, in a way, that Young Tam was no longer with them. True, he would always do as Felder told him, and he was strong, and good with his fists, but Felder's ambitions did not allow for a mental cripple. Billy Hill had no idiots working under him, because idiots wouldn't make a man rich. Early in the war, Hill's gang had used a car to break into Carrington's of Regent Street and nab six thousand pounds' worth of jewellery, a sum that boggled Felder even now. Hill was selling everything from silk to sausage skins, and it was whispered that the war had already made him a millionaire. By contrast, Felder's biggest score had come in 1941, when he and Knight had been fortunate enough to find themselves only streets away from the Café de Paris on Coventry Street as the supposedly secure basement ballroom was blown to pieces by a pair of German bombs that descended down a ventilation shaft, killing over thirty people. Under the guise of evacuating the wounded, Felder and Knight had stripped the dead and dying of rings, watches and wallets. They'd made hundreds on that one night, but things were never as good for them again.

Now he and Knight stood on a patch of waste ground that had once been a redbrick terrace, and stared at a house silvered by moonlight. It stood like a single jagged tooth in the ancient mouth of the street. Its survival had no logic to it, but then Felder had long ago learned that, like the mind of God, the nature of bombs was ultimately unknowable. Some hit and did not explode. Some took down one house or shop while sparing all else around, or, as the unfortunate patrons of the Café de Paris had learned, struck with an uncanny precision at the only vulnerable point in an otherwise secure structure. And then there were bombs that annihilated whole communities and left, as in this case, a single residence standing as a monument to all that once had been. The house was slightly larger than the ones that had been lost, but not unusually so: a lower-middle class house in a working-class street, perhaps. But Felder had cased it after his keen eye spotted the quality of the curtains on the windows, and a quick glance through one of the front windows had revealed what looked like original paintings on the walls, shelves of books, and, most enticing of all, a sideboard full of polished silverware. Discreet inquiries established that it was the home of a widow, Mrs Lyall, and she lived alone, her husband having departed to the next world during the final days of the last war.

As a rule, Felder tried to avoid burgling occupied houses: it was too risky, and brought with it the likelihood of violence if one of the occupants awoke. Felder wasn't above inflicting violence but, like any clever man, he avoided it when he could. Still, times were hard, and growing harder by the day. Despite his ambitions, Felder had resigned himself to the fact that he needed to ally himself to another for a time if he was to improve his position in life, and Billy Hill's gang seemed to offer the best opportunities for wealth and promotion. Hill would require an offering, though, a token both of Felder's potential and his esteem for the crime boss. That was why, after some thought, Felder had elected to cut Greaves out of the evening's work – in fact, to cut him loose forever. Greaves was weak and slow, and too good-natured for the likes of Billy Hill. He also had principles, to the extent that he had refused to accept a cut of the Café de Paris proceeds offered to him as a gesture of goodwill by Felder, even though he had not been present on the night in question. Robbing the houses of the dead was one thing, it appeared: stripping their bodies was another. Felder had no time for such sensitivities, and he doubted that Billy Hill would either.

Felder had a cosh in his coat pocket, Knight a knife and a homemade knuckleduster fashioned from wood embedded with screws and nuts, which he preferred to the more traditional models easily available on the street, Knight being a craftsman in his way. The weapons were only for show. Neither man anticipated much trouble from an elderly woman but the old could be stubborn and sometimes the threat of violence was required to loosen their tongues.

Felder turned to Knight.

'Ready?'

'Aye.'

And together the two men descended towards the house.

Later, as he was dying – or rather, as one of him was dying – Felder would wonder if the house and its occupants had been waiting for him, if, perhaps, they had always been waiting for him, understanding that the laws of probability, the complex crosshatching of cause and effect, suggested his path and theirs must surely cross. He didn't consider Knight's part in the process. Knight did as he was told, and so Felder's decision to target this particular widow was the moment at which the die was cast. But Knight could have made a determination of his own at any of a hundred, a thousand forks in the road between Felder's conversation with him about the house and the moment that they entered it. After all, thought Felder, as he bled from wounds unseen, wasn't that the old woman's point? Not one, but many. Not infinite, but as close to infinity as made no difference to a man like Felder, especially not at that most crucial juncture of all, the line between living and dying, between existence and non-existence.

And, yes, some small consolation might have been derived from the knowledge that this was the end for only one Felder, had it not been the end for the only Felder he had known, and would ever know.

But all that came later. For now there was only the house, its windows hooded, like the eyes of hawks, by the ubiquitous blackout curtains. They did not enter by the front door but climbed the still-intact wall that surrounded the back garden and found, not entirely to their surprise, that the kitchen door was unlocked. Once inside, they saw that the tidy little kitchen, with its pine table and two chairs, was lit by a candle encased in a glass lamp, and there were similar candles in the hall, and halfway up the stairs. Beneath the stairwell was a locked door, leading down, they presumed, to a basement. They heard no sound but the ticking of an unseen clock.

It was Knight who first noticed the patterns on the walls in the hall, taking them initially to be some strange manner of floral wallpaper and then, as he drew nearer, deciding – still erroneously – that what he was seeing was a network of cracks in the plaster, almost like the craquelure on the surface of a painting. (Knight had shared little of his background with Felder and the others. Equally, they had not troubled themselves to inquire into another man's business if it did not concern them, especially when the man in question gave no sign that such an intrusion would give him great pleasure in any case, but Felder had come to realise that Knight knew something of art and literature, and was better educated that his thick dialect might have led one to assume. In fact, Knight came from a house filled with paintings, and a family that talked easily of abrasure and blanching, gresso and glair. Had he been privy, before he died, to the insights gifted to Felder, then he might have appreciated more the story told by the patterns on the walls.)

Both men drew closer, Felder's fingers reaching out to trace what was gradually revealed to be ink work on the otherwise unadorned walls of the house, an intricate design that resembled most closely the thin branches of some form of creeping briar, as though the interior had been invaded by a pestilential vegetation, its greenery now lost to the breath of winter, had it ever enjoyed foliage to begin with. The effect was further enhanced by the addition of red dots at apparently random points, like winter fruits somehow clinging to a dead bush. Beside each red sphere was a pair of initials: E.J., R.P., L.C., but never the same combination of letters twice.

And although it was impossible to find a logic to the entirety of the tracery, it did seem to Felder and Knight that, on an individual level, its creator began with a single line which then split after an inch or so, one line continuing on to divide again while the other terminated in a horizontal dash over the vertical, like a dead end. Yet even here deviations from the norm sometimes occurred in the form of a series of dashes that, on occasion, eventually found their way back to the main thread. Similarly, numbers were appended to certain lines, which Felder took to be dates or, in particularly involved cases, hours, minutes and seconds. The designs covered the walls up to the ceiling, a few even extending on to the ceiling itself, a stepladder by the front door permitting access to such heights. They continued along the wall beside the stairs, and Felder presumed, up to the floor above their heads. The kitchen, by contrast, appeared devoid of any adornments, largely because it was barely spacious enough to accommodate its cupboards, sink and a four-ring gas cooker, until Knight, in a fit of curiosity, returned there and opened one of the doors on the wall, revealing a further network of bifurcating branches drawn, and even cut, into the interior panelling.

Again, waiting for death – a death – to approach, Felder saw another crucial juncture here, a point in events when lives might have been saved, when both men could have turned and left the house, for although they had not yet spoken, still their shared unease was evident on their faces. Then Felder thought of Billy Hill, and a share in the wealth that the war was bringing to those ruthless enough to seize opportunities when they were offered. Hill would not have turned away in the face of such inky manifestations of madness. Instead he would have reckoned the creator more vulnerable still to his predations, and honed in on easy pickings.

Beyond the kitchen lay a dining room, empty and dusty, with a closed pair of interconnecting doors leading to the front room. As with the hall, the walls were covered with lines.

Only now did Felder become aware of a presence in the front room, the one in which he had earlier glimpsed the books and paintings and, most interesting of all, the glass-fronted cabinet filled with silverware. It was the merest shifting of shadow against shadow, and the slightest exhalation of breath. A chair creaked, and Felder recognised the sounds of a sleeper responding to some small disturbance, such as the unfamiliar noise created by two men entering a house that was not theirs. Footsteps shuffled on carpet. The door began to open.

Knight reacted first. He was past Felder before the older man could even make a determination of the situation. Knight pushed hard against the door. There was a single shout – a female voice, old, querulous – and then a series of muffled impacts beneath which Felder discerned the breaking of fragile bones, like a quail being consumed behind closed lips.

Felder entered the room to find Knight straddling an old woman on the floor, one knee on her chest, his fist raised to strike again, her eyes already assuming the strange vacancy of hurt and shock. Felder gripped Knight's wrist before he could strike her again.

'Stop!' he said. 'For Christ's sake, you'll kill her!'

He felt the downward pull of Knight's right hand, the urge to harm, and then the tension went out of the younger man. Knight rose slowly and wiped his hand across his face. It left a smear of the woman's blood on his nose and cheeks. Knight rarely acted in this way, with heat and anger. He was, by nature, a cold being. Gradually, the rage went out of his eyes.

No, not just rage, saw Felder: fear too.

'I – ' said Knight. He looked down on the old woman and shook his head. 'I – ' he repeated, but nothing more came to him.

Felder knelt and gently took the woman beneath the chin, turning her head so that she was facing him. Her nose was broken, that much was clear, and her left eye was already closing. He thought that Knight might also have broken her left cheekbone, maybe even damaging the eye socket itself. Her mouth was bloodied, the upper lip split, but, as with Knight, something of her true self was now returning after the attack. Her right eye was bright.

She tried to rise. Felder helped her to her feet, aided by Knight, even though the woman weighed little more than the clothing she wore, and they almost carried her to the armchair in which she had been dozing.

'Get her some water,' said Felder, 'and a cold cloth for her injuries. Jesus.'

Knight did as he was told. Tenderly, Felder brushed a length of grey hair back from the woman's face and tucked it behind her right ear.

'I'm sorry,' he said. 'That wasn't meant to happen.'

The woman didn't respond. Her single undamaged eye merely regarded Felder with a kind of disappointment.

Knight returned, a dripping tea towel in one hand, a cup in the other. From the right pocket of his jacket, Felder noticed, peeked a bottle of brandy. Felder reached for the cloth, but Knight paused at the door, his eye fixed on the wall in which the window lay. Felder followed his gaze. More lines, more forks, more patterns, more red, inky berries. On three sides the walls were filled with bookcases and cabinets. Only here, around the window, was there space to continue the house's peculiar decoration.

'Never mind all that,' said Felder. 'Give me the towel.'

His words broke the spell, and Knight handed over the damp towel and the cup of water. Felder used the cloth to clean away some of the blood. He had hoped that its pressure might also keep some of the swelling down on the damaged eye, but when he touched the towel to the area the woman gave a pained yelp, and Felder knew that his initial suspicion had been correct: Knight had broken some of the bones in her orbital rim. Felder forced her take water, then emptied the rest on to the rug and indicated that Knight should fill the cup with brandy instead.

Knight opened the bottle, took a long draught for himself, and then poured two fingers of brandy into the cup. Felder made the woman drink once more, and used the cloth to wipe away the trickle that dribbled down her chin.

'It'll help,' he said.

He hooked her hand around the cup. Her respiration was shallow, as though it pained her to take deep breaths. Felder saw again Knight's left knee buried in the woman's tiny, flat chest. He held his hand over the spot, not wanting to touch her breast.

'Does it hurt here?' he asked.

She gave a small nod. Felder looked away.

'You should go,' said the old woman. She spoke the words on an exhalation, wheezing them out.

'What?' said Felder.

'You should go. They won't like it.'

'Who?'

'You told me that she lived alone!' said Knight. A clean blade appeared in his hand, extending itself like tempered moonlight.

'Shut up,' said Felder, his attention fixed on the woman. 'Who?' he asked again, but she did not reply, and her right eye flicked away from him to the bookshelves over the fireplace.

Felder stood. He turned to Knight.

'If anyone else lived here we'd have heard from them by now, with all that racket you made,' he said. 'Still, search the house. We're in this now, and we may as well milk it for all we can. Jewellery, money, you know the drill.'

'Why don't you ask her where she keeps it all?'

'Have you seen the size of this house? It's not Buckingham Palace. There can't be more than a few rooms upstairs.'

'I know, but – '

'Maybe you want to hit her again, see if you can kill her this time.'

Knight looked away.

'What are you going to do?' he asked.

Felder reached under his coat and untied the strings that held the sack in place. He indicated the silverware with his chin.

'I'll take care of that lot. Now get a move on.'

Knight appeared to be on the verge of saying something more, but he knew better than to argue with Felder, especially with the wreckage of the old woman bleeding away before him. Felder would take him to task for his little loss of control later, once they were safely away from here. Knight left the room, and Felder heard his heavy tread as he ascended the stairs. When he looked back at the old woman, she was smiling at him.

'Thank you,' she said.

'For what?'

She coughed, and a spray of red blood shot from between her lips.

'For killing me.'

Under the gaze of the old woman, Felder emptied the silverware into his sack. It was good stuff. He'd been a little worried that it might turn out to be only plate, although his eye, in that first short glance through the window, told him otherwise. The weight of it was considerable, but the sack was thick and strong, and had not let him down yet. His only concern now was to get it all to safety without being stopped by the police or the wardens, for there would be no way to explain away to the law a sack full of silverware.

Felder had chosen to ignore the woman's recent words to him. She'd taken a couple of blows to the head, and who knew how badly it had scrambled her thoughts? Once the cabinet was empty he made a cursory search of the shelves and drawers, but found only a few florins and half crowns wrapped in a handkerchief, and a gent's gold pocket watch engraved with three initials and a date in 1912. He considered putting it in the sack as well, but then slipped it into his own jacket pocket for fear that it might be damaged amid the silverware. From upstairs he heard the sounds of Felder rummaging through wardrobes and drawers.

Felder lit a cigarette and, through its smoke, viewed the patterns on the walls. During his search of the room he couldn't help but notice the nature of the books on its shelves. None of them were titles that he recognised, not that Felder was much for literature, but most appeared to be books on science.

'Were these your husband's?' he asked the woman. 'A son, maybe?'

The bright right eye fixed itself upon him.

'Mine,' she said.

Felder raised an eyebrow. In his world, women didn't read books on science. They hardly read anything at all. Like rumours of lost tribes in Africa, and monsters in Scottish lochs, Felder had heard of women scientists, but he had yet to meet one himself, and so remained uncertain of their actual existence.

'You a scientist, then?'

'Once.'

'What kind?'

'A physicist, although I have qualifications in chemistry too.'

'What are you, then: Professor Lyall?'

If she was surprised that he knew her name, she did not show it.

'Doctor Lyall,' she said.

'Doctor Lyall the physicist. And all this' – Felder gestured at the patterns on the wall – 'is physics?'

Lyall gave another cough, but there was only a little blood this time. Her breathing seemed to have eased somewhat. It might have been a sign that her condition was improving, but Felder doubted it. He suspected that it was her body relaxing into death. He wanted Knight to hurry up. Once they were away from the house, they'd find a telephone box and call for help. It might not be too late to save her.

'Quantum physics,' she said.

'What's that, then?'

'The study of the universe at the smallest levels.'

'Huh.' Felder took another drag on his cigarette, and moved closer to the wall. 'But what does it all mean?'

He saw her almost smile.

'You want science lessons from me?'

'Maybe, or it could be that I just want to keep you talking, because if you're talking then you're awake, and alive. We'll get help for you, I promise. It won't be long now. But just try to keep talking.'

'It's too late for that.'

'No. Tell me. Tell me about these quantum physics.'

She took another sip of brandy.

'There is a theory,' said Lyall, 'that there are an infinite number of possible existences, and each time we make a decision, one of those possible existences comes into being. But equally, alongside it may exist all other possible, or probable, existences too. It's more complex than that, but I'm keeping it as simple as I can.'

'Because you think I'm an idiot?' He said it without rancour.

'No, because I'm not even sure that I fully understand its implications myself.'

Felder was not an unintelligent man – poorly educated, yes, but not stupid. What he was hearing, though, seemed to him to be the stuff of fantasy stories: improbable, but fascinating nonetheless.

'So you're saying that, when I woke up this morning and decided to make a cup of tea, there was another version of me that just stayed in bed and snoozed for an hour?'

'In theory. Or when you decided to break into my house, another version of you simply turned away, perhaps determined to live a better life.'

Felder couldn't help but laugh.

'Are you trying to make me feel guilty?'

'No. The fact that you asked the question suggests that you're already well acquainted with guilt. You don't need me to torment you further.'

'You're quite a woman, I'll give you that.'

Felder examined once again the pattern of lines on the wall.

'So each of these forks represents a decision?' said Felder.

'That's correct.'

'It's your life,' he said, and there was a hint of wonder in his voice. 'All of these lines, these forks and dead ends, they're decisions you've made. You've mapped them out, all of them.'

'Yes.'

'Why?'

'To understand.'

'Understand what?'

'Where I went wrong,' she said. She took as deep a breath as she dared, readying herself for a longer speech. 'Because some decisions, some actions, have greater ramifications than others, more damaging consequences. And I think, perhaps, that if they're repeated often enough, the fabric of reality is altered. I call it "confluence". If I'd lived long enough, I might even have published a paper on it.'

'Confluence.' Felder repeated the word, liking the sound even if he didn't understand it. 'But what kind of bad things could an old woman like you have done?'

She frowned, and her voice rose slightly.

'I don't regard them as bad. Some might, but I don't. Still, they had consequences that I could not have foreseen. Confluence occurs at extremes, and nothing is more extreme that the possibility that, by one's actions, the nature of existence is altered. I did nothing wrong. I helped. But all paths fork, and some paths may lead into shadows. And things wait in the shadows.'

'What are the red dots supposed to be?' asked Felder.

He received no answer. Turning, he saw that Dr Lyall had closed her eyes.

'Hey,' he said. 'Hey.'

He did not move, but watched as the breathing grew softer and softer before ceasing entirely. The cup of brandy fell from her hand and bounced on the tiles of the fireplace.

And suddenly Felder noticed that he could no longer hear Knight moving above his head.

The house had four rooms upstairs – a bathroom with a toilet but no tub, two bedrooms and a third room so small that Knight couldn't quite figure out why it had been put in to begin with, since it was too small to take a bed and resembled more closely a telephone box than an actual inhabitable space. It was piled high with the detritus of the house: broken suitcases, old newspapers, the frame of a lady's bicycle, and more books. Books also occupied much space in the two bedrooms, and even in the loo, but unlike in the living room downstairs, they stood in teetering columns on the floor, the better to free up wall space for more of those infernal branching lines on the walls.

Knight was still struggling to understand why he had attacked the old woman – not that it wasn't beyond him to strike a lady, or even the odd girl who in no way resembled a lady at all, but it was the ferocity of his assault on her that surprised him. For a few seconds he had been overcome not only by an anger that burned like a wound, but also a deep and abiding sense of fear. The patterns on the walls alone could not have caused him to lose control of himself in that way. They were odd, and unsettling, but no more than that. Knight wondered if he might be coming down with something, but he had been fine until he and Felder had entered the house. There was a miasma to this place, he felt, as though the very air were polluted, even if it smelt no better or worse than any other house he knew in which an old woman was living – or slowly dying, depending on one's point of view.

Nevertheless, his looting of the rooms had not proved unproductive. In the main bedroom he discovered an assortment of jewellery, most of it gold, including an ornate pendant studded with rubies and diamonds, and a tin box which, when opened using the blade of his knife, was found to contain over two hundred pounds in notes, and a small roll of gold sovereigns. Knight immediately liberated two of the sovereigns and stashed them in the lining of his coat. He was aware of Felder's plan to hand over to Billy Hill most of the proceeds of the night, and largely approved of it, but that didn't require him to abandon common sense entirely. The possibility existed that Hill might simply relieve them of their offerings and throw them back on the street, perhaps with a beating to remind them of the extent of their delusion if they thought they could buy their way into his favour. If nothing else, the sovereigns would ease the pain of rejection, both physical and metaphorical, and provide him with some security if he chose to abandon Felder in the aftermath. And if Billy Hill accepted them, well, then all to the good: the sovereigns would form the basis of greater wealth to come.

Knight was just storing the jewellery and the rest of the money in his various pockets when he heard footsteps on the bare boards outside the bedroom door. Felder, he thought at first, but the steps were too light, and Felder would have known better than to approach him without warning in a strange house. Knight turned just in time to see what appeared to be a small child's bare left foot and leg disappear from sight, as though the child had been watching him and now feared being caught. A boy, Knight thought. But where could the child have been hiding? There was nowhere to conceal oneself in the downstairs rooms, and Knight had searched this floor thoroughly. Could the boy somehow have secreted himself among the rubbish in the tiny spare room? It was possible, but unlikely, not unless he had actively conspired to bury himself beneath the books, bags and cases.

Then it came to him: the cellar. They had checked it, and found it locked, but Knight could not recall seeing a key. Perhaps the boy had spotted them as they entered the house and, in fear, slipped into the cellar and locked the door behind him. Yes, that was it. There could be no other explanation. Somehow the boy had managed to get past Felder and come upstairs, although Knight wondered why he had not instead left the house and gone to seek help. But who could understand the thought processes of a frightened child?

By now Knight was already in pursuit. He wrenched open the bedroom door, stepped into the upstairs landing, and stopped.

It was no longer the same house. The landing was dark, the walls entirely unadorned except for patches of faded wallpaper that hung stubbornly to the plaster, hints of funeral lilies beckoning to Knight in the dimness. He could see no inked lines, no initialled dots. The landing was still partially lit by candles, but it was now part of a much larger structure, and Knight counted at least eight doors before it ended at a flight of stairs. One of those doors, halfway along on the right, was slowly closing before Knight's eyes.

'Felder?' he called. 'Felder, can you hear me?'

But there was no reply.

Knight reached into one of his pockets and once again withdrew his knife. It was of Japanese manufacture, and was among his most prized possessions, as well as being one of the few items he had taken from his childhood home before fleeing it for the mainland. He kept it keen, and even to touch its blade carelessly was to risk the kind of wound that would require stitches to heal. Opening the old woman's lock box had not left even a scratch on the steel. Holding it in his hand gave Knight some small sense of reassurance, even as his mind struggled to comprehend how he could enter a room in one house and apparently emerge from it into another house entirely.

'Felder!'

This time his cry elicited some response. It came in the form of a childish giggle, and then a hushing sound. Not just one child, then. Two, at least.

Knight moved silently along the landing, testing the doors as he went. All appeared to be locked, all except that door on the right, which stood slightly ajar. As he drew nearer to it he heard the sound of running from behind it, as of children moving farther into its reaches. The footfalls echoed slightly before they faded away, as though the room beyond was very long, and its ceiling very high.

Knight stood before the door. He reached out his left hand and pushed. The door opened without a noise. Ahead of him was a wall inset with a series of large windows, although he could see nothing through them because of the blackout curtains. Below the windows stood a line of children's cots, all apparently unoccupied. Knight stepped into the room and saw more cots lined up against the wall opposite the windows. A single lamp on a nightstand by the door provided the sole illumination. Knight counted twelve cots on either side and then, as his eyes grew more accustomed to the dark, still more stretching away into the darkness. He could not even begin to guess the size of the room, nor the height of its ceilings, which were taller than the ceilings of the landing outside.

The windows drew his attention again. Yes, there was blackness beyond them, but surely that meant the curtains had been hung outside the windows. He approached them, the knife still clutched firmly in his right hand. He glimpsed his reflection in the glass, marooned in the darkness like a spectre of himself. He touched his fingers to the pane. It was painfully cold, although the room itself was tolerably warm. And what he felt, as his reflected self stared back at him, and his fingertips grew numb, was that the blackness beyond the window was not caused by drapes, or natural dark, but by a kind of nothingness given form, as though all the stars had been plucked from the night sky and hidden away, and the house was floating in the void. Knight was overcome by a sense of terrible loneliness, of a hopelessness that only oblivion could assuage. Hypnotised by the vacuum, he understood that a man might stand here and allow the emptiness beyond to drain him slowly and methodically, leaving only a husk that would, in time, fall to the floor and crumble slowly like the desiccated form of an insect sucked dry by a spider.

Knight heard movement far above his head: a soft scuttling. He began to tremble. He feared that, in envisaging a spider and his prey, the great room had taken the image and given it substance. Slowly he raised his face to the ceiling. The lamp by the door grew brighter, its light spreading outwards and upwards, until it was reflected at last in a multitude of black eyes like flecks of obsidian embedded in the plaster. Knight saw movement too, pale, naked forms intermingling, clinging to the ceiling with fat, truncated limbs; and now descending along the walls, crawling like insects, their gaze fixed on Knight.

They were infants, hundreds of them, each no more than a few months old and each alive yet not alive, their bodies mottled slightly with corruption. Knight stared at them as they came, flowing down the walls. Behind him, and unseen, a small hand reached out and touched a finger softly to the back of his neck. He felt a sting, a spider's kiss. The blade fell from his hand and he followed it, dropping to his knees as the pain spread through his system. He collapsed on his right side, his eyes open, unable to move, to speak, even to blink. They came to him, hands reaching for his nose, his mouth, his eyes, exploring, testing, more and more of them, until he was lost beneath them and died in stillness among creatures that basked in the novelty of his fading warmth, and wept when it was gone.

Felder went to the door of the living room and called Knight's name. When no answer came, he stepped into the hall. The stairs to the bedroom were still there, but they now ended in blackness, with nothing beyond them. Where once had stood a front door, now was only a wall upon which hung a long mirror. The kitchen, too, was gone, and another mirror had taken its place, so that Felder stood trapped between infinite versions of himself. He looked back at the body of the old woman, but that too was now changed – or, the thought struck him, unchanged, for her face was unmarked, and she was merely sleeping. She moved in her dreams, the chair creaking, her mouth emitting a small snore, but she did wake, and no Knight appeared to pummel her with his fists. Only as the door began to close in front of Felder did she open her eyes, but he could not tell if she saw him or simply dreamed him before she was lost to his sight. He heard a key turn in the lock as, in the mirrors, all reflections disappeared, and the wall before him began to crack. He watched the cracks advance – forking, diverging, progressing, ending – and saw the ink dry against the plaster as the pattern of his life was drawn for him.

And as one door was locked, so another was opened. He heard the cellar door creak, and the sound of light footsteps descending. Felder did not rail. He did not fight, or scream. He simply followed the sound.

Knight was in the cellar. He sat slumped in a chair, his head back, his eyes, now ruins in their sockets, staring sightlessly at the ceiling. The walls of the cellar were lined with jars, none of them empty.

They won't like it.

On a workbench rested a bag, and beside it a set of clean, bright surgical instruments. Felder saw unmarked potions in bottles, and powders and pills ready for use. He looked again at the jars, and at what they contained, floating in preservative. He had heard of women like Dr Lyall. Young unmarried girls with reputations to protect, wives who could not explain away a new child when their husbands were fighting in foreign fields, mothers with bodies so worn that another baby would kill them, all came to Dr Lyall or others of her kind, and they did what the doctors would not. Felder had never considered the price that might have to be paid, the burden to be carried. She had marked them all on her wall, the red dots of her visitations.

Thank you.

Confluence. Existence and non-existence, tearing at the fabric of reality, at the walls between universes.

For killing me.

One more mirror stood in the cellar. Felder saw himself reflected in it: this Felder, this moment, fixed by the decisions and actions that had led him to this place. The walls drew away from him, leaving only shadows behind, and out of those shadows emerged children, some little more than crawling infants but others older, and more watchful. Their rage was a cold thing, for there is no rage quite like that of thwarted youth, and he experienced it as a multitude of surgical hooks and blades cutting into his flesh. His reflected self began to bleed, and he supposed that he must have been bleeding too, although he could see no wounds. He could feel them, though. They were all inside: deep inside.

He died slowly, or one of him did, the only version of himself that he would ever know. In the logic of his dying he understood that, in another universe – in many universes – the torment of Dr Lyall by her children would continue, but in this one it had ended, just as his own must surely, mercifully end.

As the life faded from him, a line of ink moved inexorably across the filthy floor, then faded away to nothing.

YRSA SIGURDARDÓTTIR, born in Iceland in 1963, works as a civil engineer in Reykjavik, as well as writing crime novels and children's fiction. She is best known for her six crime novels featuring Thora Gudmundsdottir, an attorney and single mother, the latest of which is *The Silence of the Sea*. The series has been a bestseller across Europe. In 2012 she published her first horror novel, *I Remember You*, combining crime and the supernatural.

Black Sky

Yrsa Sigurdardóttir

The message was disturbing. It began with electronic crackle and ended with a plea. 'Help us. Please help us.' The piteous voice sounded almost rusty, as if the radio waves had gathered dust on their long journey. And the words were out of place. There was nothing wrong and no one needed any help. Dixie pricked up her ears in case more was to follow, but in return she got nothing but a dense silence. The frequency and wavelength of the communication was still visible on the radio dashboard but gave nothing away. No one on her team had been given this wavelength, or anyone from the new base. Since there were no other people around, this implied that the strange message had either come out of nowhere or did not exist at all. Which was ridiculous. She had heard something. Some statistical anomaly must have aligned electric disturbance in such a way that it came out as words. Dixie relaxed. That was it. She had read too much into the sounds, imagined a voice where there was none. She was, after all, in a place where the senses could easily be confused. It was a known fact and believed to relate to lack of stimulation. There was little to see, little to hear and almost nothing to smell. But despite this knowledge, the echo of the eerie voice in her head made her long to rip the headset off, throw it into the farthest corner of the control room and stamp on it until it became one with the colourless flooring.

'David? Is that you?' No reply.

Dixie linked up to the system operator. 'Jenna. I just got an odd message over the headset. Can you check it for me?' She read out the frequency.

'Must have been a glitch. It's not from us or the commissioning team at Base-3. Don't know who it could be. Want me to recover it for you? I can also trace where it's coming from. Get you a direction and distance.'

'No.' Her reply was curt, more so than Dixie intended. 'It was nothing.'

'OK. Whatever.' As always Jenna sounded uninterested. Nothing outside the world of signals, pixels, processes and fragments held any importance for her. 'I'm up to my neck here anyway. There seems to be something wrong with the communications systems. People can't reach home. Most likely your thing had something to do with that.' The line went silent as the connection was cut. No small talk. No goodbye.

Dixie got back to work, forcing the message out of her head. The last mining shift she would ever supervise was about to wrap up. Only five hours of sunlight remained, to be followed by a little over two weeks of total darkness. It was a still darkness unlike any night anywhere on Earth and the long day's departure was not marked by twilight.

The sun simply vanished from the black sky, slowly disappearing behind the rounded corner of the horizon and cutting off visibility. Day, night. Night, day. There was no need to celebrate the never-ending cycle with any fuss. Life was never meant to set foot here, much less make itself comfortable and stay. In the original scheme of things, the moon was meant to be barren, simply to serve the purpose of powering tides on earth thereby ensuring that oceans did not become stagnant and toxic to marine life. Aside from this role the moon was of no consequence. And it showed. Beauty had found no foothold here; nothing remotely appealing was to be seen aside from the starry sky. Even the grey colour of the regolith was monotone, showing only the merest hints of variety in its hue. Nature's artistry had been left out of the picture and even the most gushing of bleeding hearts would find it hard to muster up enthusiastic complaints about the strip mining that took place here. This made Dixie's life a lot easier. She had no qualms about her job, even when looking over the seemingly endless ground they had covered since her assignment began just under a year ago. Within the perimeter of the mined area the ground looked pretty much the same as it had when virgin. Grey. The works left the terrain a little smoother, removing the occasional small crater and any bumps or rocks and replacing them with uniform ripples. It was almost as if they were striving to produce the solar system's largest Zen garden, not harvesting helium-3 for Earth's bottomless energy production requirements.

Dixie looked away from the control room screens that provided her with an overview of the outside. She blinked, fighting off a fatigue that had appeared out of nowhere. She had slept well, as she always did thanks to the sleeping aids administered religiously to the entire crew. This yearning to lie down had nothing to do with lack of sleep. Neither was it related to physical exhaustion; to her recollection, she had done nothing strenuous since waking up and strapping on the weights that kept her from walking as if her feet had been replaced with coiled springs while she dozed. The day had been the same as countless others. The lethargy was most likely a result of her body's increased tolerance for the medication required to get by here. The in-house doctor had told her to look out for this but she had pushed the creeping signs away, not wanting to take more. Already the small pile she swallowed in the morning left her not wanting breakfast. One more pill added to the fistful would most likely cause her to throw up.

She vaguely recalled being worried about the effects of the medication when she first arrived. Now it seemed so trivial and ridiculous that she couldn't help but smile. The radiation tracker she carried showed she had so far accumulated radiation that amounted to her having had about seven chest x-rays a day since her arrival. About twice the annual dose she would have received to date down on Earth, but per day. Seven hundred and thirty times more if you measured it by year.

Perhaps the effects of this had now come home to roost. Her overwhelming feeling of tiredness was compounded by this depressing thought and the conditioning imprinted on her during training kicked in, forcing her into thinking positively. Find something good and focus on it. Focus. Focus. Focus. Her mind came up blank until she finally caught hold of a positive recollection. At least they had lost no one to a radiation burst from solar storms. The warning systems had proved their worth and all outside had managed to shuffle into the underground chambers of the station in time. Chalk up one for her team. Screw radiation. Screw the fact that she'd never be able to bear children. Worse things had happened.

Dixie repositioned her headset and selected the line that would connect her to David, the foreman currently winding up the shift outside. The final shift. Soon she and the rest of the crew could go back home to Earth. To normality. To life. If her ravaged insides hadn't planned for death in its place. Or if the pressurisation unit in the shuttle bringing her and the crew back didn't break down and kill them all, as had happened to one of the Base-1 teams years ago. She made a mental note to see the doctor. She was obviously showing signs of depression and another pill or two wouldn't kill her. It would even be good practice for her resumed life on Earth. She didn't expect the pile of tablets to shrink once she got back home. This she knew for a fact after being allowed to speak to some of those that had manned her position in the past. Not that they had been particularly forthcoming, answering her questions as briefly as possible. At the time she'd felt as if they were merely counting down the minutes until her interview was over. Now she realised she would have been exactly the same. Her contract stipulated one half hour – annually – if future candidates wished to question her. She would give them precisely that. Not a minute more.

'Hi, David. How's it going?' The niggling feeling that something was wrong weaselled itself in between her scattered thoughts. Her mind was suddenly filled with images of one of the workers ripping his suit, his body bloating and the saliva in his mouth starting to boil on his tongue. She had been made to watch footage of such accidents before coming here, in preparation. At the time she could not line up the incidents in a worst to least worst scenario. There was no best. Everyone that died here, died horribly.

The company had always been clear on this. Never once did they try to sweep the hardships of the job under the rug – the moon is only for those tough in body and mind. The weak will die. Only the strong were selected. In the case of her team, those the screening process misjudged had paid for the error with their lives. In the year that had passed two people had died, one who turned out to have a low tolerance for radiation and one of a heart attack after panicking when the temperature control in his suit went haywire. Their bodies had been reduced to dust and gases in the heating chambers as the cost of the trip back to earth was exorbitant, a luxury only allowed the living. The dead stayed behind. It was some consolation that the death toll on her watch was way below the average. Usually a high percentage of the crew members died during the last month of their stay, but she had lost no one since the second death three months ago. Their safety figures were the best to date if you ignored the last crew to work out of now decommissioned Base-1, who all died in an accident on the way home. While still mining they had only lost a single crew member, though.

'Did you hear me David? How is it going?'

'Hxxtr.' The reply was distorted and the software installed to fix that kicked in. The man's crisp voice suddenly sounded as if he was standing next to her. 'Yeah, yeah. We're OK. I'm making my way back now. The helium-3 containers have been sent by rail to the mass driver and the mobile miners have also been mobilised. The operators will follow them for a while in case something goes wrong at the onset. They are under instructions to be back before nightfall. I'm a bit

YRSA SIGURDARDÓTTIR

worried about mobile miner one though. The conveyors stalled and since there is so little time left we didn't have time to locate the problem, let alone fix it in situ.'

Dixie didn't waste time discussing his decision. He'd made the right call and he knew it. It wasn't as if an extra hour of operation of one machine of the three would make much difference to the yield. 'How far off mark are we?' His answer was much as she had expected. Perhaps a little lower. The best areas within reach from the base had already been exhausted. The area they now had to work with contained a mere thirty parts per billion of the precious helium-3 the Earth craved. As a result, for the past four cycles they had not been able to meet the expected quota although she had childishly hoped that this last cycle would somehow and miraculously exceed expectations: that the site would go out with a bang. When Dixie and the crew first arrived they had still been working within the area that yielded twice as much. That was before they'd had to start making calls to the company, explaining that they would come up short.

Dixie shifted one of the external cameras to show the procession of the massive mobile miners to their new home. They looked worse for wear, having spent ten years slowly passing over the moon's surface, running the regolith through a heating process that separated valuable elements from the loose material covering the surface. In addition to the helium-3 payload they were here to acquire, these elements also included the oxygen and nitrogen necessary for life support at the base. Everything here revolved around these monstrous, looming machines. They worked non-stop during the bright two-week-long lunar day, undergoing routine maintenance during the corresponding two-week night. During this non-productive phase the helium-3 that had been processed was sent to Earth using a mass driver situated at the edge of the dark side, a thirty hour journey away from the base. The capsule sent hurtling into space every two weeks was intercepted by the company's space station and shipped from there to Earth where the helium-3 was used for electricity production via a pollution-free fusion process. Dixie did not want to consider the implications of the shortage if the new site did not meet expectations. The world was now completely dependent on the shipments arriving. Fully loaded, not partially.

As captain of the base, she was responsible for everything running smoothly. And now her tour of duty was as good as over, as was the useful lifetime of this particular station. Next week the new mining base would take over and the base they had called home would become derelict. Despite the extreme cost of shipping materials over from Earth nothing aside from the mobile miners and some of the heaviest equipment would be recycled, as this would mean a halt to operations while the bones of the station were picked over, and the Earth could not afford to lose its constant supply of energy fodder. So this base was destined to become a relic, like the preceding station which they could see on the edge of the horizon, slowly being eaten away by radiation bursts from solar winds. The same solar winds that had peppered the moon's surface with helium-3 particles for billions of years. Unfortunately these were rejected by the Earth's protective atmosphere, so mining there was out of the question. In addition, the so-called 'dark side' of the moon received more of these particles than the side facing the Earth so mining was banished to the God-forsaken place visible on the screens. It would have been too easy any other way.

'Come and see me when you get back.' Dixie needed to go over the remaining tasks with the foreman. It would not take long; the tasks were few and clear-cut. They were to write a final report providing the new team at Base-3 with a summary of lessons learned during their year of operations. They were also to be on call in case something went wrong on the mobile miners' long journey to the new base. The handover of the equipment would not be face to face as the new base was situated far enough away to make human accompaniment impossible. They had no vehicles or spacesuits able to provide breathable air for the ten-day trip. Which wasn't all bad as it meant the entire crew would spend their remaining days here indoors. They had already had their full share of exposure to the atmosphere these past twelve months. Despite advances in every field since humankind first mastered space travel, man had yet to conquer the effects of prolonged living outside Earth's protection. A year-long assignment was already pushing the limits. Dixie could feel the effects of low gravity on her bones and muscles and the effects of the artificial atmosphere on her lungs and heart. Effects that time and proper therapy would mostly correct back on Earth. But never fully.

Of this she had been repeatedly warned during the recruitment phase, the last and final time when signing the actual contract and sealing her decision. But the words had faded to a whisper as she focused her eyes on the huge sum she was to be paid. Not to mention the bonus if she stuck it out for the full year. She would never have to work again, and could live the kind of life most yearned for but would never attain. She deserved it. Until now she had spent her life studying hard, training and toning her physique and obtaining the mechanical and management skills that this job required.

And now it was time to reap the rewards. Like those who had come before her, Dixie would enter the ranks of the privileged. She would be allowed to travel and be provided with a larger share of Earth's diminishing resources than the average civilian. At the time these privileges had seemed irresistible. Now what she longed for most was a blue sky.

'Is it OK if I take a rain check?' David's voice sounded hollow. The removal of static from the transmission also leached every trace of humanity from his voice. He was one of the calmest people she'd ever met, taking everything in his stride and able to deal with the most difficult of situations without missing a beat. 'I was going to make a trip up to the old base if you don't mind.'

'What?' Dixie wondered if she had misheard. Few had ever shown any interest in the abandoned station and those that had never suggested a field trip over there to have a look around. The people working here were not that type. Their lives were on hold. They worked, ate and slept while counting down the days until they could get back to Earth and resume their real existence. She hoped they were different people there, if their personalities since they arrived were anything to go by. It was hard to tell. This place had a way of suppressing any personality quirks or defining characteristics. For example, no one had ever thought of giving names to the objects or areas they commonly referred to. Instead they used numbers. Miners 1, 2 and 3. Bases 1, 2 and 3. Areas 2-1, 2-2 and so on. It had been this way since they began mining here. She should probably count herself lucky that she and the crew had not begun referring to each other with numerals during their mission. She wondered what number she would have picked if they had. Number one would have been too obvious. Seven, maybe.

The 'strong leadership skills' that had been so high on the recruiters' list were almost laughable, all things considered. The crew did not really need a leader. They just needed to be told what to do. The company could have saved themselves the money spent on devising tests and questions meant to assess Dixie's management qualities. And she could have done without the stressful interviews conducted by men and women in pricey suits. Interviews that had nothing to do with her technical expertise, crammed with questions about largely implausible scenarios. She couldn't hide behind her top grade degree and impressive CV while she struggled to come up with one insightful answer after another. A complete waste of time.

'David? Can you hear me? Why would you want to go there? It's over an hour's drive. On high propulsion.'

'I've been picking up odd signals. They're coming from there.' 'Odd' could mean anything, here on the moon. David's voice gave no hint as to what he meant by it.

'What do you mean, odd?' Dixie sat up straighter in her seat.

'Just odd.'

Dixie did not press the point. A signal coming from a base abandoned over five years ago was odd enough in itself. She would sound stupid if she made him explain himself in more detail, more so if she asked whether the message had been a plea for help. It couldn't be the same thing she had heard. But who knew? 'I'm coming with you. Pick me up by airlock bay 5.'

A very still silence followed and Dixie wondered if they had been cut off. 'You don't have to. It's probably nothing.'

'I agree with you there, but I want to come anyway. We can discuss the schedule for the next days on the way.' She listened to his breathing and thought it sounded almost relieved. Not that you could tell much from breathing. 'Airlock bay 5. I'll be there in ten minutes, ready for pickup.' After making an unsuccessful attempt to reach the control station down on earth to let them know she and David were going over to Base-1, Dixie turned off the headset and made her way upstairs. Long distance communications were obviously still down.

The spacesuit felt clammy and cold, as always. Before she had tried one on, the seamless, skin-tight one-pieces looked sleek and light. In reality they were anything but. This one now smelled of the regolith dust it had collected during her last outing. It was the smell of something singed, as if the grey sand covering the moon's surface were ashes from a massive fire. The smell of a billion-year-old inferno. Dixie shook the particles off in an attempt to disperse the odour. She lay the suit down and undressed; then began the lengthy process of putting it on, reminding herself that she could now count down the number of times she would be forced to wear it. Five, maybe six times more. She would need to go out once or twice to conduct measurements. The final time she would have to wear it would be a week to ten days from now, when the shuttle arrived to pick them up. Once back on Earth she would shred it, not have it mounted in a frame at company headquarters like other mining operation captains. Unless she changed her mind on the trip home and began to view it with fondness. The sort of strange nostalgia that time whipped up even for negative experiences.

On the way from the equipment room to the airlock she passed the station doctor, a man around twenty years her senior. His qualifications far exceeded what was required of him and having access to the personnel files of her staff, Dixie knew the reason for his peculiar career choice. It had nothing to do with the money on offer; the man had administered an unapproved drug to his patients and some of them had died. This job saved him a public trial and the humiliation of almost certain incarceration. The company had more clout than most political or bureaucratic organisations and had used it to get the man on board in exchange for making his judicial problem evaporate. Dixie and the doctor exchanged empty greetings and the man went on his way, the white medical coat he wore slapping the air behind him. Like everyone else on the team he was a quiet man, although he always seemed to be in a rush to go somewhere else within the small confines of the base. Dixie couldn't help but feel he was running away from the past, hoping if he could keep moving quickly enough it would not catch up with him.

She entered the airlock and waited for permission to open the outer door. She checked the small monitor on her sleeve, reassuring herself that the suit was airtight and her helmet properly sealed. She heard the click of the mechanism in the door through the globe dulling her senses, and engaged the opening process. She stepped outside and the airlock closed behind her. The heat outside wrapped itself around her body, malevolently welcoming her back from the confines of the underground bunkers. The suit's cooling system kicked in and it immediately ceased to be an object of hatred. A few of the brighter stars glittered weakly in the black sky, now that the sun had begun to wane at the horizon. She felt insignificant and vulnerable, as always when outside. Life's place was on Earth.

Dixie got into the seat next to David who acknowledged her presence with a nod of his helmet-clad head.

His suit was clunkier than hers as he spent more time outside and needed more protection. She closed the hatch-like door behind her and the vehicle lifted itself from the ground and began to propel itself forward, silently. The lack of atmosphere made generation of sound impossible, communication with those outside only possible through radio-waves. Even the colossal miners moved, crunched and boiled the ground without so much as a creak or rustle.

The vehicle picked up speed and soon the greyish landscape started to blur. A green light blinked in the dashboard, indicating that the inside of the vehicle now contained breathable air. This released the lock on their helmets and both Dixie and David removed them. Her shoulders rejoiced without the weight. 'Tell me about the signal.'

David did not turn his head. He stared at the endless grey regolith spread out before them and the silhouette of the abandoned base in the far distance. 'It wasn't very clear.' She did not have to see his face to know he was lying. Maybe not lying but leaving something out. Much like her. It wasn't as if she was telling him anything.

'How can a signal be coming from there? The place has been abandoned for five years now. The power can't still be on. It should have run out soon after it was abandoned.'

'I don't know. I was wondering if the collector beam might have passed over their receiver during the disman-tling process and set the system going again.' Mirrors that collected sunlight were situated in various locations along the perimeter of the mining area. They reflected the light onto a single spot where it was further projected via a collector beam to a receiver situated beside the station. It was meant to act as an emergency energy source, providing the station with enough energy to operate life-saving systems within the base if the helium-3 power generator broke down. No one ever spoke of what would happen if the generator malfunctioned during the thirteen days of darkness. It was not good for morale. If she ever came across any of the leadership interviewers she would suggest they add that question to their artillery. 'It's the only explanation I can think of and it seems to make sense.'

Dixie shrugged. 'Possibly, if the old systems are still intact.' She shifted uncomfortably in her seat, the five-point harness securing her in place pinching her shoulders. 'But if the beam merely passed over the station, the power wouldn't have been on for long.'

'Well, that fits with the signal. It only lasted a very short time. It repeated itself twice, both times while we were working on the collector apparatus with the projector positioned in the direction of Base-1, so I think my theory holds.'

'And what did you hear?'

'A voice. Not particularly clear.'

'A voice?' Dixie did not sound as incredulous as she had hoped. 'A human voice?'

'A man's voice.'

'But that's impossible. There's no one stationed there. There can't be.'

'Could be an old signal. Something they put on the air before shutting down.'

'Why would they do that?'

'I don't know. Why does anyone do anything?' David stared straight ahead and his hands were steady. He seemed perfectly sane. 'I must have misheard the words though.'

'Why? What did they seem to say?'

'Base-2. We are not going back. I repeat, we are not going back.' David swallowed. His Adam's apple bobbed twice up and down before disappearing under the helmet brace collar of his suit. 'I might have misheard that bit. But the rest was crystal clear. He said: Help us – please help us.'

Dixie said nothing. So her ears had not been playing tricks on her after all. Two people could not have an identical aural hallucination at the same time. Or could they? No, of course not. She wondered if she should tell him she had heard part of the communication, but decided not to. It wouldn't make any difference. 'Well. Maybe we will find an explanation when we get there.'

'Maybe.' David didn't sound optimistic. For the remainder of their journey they discussed what needed to be done before they left. When that topic was exhausted they switched to discussing the decisions they now faced regarding the homes the company would arrange for them, interior furnishings, gardening, vehicles and whatever else their hearts desired. Dixie was happy to hear she was not the only one already tired of the endless lists and photos they were being sent. There had even been one containing a selection of pets. That one she hadn't bothered opening. She didn't need a pet. She needed time to adjust, then time to find someone to love. Someone with whom to share all the perks of her new life. In that respect David was better set up than she was; he had a wife and two children waiting with increasing impatience for his return, while all she had was a set of rather undemonstrative parents and a much younger brother she hardly knew.

They made the last ten minutes of the journey in complete silence. David reduced the vehicle's speed and they watched solemnly as the entrance of Base-1 came into view. It looked dusty and had taken on the colour of it surroundings. Grey.

The round airlock looked like an open mouth. Open to let out a scream. Don't leave me here. Take me with you.

'Shall we get out?' David stared out of the arch-shaped window while he spoke. His face showed no emotion but a small tic had overtaken his right eye. A sign of stress. He cleared his throat and replaced his helmet. Practised finger movements clicked and pressed in all the right places until the suit gave a beep to say he was safe to disembark. Dixie did the same, although less nimbly. Her beep sounded as an echo of his. They turned on the communication systems and passed test words between them until satisfied everything was working properly.

When they emerged, the same heat enveloped Dixie's body as outside Base-2. Her heartbeat increased when it seemed as if the suit's cooling system wasn't going to engage, but went back to normal when it did. She licked a droplet of sweat from her upper lip. She was not going to die here. Not when home was so close she could almost smell it. They moved towards the airlock until they stood facing it, neither seeming to want to touch the outdated mechanism. It felt as if they were about to desecrate a grave or a holy place. One not meant to be revisited. 'Do you think it will open?' Dixie almost hoped David would say no. If they found anything inside, it wasn't going to be a nice surprise.

'I think so. It's obviously a bit different than ours, being over ten years old, but the workings are the same. There should be a manual lever somewhere.' David ran his hand over the various switches. He tried two before he found the correct one and the two of them used their combined strength to nudge it into an open position. They then did the same to pull the huge hatch towards them until they had secured an opening large enough for them to squeeze through without snagging their suits. As soon as they entered the dark enclave behind the steel the lights on their helmets and suits automatically turned on and they were able to see the other airlock hatch opposite the first. Again they struggled to open it, having to disengage a lock that was meant to keep it closed while the outer hatch was open. Neither of them wanted to make the task easier by closing off their way out.

Stepping though the second opening was hard. Not physically but mentally. The lights on their suits were not powerful enough to light up the corridor in front of them and Dixie couldn't help but feel that something disturbing was hovering just outside the reach of the lights, stepping silently away as the pair of them proceeded further and further inward and down into the underground chambers. The few objects lying around caused shadows to dance enticingly around them, daring them to continue on this fool's errand. 'Should we go back?' David had stopped, looking around as if he expected non-existent aliens to attack from the darkness.

'I wouldn't mind.' Dixie smiled but it did not stick. They had come all this way. 'How about we check the communications room and leave it at that? A recording would have to come from there if the emergency generator system had anything to do with that strange message. Individual devices wouldn't be hooked up to that.'

David agreed, though he didn't look thrilled. He was probably only going along with her because she was above him in the pecking order as leader of the crew. A leader who had yet to discover if she had any leadership skills. Their progress was slowed down with every step, each one more difficult to take than the previous. They passed the nursery and stopped to peer through the glass wall separating it from the corridor. Inside the plants that had striven to produce oxygen and fresh food for past crews had lost all colour; dead and dried out like ghosts of the lush vegetation that had once filled the space. 'Shit.' The word spilled out of Dixie's mouth without her having intended to give away how disquieting she found the sight.

'Yeah. Shit.' David's voice became more agitated. 'Shit. Shit. Shit. Look over there.' He pointed to a tangle of leaves and stems. Dixie strained her eyes and saw what had so disturbed him. The sole of a shoe was discernible amongst the dead vegetation. And the shoe was at the end of a leg, clad in what had once been a white spacesuit.

'Fucking hell.' Dixie exhaled and stepped away from the glass. There were more shoes, feet, hands and even faces hidden in the tangles now that she knew what to look for. 'What's going on?'

David seemed to have no answer. He looked away and pointed ahead. 'If the layout is the same as at Base-2 the communications room should be just ahead. Shall we see if we can find an explanation there?' He turned back and looked at the footprints they had left in the fine dust covering the floor of the corridor. It was obvious which way he really wanted to go.

'Yes.' It was the opposite of what she wanted to say. But she had to. She didn't want him to remember her as a coward. She even made sure to keep one step ahead of him. The pleading voice found its way into the forefront of her mind and she had to remind herself over and over again that she was not actually hearing it, simply recalling the words. Help us. Please help us.

The door to the communications room was finally in front of them. The engraved lettering on the sign marking the door had become flush with the panel, filled up with the same grey dust that covered the floor. Neither of them was able to blow it away because of the helmets. Dixie reached out and slid the door to the side, fully exposing the darkened room behind it. She gasped as the beams from their suits and helmets lit up the space. The equipment and screens placed on the walls and standing around on various tables looked old-fashioned and clumsy compared to their newer, sleeker versions. But neither of them wasted any time pondering the advance of technology.

It was the man sitting in front of the main radio that had their full attention. He was dead, of that they could be certain. He had succumbed with open eyes, now shrivelled into his head that had fallen over the back of the chair. He stared blindly at them, neck taut and mouth agape like some sort of deranged contortionist. 'I know that man.' Dixie made no attempt at keeping the horror from her voice. 'I know who he is.' Even the sunken eyes and mummified nose could not disguise his face. It was the captain of the last Base-1 crew, the crew that had supposedly died during their transportation back to Earth. Dixie's senses heightened for the first time in months and the picture in front of her became crisper and clearer than before. She could even hear the rustling sound her body made against the inside of her spacesuit. She stepped in and walked up to the man. David stayed behind and watched as she picked up a sheet of paper lying on the desk in front of him. She used her fingers to dust the page and read what the man had written. Just before he died, alone and abandoned by those that placed him here. The company. The fucking company.

Dixie read the words, digesting the letter's content in its entirety. 'We're not going back, David. We will die here.

Back at Base-2. Most of us in the nursery, where we'll think we can hold out until help arrives. But none will come.'

'What are you talking about?' David still stood in the doorway, his face behind the helmet's dome a grimace of stunned disbelief. 'What does it say?'

'The company left them here. Cut off all communication and just left them. There was never any shuttle. It was probably too expensive and better for the bottom line to make up a story about them dying on the way over. No matter how high the compensation they paid the relatives, it would always be a thousand times cheaper than sending a special mission over to get them.' Dixie placed the letter carefully back where it had lain. Maybe someone else would find it later. Someone who could get the message across. She certainly wouldn't be able to. Its contents would die with her, here on the moon. Under a black sky. She looked away from the page. 'They were the last crew in this station. The other crews that preceded them went home because they took the seats of those that were sent over to replace them. But these poor bastards didn't need replacing. Any more than we do. Shit.'

'I don't believe it. I don't believe it. You're making this up.'

'Of course I'm not. I'm not an idiot.' But perhaps she was. She had swallowed the whole spiel. But then again, why wouldn't she? The company made every effort to keep them in the dark. Sending them pictures of houses they would never live in and pets they would never stroke or feed. 'I'm telling you. We're dead men walking.'

'Come on Dixie. It can't be true. It … can … not … be … true.' David's breathing had become erratic but he was clearly making an effort to calm down. 'OK, if what you're saying is correct then why didn't they simply transport these men over to Base-2 when the shuttle arrived with the first crew to man that station? Can you tell me that?'

'Sure I can. Don't you remember? The first crew to arrive to Base-2 arrived over a year after Base-1 was shut down. This was six years ago. The Earth had enough helium-3 to last them a couple of years. There was no rush. But these men would never have survived the wait, even if all systems had been kept running. No one can stay alive here for two years. You know that.'

'But it's different now. The new crew for Base-3 will arrive soon. They can bring us back on that shuttle.' He was pleading. As if Dixie had any control over the situation.

'No they can't. That shuttle is staying here and taking the payload back after the first mining yield is in. There's a shortage looming down on Earth and the company can't wait for the lengthy process involving the mass diver and the space station interface. And we can't get there to force them to take us back. It's too far.' If only their most recent returns had been better. If only. 'Now that I think about it, the deaths I read about towards the end of most of the other crews' missions were probably staged by the company. That way they had space in the shuttles for things that inevitably needed to be transported back to Earth. Cores from the geoscientists' research work. I can't recall a single instance when they've needed two shuttles, despite the bulk of that stuff. Our good safety figures just show that we were never meant to go back. It would have been a waste of effort to weed us down to a manageable number. Same as with these guys. They lost precious few men while in operation. None during their final month. Just like us. Oh, God.'

Dixie straightened her back. Suddenly she knew why it had been so important to establish her command of leadership. She was the one that would lead her crew of fifteen men and women through the rough road ahead. The road to certain death. Paved with sorrow, loneliness, regret and anger. That would certainly test her management skills. Particularly when the small amount of helium-3 they had left aside ran out and the power went. They had foolishly sent everything they mined back to Earth as they believed they only needed enough to run the station until the non-existent shuttle was to pick them up. They had dismantled the back-up power system and loaded it onto the miners. Not that it mattered, as night was about to fall. 'Come on. Let's get back. I need to break the bad news.' She turned around and took a photo of the letter with the camera mounted on her helmet. She also took one of the body of the former Base-1 captain and a few of the other dead lying amongst the dried-out plants in the nursery. Otherwise her crew might not believe her.

They exited the abandoned base, closing the airlock behind them. Neither said a word on the drive back. There was nothing to be said.

Two hours remained of daylight. Then two weeks of night.

Afterword

Mark Goldring

OXFAM CHIEF EXECUTIVE

Crime fiction has always reflected the human instinct to face down injustice, and that instinct has always been at the heart of Oxfam's work, too. We might not employ detectives or solve cryptic clues, but our staff have long been motivated by a similar determination to identify, address and eradicate injustice.

That injustice can take many forms. Today, for example, 57 million children – mostly girls – still don't have the opportunity to go to school. Hundreds of millions of people aren't able to drink clean water. And the families who are already facing the impact of climate change are the ones who have done least to cause it.

So in the face of this injustice, we respond, standing alongside people all over the globe as they push for lasting change. We work locally, which in the examples above might mean supporting education projects, building clean water supplies and helping communities prepare for changing weather. And we campaign nationally and globally too: applying the pressure on systemic inequalities that cause and perpetuate poverty.

For me, our work to tackle injustice comes down to removing the barriers that prevent people from taking control of their own lives. Throughout the world, our work involves supporting people – particularly women – to speak out and have a say in the decisions that affect their lives. This work can play a major role in creating an environment where everyone can prosper in the long term. And, once again, this work is ultimately about finding and fighting injustice.

By buying this book, you've joined that fight. You've joined the battle for a better future. And you've backed our work to lift lives for good, driven by the unwavering certainty that injustice is never permanent. Thank you for your support.